Sarah Challis, whose father is the distinguished cinematographer Christopher Challis, travelled widely with film units as a child. She has since lived in Scotland and California, but is now happily settled in a Dorset village. She is married with four sons.

JUMPING TO CONCLUSIONS

Sarah Challis

headline
review

First published in hardback in 2005 by REVIEW
An imprint of Headline Book Publishing

First published in paperback in 2006
by HEADLINE REVIEW

1

ISBN 0 7553 2855 8 (A format)
ISBN 0 7553 2166 9 (B format)

Typeset in Meridien by
Palimpsest Book Production Limited, Polmont, Stirlingshire

Printed and bound in Great Britain by
Mackays of Chatham plc, Chatham, Kent

Headline's policy is to use papers that are natural, renewable and
recyclable products and made from wood grown in sustainable forests.
The logging and manufacturing processes are expected to conform to
the environmental regulations of the country of origin.

HEADLINE BOOK PUBLISHING
A division of Hodder Headline
338 Euston Road
London NW1 3BH

www.reviewbooks.co.uk
www.hodderheadline.com

For Raphael and Esme, with love.

With thanks to John and Teresa Dufosee,
and all the staff at Nyland Stables.

Chapter One

Tom knew there was something wrong as soon as he saw the mare in the paddock. It took two men to lead her up, and even then she swung her quarters about, her back arched like a cat, her neck dark and steaming with sweat. Tom caught hold of the stirrup leather. 'For God's sake, Jess!' he pleaded. 'Get off while you can! She's bloody dangerous!'

'She'll be all right,' Jess muttered, resenting the interference, her face pale and set under the bright blue silk of her helmet. Ignoring him, she collected up the reins, concentrating on keeping her balance on the tiny racing saddle which was slippery and wet from the slanting February rain. 'She's only a baby. It's her first race. She'll settle when we're away from the crowds.' Leaning down the mare's neck, she spoke to the owner, who was bracing his shoulder against the mare's chest in an attempt to keep her steady. 'Ask if I can go down to the start early, Mr Dawlish. She'll get worse here in the paddock, with the other horses and the people.'

The man looked up and nodded and the drops of rain which had collected on the peak of his cap shook themselves free to bounce down the front of his waxed jacket.

Tom let go his hold, knowing he was wasting his time. Jess would do what she wanted as usual. She wouldn't listen. He watched as Ted Dawlish and his burly son, both farmers and heavy plant contractors, who trained the horse at home on a bleak Dorset hill, hustled the frantic mare onto the track and let her go, scuttling out of range of her flying heels as she bounded and bucked away from them.

With any luck Jess will fall off before she gets to the start, thought Tom gloomily, turning up the collar of his coat. It was freezing, with an icy wind blowing grey sheets of rain out of an iron coloured sky. The nylon knees of his breeches clung to his legs in a wet, transparent film and his thin-soled racing boots were sodden. Ted Dawlish came to stand beside him, carrying the lead rope, his son folding the blanket they had whipped off the mare's back in the paddock.

Sensing Tom's disapproval, he said, 'She'll settle all right. That's a good little mare, that is. Full sister to Flying Fish. She'll win a race, she will.'

'Not this one,' said Tom dourly. 'She shouldn't be on a racecourse yet. She's not ready.'

'That's your opinion.' The two men turned their backs, squinting into the stinging rain, to watch their mare's erratic progress between the white rails of the track.

Tom threaded his way through the punters who had gathered round the paddock to have a look at the horses for the maiden race. At this late stage of the afternoon the point-to-point crowds had thinned and only the diehards remained, hunched into waterproof coats, backs turned to the wind, damp racecards gripped between numb fingers. The ground beneath their feet had been turned to mud and was littered with the bright shreds of discarded betting slips.

Jumping to Conclusions

The commentator's voice was announcing the runners and riders, fourteen in all, with Miss Jessica Haddon on Mr Edward Dawlish's Flying Fancy gone down early to the start.

Tom ducked under the rails and crossed the track to the far side, away from the flapping white trade tents where the displays of saddlery and racks of outdoor clothes were being dismantled and loaded into the backs of vans. It would have been a bad day for the retailers, he thought. Nobody wanted to browse round the stalls in this sort of weather. From the far side of the course he could look away over open country, across the vale to the west, from where the weather was coming. The distance was swallowed by pillows of cloud, the grey of the sky melting into the grey of the winter fields. A line of crooked thorn trees, hunched against the wind, marked the top of the ridge to his right. Down below, in the wet of a winding valley, he could just see some bedraggled ewes, their heavy fleeces dirty and hanging from their bellies in shreds, and the tiny white scraps which were their lambs. Poor little buggers, he thought. What a miserable start to life.

Using his binoculars, he could see down to the start of the course. Jess was trying to steady Fancy, riding her in circles, but she was spooking and shying, her head in the air, fighting the bit, not listening. Tom felt a knot in his stomach but he knew that had it been him down there he would not have felt this fear. Jess would only be aware of the strung-up animal beneath her. She would be concentrating on trying to give the horse confidence, to calm her nerves, to get her to settle.

He wiped his wet hair out of his eyes and noticed his

hands looked purple with cold, his knuckles white. He had to lose so much weight to race ride that the bones of his wrists jutted in knobs from his strong forearms. He looked like a concentration camp victim, his mother complained, hating to see the hollow angles of his face and his eyes sunk in their sockets. 'It's only for a few months, Mum,' he'd said. 'You can fatten me up again in June.' Still, it was a struggle that got harder as he got older. Over six foot and now twenty-seven, it took determination and iron will to get down to under eleven stone. It was different for Jess who was as slim as a reed, although she was quite tall. She had to carry a weight cloth, even with today's ten-pound allowance for a five-year-old mare.

Now the huntsman, his black horse cantering crabwise, head down into the weather, ears flat back, was escorting the other runners down to the start. The sound of the horn floated away on a vicious gust as the splash of the red hunt coat led the field of bright racing colours, yellow, pink, orange, green, into the grey distance.

Tom refocused on Jess's mare who stood rooted to the spot, transfixed by the other horses cantering towards her. She'll explode in a minute, he thought. She won't stay still for long.

'What the hell is she riding?' said a voice at his elbow. He looked round to see two of the girls who worked with Jess at Ken Andrews' point-to-point stable: little Moira, her dark hair wet against her cheeks, the hood of her waterproof coat pulled low, and the head lass, Rhona, who was known to prefer horses to men by a wide margin. Her nose was red from the cold and her glasses were streaked with rain.

'A youngster of Ted Dawlish's. It's never run before.'

'Jesus!' said Rhona, shaking her head.

'She got offered the ride just before the race,' said Tom. 'You know Jess. She won't turn down anything.'

'How did it behave in the paddock?'

'Mad!' sighed Tom. 'Dawlish and his son couldn't hold her. She was nearly climbing over the rails. Jess asked to go down to the start early.'

Rhona sniffed and pulled a disapproving face. 'Those two couldn't train water to run down a drain,' she said. 'That mare's not ready to run, is she? She's too ignorant.' She saw it at the start of every season, these hair-raising introductions of young horses to racing. 'Jess is good, though, Tom,' she added. She could see how he was feeling. His face looked white and strained. 'She's a sensitive rider. You know that. She'll get the best out of the mare. I hate to see Carl or one of the other blokes bullying a youngster round. Jess won't do that.'

'If you ask me, she's nuts,' said Moira. 'I'm surprised she does it, to tell you the truth, what with Izzy and all. It seems, like, irresponsible.'

Tom said nothing. He knew that Moira and Jess did not get on. He wasn't going to criticise Jess in front of her, anyway.

'Are they here?' asked Rhona. 'Izzy and Jess's mum?'

'No, thank goodness,' said Tom. 'Belinda hates it when Jess is riding. She can't bear to watch. Izzy wanted to come but Jess persuaded her it was too cold. She's only six, remember.'

'They're lining up,' said Rhona, peering down the course. 'They'll be off in a minute.'

Moira turned her back on the driving rain. She could not pretend she was interested. As far as she was concerned, Jess could break her neck if that's what she wanted. You had to be off your head to sit on an unknown young horse for the first time and set out to gallop for three miles over eighteen stiff brush fences in the company of a lot of other novices. It annoyed her to hear everyone saying that Jess was so brave, as if it was something to be proud of. Foolhardy, she'd call it, and wanting to draw attention to herself. Wanting to win. That's what got up her nose.

She glanced at Tom who had his field glasses concentrated on the start. She had always fancied him. He was tall and lean with a lot of wild, curly, dark hair which he wore in a shaggy mop, more out of not caring what he looked like than affectation. His face was long and thin with lines running down his cheeks which deepened when he smiled. He looked somehow poetic and romantic, she thought, like an old-fashioned hero who would come cantering up on a white horse and doff his tall hat at simpering girls in bonnets and empire-line dresses. He wasn't the type she usually went for – loud, joshing, red-faced young men who got dressed up for Saturday night and drank themselves stupid with their mates. Tom was quiet, a bit serious; and sharp-faced, clever little Moira knew instinctively that he was a good bet.

He was classy, that was it, she thought. He had a posh voice, but not like some of them she'd come across, not braying like a bloody donkey, and he had good manners. He could muck around and have a laugh but you knew he'd never take it too far because there was a gentleness about him. He really was like a bloke in a film, she thought. One of those films where the hero is a bit hopeless but you can see from the beginning that he has potential. He's only got to meet the right girl, take his glasses off and square his jaw, and suddenly he's a sex god. Anyhow, he was wasted on Jess, who was so busy proving herself that she didn't have time for anybody else. Moira nestled in close behind him.

'I'm sheltering, Tom,' she said, leaning her head against his wet coat. Being small and pretty, she hoped to bring out his protective side, which, God knows, Jess wasn't interested in.

Down at the start Jess was conscious of nothing but the chestnut mare. She could sense the tension, made up in equal parts of fear and excitement, pulsing through Fancy's body like an electrical charge. She talked to her softly, keeping a hand on the trembling neck where the veins stood out like ropes under the thin skin. She kept a gentle pressure with her seat and legs, trying to keep her moving forward while staying out of the way of the other horses, which were all inexperienced, all unpredictable, wheeling and fretting along the start line, several striking out wildly with hind legs in a frenzy of excitement.

The rain was coming in almost horizontally but at least they would have it at their backs for the first half-mile or so, before the loop at the bottom of the course and the long haul back up the hill. Jess pulled her goggles down over her eyes with one hand and adjusted her whip. She had to be ready for the starter's flag, ready to give the mare the signal to set off and then try to settle her down as well as she could towards the first fence. She aimed to tuck her in behind the other horses and keep to the rails, well out of the way. Mr Dawlish said she jumped like a stag, but Jess knew enough about owners to discount that as any true indication of the mare's ability.

The horses milling in front of her were suddenly involved in some sort of nervous fracas. She could hear swearing and the starter shouting for them to get back and then the flag came down and they were off.

Fancy began badly, unwilling to start and running sideways across the track before Jess got her straight and moving forward. By then the others were galloping away from her and she was caught in their slipstream of flying mud and clods of earth. Jess managed to get in by the rails but the mare was still resisting, throwing her head in the air to avoid taking up the bit. Jess kept calm, pushing her forward gently until suddenly, realising that she was being left behind, Fancy lowered her head and bounded down the track, chasing after the others, desperate to catch them.

Jess pulled at the wet reins, trying to establish some sort of contact to make the mare slow down. A working gallop was what she wanted but now she was being run away with down the course and it seemed no time before the first fence was approaching as a dark line, growing thicker and higher with every stride. Up in front, the leaders met it in a bunch and flowed over but a following horse refused at the last moment, sliding into the groundboard, causing the one behind to run out through the wings. The white plastic tubes buckled and gave way and the jockey fell off at the feet of the St John ambulance men.

Jess was conscious of the commotion but could not take her eyes off the point where Fancy must take off. Although she was tugging hard on alternate reins she was having no effect on the speed at which they were bearing down on the fence. God, we're going to crash, she thought, with a sudden stab of real terror as the mare ignored her signal to take off and rushed in too close, almost into the bottom of the fence. Then, at the last moment, Jess felt her gather herself to leave the ground and somehow her speed was enough to fling her over, but only just. They landed in a heap on the other side with bits of brush flying through the air behind them.

Jess was thrown up the mare's neck as she scrabbled to keep her feet and by the time she was back in the saddle, Fancy was galloping again in another wild, uncontrollable flight after the others.

A shower of mud splattered against Jess's goggles as they overtook a back runner and Fancy pulled and snatched at the bit, the wet reins sliding through the fingers of Jess's sodden gloves. The next fence was close and they were still galloping flat out. There was nothing Jess could do but sit tight and hope that speed would get them over once again. The dark slope of tightly packed birch loomed ahead but the mare had her head down now, nearly between her knees, boring along. Jess shouted out loud as she gave her the signal to take off and, miraculously, she did, too low, too fast, but enough to get them over, ready for the long run to the open ditch.

This was the moment to try and settle her, now that the

frenzied galloping had taken the edge off her nervous energy. Jess worked hard to bring the horse between her hands and legs, to soften her iron hold on the bit and to tuck her hindquarters under to steady her stride, and gradually she felt her respond. They were coming up to the public enclosures and she was vaguely conscious of crowds against the rails and the loudspeaker, and of the horses ahead of her and a few behind. Another hundred yards and they were closing on the next fence, the orange ground rail marking the ditch before the jump. The mare was going beautifully, coming in straight, head up and ears pricked, concentrating for the first time. Jess knew she was going to get it right and, sitting down, she drove her forward and felt her leap, soaring over the fence and landing galloping on the other side. The speed and power hit Jess like a blow on the chest and she cried out in exhilaration. If she could keep Fancy jumping like that they would be fine. They would get round safe and sound.

Now they had reached the bottom end of the course and as they swung round the curve of rails, she could see the rest of the runners ploughing up the long hill in front of them and then the force of the weather hit her head on. Her goggles streamed with mud and water and she ducked her head lower as they ran into the buffeting wind.

As they closed on the next jump, it seemed as if they would overhaul a grey horse which was labouring through the heavy ground and had already run out of steam. It was making a lot of effort but hardly going forward and they came into the fence almost side by side. When the grey refused and swerved to the side, Jess tried to remind the mare what she had to do, but Fancy was distracted and unbalanced and at the instant when she should have taken off, Jess knew that their luck had run out. Fancy hardly left the ground, hit the guard rail with a crack like an exploding gun and catapulted over the fence. Jess was flung out of the saddle and into an arc through the air and as she started to fall she saw the mare's hind legs upside down against the grey sky above her head. The next moment she smacked into the ground and her mouth was full of mud.

'Come on, Izzy! Get a move on!' said Belinda Haddon to her granddaughter, but Izzy was not to be hurried. Squatting down in front of the hen house, she peered into the dark interior, breathing heavily as she counted the scaly legs which she could see in neat pairs on the perch within.

'Come on, Izzy! It's freezing. They'll all be inside on an afternoon like this.'

'I have to check,' said Izzy in a reprimanding tone. 'You never know. Just think if one of them *wasn't* and was shut out all night long in the rain!'

Oh dear, thought Belinda, she does make heavy going of everything. She tucked her hands deeper in the pockets of her old jacket. It was the nastiest sort of February afternoon. The sort of damp cold which got into your bones. At last, Izzy stood up, satisfied. Her round, freckled face under the hood of her coat was pink from the cold and her glasses were streaked with rain. Painfully slow, she shut the flap door and secured the bolt, while Belinda tried to be patient. At last the job was done and she caught hold of Izzy's wet mittened hand and turned back towards the cottage.

It was nearly dark although it was only half past three. Squares of golden light shone into the gloom from the kitchen and sitting-room windows. Belinda longed to be back beside the fire but first they must fill the log basket and then take Snowy a little way down the lane. They had already thrown some hay over the fence for Bonnet, Izzy's small square pony, who stood stoically with water pouring down her woolly sides, bottom thrust into the shelter of the hedge. Jess was supposed to have left a hay net ready but, typically, she had forgotten, and Belinda was not going to hang about outside for any longer than was necessary.

She was surprised that Izzy had allowed her to get away with a short cut like that. She had only protested a bit, saying, 'But Granny, it's *wasteful*. Bonnet'll stand on the hay and it will get muddy and spoiled.'

'Oh bugger that!' Belinda said under her breath, and out loud, 'It won't matter, darling. Not just for once. Bonnet won't mind. She'll just be glad to have her tea.'

Calling Snowy, the cheerful white mongrel with a patch over one eye and one black ear, Belinda and Izzy let themselves out of the gate onto the lane. The gate was rotting, like everything else, thought Belinda, and had to be pushed hard to open. It was no use complaining to her landlord when she knew from bitter experience that he would do nothing about it. The rent of Rosebay Cottage was low in recognition of the fact that he spent as little as possible on maintenance.

The lane wound away between tall naked trees, oak and sycamore, and the blackthorn hedge reared up gloomily on either side. The ditches were full and overflowing so that the surface of the lane streamed with water and eddies of small stones and twigs. Snowy trotted along gaily, undeterred by the weather, his tail in the air, his rather rude bottom looking cheerful as usual. Wreathed in smiles was how Belinda thought of it. Once an inner-city stray, Snowy treated every day of his rescued life with a determined and touching optimism.

Surreptitiously, Belinda consulted her watch. The last race would be over now and she could begin to relax. As far as she knew, Jess had three rides and, all being well, would now be drinking coffee and eating ham rolls in the lorry with the other yard staff, her job done for the day. She could imagine the steamed-up windows, the laughter, the horses rugged and bandaged, their manes crinkly from the loosened plaits.

Of course, it didn't always end like that. Belinda did not like to think of the horses which hobbled home or, worse, the empty space in the lorry, the empty stable on the yard. She had seen too many heartbreaking sights to want to go and watch her youngest daughter hurtle along at forty miles an hour on a ton of unpredictable muscle and bone. Three and a half miles over eighteen fences nearly four feet high. It was a mad, dangerous, perilous sport and she wished more than anything that Jess would not do it any more. But it was a waste of time wishing that Jess wouldn't do something that she wanted to do.

Thank goodness Izzy did not seem to worry. She had not asked what time her mother would be home or even what races she was riding in. Earlier she had been diverted by the jumble sale in the village hall. She'd bought some old-fashioned animal stories and a copy of *The Water Babies* which had kept her happy all the afternoon. She's such a funny little thing, thought Belinda, looking down at the red hooded figure which bobbed along beside her. She could see that Izzy was walking in a special way, turning out her right boot at every other step and then giving a small hop, looking down at her feet and concentrating. Belinda wondered what interior, private game she was playing. She was such a serious, stolid sort of child with none of Jess's naughty, wild spirit. It was hard to believe that they were mother and daughter. Her father must have been a very different sort of character, Belinda thought, as she so often did. She had a pretty good idea who Izzy's father was but Jess's silence on the subject was permanent. It used to bother her in the early days. Partly it was the unfairness of it all – that Jess at nineteen should be wholly responsible for the furious, red-faced bawling bundle that was Izzy. But after swanking round the point-to-point yard with her new baby, giggling with the other girls about the indignity of childbirth and joking about bathing Izzy in a stable bucket, Jess shed the responsibility as soon as she could and it was only a matter of weeks before Izzy was left with Belinda for longer and longer periods.

'You're much better with her than me, Mum,' she'd said. 'I don't know what to do with a baby.' It was hard then not to retort, well, you should have thought of that nine months ago.

In fact, she was a good mother in some ways, thought Belinda. Good at games and stories, good at bikes and swings and teaching Izzy to ride but it didn't help that Izzy grew up slow and cautious, careful and solemn, and it wasn't

long before Jess lost patience with the sort of games Izzy
liked best

But oh, how Belinda loved her granddaughter. Just
feeling the tug of her hand as she hopped down the lane
overwhelmed her with such a weight of love that it was
hard to breathe. Her solidness, the pink, freckled face, her
often surprising humour, the slow smile which, when it
came, bunched up and dimpled her round cheeks, her undemanding nature – sometimes Belinda could not think of
these things without tears springing into her eyes, because
what sort of future did the child have? She should have
been growing up in a proper family, with a mother and a
father and brothers and sisters, not brought up any old how
by her grandmother and her profligate unmarried mother,
who had not a bean between them.

'We'll turn back at the top of the lane, shall we?' she
said. 'It's getting dark so quickly.'

Without replying, Izzy nodded her head. 'Granny,' she
said, addressing her boots, 'is time always the same length?
Are minutes always the same?'

Belinda considered. 'I expect a scientist would tell you
they were,' she said. 'But some seem to go faster than others,
don't they? There's an expression that talks about time dragging, and I certainly know what that feels like, don't you?'

Izzy looked up and nodded. 'Time dragging,' she said
thoughtfully. 'Like as if you're pulling it along behind you and
it's really heavy.'

'That's it,' said Belinda.

'Would you say that this afternoon you and me had been
dragging time?'

15

Belinda looked down at her granddaughter. 'Well, it's been a dull sort of day because of the weather,' she said.

'And because of Mummy,' said Izzy in a little voice, looking down and concentrating on her hop and skip.

Belinda tightened her hold on the mitten in her hand and then said, 'Maybe. A bit. But then, Izzbug, I never think time spent with you is a drag.'

Izzy said nothing. What is she thinking? wondered Belinda. She was so undemanding and undemonstrative that it was hard to know what was going on beneath the placid exterior.

'Shall we toast some crumpets when we get home?' Belinda asked after a pause. Rather a greedy child, Izzy was always cheered by food.

'That's a good idea, Granny. Yum, yum. Come on, Snowy.'

When they got in, and as Belinda was stacking logs in the lean-to by the back door, she heard the telephone ring.

'Answer that, will you, darling,' she called and heard Izzy pick up the receiver.

Rhona started to run as soon as she realised that there had been an accident. Tom was in front of her, his long legs carrying him further and faster and when he glanced back for her, she waved him on and shouted, 'Don't wait for us!' Then she realised that Moira had left her side and melted away into the crowd. It was no surprise. She can't be bothered, she thought as she ran. She doesn't care what's happened to Jess.

Her legs felt weak and ungainly and her long mac caught round her thighs, slowing her down. The turf was cut up by the day's racing and she tripped and slithered on the

mud and ruts. Stopping to catch her breath, she saw with
relief that the mare was up on her feet and two men were
trying to catch her, running with spread arms while Fancy
galloped about in front of the fence. Jess was still on the
ground and Rhona could see that the two St John ambulance men were bending over her.

Rhona started to run again. Oh, please God, she prayed,
let her be all right! Jess must be hurt not to have got to
her feet and now Rhona saw that the field ambulance was
bouncing slowly towards the fence. Nobody else standing
along the rails seemed to be taking any notice of the drama
that was Jess; their eyes were following the runners who
were coming round again for a second time. Rhona could
hear the growing thud of hooves behind her and she ducked
under the rails as the horses flashed by, a blur of muddied
colours and a rush of snorted breaths.

She was out of breath herself and the blood thumped in
her ears, but she began to run again as soon as the horses
had passed. She saw that Tom had caught the chestnut mare
and was leading her round, away from the fence, and that
it looked as if they had put Jess on a stretcher and were
lifting her into the ambulance. She could see the doors open
and a flash of red blanket and then the doors were slammed
shut and the ambulance started to move, turning slowly
and bumping its way across the field towards the first aid
tent. Rhona stopped. There was no point in going on now.
She saw Tom vault onto the mare and start to ride her back
towards the lorry park, his long legs dangling free of the
stirrups. At least the horse is all right, she thought. That, at
least, was something.

She'd worked with Ken for seven years and point-to-pointing was her life, but it still made her heart stop to see a fall like that. It took her straight back to when Robert, her fiancé, broke his back, and was turned at that moment from a young man with everything to look forward to into a mumbling vegetable. Eighteen months he'd been like that in the head unit in Bristol before he had the stroke that finally killed him. She'd wept then, for the first time, partly for herself and the white dress which hung under a plastic cover in the wardrobe of her mother's spare bedroom and partly out of relief for him, that it was all over and he was no longer trapped in that broken body.

It was a mad and dangerous sport and you weren't in it unless you could take it, that knife edge between glory and disaster. It was the same every time, every race. If anyone asked you why you did it, when so many hours and so much effort culminated in this desperate need for it just to end safely, you couldn't give an answer. You just did it because you loved it. With this in her mind, Rhona turned into the driving rain and, head down, began the long plod back to the tents.

'Who is it, Izzy?' mouthed Belinda, making a querying sort of face at her granddaughter who was holding out the telephone receiver towards her.

Izzy put the receiver back to her ear. 'Who is it speaking, please?' she asked politely. She listened to the reply and then said to Belinda, 'It's a man with a funny name. Mr Victor.'

Who? wondered Belinda. She kicked off her rubber boots

by the back door and threw her wet coat on the floor.

'Hello, this is Belinda.'

A man's voice, a deep, mature voice which she did not recognise, said, 'Hello, Mrs Haddon. Belinda.'

'Who is this?' asked Belinda, bemused.

'Victor Bradford.'

'Who?' Belinda was aware of being rude, of perhaps not recognising someone she should know. 'I'm sorry,' she said, to give herself time. 'Victor Bradford?'

'From the garage.'

'The garage?' How stupid she was being. What garage? What Victor? Izzy was standing next to her, intrigued, and Belinda reached out and combed her fingers through her soft, peach-coloured hair, untangling the silky threads. 'Crumpets,' she mouthed at her. 'Get the crumpets out of the larder.'

'You brought your car in last week. For an MOT,'

'Oh, yes!' Now she knew. She remembered now. The big man who owned the garage outside the village. She remembered standing in his overflowing office, writing out an enormous cheque, and how they had talked about the weather, how cold it was. He was rather a nice man, she recollected. He had been apologetic about the size of the bill and had gone through it with her item by item, as if that would make it better.

'Oh, yes,' she said again, searching in her mind for a clue as to why he should be on the telephone. She watched Izzy fetch the crumpets and set about trying to open the tough cellophane packaging with a knife.

'I hope you don't mind me telephoning,' he said.

'No, no,' she said brightly. What *did* he want?

'I just wondered if you were doing anything next Wednesday evening.'

'Doing anything?' repeated Belinda. What did he mean? Was he asking her to work in the garage, or something? She imagined taking the place of the large blonde woman she had assumed was his wife, who sat behind the counter in the little shop, spilling over the chair on which she swivelled between the till and the portable television set up on the wall.

'Yes, I wondered if you would like to come to a concert. I've been given tickets for a show at the Pier Theatre in Bournemouth.'

Belinda was astonished. Was the man, this Victor, asking her *out*? *On a date?* It sounded like it.

'Well, how very kind of you,' she said, recovering her manners. 'That's such a lovely thought and I'm so sorry that it won't be possible.'

'Won't be possible?' He sounded disappointed.

'No, I'm so sorry.' She would have to do better than this. 'You see, I'm afraid that . . .' What could she say? 'My daughter is out that night and I'm looking after my grand-daughter.' Relief. That sounded quite plausible and was almost true.

'Oh. I see. Well, that's a pity. We could have had a bite of supper after. Maybe another time?'

Belinda put a hand to her mouth. Was this a joke? Was someone making fun of her? No one had asked her out for years. She couldn't remember when.

'I know you're a widow, see, and I lost my wife two years ago.'

Belinda murmured sympathetically.

'So, I thought . . .'

'Yes, well, that was very kind. A kind thought.'

'So you wouldn't mind if I asked you again?'

'Um, well.' What could she say? It was so hard to be discouraging without sounding rude. 'It might be difficult.'

'Oh, so there's someone else, is there?'

This was becoming absurd. 'No.' She laughed defensively. 'Certainly not. No, no one else. You see, I'm not really interested in that sort of thing.'

'Ah,' said Victor. 'I see. Well, I might just keep trying then. Keep hoping. Maybe you'll change your mind. Just friendship, that's all. Just for the company.'

'Yes, of course. Well, it was very kind of you. Really it was. Now, I'm afraid I must go. My granddaughter is about to have a serious accident with a kitchen knife!' She laughed brightly to cover her embarrassment.

'You'd better go then,' said Victor in a solemn tone.

'Yes, well, goodbye then.'

'Goodbye.'

Belinda put down the telephone and met Izzy's offended stare.

'Granny,' she objected. 'I'm not! I'm not about to have an accident. I'm being careful.'

'I know, darling. I had to say that. To get off the telephone.'

'Who was it?' asked Izzy. 'Who was that man? He'll think I'm a silly baby now. What did he want?'

'Oh,' said Belinda. 'I don't know what he wanted, really. I don't know him at all, but he asked me if I would like to go to a concert with him.'

21

'Why don't you want to?' asked Izzy. 'It would be nice, wouldn't it?'

'Oh no, I don't think so. We wouldn't have anything to talk about. We don't know each other, you see.'

'Oh,' said Izzy. 'That's funny. Asking people you don't know.'

She was too clever by half, thought Belinda. 'Come on,' she said, to change the subject. 'Let's put a log on the fire and toast those crumpets.'

What an extraordinary thing, she thought as she knelt over the hearth plying the toasting fork and feeling the welcome heat on her face. Asking me out. What was he thinking of? She tried to remember Victor Bradford. A tall, well-built man. No overalls – wearing a sweater, she thought, jeans, work boots, and a woolly hat. She remembered the woolly hat. He had a slight Dorset accent, a softening of the edges of his words.

What would her mother-in-law say? Belinda smiled, thinking how unsuitable the snobbish old lady, a canon's widow, would deem a man like Victor Bradford. That would almost be reason enough to accept his invitation, she thought, had she wanted to go out with a man. Which she most definitely didn't. Not again. She was past all that.

'Here you go, Iz,' she said, hot-fingering the crumpet off the prongs of the fork. 'Put the butter on while it's warm.'

All the same, she had to admit to herself that it was a pleasant surprise to discover that a man, any man, come to that, had taken an interest in her. What had she been wearing on this MOT occasion? She couldn't remember. Usual old gear, she supposed, jeans, sweater, old sheepskin coat. Lipstick, though. She always wore lipstick. Izzy said she would even put lipstick on for Snowy, and it would certainly be the thing she would grab if the house burned down.

How Jess would laugh when she told her. Asked out by the garage man! It made her smile, thinking about it.

Rhona pushed through the crowds who were streaming back to the car parks now that the last race was over or jostling into the beer tent where the ground had been turned into a soupy mix of mud and beer and the rain dripped steadily from the awning. The winning horses, being led into the winners' enclosure, were of no interest except to their owners and trainers who, ignoring the dismal weather, crowded round them, talking excitedly, lit up by success.

She dodged through the frozen bookies who were in a hurry to dismantle their stands, load their suitcases into the backs of their cars and get inside and get the heaters running. No one in their right minds would want to hang about on such an afternoon. Ahead, Rhona could see the first aid tent next to where the jockeys weighed in. The ambulance was drawn up outside, its doors still open. That was where they would have taken Jess.

Before she got there, she was joined by Ken Andrews' wife, Mary, her face solemn with anxiety. 'Is Jess all right?' she asked. 'I didn't see what happened but Ken said she had an awful fall.'

Rhona shrugged. 'I don't know. The horse turned right over. They've got her in there.' She indicated the tent where an ambulance man stood guarding the entrance. The two

women exchanged glances, both fearing the worst, but as
they got closer, above the whacking noise of the wind
banging the canvas, they could hear a raised voice. Jess was
arguing with the doctor.

'I was only winded!' she was saying, arms akimbo, still
holding her whip in one hand. She was so covered in grey
mud that it was hard to know what colours she'd been
riding in. She had removed her helmet and a wet length of
dark hair hung down her back. 'That's why I didn't get
straight up. I wasn't concussed. Not for one second!' She
looked round to see Rhona and Mary crowding in the
entrance and said, 'I'm just telling the doctor that there's
nothing wrong with me.' Opposite her, a calm middle-aged
man in waterproof jacket and trousers held Jess's Jockey
Club medical record book in one hand. 'I would have walked
or ridden back if it hadn't been for these kind men offering
me a lift. I promise you. I'm perfectly all right.'

'You're just a bloody idiot, that's all!' said Mary. 'Riding
an animal like that! Are you out of your mind?' The doctor
looked round, startled by her tone.

'She *is* all right, you know,' he intervened kindly. 'There
really isn't any harm done. She'll be stiff tomorrow, a few
bruises, but nothing broken.'

'That's not the point,' said Mary. 'OK, so she's escaped
this time, but what's she intending to do? Go on riding
maniac horses until one *kills* her?'

The doctor shrugged. That wasn't his business. He handed
Jess her medical record book. 'There you go,' he said. 'It
wasn't a recordable accident. You're fit to ride.'

'Thanks,' said Jess, with a grin, sweeping the book out

of his hand and turning to pick up her helmet. 'Anyway, Mary, you should be glad I wasn't hurt, not furious.' She smiled at the ambulance men. 'Thanks for the lift,' and she ducked out of the tent. Mary and Rhona stepped back to let her pass.

'You shouldn't do it, Jess,' said Mary, kinder now. 'It scares the pants off me, hearing you've had a fall like that. I feel responsible for you. What would your mother say if she knew?'

'There's no need for her to know. I don't know why you mind more about me than Carl or Tom. I don't have any more falls than they do.'

'Riding our young horses is one thing. At least you know they're well prepared. You didn't know anything about that horse except that it had it all to learn. But most importantly, you've got a *child*, for God's sake!'

A female jockey, wearing a long mackintosh over her breeches, intervened.

'You all right, Jess?' she asked.

'Yeah, thanks, Annie,' said Jess. 'Had one hell of a crash though. Did you see?'

The girl nodded. 'So I hear. Horse OK?'

'Yes, thank goodness. I'm just going to check on her now.'

'Going to Black Forest Lodge next week?'

'Yes. See you there.'

Mary shook her head in despair. 'Come on, Rhona. I'm wasting my breath. Let's get back to the lorry. My feet are like blocks of ice.'

They're a different breed, she thought, as they battled back towards the lorry park, these tough, horsy girls whose passion is racing. They had had a few of them through their yard, willing to work more for love than money and then risk life and limb on the racecourse. After a few falls and a couple of tough seasons, they'd usually had enough. They weren't all as determined as Jess Haddon. What bothered Mary was that in Jess's case she did not appear to take into consideration the fact that she had a six-year-old daughter to think about, a daughter, moreover, who had no acknowledged father.

Rhona, too, was thinking of Izzy. Mary's words had taken her back to when Jess's child was newborn and how she had held the little red creature with her creased and ancient baby face and felt a contraction of tenderness that had silenced and shocked her. Jess, meanwhile, had sat up in the hospital bed wearing a T-shirt with the words Kiss My Ass across the front and said, 'What do you think, Rhona? Hideous, isn't it? Give me a puppy any day!'

That was typical of Jess, but she was joking of course, and Rhona was not deceived. Jess had even breastfed the baby for a few months, bringing her to work in a pram, which she parked in the yard if it was fine and in the farmhouse kitchen when it wasn't. Mary used to yell across the yard for her when Izzy cried and Rhona had watched entranced when Jess freed a round breast and plugged her crying baby to the nipple, whereupon the squalling had promptly stopped.

The tenderness and closeness were what Rhona remembered. She saw it in the baby's unfocused eyes that sought her mother's face, in the first milky smiles, in Jess's uncharacteristic gentleness as she offered a finger to the tiny hand with its starfish fingers and perfect transparent nails like minute, pearly shells.

It had been a surprise to her, to feel like that. She thought she had sealed over any tender feelings after Rob had died. Later, when she made a fresh beginning and started work for the Andrews, she had acquired a reputation for toughness, for preferring the horses she looked after to any man, for scoffing at the idea of marriage or motherhood. This was her armour and her shield so that when she shut the door of the mobile home she lived in behind the hay barn, and took Thomas, the yard cat, onto her lap, she could tell herself that she had all that she wanted and that there were no yawning gaps in her life.

Mary was right, she thought, as she followed her ample behind up the steps of the lorry into the steamy warmth and smell of horse. Jess should take better care of herself. She had a lot to live for.

Chapter Two

The horses done for the night, Jess pushed open the back door of the long, low farmhouse which ran along one side of the racing yard. She kicked off her boots in the flagged washroom and hung her sopping coat on a peg. Not bothering to knock, she went through the inner door into the kitchen, a low-ceilinged room which glowed with light and warmth. Tom was already there, leaning up against the Aga alongside Carl, the other lad who rode for Ken Andrews, both holding mugs of soup, cigarettes in their free hands, laughing and talking. The long table was littered with the remains of a picnic, a fruitcake in a tin, a loaf of bread on a wooden board, butter, cheese, pickles and a bottle of whisky. Ken, a slightly built man with thinning, sandy hair and a shrewd, ruddy face, sat opposite Mary and the other stable girls, red-haired Susan and dark Moira. A nest of three Jack Russell terriers snored in a sagging armchair in the corner by the old-fashioned sideboard laden with silver cups and trophies.

Jess knew the talk would be about the day's racing, analysing how the horses had performed, exchanging gossip, planning future outings. If the horses had run well, it was the best part of the day, everyone relaxed and tired, the tension spent, the work done; but sometimes jockeys had to brave grim-faced silence if they had bogged up and got things wrong or, worse, if a horse had been injured. Tonight there was nothing but satisfaction in the air. Tom had ridden two winners, Carl had a second place and Jess had brought a tricky novice home fourth in a hotly contested ladies' race. It had been a good day, given the state of the going and the fact that all the horses were still a whisker off peak fitness so early in the season.

Jess had had the only fall and as she sipped at the mug of soup passed to her by Tom, she gingerly felt her elbow and ribs which were bruised and sore.

'Stiffening up, Jess?' asked Mary. She was kinder now that the fright Jess had given her had worn off.

'I'm OK. A bit battered.' It wasn't done to make a fuss and Jess was always conscious of the need to prove herself to Ken and Mary. They had seen a good few young men and women ride for them over the years and their judgement counted more than anything. Above all, they had to know she was tough enough to do the job.

'She jumped that third fence well,' said Ken, adding a trickle of whisky to his tea. 'Flew it. She'll learn, that little mare. Got the breeding to turn into something useful.'

Jess knew she could take this remark as the only sort of compliment she would get from him.

'Yeah. She'll do better next time out,' she said.

'Hmm,' said Mary, making her disapproval obvious. 'What did Ted Dawlish have to say?'

'Not much,' said Jess. 'You know him. He's a man of few words and most of them are offensive. He said I took her into her bleeding fences too fucking fast.'

They all laughed.

'Bloody cheek,' snorted Mary. 'I know for a fact that mare hasn't been backed five months. He was lucky to get anyone to ride her. She earned quite a reputation for herself out qualifying with the South Dorset. She's hardly had a saddle on her back.' All point-to-point horses had to put in a regular appearance on the hunting field in order to be eligible to race. The hunting season began in September when the corn was cut and the fields were clear and after December the qualifiers disappeared as the racing season absorbed them.

'They saw Jess coming,' sniggered Moira. 'She's got "Sucker. Try me!" written across her forehead.'

'I can't afford to be picky,' retorted Jess defensively. It was annoying to hear that sort of remark from Moira whose own nerve was shot, who didn't race herself and who would only exercise the quietest horses and therefore did not really pull her weight on the yard. 'If I don't take up the rides I get offered, I'm liable to lose the good ones along with the rubbish.'

'That's right,' concurred Ken. 'That's the way it goes. There aren't any short cuts in this game. The good rides are earned the hard way. Anyway, owners want the best riders for their young horses. That's why Mrs Toynbee insists on Tom riding Cinders.' He winked at Mary across the table so that Jess could not avoid seeing but she chose to ignore his intention to wind her up. He knew that Mrs Toynbee's preference for Tom as a jockey rankled with her. Cinderella Slipper was one of the horses which had had a comfortable win that afternoon. A big, brown mare, she was bred to race and already showed good form in her first season. She was a ride that Jess wanted more than anything. However, her owner, a grand old lady who had had horses in training with Ken for thirty years, insisted on putting Tom on board.

'I bet she was pleased with how she ran today,' Jess said, trying to sound casual. Of course she was jealous, she couldn't help it, even though she wanted to be glad for Tom.

'Yes, she was pleased,' said Tom, 'although she always gives the impression that it was only what she expected and she would want to know why if she hadn't won.'

'That's a bloody good horse, that's why,' snorted Ken. 'If she hadn't won, it would have been your fault.'

'Thanks, Ken,' said Tom. 'So I just sit there, do I? Go along for the scenery?'

They all laughed again and Ken leaned over to pour some whisky in Tom's mug of tea. Tom had been riding for him since he was fifteen and the insults which passed between them were joshing and friendly.

The door opened and a young woman put her head in, her face round and rosy, framed by her striped woollen hat.

'That's me done, Ken,' she said. 'I'll be off now, before the kids forget what I look like. See you on Monday. Bye, Mary. Bye, everyone.'

'Bye, Lisa.'

Mary got to her feet and picked up an oven glove. She pushed the two young men out of the way so that she could open the door of the Aga and peer in at a casserole. Jess drained her soup and put the mug in the dishwasher.

'Thanks, Mary. I'll be off too. Can you take me, Tom?'

'You coming out later?' asked Moira. 'We're going down the Cricketers at Pulham.'

'I'm not, no,' said Jess, pulling a face. 'I'm bloody knackered. I want an evening in. Early bed for me.'

'What about you, Tom?'

Tom hesitated and looked at Jess. Moira smirked. 'Early bed for you too? If you're lucky?'

Jess ignored her. 'Come on, Tom,' she said. 'Let's get a Chinese on the way home.'

Moira shrugged. It really annoyed her that he let himself be pushed around like that.

'Bye, you two,' said Susan peaceably. 'See you on Monday.'

The door opened again and Rhona put her head in, her plain face dominated by her cold, red nose, her waterproofs shining with wet.

'Tod's leg has come right up,' she told Ken. 'I've hosed it but I'd like you to come and have a look. I think he should have a shot of antibiotic.'

Ken sighed and got to his feet, reaching for his coat and cap which had been put by the Aga to dry. There was always something that needed doing, a horse to be seen to, a problem to be sorted. Together they trooped out into the filthy night.

Later, in his old Land Rover, Tom glanced sideways at Jess, trying to assess her mood. She had her father's face, square-jawed and determined but with her mother's long, sensitive, mobile mouth and deep-set, downward-sloping brown eyes. It was an unusual face which seemed assembled of mismatching parts, the bone structure suggesting a toughness which was contradicted by the soft and dreamy eyes and mouth; not really pretty, but attractive, the sort of face that made you want to look again. She could appear solemn and slightly sulky until she smiled and then three deep little dimples caught at each corner of her mouth and transformed her appearance. Instantly she looked merry and wicked. It was an enchanting smile, and the one thing about Jess that Tom saw Izzy had inherited.

'Are you really OK?' he asked over the noise of the wind-screen wipers.

'Yeah. I keep telling everybody I am. I've got a stonking headache, that's all. Not from the fall, just the cold and the whole bloody shenanigans.'

Tom knew what she meant. There was a lot of tension built into a day's racing, quite apart from the physical demands. This time of the year was the worst when the new horses were raw and inexperienced and the weather was so often foul. It got better as the season wore on into the spring and point-to-point meetings became a pleasurable day out with a carnival atmosphere and work on the yard was less of a grind.

Tom also knew that there was more to it than that. Jess had set herself the goal of making it as a leading lady rider, maybe even winning the area championship, and today would have earned her only a few extra points. This year was crucial, she reckoned. She thought that soon she would be too old, over the hill, and unless she made her mark now, she never would. Of course it all hung on what rides she was offered and it was irritating to her that Ken consistently put up Tom or Carl on his more favoured horses.

'You're not as experienced and you're a girl,' he would point out calmly.

'Ken, you can get reported for saying that sort of thing,' Jess complained. 'The equality police will come and take you away.' He just smiled and pencilled Tom or Carl's name alongside his entries.

'You can have all the ladies' races,' he said, 'and the odd confined and open race along the way, if the owners are happy to give you the ride, but I'm not putting you up on the really dodgy novices and that's that. I don't want your mum after me.'

So Jess had to resort to picking up extra rides here and there, horses like Flying Fancy that later on would stand a chance of winning, and would probably have another jockey on top when they did so. It was maddening and unfair in her view and she chafed against it.

Tom sympathised in part. He understood the competitive, killer streak that you had to have to be a successful point-to-point jockey although, having ridden for as many years as he had, he himself no longer felt driven in quite the same way. He had nothing to prove these days, and was happy with his life – part-time farmer on his own small acreage, and jobbing handyman the rest of the time. A bit of fencing and ditching, tree clearance, and a stream of young horses that he bought wisely, schooled, hunted, introduced to eventing and sold on. No doubt it was not quite the life his parents would have wished for him after an expensive school and university reading English, but it was what he wanted and he made a small living and it was, he felt, a case of reverting to type. His grandfather had been a farmer and horse coper and Tom was much more like him in character and appearance than his uptight, upright, solicitor father.

Tom tried to assess the atmosphere in the car, like dipping a toe into a swimming pool to test the temperature of the water. Jess was silent. He never knew how to get close to her when she was like this. Sometimes she seemed grateful for his tentative offers of consolation and sympathy and then they shared a period of warmth and closeness which made his heart expand. He couldn't hide the fact that he loved her, even though the other women in his life, his mother and sisters, said it was a mistake. Treat 'em mean, keep 'em keen was not an attitude he could ever adopt, even if he wanted to. He wore his heart on his sleeve. That was the expression he had heard used about him and he didn't know what he could do about it. It made him think of the achievement badges he had earned in the village Cub Scout troop when he was at primary school and how his mother had patiently stitched them onto the sleeve of his uniform. Woodland Craft was one, and Kitchen Skills another. He imagined his heart alongside those two.

If he gauged it wrong now with Jess she would retreat further, shutting him out completely, and it would be no use trying to close the gap. When she was like that he had learned to go quiet himself and let her mood run its course.

He could understand what was eating at her tonight. It was Moira's stupid remarks and the fact that she was getting little encouragement in her efforts to get good horses to ride. It didn't seem to matter how well she rode – and she was good, there was no doubt of that, and improving. She was brave and she could think her way round a track, ride a clever race, time things right, see spaces and use them, but it was hard for her to demonstrate this skill when she got no further than the fifth fence because of an unlucky fall, or was on a horse that simply didn't have ability.

Ken's attitude was understandable, too, and came from his quite genuine concern for her safety and because he held the old-fashioned view that things were different for a girl. But if racing was what you wanted to do, if it possessed you, as it did Jess, with a consuming passion, then nothing short of injury would stop you. You put up with all the shit – the weary, tedious round of stable work, the early, slow, boring build to fitness, the road work, the trotting. You shrugged off all the painful little injuries like bruised ribs after a fall from a skittish horse just up from grass, a toe crushed by an ill-mannered youngster, the pulled muscles from the lifting and carrying, and later, when the winter took hold, the flaming, itching chilblains on frozen toes and fingers. There was no glamour in it, that was for sure. No money and no glamour. Poncing about in racing colours and white breeches on race days was as close as it came – that and the beauty of the horses.

More fun were the early days of qualifying with the local hunts, the misty September mornings spent on sweating young horses, mad with excitement at their first sight of hounds. The real reward came with the much more enjoyable half days on the seasoned pointers who knew the ropes and loved their hunting and took you zinging across country, flying the mighty blackthorn hedges of the Blackmore Vale to make your heart sing. All this because, at the end, soon after Christmas, there was racing.

There was nothing to touch it, nothing to beat it for fear and excitement, and when it all came magically right – the race, the horse, the course, the weather, the ground – when all these things were in your favour, it seemed as if the gods were smiling and you were lifted into a state approaching euphoria. Tom had once come across some lines of poetry – Rupert Brooke it was – and they jumped out from the page at him because they so poignantly described that feeling which 'caught our youth and wakened us from sleeping, with hand made sure, clear eye and sharpened power, to turn, as swimmers into cleanness leaping'. Then, when he read on, he felt ashamed when he realised the poet was talking about young men dying in the First World War while he was thinking merely about the thrill of racing.

He knew how Jess felt and understood why she wanted to win. They had a lot of other things in common as well. They both loved animals, the countryside and the sort of life which involved both. Neither cared much for material success or its trappings. They both drove clapped-out old cars and Jess still lived at home while he rented half a ramshackle farmhouse. Judged by the successful careers of people he had been at school with, Tom reckoned he could be written off as a failure in most respects, but he was happy and loved what he did, which was what really mattered. And he loved Jess, who was at the middle of everything, the core of his life. His relationship with her was what anchored him here in this small place with its close horizons and familiar, unchanging routines. If it hadn't been for her, who knows, he might have buggered off to Australia or New Zealand or South America, somewhere with wide open spaces and room for people like him who were becoming oddities in an increasingly urban England.

What Jess felt for him was another matter and he had learned to keep quiet about his feelings because if he expressed them, she shied off with the usual complaint about being pressurised and not wanting to make promises she might not be able to keep. But then, she seemed to rely on him, to need him there, like tonight when she had turned to him for a lift and for company. The fact that she slept with him on a fairly regular basis further confused him. He was often aware of some sort of gender role switch. These days, wasn't it supposed to be the man who never felt ready to commit to a relationship? Yet here he was, a big pushover, hanging around, hoping that one day Jess would want him.

He felt like one of those stoical Thomas Hardy characters who, unappreciated by the object of their affections, plod along with their simple, Dorset country life, cutting turnips or chopping wood or trudging about after sheep, all the time patiently waiting for the penny to drop and the girl to recognise their worth. He had just finished rereading *The Woodlanders* and it was a bit depressing to be reminded that Giles Winterbourne had to die in a miserable shed, covered by a wet sack, before Grace realised that she loved him.

Beside him, Jess stirred in her seat, like a dog shaking off the rain.

'Tell you what,' she said, in a moderately more cheerful voice, 'I'll give Mum a ring and see if she and Izzy want to share a Chinese. A crispy pork ball is currently Izzy's idea of heaven. We could stop in Sharston and pick up a take-away.' She fished in her old denim bag for her mobile telephone and tapped in a number. Tom felt relieved. She was all right then. If she wanted a sociable evening with her family at Rosebay Cottage, she was all right. He smiled across at her in the dark.

'Got any dosh?' she asked him. 'Can you lend me a tenner?'

Later, the plastic bag containing the foil boxes of hot food on Jess's knees, they drove out of the little town towards the village. It was pitch dark and the lane which wound between the looming hills ran with water and shone like a river in the headlights. Round the next bend the lights of the village were a smear of gold in the dark although most of the cottages had their curtains drawn snugly against the evening cold. At the crossroads Tom turned right and followed Church Lane past the Old Rectory and the new, modern vicarage and the row of thatched cottages now knocked into one. A few more houses and the village petered out and the lane climbed into blackness. The trees on the left hung ghostly branches over the road and on the right the hill dropped away steeply. At the top, the wood was broken by a park wall and then one of the pair of cottages which was home to Belinda, Jess and Izzy. Jess was glad that her mother hadn't drawn the curtains and two rectangles of golden light shone through the gloom and that the lamp over the door beckoned. Tom pulled up to the side of the cottage and turned off the engine. Collecting her things from the cab, Jess got ready to make a dash to shelter when the back door opened and against the stream of light she saw Izzy peering out into the blackness. Then, realising who it was who had arrived, she began jumping up and down in her red elephant slippers, with Snowy barking beside her.

Jess slammed the Land Rover door and ducked into the wind and rain. Through the weather she could just hear Izzy's piping voice.

'Mummy!' she was calling. 'Hurry, hurry! We've been waiting for you!'

Belinda was in the kitchen when she heard Tom's car pulling off the lane. It had been a relief to get Jess's telephone call suggesting a takeaway and not to have to think about supper. Although she disapproved in principle of fast food, horrendously expensive and stuffed with E numbers and monosodium glutamate, it was nevertheless a treat. She loved prising the lids off the foil boxes and finding them filled with squashed rice and noodles and pale lumps of chicken and prawn swimming in slimy dark liquid. Even better was being able to chuck the boxes out afterwards and dispense with any form of washing-up.

This evening she was feeling particularly worn out. She felt the strain when Jess was racing and the telephone conversation she had just had with Jo, Jess's older sister, didn't help. Jo was sensible, a trained solicitor, married to a civil engineer and living in Reading, and she disapproved of Jess vehemently and took every opportunity to tell Belinda so. This did not help in any way, just notched up the stress level and made things worse, in Belinda's view. This evening Jo's voice had taken on a challenging, slightly self-righteous tone and Belinda felt driven into a corner.

'I know, I know,' she'd said. 'I agree entirely. Jess shouldn't be racing these novices and it worries me terribly.' She had kicked the kitchen door shut so that Izzy, who was still engrossed in crumpet toasting, shouldn't hear. 'But I can't stop her. What would you suggest I do? It's no use banging on at me about it!' Jo had harangued her then about irresponsibility and no provision being made for Izzy's future until Belinda's head was spinning. Jo going on like that made her feel as if their entire existence was precarious, as if the three of them, herself and Izzy and Jess, were teetering on a precipice – too small an income, a tiny pension, old age around the corner. It was depressing and she didn't want to be reminded of it.

At her age, and as a widow, she might have hoped to be living peacefully and quietly on her own, occupied by gentle middle-aged interests in gardening or antiques or charity work, not still being buffeted about between these two strong-willed daughters. She couldn't imagine bothering her own parents in the same way when she was their age. It seemed that today's grown-up children were never to develop the distance between the generations which she remembered. Many of her friends remarked on this phenomenon. Their adult children always seemed to be there – borrowing money, occupying what should by now be spare bedrooms, nagging, bossing, criticising and generally involving their parents in their lives, while at the same time making it quite clear they had not the slightest intention of listening to parental advice.

Really, she felt a strong inclination to forgo the takeaway and sneak upstairs for a long bath and bed. She loved her bed more than anything these days. In fact she would choose it as her one luxury on *Desert Island Discs*. She didn't like to consider what this might say about her. Perhaps she was suffering from a vitamin or mineral deficiency and needed the sort of supplements advertised in the Sunday papers. Ginko root or Devil's Claw. The advertisements always had a trim, silver-haired, middle-aged couple hand in hand or with their arms loosely circled round each other's shoulders, leaning on the deck rail of a cruise ship, smiling into the distance and clearly enjoying every moment of their supple joints and regular bowel movements.

When Jess and Tom appeared in the kitchen, blinking in the light, they both looked bleary with fatigue. Tom was holding a white plastic carrier bag which brought with it a hot steamy smell almost like wet dog. Despite herself, Belinda felt a wave of tenderness and pleasure. It was lovely that they wanted to come home, she thought. It was the best thing in the world to have one's family around and thank goodness for Tom that he was happy to spend an evening with them.

'Mummy! Mummy!' shrieked Izzy, pulling at Jess's hand. 'I got some books at the jumble sale. Some animal stories and *The Water Babies* with pictures. Come and see! Come and see!'

'Whizzo Izzo! Ouch! Don't touch my ribs. I'll come in a minute.'

'Oh, darling,' Belinda couldn't help saying. 'What happened? Not another fall?'

'Don't bloody start,' said Jess rudely, opening the fridge and taking out a bottle of milk.

Tom stepped forward and kissed Belinda on the cheek and hoisted the plastic bag in the air.

'No, all right. I won't say anything, but you know how

43

I feel.' She turned to Tom. 'The plates are warming in the oven, Tom. Shall we eat next door, by the fire?'

'You bet. I'm still not thawed out,' said Jess, pouring herself a glass of milk.

'Mummy!' said Izzy, still catching at Jess's hand and clamouring for attention, 'How was the races? Tell me, tell me.'

'Hang on, Titch. Let me get all these wet things off,' and Jess started to peel off her sweaters. 'Iz, run up and get me my tracky bums and jersey. I want to feel toasted while I eat my supper.'

Izzy scuttled off, glad to have a mission, and while she was away, Belinda said, 'She's been so worried about you.'

'Well, that's your fault,' Jess shot back. 'She gets that from you. You put it into her mind that I might get hurt. It wouldn't occur to her otherwise. It's you and Jo.'

Belinda was silent. In a way, Jess was right. Anxiety was catching.

Tom began unpacking the foil boxes, opening lids and sniffing the contents while Belinda bustled about getting the plates out of the Rayburn and putting them on a tray with a roll of kitchen paper.

'Got any more soy sauce?' he asked Belinda.

'In the cupboard behind you. Bottom left.' She slid her arm round Jess who was standing unselfconsciously in bra and pants, chucking her wet clothes in the general direction of the washing machine.

'Anyway,' she said. 'Glad to have you home in one piece.' For a brief moment her tall daughter dropped her head onto her shoulder in a small gesture of affection which signalled the end of hostilities.

'Here, Mummy,' called Izzy from the sitting room. 'Here are your tracky bees.' She caught sight of the food. 'Oooh. Lovely battered bollocks!'

'Izzy!' protested Belinda.

'She gets that from Tom. That's what he calls them,' said Jess as they trooped from the kitchen to the fire.

After they had eaten they slumped back in that curious state, which Belinda found was usual with Chinese food, of feeling stuffed full but somehow unsatisfied, and watched an appalling television game show. Belinda had opened a bottle of wine which she shared with Tom, and the effect was to make her feel momentarily at peace. It was a cosy scene with the flames warming the pale walls and casting deep shadows in the corners, disguising the shabbiness of the worn chair covers and the threadbare carpet.

Belinda suddenly remembered that she hadn't told either Jess or Jo about Victor. Now, for some reason, she found that she didn't want to make a joke of it. She didn't want to hold him up to ridicule and to laugh at his expense. She felt that by virtue of his widowhood and age he was more on her side than on theirs. He would understand her worries about the young and about her own future because he, no doubt, had grown-up children of his own and very likely anxieties about his business. He would be an ally. It was ridiculous thinking like this because they would never be friends. Victor. It wasn't a name she liked. She had never known anyone called Victor. Not as a friend. So Victor remained her secret. Hers and Izzy's. An untold joke.

Izzy should be in bed. It was disgracefully late and this television programme they were watching was so loaded with laboured sexual teases and suggestiveness that it was quite unsuitable, but she was happy, curled up with Jess and Tom and that, after all, was what she most needed. A sense of belonging.

They looked like a family, sitting there, Tom in the middle, with one arm looped round Izzy who had her head on his chest, and the other round Jess, and yet they weren't. They were held together by the loosest of connections, which could be broken and put aside should either Jess or Tom grow tired of their relationship. It was a situation that was quite outside Belinda's experience. There had been no option when she was young but to get married and when she was Jess's age she had three young children, and thought of herself as settled into a union which would last for ever. Things were so different now. Even steady, conventional Jo had lived quite openly with her future husband, Nick, from university onwards, while Charlie, the eldest child, moved between a series of live-in girlfriends whom she swapped as regularly as he changed his socks.

Did this change in the moral climate make for more happiness and ultimately more successful relationships? How could she say? When she had walked down the aisle beside David she was nineteen and knew nothing about life or love. The profound shock she had experienced as the euphoria of her wedding wore off, the misery over her inadequacies as a wife, the unsatisfactory fumbling in bed, the loneliness of army housing with a husband posted abroad – none of these things applied to her own children. Looking back on her decision to marry she had come to the conclusion that it was because she was desperate to leave home and desperate for a wedding list at Peter Jones, at the top of which was a Wedgwood dinner service and a Kenwood food mixer. She got what she wanted, with David thrown in, like part of a job lot. Almost any reasonable man would have done and she was lucky that David turned out as he did.

Later on, when she had given up all the silly yearning for romantic love, they had grown closer and a fondness had developed between them which had augured well for their middle age. Then came the heart attack out of the blue while he was sitting at his desk at Blandford camp opening his mail, aged forty-five. Fifteen years ago. Now most of the china had been broken but the food mixer was still going strong.

These days David's death was too far away to feel the shock and pain and regret. She had had to get on with life because of the children. She had discovered that David hadn't in fact been very good with money, that there were debts to be paid off and very little life insurance, and that for years they had been living beyond their means. She had had to face unpalatable facts and shoulder certain responsibilities for the first time in her adult life. The house had to be sold and the girls moved from their boarding school; somehow or other she had to keep the whole rackety show on the road. She wasn't very good at it, and sat weeping night after night, not from grief but from anger. What had been the point of David, after all? He had turned out to have been hopeless at all of these things. She felt as if he had let her down badly, that he had not kept his side of the bargain, which was how she had come to see her marriage. It had never been a love match, she had known that when she walked triumphantly down the aisle on his arm, but she had always believed it would be a bulwark against an uncertain world, against insecurity and poverty and loneliness, but she and the children were pitched head first into all those things. Damn you, David, leaving me with all this mess, she had thought grimly, weeping onto the shoulders of her friends who assumed, incorrectly, that she was convulsed with grief.

Belinda suspected that Jo had suffered most when David died and things had been so rocky for a time. She had been fifteen and about to take her GCSEs but in true Jo fashion she had sailed through her exams and not complained when she had had to leave her expensive school that summer. After that she had gone to college in Yeovil where she got her A levels but had no fun as far as Belinda could see.

From then on Jo had sought security as if she wanted to catch hold of the future and nail it down. She roped in reliable Nick as a steady boyfriend in her first year at university. She got holiday jobs and invested her student loan so that she freed herself from debt years before any of her friends and then organised Nick into marriage when it made sense from a taxation point of view. Belinda suspected that they were now considering starting a family – and what a planned baby it would be. Unlike poor little Izzy. A careful cost exercise would have been done, taking into account a private birth and subsequent childcare, in order for Jo to return to work and earn the money to set up a trust to pay school fees from nursery onwards. All this was admirable and made Belinda very proud of Jo, but she wondered whether at some point in her life Jo would not feel that she had wasted her youth, or had it stolen from her.

Charlie had suffered least although, being a boy, he had reason to miss his father most. He had been awarded a bursary to finish his schooling and scraped enough A levels to go off and learn to be an estate agent. He had been buoyed along by his gang of cheerful, rule-breaking, beer-drinking friends who would not allow him to mope or be left out of anything. He spent holidays loafing about between their well-off homes and came back to his mother and sisters less and less often. He hated the cramped, rented cottage and the scrimping lifestyle they had to adopt, and released himself as soon as possible.

Now he was doing well at work and lived a noisy, laddish life in London. He was a dutiful son, telephoning to keep in touch and turning up at Christmas and Easter. Belinda suspected that he found Jo and Nick dull, but he got on well with Jess and was the only member of the family to encourage her racing. Every now and then he would turn up at a point-to-point with a gang of friends to watch her ride, and he and Tom enjoyed an easy, teasing relationship.

Jess had been the real worry. She had moved from boarding school to the local school in Sherborne, hating both equally, and was lazy and uncooperative about every-thing but horses. Moving to the cottage had been a bonus for her because it came with a field and a stable and she soon had the loan of an old pony. From then on she had poured everything into riding and had insisted on leaving school at sixteen and going to work in the racing stables, which alarmed everyone. She must get some qualifications, they all said. There's no future in point-to-pointing, she's throwing her life away. What can I do? Belinda had wailed. She won't listen to me.

Meanwhile Belinda had no option but to make the best of things and gradually this was what she had done. Finding a menial job in a dress shop in Sherborne and going to evening classes to learn how to use a word processor was the beginning and gradually things got better. She changed jobs and started to work as a part-time secretary for financial consultants in the same town, earning more money and proving to be efficient and reliable. She began to enjoy her independence and as the years went by she got used to being on her own, and now suddenly here she was, with the children grown up and Izzy nearly six, and life pottering past at an alarming rate.

Belinda yawned and stretched and looked at her watch.

'Jess, it's nearly ten o'clock. Izzy should have been in bed hours ago.'

'Go on then, Iz,' said Jess sleepily, pushing her daughter off her lap. 'Up to bed.'

Izzy, tired past being reasonable, began to whine. 'I don't want to go on my own. Take me up, Mummy. Read me a story. You haven't looked at my books, Mummy.' She pushed *The Water Babies* into Jess's lap.

Jess ignored her, her eyes glued to the screen.

'Please!' wailed Izzy.

Jess gave her a push with her foot. 'Oh, go to bed, Izzy. Stop being such a pain or I won't let you stay up late again. I'm not coming up with you. I'm too tired to move.'

'Come on, Izzbug,' said Belinda. 'Gran's about to peg out.

Let's go up together, shall we? Bring your books. I'll read you a bit in bed. Jess, turn off the lights and put Snowy out before you come up. And put the guard in front of the fire.'

'Oh, Mum,' moaned Jess. 'Stop fussing. You'll be reminding me to clean my teeth next.'

Upstairs Belinda wiped off her make-up while Izzy draped a damp flannel over her face. 'I'll wash in the morning,' she said from under it. 'It can wait until then, can't it, Gran?'

'You're a dirty little grub,' said Belinda, 'but I don't suppose it matters for once. Come on. Heavenly bed. My favourite place to be!'

'Can I come with you?' wheedled Izzy. 'Just for a little while? I'll help to get your bed cosy for you.'

'I switched on my electric blanket half an hour ago, but you can come for a bit.'

Izzy hopped up into the big bed while Belinda undressed and then gratefully climbed between the sheets beside her granddaughter. It felt embracingly warm and welcoming. Bliss, she thought, settling back and reaching for her night cream. Izzy was already curled into a drowsy ball, sucking her thumb and twiddling a curl of hair round the fingers of her other hand. She had stacked her books beside her. 'Read to me, Granny,' she commanded sleepily.

Belinda picked up the first of Izzy's books. It was a large, old hardback with a faded green cover and *Tales from the Animal Kingdom* printed in gold letters. She flicked through the pages and saw that it was far too old for Izzy and that the drawings were rather dull pen and ink. There was not much to entertain her here. She was just about to close it when she saw that a child had already written its name on the frontispiece in a large, round hand.

'This book belongs to John Thomas Bearsden,' she read. 'Christmas 1972. The Grove, Kington, Dorset, England, Europe, The Western Hemisphere, The World, The Solar System, The Universe.' Horrified, Belinda snapped the book shut.

If Tom stayed the night, Belinda did not know it. When she went down to make her early morning cup of tea, his Land Rover had gone and the back door was unlocked. She let Snowy out into the garden and was glad to find that the wind and rain of the previous day had given way and that, although pitch black, the morning had a different, more gentle feel. A sifting of dried winter leaves and twigs had blown into the porch by the back door and the garden path was littered with debris from the surrounding trees but now there was a stillness in the air and the bitter, raw cold was gone. A smell of wet wood and earth, mushroomy and intense, came through the open door while she waited for the kettle to boil and a cock pheasant burst out of the trees behind the cottage with a saw-edged call of alarm.

From the sitting-room door Belinda could see that Jess hadn't bothered to set the room to rights before she went to bed the night before. The sofa cushions were flattened or on the floor, and the carpet was strewn with mugs and discarded bits and pieces. The fire had burned down to a mound of grey ash. The room looked dreary and depressing and Belinda felt compelled to start plumping cushions and picking things up and sweeping the hearth with the little brush. There were still one or two red embers among the wood ash, and by dropping a few pieces of kindling onto the fire and fanning it with a newspaper, flames sprang to life and she fed the blaze with some coal and larger pieces of wood.

Settling back on her heels, watching the flames, she wondered where the compulsion came from to be always putting things straight when the inevitable progress of daily life meant that it was wasted work. It couldn't just be an inborn female trait – or if it was, it had bypassed her daughters. However, like a Pavlovian dog, Belinda had to go through the motions of clearing, tidying, putting away in order to achieve a sense of inner calm and order and to be able to sit and enjoy the first cup of tea of the day.

She fetched the tray from the kitchen, settled in the chair by the fire and put her feet up on the fender. In the pocket of her dressing gown were her needlework scissors and piled on the floor beside her were the books Izzy had bought at the jumble sale. A quick glance last night had revealed that Johnnie Bearsden's name appeared in three, and it was these that she was about to take the scissors to. Working carefully, she cut the pages as close to the spine as possible. Then she fed the offending flyleaves into the flames.

John Thomas Bearsden. Seeing the name like that on the page and so unexpectedly had been a shock. It seemed incredible that of all the children's books piled on the trestle table in the village hall, bright comic books, modern stories based on television programmes, cheerful annuals, contemporary retelling of fairy stories, Izzy should have picked out these particular books. They must have been stacked together and she supposed that Mrs Binns, who manned the stall, had let her have them all for the pound coin that Belinda had given her to spend.

John Thomas Bearsden. The name would mean nothing to Izzy, nor Mrs Binns come to that, but it wasn't only Belinda who believed that Johnnie was Izzy's father. Several people had come to that conclusion when Jess announced that she was pregnant.

Jess had loved Johnnie, Belinda was sure, since she was about twelve years old and he was the glamorous young army officer who trained the Pony Club cross-country team. He was one of those men, remembered Belinda, who was mercilessly charming and endowed with such confidence that women found him attractive, especially the little horsy girls, who flirted with him in that dangerous, half-knowing, half-innocent way. Belinda had never felt comfortable with him. He was too smooth, too conscious of his attractiveness, but what she felt about him hardly mattered, one way or the other, because their lives barely touched except for that summer when Jess was in the team. Evenings and weekends had been taken up with practices and Johnnie would whistle down from London in his sports car whenever he could. Belinda remembered how the Pony Club mothers took to wearing scent and clean, tight jeans, and even old Mrs Vaughan, the district commissioner, became pink and girlish in his company, as the beam of his charm swung across them all.

The Pony Club competition came and went and he disappeared for several years, busy being a soldier, she supposed, before turning up after Jess had left school and was working at the racing stables. He was married by then with a child, but as dashing as ever, and for just one season he kept a half-share of a racehorse with Ken. He was still in the Army and living in London and he would arrive on a Saturday morning to ride before belting back after his race. Belinda imagined that his life was a whirl of glamorous events because it was clear that he had outgrown the local social scene and was now moving in smarter circles, but he continued to be his usual charming self and to exercise his fairly harmless compulsion to make girls love him.

And Jess certainly did, in a starry-eyed, infatuated, teenage sort of way. She looked after his horse at Ken's and it seemed to Belinda that Johnnie paid her special attention, tipping her generously, sending her a huge box of chocolates when his horse won and once or twice taking her out to a pub supper when his wife was away.

Belinda had wondered since about this shadowy wife. She was American and wealthy, according to local gossip, and older than Johnnie. Because he had always had a taste for living way beyond his means there was the suggestion that he had married her for her money and this seemed perfectly plausible to Belinda. She imagined the marriage already showing signs of stress, of Johnnie's charm wearing thin, of his lifestyle cramped by the arrival of a baby and of a wife bored by army life who seemed to spend a lot of time back home in the United States.

This was the only evidence that Belinda could cite that Johnnie and Jess had had an affair. Jess had certainly not had any other special boyfriend at the time. She went out with a gang of young people from the yard and the neighbourhood and she did not drink so couldn't even be excused on the grounds that some man had got her drunk and taken advantage of her. She just announced that she was pregnant and that was that – no explanation and no regrets. In the absence of anybody else it was Johnnie Bearsden's name that came up as the likely father of her baby.

He had been in the right place at the right time and Jess adored him. If she was absolutely truthful, he was also the one whom Belinda would have chosen. It was snobbish of her, she knew, but she would rather it had been Johnnie than any of the deadbeats and rogering adventurers who hung around racing yards. Johnnie was related to a semi-distinguished family who once owned a small estate close by, and there was a sort of Jane Austen romance to it. It would be nice for Izzy to find that she was related to an old landed family and one day, maybe, be acknowledged.

It was shallow, Belinda knew, to care what people said behind her back, but she did mind, and it seemed she felt all the shame which Jess herself defiantly refused to share. She wouldn't even weep and confess that it had all been a terrible mistake but instead accepted her condition with a matter-of-factness which drove Belinda mad.

Film stars went in for that sort of thing, and poor, hopeless, ignorant teenagers, but not ordinary, well-brought-up, educated girls like Jess. It was so unnecessary. Contraception was so widely available that to have unprotected sex with some man who, for whatever reason, could not take on the role of father was utterly stupid. Belinda had railed and raged privately, while trying to suppress these feelings in her dealings with Jess who was as sulky and touchy as most teenagers could be.

They got through her pregnancy somehow and when Jess announced that she would look for somewhere else to live, Belinda persuaded her to stay until after the baby was born. Then Izzy arrived and changed everything. She released such love and tenderness that Belinda's heart was lost and even Jess softened and glowed with motherhood, for a short time at least.

The situation did not alter. Jess continued to work at the yard at not much above the minimum wage and Belinda's worries about the future were compounded now that there was a baby to consider. That, and the fact that Izzy did not have the sort of home and family that Belinda felt was every child's due were her chief concerns.

This worry was still with her. She thought about it most days; it was always at the back of her mind, this big aching anxiety that Izzy was missing out and that however much she loved her granddaughter, there was nothing she could do to fill the void that having no father left in her life. It wasn't as if Jess furnished Izzy with even the barest of details. Surely she could tell her that her father was a man whom Jess had once loved but who had moved away, gone abroad, died, anything other than this blank?

Sometimes Belinda wondered whether Jess had no idea herself, whether she had slept with numerous men and Izzy's father could be one of many. This was an ugly and disturbing thought; she couldn't believe it of her daughter. There was nothing in her behaviour to suggest that this was true. In fact, if anything, Jess seemed relatively uninterested in men.

She didn't go to parties much and didn't dress or behave in what Belinda thought of as a tarty way. Even in staid Dorset, girls went around in low-cut jeans, their bellies bared almost to their pubic hair and their bosoms bursting out of strappy tops, but Jess had never been provocative like that. She was very rarely out all night, and if she was, it was generally with Tom, and dear Tom was not Izzy's father, Belinda knew, because he had been abroad, working in a racing yard in the United States, when Jess became pregnant.

Eventually Jess was going to have to tell Izzy something. Immaculate conception was not a pretence that could be sustained for ever.

Meanwhile, here she was, destroying evidence of Johnnie because Jess would never believe that she had not had a hand in Izzy's choice, and if Izzy's curiosity led to questions, God only knew what a can of worms that would open.

How the books had found their way into the village jumble sale, Belinda could only guess. Quatt Lodge, the Bearsdens' old house, had recently been sold after Johnnie's ancient uncle died. Perhaps a job lot of junk had been cleared out and found its way into the sale. That could be the only explanation.

Belinda's thoughts were interrupted by the door opening and Izzy herself appearing, her face still crumpled with sleep, barefoot and wearing her stripy nightdress. She made a wobbling half run across the room to climb into Belinda's lap, putting her cold, smooth little arms round her neck. Belinda stroked the tangled tangerine-coloured hair off her face, marvelling at the fine skin, palest pink from sleep and marbled on her forehead by faint blue veins.

'Good morning, darling,' she said. 'You're awake early.'

'You moved me,' Izzy complained in a sleepy voice. 'You moved me, Gran. Out of your bed.'

'Because you kick, darling. You kick like a little horse in your sleep. You'd have kicked me out.'

Izzy snorted with laughter. 'When did you?' she asked. 'When did you move me?'

'Middle of the night. Kick, kick, you went. I lifted you out and put you in your own bed and you never woke up.'

'Was I dreaming, do you think? Of being a horse?'

'You must have been. A very badly behaved one.'

'I'd like to be a naughty horse.'

'You would? Why's that?'

'I could kick and bite people.'

'Izzy! Why do you want to do that?'

'I just do, sometimes.'

Belinda laughed. 'Who in particular would you like to kick and bite, darling?'

Izzy looked up at her with clear grey eyes. 'Boys at school who call me a bastard. That's rude, isn't it?'

Belinda felt something like a knife slice through under her ribs, deep into the centre of her body, with a real physical pain.

'Which boys?' she asked quietly, stroking the fine strands of hair from Izzy's forehead.

'Rupert and Hugo,' said Izzy. 'It's always them.'

Yes, it would be, thought Belinda. It would be those snot-nosed, ugly little twins, offspring of a London banker and his smart wife. It would be them. They were only at the village primary school until they were old enough to be sent off to a smart local prep school. That sort of remark wouldn't come from the other ordinary children with the usual backgrounds, children with single mothers and missing fathers and stepfathers and half-brothers and -sisters. The wretched twins would have heard the word at home from their mother, the stuck-up, smug Carina, with her loud voice and her hunters and Range Rover and her week's skiing in the New Year and holidays in Sri Lanka.

'Yes, it is rude, and they're rude,' she said, 'and they deserve a good kick. I'd give them one myself given half a chance!'

Chapter Three

Later, sitting in church, she regretted her response. She should have said something more circumspect. She should have said that reacting with violence never solved anything and that kicking and biting were wrong, but the truth was that she felt the same as Izzy. She would have liked to get the two little beasts into a corner and teach them a lesson.

It was exactly what she had feared Izzy would have to go through as she grew up and she was frightened that it had started already. Sitting in the icy grey interior of the little stone church, Belinda tucked her hands into the sleeves of her coat and hunched her shoulders. The name-calling and Johnnie Bearsden's childhood books appearing in such an unexpected way seemed ominously linked, although she couldn't think how.

She didn't hear a word of the sermon and suddenly the congregation, only eight of them, the old diehards, were getting to their feet and scrabbling for their collection envelopes to put in the plate which was being passed around by Alison Busby in a large ginger fur hat like a big tom cat on her head. Belinda, whose job it was to clean the church brass, noticed that the plate was nearly green and dull with tarnish. Something else to put on her list of things to do.

'Our closing hymn, number sixty-four,' announced old Canon Hobsworth, looking over his half-moon spectacles. Belinda saw that he was wearing rubber boots under his cassock. The lane from his cottage by the old packhorse bridge at the bottom end of the village must be flooded again.

'No, it's not,' contradicted Jean Rooke in a ringing voice from the organ seat. 'It's number eight-one. "Lead Kindly Light".'

'Any advance on eighty-one?' asked the canon cheerily. 'Right we are, eighty-one it is,' and the organ creaked into action.

As the hymn churned on – surely something more uplifting could have been chosen – it occurred to Belinda that she had not discovered from Izzy whether she knew what the term 'bastard' actually meant. With any luck she didn't, and neither did those horrible twins. They just knew it was abusive and insulting.

When the congregation trooped out, the air was soft and springlike. It had been much colder in church. All along the path, snowdrops dipped their delicate white heads and tucked under the wall, clumps of pale yellow primroses dappled the bleached winter grass like sunshine. Birdsong trembled in the light, pearly sky above the bleating voices of ewes and the piping of their lambs in the yard behind Church Farm. It felt as if spring had come with a rush.

Belinda hurried round the little knots of people on the path. This morning she did not want to chat. 'Good morning,' she called. 'Sorry to rush. I haven't forgotten, Alison, about the roof fund meeting. All well, Jean?

62

Morning, Canon. Lovely, isn't it? But what a day we had yesterday. Yes, the family are fine, thank you.' With relief she reached her car and set off home.

After the lane wound out of the village and began the steep climb to the top of the ridge, Belinda was, as usual, spellbound by the view. This morning the wide vale below glimmered in the watery sunlight, the small grass fields silvery green and the hedges and trees blue. The sky seemed so high and airy and it was fluffed with palest pink and violet clouds. After the gloom of yesterday when it had pressed down, iron-grey like a saucepan lid, Belinda felt her spirits lift. She looked forward to getting lunch ready, to the delicious smell of roast lamb and garlic and sizzling roast potatoes. The routine of Sunday would settle her nerves and re-establish a sense of normality, and today she had Dinka, her best and oldest friend, coming to lunch on her way back from a photo shoot in Cornwall. Afterwards, perhaps they would all go for a walk before Dinka started off back to London.

As she pulled into the space beside the cottage she saw that Dinka's smart little silver car was already parked. The doors and windows of the cottage had been opened to the morning and Snowy was basking on the concrete path. He jumped up and ran to greet her as she got out of the car.

'Dinka!' she called, hurrying inside. 'Sorry I wasn't here when you arrived.'

The little kitchen was bright with sunshine when she went in and Dinka was sitting at the table, smoking a ciga-rette and turning over the pages of the Sunday newspaper. She looked up and smiled, her dark glasses perched on her sleek blonde hair, her legs in tight jeans thrust out in front of her. She had an attractive face with narrow, slanting brown eyes set quite close together above a long, elegant nose with a tilt at the end and a full mouth of large, white, even teeth. It was a sharp, intelligent face, slightly simian in its alert expressiveness. She got up to embrace Belinda, who felt the softness of her cashmere sweater and caught the delicious whiff of familiar scent. A slide of solid bracelets clinked as Dinka lowered her arm.

'Dinka, you look wonderful as usual. How was the shoot? Did it go well?'

'Ghastly. Don't ask. You must have noticed the weather. It poured with rain for two solid days, and in the end we gave up. It was a garden piece, after all, and you couldn't see the bloody garden for swirling sea mist. Then look at today! Perfect, but too late. The saddest words in the English language. We'll have to come back later in the spring.' Dinka worked as features editor for a glossy magazine and led the sort of life that Belinda could only guess at.

'How was church?' Dinka asked, settling back at the table. 'I hope you put in a good word for me.'

'Same as usual. Nothing much changes down here. I wish it was twelve o'clock and we could have a drink,' said Belinda, consulting her watch. 'Church always makes me long for a large gin.'

'Oh, honestly! Who cares what the time is! Anyway, it can't be far off midday,'

'Oh no, we must wait,' said Belinda. 'It's a slippery slope otherwise. A terror for women like me, living alone, watching the clock for when they can have the first drink of the day. A lunchtime gin is my Sunday treat. I always feel I've earned it, somehow, if I've been to church.'

'Oh, I see. Although you hardly live alone, do you? Jesus turned water into wine so I'm sure he'd be sympathetic. He understood the need for a drink. Actually, I've got some wine for you in the car. I'll go and get it in a minute. We can have it at lunch.'

'That's kind of you. I'll put the meat in the oven right away. Have you seen Jess and Izzy? Where have they got to?'

'Gone to help that lovely Tom with some lambs. Apparently he's got two sets of triplets which he's got to keep an eye on and Izzy was very keen to see them. She and Jess seemed well and bouncy, both of them. Izzy's grown since I saw her at Christmas.'

'Yes, I think she has, but oh dear, Dinka, I'm so worried about her. But I won't start on that now. Not until we've had a drink, anyway. Will you have to dash off after lunch? Have you got time for a walk? It's such a heavenly day.'

'We'll see. I'm not wildly keen on exercise, as you know. A little wander along the lane would be quite enough. Now what's all this about Izzy?' Dinka drew on her cigarette, narrowing her eyes, a quizzical expression on her face.

'She's being teased at school. She told me this morning. Name-calling, that sort of thing. Being called a bastard. It's what I've always dreaded would happen.'

'Belinda, get real.' Dinka snorted. 'Children these days are incredibly foul-mouthed. They call each other much worse things than that. You should hear them going past my house in London on the way to All Saints primary down the road. They eff and blind worse than merchant seamen.'

'But this is a *pointed* insult, Dinka. The horrid little boys who have been teasing her know exactly what they're saying, I'm sure. They'll have got it from their mother, who is a fearful snob and gossip. She's always been horridly interested in Jess, asking questions which are supposed to be sympathetic but are really prompted by a salacious curiosity.'

'So what? It's fashionable to have an unknown father these days. Don't make such a big deal of it.'

'That's all very well for you to say. It's different in London. And that's not the only thing. Yesterday Izzy bought some books at the jumble sale in the village, old children's books, and the extraordinary thing is that when I was reading them to her last night I discovered that they had belonged to Johnnie Bearsden! His name was in the front cover!'

'Johnnie who?' Dinka looked nonplussed.

'Dinka, you know. The man I'm sure is Izzy's father.'

Dinka stubbed out her cigarette. 'Look, I'm sorry if I am being a bit slow but, frankly, so what?'

Belinda stared at her, amazed that she hadn't got the point. 'Well, what were they doing there? In our village jumble sale? It seems so peculiar, and that Izzy, of all people, should buy them.'

Dinka shrugged. 'I can't see what you're getting at. Pure coincidence, I would say. Didn't his family come from round here?'

'His parents lived the other side of Dorset but his great-uncle lived at Quatt Lodge only a few miles away. Johnnie used to come and stay with him when he was in the Army, and he hunted with the Blackmore Vale and got involved with teaching in the Pony Club. That's how we met him and then, later, after he was married, he kept a racehorse with Ken Andrews, where Jess works. But that was years ago. Exactly when Jess became pregnant. Why should the books turn up now?'

'I've no idea but I can't see that it's at all significant. Izzy picking them out was pure chance.'

'It just makes me feel uneasy and unsettled.'

'That's because you're hyper-sensitive on the subject. What did Jess say?'

'Jess? You don't think I *told* her? I spent ages this morning cutting the pages out of the books before she could see them.'

'Why?'

'Because I couldn't face the upset it would cause. Jess is terribly touchy about Johnnie. She doesn't like his name being mentioned.'

'Bloody hell, Belinda. What a can of worms this all is. Are we going to have that drink? Although it pains me, make mine long and weak because I'm driving.'

Belinda bustled about getting the gin bottle out of the larder and looking for a lemon.

'Actually,' said Dinka, as they clinked glasses, 'speaking of Jess, I think she mentioned taking Izzy out on that square brown pony after lunch. Didn't you say it was ancient, by the way? It would make the perfect rug for my hall. Could I put my name down for it?'

'Dinka!' laughed Belinda. 'Don't let Izzy hear you!'

'The point I am making is that you're for ever moaning that Jess is a negligent mother, and so I was rather impressed with all this Izzy-centred activity. She's a bloody sight better mother than mine was, or most mothers when we were growing up. The concept of "doing things" with one's children hadn't been thought of then.'

Belinda considered. It was true. She could remember Dinka's stylish, divorced mother from their school days and how appallingly neglected her friend had been. She was frequently abandoned for weeks at a time while her mother was in the south of France, staying with friends, or something equally diverting and child excluding. One Easter holiday when Dinka complained that her shoes hurt her toes and she had grown out of her clothes, her own mother had taken her to London and bought her new school uniform from Daniel Neale's.

Belinda had been envious of her then and hungry for a bit of glamour in her own home life which seemed so austere and dull by comparison. At that age she hadn't appreciated the benefit of a stable and ordinary family and would have gladly exchanged her own for Dinka's solitary state.

'I *did* have a good mother,' she said, 'but I used to pray to be orphaned, which I thought was the most romantic thing ever. I wanted my brothers to be bumped off at the same time so that I could be entirely alone in the world. I could make myself cry just thinking of the wonderful pathos of it.'

'There you are then,' said Dinka, as if something had been proved. 'So stop worrying about Izzy. The one thing that child knows is that she is loved. Now let's have a top-up.' She sloshed more gin into each of their glasses.

'I've got something else to tell you,' said Belinda, throwing new potatoes into the sink and taking up a knife to begin scraping them. 'A man has asked me to go out with him!'

'Belinda! Now we're talking!' said Dinka with enthusiasm. 'I hope you said yes. I'm not offering to help with those potatoes. I can't afford to ruin my nails. I'll set the table in a minute.'

'No, I didn't. I did my best to put him off.'

'Oh Belinda! Why, for heaven's sake? What's the matter with him?'

'Nothing. He's the man from the garage where I get my car sorted out. He took me completely by surprise. Izzy answered the telephone and when she passed it over to me, I couldn't think who he was. I've hardly spoken to him before although I've seen him lots of times. He's always about, but not to have a conversation with.'

'But why did you say no? Is he married already or something? I think a motor mechanic could be a wonderful lover. There's something quite raunchy about oil-stained overalls and the manly mastery of the internal combustion engine.'

'No, he's a widower, but I don't know him, for one thing, and for another, well, I don't really want a man in my life. I'm quite happy as I am.'

'Don't be ridiculous. You can't be. No woman is. You did your mother hen stuff one time around, you don't need to throw yourself so wholeheartedly into a second circuit with Izzy. You should have a grown-up life now – and that includes some wonderful sex.'

'Thank you, Dinka. I do have a life. Stop making me sound like a sad case.' The two friends clinked glasses again. This conversation was taking a familiar turn. Dinka's recipe for happiness always included a man, although as Belinda knew all too well, most of her amorous adventures ended in tears. Childless and divorced for over twenty years, her current lover was a Spanish photographer, fifteen years her junior.

'I have to admit that I am rather flattered that he saw my potential, as it were,' Belinda admitted, dropping a yellow, scraped potato into the saucepan at her elbow. 'Although I keep reading that fifty is the new thirty, so I suppose it's quite possible that I could go on the pull, or whatever it is you call it. Anyway, I thought you would be amused.'

'Amused, maybe, but not a bit surprised. Stop being so bloody *humble*, Belinda. You sound *grateful* that this man should have noticed you. Why can't you accept that you're attractive and that a man should be interested in you?'

'Because there hasn't exactly been a rush of eligible men to my front door, and because I really do feel slightly past my best-before date.'

'Don't be ridiculous. You're exactly the same age as me and I have Javier, a delicious thirty-five-year-old, who dotes on me. It's all a matter of confidence.'

Maybe, thought Belinda, but at what price? The upkeep, for one thing. Dinka was permanently under refurbishment and modernisation, undergoing nips and tucks and Botox and liposuction. Is it really worth it, she wondered, when at best she can only hope to look good for her age? She looked wonderful, but the world was full of radiant twenty-year-olds who didn't have to do anything to look younger and better.

'But my garage man would have to be happy with me exactly as I am – unimproved,' she said, 'and anyway, he isn't anything very glamorous himself.'

'What does he look like?'

'I can hardly remember. Tall, well-built. Nice, craggy face. He's got a Dorset accent.'

'He sounds perfect. You really should give him a go.'

'You make him sound like a fairground ride.'

'Hmm. The Big Dipper. Come on, Belinda. Say yes. It would do you good.'

Sunday lunch over, the three women sat on at the table, drinking coffee and picking at a wedge of local cheddar cheese which Belinda bought at the village post office. Dinka produced a box of luxury chocolates and they drooled over them as they talked.

Izzy, who had been allowed to get down and was drawing on the sitting-room floor, came through to the kitchen and hung on the back of Jess's chair as she chose from the box, her fingers hovering over the chocolates in an agony of indecision.

'What were you drawing, Izzy?' asked Dinka. 'Can we see?'

'It's Mummy on her racehorse,' said Izzy, bringing the paper to the table. 'Winning this big gold cup. See? When I've finished I want you to put it on the wall, Mummy.'

'OK, Izzo. Let's hope you're right and I will win a big gold cup. Here, colour the horse a nice brown and make its legs a bit longer. It looks like a corgi at the moment. I'd never win anything on that.'

Izzy looked crestfallen but Jess appeared not to notice.

'When do you have to leave, Dinka?' she asked.

'Soonish. That reminds me, I've got a bag of sweaters for you, Jess, in the back of my car. Izzy, can you run and get them for me? They're in a big yellow bag.'

Izzy trotted off.

'Great,' said Jess. 'Your cast-offs are the mainstay of my wardrobe.'

'They'll be OK for work, anyway,' said Dinka.

Izzy banged through the kitchen door clutching a large, bright yellow Selfridges carrier bag. Excitedly, she dived in and drew out a pale grey cashmere polo neck which she draped on her mother's front.

'Lovely Mummy. Like a rabbit!'

'This is a bit posh, isn't it?' said Jess. 'Not exactly suitable for mucking out.'

'Well, you can wear it sometime, can't you?' said Dinka dismissively. 'Grey is a bit last year, but I don't suppose the horses will mind.'

'It's beautiful. Thank you.'

Izzy pulled out three more sweaters, a striped lambswool and another two polo necks.

'Thanks, Dinka,' said Jess.

Belinda whisked up one of the black polos and said, 'Can I lay claim to this? It would be perfect for work.'

'Oh, fight it out between you,' said Dinka. 'She whose need is greatest sort of thing.'

Jess caught hold of Izzy and, drawing her between her legs, held her fast. 'Do you want to take Bonnet for that ride?' she asked. 'I'll come with you on my bike.'

'Yes please. Yes please!' said Izzy, hopping about.

'Thanks for lunch, Mum,' said Jess. 'I'll help clear up later. Go and get changed, Iz.'

As if the washing-up would still be there when she got back, thought Belinda, but there was no point in making a remark along those lines. It would just make Jess cross.

'That's OK, darling,' she said instead.

She met Dinka's eyes across the table and knew what she was thinking. At least Jess had suggested doing something with Izzy. Belinda smiled at her friend. Dinka always managed to help her keep things in proportion.

By the time she had made another pot of coffee and Dinka was upstairs using the bathroom, Belinda could see from the kitchen window that Bonnet was tied up to the gate of the field with her saddle on while Jess was apparently showing Izzy how to plait her mane. It was a happy scene, the sunshine, the sturdy little pony and the two of them intent on what they were doing, their heads close, their hands touching.

Belinda went out of the back door and Izzy glanced up, her face pink with excitement and pleasure under her riding cap, the peak low over her round spectacles.

'Mummy's going to ride her mountain bike and I'm going to canter,' she told Belinda importantly.

'You be careful, darling,' she replied, and then regretted it as Jess shot her an accusing look – there you go, instilling fear again, it seemed to say. Belinda went over to the gate to stroke Bonnet's nose. The little pony's eyes were half closed.

'Look, she's nearly asleep,' laughed Belinda. 'She's nodding off in the sunshine.'

'Well, she is an old age pensioner,' said Jess, putting a neck strap over the neat little brown head. 'She's twenty-two, remember. A lot older than you, Mum, in horse years.'

'Oh, I do sympathise,' said Belinda. 'I wouldn't want to be going for a canter if I could doze in the sun instead. Especially after lunch. Have a nice ride, darling.'

'Watch me, Granny!' commanded Izzy excitedly. 'Watch me get on.'

'All right. Here, Snowy! Don't think for one moment that you're going too.' Snowy had perfected the art of making a nuisance of himself out riding, snapping and barking at Bonnet's heels when she was persuaded to go faster than a trot. Belinda took hold of his collar as Jess gave Izzy a leg-up. How tiny she looks, thought Belinda, observing her grand-daughter's little legs sticking out from Bonnet's hairy sides. She could tell from Izzy's intent expression that she was half scared, half loving it. She took up the reins and beamed across at her grandmother, wanting to be noticed up there on Bonnet's back where she felt big and important.

'Bye, Gran. Bye, Snowy. I'm going to canter! Mummy says I can!'

Jess wheeled her mountain bike from the shed and swung her leg over the crossbar. With her hair tucked into a base-ball cap and in her old jacket and jeans and dirty trainers, she looked hardly more than a teenager.

'OK, Iz, shorten the reins. No, shorter than that. Wind in the knitting. Come on, Bonnet. Off we go.' Belinda watched them turn out of the drive and onto the lane before dragging Snowy, who was whining in protest and looking longingly over his shoulder, back into the cottage.

Dinka was standing at the window, a fresh cigarette in her hand, looking thoughtful.

'That pony would be perfect,' she said. 'Exactly the right shade of brown.'

Chapter Four

Along the lane from the cottage, further along the ridge, a small farm perched on the side of the hill, its corrugated barn full of pregnant ewes. Immediately opposite, and through a heavy five-barred gate, the bridleway started, winding between tall trees, deeper and deeper into the wood until the brush and brambles closed around the thread of path and the bare branches nearly met overhead. In the summer it baked hard and horses' hooves beat hollow on the track, but throughout the winter months it was deep and wet, black with mud and pools of water.

It was one of Izzy's favourite places. She loved the sound of the wind in the tops of the trees and the silence beneath, broken by the sudden movement of deer gliding between the thickets, stopping and turning to watch Bonnet trotting past. It was the ideal place for her to ride alone because the clever little pony knew the twists and turns and the straight places where she could break into a canter for a few strides, and at the very end there was a hunting gate where she came to a halt, turned on a sixpence and retraced her steps, faster this time, her little legs flying along through the splashy mud. All Izzy had to do was sit tight and Bonnet took care of the rest.

Jess got off her bike to open the gate. 'Hang on, Izzy. Have we checked your girth? Look at it. This would go round you *and* Bonnet.'

Izzy stuck her leg forward, tense with excitement, while Jess lifted the saddle flap and notched the girth straps up several holes.

'There you are. OK? Just go steady on the way back when Bonnet knows she's pointing home. Hang on to the neck strap if you feel a bit wobbly. I'll come behind you on the bike.' She let Izzy through the gate and Bonnet set off at a brisk trot. She knew this routine inside out, being a local pony and having been passed round various families as she became outgrown. Izzy was thrown about on the saddle and Jess groaned aloud at her ungainliness. It was an irritation to her that her daughter was not a natural rider.

'Don't bounce up and down so much!' she called. 'Try to sit still!' But Izzy was out of earshot.

I'll give her a head start, she thought, dawdling by the gate. It does her good to do things on her own. She'll never have confidence with Mum fussing about her all the time. She started to push her bike along the path and then got on and pedalled slowly. She could hear the wind sighing in the top branches of the fir trees and then, high above, the thin mew of a pair of buzzards. She could see them if she looked up, wheeling against the blue of the washed sky.

Now she had to concentrate on watching where she was going as the track turned between the trees and the furrows became full of black water and the grass was sedgey and coarse. She could see where Bonnet's hooves had cut into the ground and could smell the sulphurous stink of churned-up mud. She stopped to listen. Nothing. Surely Izzy should have reached the gate and turned back by now? She dragged the bike to the side of the track and waited. There was no sound of a pony's hooves or snorting breath. Jess looked up at the sky and watched the buzzards for a bit longer. Still nothing. Ten minutes had gone by at least since Izzy had set off. Something must have happened.

Jess struggled to get the bike back on the track and set off again, this time cycling hard, standing on the pedals to gain leverage, panic starting to mount in her chest. She stopped again to listen but the blood drumming in her ears and her ragged breathing blotted out everything else. After a moment she realised that there was still no sound and she called, 'Izzy! Izzy!' A woodpigeon clattered its way out of a tree above her head and a rook cawed, but there was no other noise.

Oh, God, she thought. Let her be all right. Please God. At the same time she felt angry. Where was she? What stupid thing had she done? Fallen off? Caught her foot in the stirrup? Gone the wrong way? Stupid, stupid, little girl. She imagined her mother's face, heard her voice, 'Do be careful, Izzy!' Bloody hell, where was she?

By now Jess was nearly at the end of the bridle path, nearly at the hunting gate, which led out over a narrow bridge onto the open field beyond. She could see glimpses of the wide space through the last of the trees, a dull bleak slope of last year's maize stalks. Round the last bend and there was the gate, unexpectedly open, and no Izzy. Jess threw down her bike and ran. She could see fresh tracks in the gateway, new hoof prints going both ways. Leaving her bike, she ran out into the field and listened again. Above the sound of crows and sheep and a cock pheasant calling back in the wood she thought she heard something else, the distant thudding of hooves and then she saw them coming over the brow of the hill, two riders, trotting along side by side. One was a larger child on a grey pony and the other, unmistakably, Izzy and Bonnet.

Jess felt a great boil of anger, and she started to yell. The stupid child deserved to be as frightened as she had been.

'Izzy! Izzy! Where the hell have you been! Izzy! Izzy!' she bellowed. As the riders got closer she could see Izzy's pink face and that she was smiling, grinning from ear to ear, unaware of the crime she had committed, and that the child she was with was a boy, who was grinning too. Jess stalked towards them, her face clouded with rage.

'Hello, Mummy,' called Izzy, in an excited voice. 'I've been round the field with Mikey. Mummy, this is Mikey. He's come to live here from America.'

The boy turned to stare at Jess. 'Hi,' he said and pushed his riding cap back from his face. His glasses winked at her in the sun and Jess, turning to glare at him, was struck suddenly and dreadfully by his appearance. Her anger was displaced by shock. She had to turn away to prevent herself from staring.

To cover her confusion, she turned angrily to Izzy. 'You shouldn't have gone beyond the gate. You know that.'

'I met Mikey. He said we could canter up the field to his mummy, but Bonnet wouldn't canter, Mummy. I tried and tried but she wouldn't.'

'Of course she wouldn't. It's away from home and she knows you shouldn't go on. It was very naughty of you.'

Izzy's mouth drooped and Jess turned back to the other child. She needed to reassure herself that she had been wrong, that her eyes had deceived her.

'She shouldn't have gone with you,' she said. 'She's not supposed to go beyond this gate.'

The boy shrugged. He had a strange sort of composure and assurance for a child who looked no more than about nine. There was nothing in his manner to suggest that he noticed or cared that Jess was cross.

'We only went to my mom,' he said, waving his hand up the field. 'She's just up there, by the gate.'

'She's an American lady, Mummy.'

Jess snorted and took hold of Bonnet's bridle. 'Well, you'd better be going back to her,' she said curtly to the boy. 'Come on, Izzy, we must go.'

'Bye, Mikey,' called Izzy, but he had turned his pony and was flying away from them, mud splattering from the churning hooves.

'Come on, Izzy!' said Jess irritably, dragging Bonnet back to the wicket gate into the wood. 'You should be able to shut this on your own by now.'

'I can't, Mummy. It's too difficult for me. You must do it. Anyway, how can I learn to close it if I'm not s'posed to open it?'

'Don't be cheeky, and don't ever go off like that again.'

Izzy's face took on a closed, determined look. Her cheeks were still pink and glowing with the thrill of riding off with the boy, right up to the top of the field where she had never

81

been before. She was used to her mother's change of moods and was not going to let her spoil her adventure.

'That boy's name was Mikey, Mummy. He's going to be my friend. And his pony's name was, was, um, I've forgotten. His mummy was smoking a cigarette and she said, "Why, hello there."'

Jess pushed her bike on ahead up the track, her mind spinning, trying to make sense of Izzy's chatter. The boy's appearance had given her a shock, but his manner and how he spoke had altered the first impression he had given her. She wondered now whether she had imagined what she saw when he pushed back the brim of his cap and stared at her, but she knew she hadn't.

Izzy was having an imaginary conversation behind her. She could hear her saying. 'This is Mrs Mikey from America. Why, hello there!'

'Where did he come from, that boy?' Jess asked her, over her shoulder.

'From America. I said.'

'Not today, he didn't. He must be staying round here, mustn't he?' Her voice was unnecessarily sharp. She couldn't help it.

'I don't know,' said Izzy vaguely. 'He was with his mummy. They were from over there,' and she waved her hand back the way they had come. Jess wondered for a moment whether Izzy had noticed, had been struck in the same way that she had been, but she didn't think so. Perhaps children were less aware of their own appearance than grown-ups. If she had observed anything peculiar, being Izzy she would never have stopped talking about it.

All the same it was a strange and oddly disturbing experience, especially coming so soon after she'd seen Johnnie Bearsden's name in those books from the jumble sale. She had noticed them last night when Izzy had first plonked them on her lap and she had flicked through them. She hadn't said anything, just shoved the whole lot on the floor and told Izzy she was too tired to read. This morning, to her intense irritation, she found that her mother had carefully removed the offending pages in a 'this name must never be spoken again' sort of gesture, exactly as if she was a character in a Victorian melodrama.

Why the hell did she have to make such a huge deal of the whole Johnnie Bearsden thing, and secretly too, so that the subject became a taboo and could not be raised between them? Now Jess felt the burden of knowing what her mother had done while Belinda did not know that she knew. It was as silly as that. Tiptoeing about each other to avoid what her mother called 'a scene'.

Round the next bend the cottage appeared, tucked into the dark shoulder of the wood. Dinka's car had gone.

'Come on, Izzo,' she called back to her daughter. 'Why don't you trot the last bit?'

Bonnet, happy to be nearly home, set off briskly. She was looking forward to the handful of pony nuts she had earned for her effort. When she was within earshot, Izzy began to call.

'Granny! Come and look! I'm coming! Granny! I met a boy called Mikey! I met his mummy, and she said, "Why, hello there!"'

*

On the other side of the muddy maize field, Michael Peregrine Bearsden was walking home on his pony, Crusader, and feeling cross with his mother who was lagging behind trying to make her two new springer spaniels behave, while talking on her mobile telephone. Since she had got the dogs from the keeper who had trained them to the gun, she had started these afternoon sessions whenever they were down in the country, and Mikey found them incredibly boring. His mother's raised voice got on his nerves, for one thing, and she did not seem to have grasped the need to give a simple command and then insist on it being executed. Instead she went on and on at Teal and Snipe. He could hear her now. 'Snipe! Come here and sit at once. I've already told you that I want you to sit and you will not listen. Come here this instant! Leave that bit of dung, you dirty dog! Leave it! Come here!' before resuming her conversation with whoever it was. Mikey could see the puzzled expression on Teal's face as he squatted at her feet and waited, quivering with eagerness, to be told what to do next.

The dogs behaved perfectly well with his father, whereas his mother worked them up into a frenzy of excitement and then lost interest. She was in a funny mood anyway. She had been funny ever since he had cantered back across the field with that little girl. She kept asking questions about her as if he was supposed to know anything. He wasn't interested anyway. The girl was only a baby. She couldn't even get her pony to canter. Her mother had been weird, too. She had glared at him as if it was his fault her kid had gone where she shouldn't. Women, thought Mikey. What a nightmare. He turned in the saddle and shouted over his shoulder. 'Mom! I'm going on. I don't want to hang about all day!' His mother, her mobile clamped to her ear, waved a hand in his direction.

The following morning as Belinda drove to work, she was thinking about sex. Over the years she had come to the depressing conclusion that she wasn't much good at it. Before David had gone to work on that last fateful morning, they had made love. At least that was how she imagined David would have thought of it, although these days she supposed it would be called a shag.

It was inevitable that she should have repeatedly gone back to the last time they were together and she always wished that it had been a better experience. She could remember it so clearly, how his hand crept towards her under the duvet and because he was not a demonstrative, stroking, holding, caressing sort of man, she had known that he wanted sex. He had moved towards her then and she noticed his breath smelled stale as he fumbled with her nightdress and then heaved himself on top.

She remembered how she had lain rigid, aware that wifely duty demanded that she show a bit of enthusiasm and encouragement, but really feeling more like a lump of pastry under a rolling pin. She knew it was as much her fault as his. She should have halted the proceedings, explained that some preliminaries were called for, initiated a bit of what she could not bring herself to call foreplay. Instead it was quicker and easier to get it over with and allow him to heave up and down for a minute or two and snort into her ear as if he were labouring up a steep hill.

Thankfully, it was over quickly and with a sudden convulsion he collapsed on top of her, crushing heavily on her ribs. A few seconds later he rolled off and as he turned away for a few last minutes of sleep before the alarm rang, he gave her shoulder a little squeeze and that was that.

How could that squeeze be interpreted? she had since wondered, over and over again. Was it a gesture of complicity, to indicate the successful culmination of an activity in which they had both been participants? Like teammates grasping one another at the end of a match? If this was so, how horribly unaware David had been of how she really felt.

Or was it offered in a spirit of condolence? Was it to say, sorry, old thing, I know that was pretty awful for you? If that was the case, why did it have to happen at all? Why did he set about the whole dreadful, humiliating proceedings with such resolution and go on poking away at her until he'd done, when he knew she was unaroused and resentful?

She liked to think that in other ways they had had a happy, strong marriage and that David was a considerate and nice man, firmly in the good husband class. It was just that these days the whole sex palaver seemed to matter so much. If she was to believe what she read in magazines and newspapers, it seemed to be the central plank of every relationship and women felt they had a statutory right to multiple orgasms and a sensational sex life. It seemed impossible to even consider a marriage as happy or successful unless sex was a thumping, humping, heaving, clutching, moaning and frequent occurrence.

Belinda's understanding of this spectacular activity was drawn almost entirely from television and the occasional film seen in the cinema by the cattle market in Yeovil. The couples involved practically devoured each other, writhed and moaned and at intervals dived under the sheets to perform acts too excessive even for modern audiences. And this, she supposed, was what people got up to, which was hard to reconcile with the couples she knew and those she saw about her in the gloom of the cinema. She and David certainly never had – even at the beginning. She suspected that he was as inexperienced as she had been when they got engaged, although he had made bluff remarks about former girlfriends to cover his fumbling overtures. Anyway, what did it really matter in the long run? Not at all, she thought, except that it was a bit like not being invited to what the whole world said was a very good party. She just wondered what she had missed and if she might have enjoyed it.

And then, eight years after David had died, there had been a chance meeting at a local party with his ex-commanding officer, James Redpath. Belinda still found it hard to think about him without pain. She had been instantly attracted to him and he had been so handsome and kind and so concerned that he should not be taking advantage of her widowed state. She allowed herself to believe that what they subsequently shared had been magical – it was a revelation to her, anyway, and James had said her innocence was wonderful and exciting to him. Their affair lasted several glorious months and all the time she had known that his next posting would take him abroad and that would be the end of it, which it was in more ways than one. After a week or two of increasingly sporadic contact, she ceased to hear from him and her letters and telephone calls went unanswered until finally he had written the briefest note to say that he was sorry but his feelings did not match her own. All this happened to co-incide with Jess's pregnancy, exactly when she felt most alone and could have done with some loving support. Instead, in the miserable weeks she spent analysing their doomed affair, she had come to the conclusion that she hadn't been good enough for him – not attractive, clever or sexy enough.

When she read in the newspapers, nearly eighteen months later, of his death in Bosnia, blown up by a car bomb, she felt a strange sense of detachment as if her grief for him was numbed because in a sense she had already mourned his loss.

She thought of this as she approached Victor's garage on Monday morning. She and Izzy had had the usual run to get away on time and she had vowed yet again that she would get up ten minutes earlier to avoid the rush. The weekday routine at Rosebay Cottage was always the same. Jess was up and away at six o'clock, leaving Izzy and Belinda another hour in bed before they left the house together at eight fifteen, having fed the chickens and Bonnet and taken Snowy for a run. Belinda dropped Izzy off at school in Bishops Barton before going on to Sherborne to be in the office by eight forty-five.

Driving alone to and from work provided Belinda with valuable little pools of uninterrupted silence and were the best times to think undisturbed. Now the prospect of going out with Victor had sparked off silly speculations about having a physical relationship with a man again. What on earth would it be like, she wondered, in ripe middle age, to put it kindly? There was the slightly crepey flesh for one thing. She had noticed that while her bosoms were still full and in pretty good shape, the skin of her cleavage had started to crinkle, like an old apple forgotten in the fruit bowl. And she had developed a thicker waist in recent years. She couldn't imagine a man putting his hands round the meaty roll that seemed to have formed round her middle. Her legs were still all right in shape, but better for being in trousers or opaque black tights; in the flesh they looked oddly puckered and lumpy.

Her hair was like that of most other middle-aged English women. She had it cut every few weeks by a local farmer's wife who had been a hairdresser in a previous life. Dinka was horrified by this information and said that if she didn't watch out she'd be thrown onto her back and have the sheep shears run over her head, but Belinda was perfectly satisfied with Janie's efforts. She wore it at that compromise length common to her age, when the long, youthful mane had had to go but there was still a fear of going too short and looking mannish, or medium short and looking like the Queen. She coloured it herself every couple of months with a vicious smelling concoction which promised her a soft velvet brown, with 'full grey coverage'. 'Rivoli' the colour was called, although the woman in the chemist in Sharston called it 'Ravioli'. On the front of the box was a young Italian-looking girl whose long, shining brown hair tumbled about her naked shoulders. This was not the unlikely result that Belinda was striving for – she'd rather have chosen Fieldmouse if there had been such a colour, a silvery, light brown which flattered fine, pale English skin and blue eyes and was what Belinda's natural colouring had been before the dreary pepper and salt took over.

Face? How was her face wearing? She couldn't remember the last time she had really looked at it with much interest. There was definitely more of a double chin these days and a loss of firmness, a slight downward sag, a bit like a sponge cake sunken in the centre from having been taken too soon from the oven. And wrinkles. Yes, lots of wrinkles, but Belinda rather liked them, liked to see where her eyes crinkled at the corners and her smile around her mouth. Her face was all right. It was a gentle face, a kind face, she liked to think, and still bore the traces of the pretty girl she had been. Her best features were her far-apart blue eyes and the wide mouth which, as in Jess, could look mournful until she smiled.

All in all, she felt she was in fair nick for her age, and healthy and strong apart from a niggling back problem which she hoped to strengthen with weekly Pilates sessions. The most obvious thing about her was her ordinariness and it was with this in mind that she pondered Victor Bradford's invitation. Why her? Of course, she was single. Maybe that was enough in itself. Maybe he was desperate.

She was passing the garage now, Bradford Motors. The pumps were busy, with several cars queuing to use them, and the line-up of second-hand vehicles for sale extended from the edge of the forecourt into the field behind. The large workshop on the other side was also busy with a horsebox drawn over the examination pit and several young men leaning into the open bonnet of a car. Checking in her mirror that there was no one behind her, Belinda could not resist slowing down and glancing in. At that moment the door from the office behind the shop opened and Victor came out and crossed the forecourt. He appeared to be calling to someone in the workshop and did not glance in her direction. It would have been terribly embarrassing to be caught staring in like that. Belinda accelerated away.

She had just had time to notice that Victor was wearing a thick padded jacket and his customary woolly hat. Proper workmanlike gear, she thought, and there was something about his brisk walk and the gesture he made to the boys in the workshop that showed he was in authority, the boss.

Belinda smiled to herself. It was quite fun to have this little, unexpected diversion. A long day awaited her at the office and apart from everything else she had a fresh worry about her elderly parents, especially after the telephone conversation she had had with her mother the night before.

Jim and Charlotte Westcott, both in their mid-eighties, still lived independently in a cottage in Suffolk and her father had apparently fallen off a ladder while trying to fix some lead flashing over a leaking bedroom window. He was bruised and scratched but otherwise unhurt, his fall having been broken by a dense escalonia bush growing outside the sitting-room window.

Belinda was horrified. 'Mother! What was he *thinking* of? How could you have allowed him to do something so stupid at his age?'

'Now, darling,' said Charlotte reprovingly. She had been

a primary school headmistress and still sometimes sounded like one. 'You know very well that nothing deters your father when his mind is made up. Anyway, we decided that if he had a fall it was as good a way to go as any. At least he would be doing something useful. We've been waiting for the roofer for six weeks.'

Belinda sighed. This sort of conversation drove her to distraction.

'Anyway, you're not to say anything,' her mother went on. 'I promised him that I wouldn't tell any of you. It gave me quite a fright to see his legs flying past the window! I don't think the bush will be the same again and it flowered beautifully last year.'

Belinda ran her hand through her hair in despair. 'Really, Mother, you're both impossible. It worries me terribly, and you live so far away from us all.'

'Oh, don't start all that again,' retorted Charlotte. 'We're as fit as fleas, the pair of us. You have to let us old people get on with it. I remember how worried we were about my mother. You know after her first stroke she became quite mad on bonfires. She had one nearly every day when the weather was suitable, up until she was ninety. We always thought she would have one of her giddy turns and have a dreadful accident and incinerate herself, but of course she was perfectly all right. Ga-ga in the end, but the bonfires did her no harm at all.'

Belinda thought about this now as she drew up in the car park behind the offices of Clutter and Savage, where she worked. As soon as she had a free weekend she must go to Suffolk to see them. Giving them a poke with a sharp stick, her father called these visits. In fact, she wondered whether she should ask for a few days off and go sooner rather than later. Tony and Leo, her two brothers, were useless. Tony, a hospital consultant, was too busy, and Leo, a schoolteacher who lived the closest, was too lazy and unconcerned. Belinda felt a heightened irritation with him. Really, given his long holidays, he should pull his finger out and go and see them more often. It wasn't fair always to leave it to her.

If only her parents could have been persuaded to move closer to one of their children while they were still young and fit enough to cope with the upheaval. It was too late now. They had got beyond the point where settling somewhere new was a possibility and they would never agree to it anyway. They had a long-established routine – her father had retired from being a GP over twenty years ago – and pottered about, bickering and grumbling companionably, united only in their determination to remain independent and to stay where they were. They both declared stoutly that the only way they would be leaving Polders End was feet first.

Belinda reached for her bag, got out of the car and turned to lock the door. It was another iron-grey, bitter morning and she was glad of the warm polo neck that she had swiped from Dinka's cast-offs. Setting off across the car park she noticed that, as usual, she was at work before her bosses. Their designated parking spaces were empty. With any luck, and it being a Monday morning, she would have the office to herself for half an hour or so, which would give her time to sort the mail and do some filing. She liked them both,

Mark Savage and Philip Clutter, cheerful, easygoing men in their late forties who had set up the financial consultancy when they grew sick of working in London and their wives wanted to live in the country.

She had been grateful for the part-time secretarial work that she had been offered at Clutter and Savage and as her competence and confidence grew, she assumed the running of the office. Over the years she had become so familiar with the financial affairs of the clients that she was able to take on more and more of the routine work of the administration of pension and trust funds and was pleased and flattered when it was suggested that she might like to move in that direction. It would have meant studying for professional exams and when she thought about it, she balked at the extra responsibility. Because of Izzy, and the amount of childcare she willingly provided, she preferred to be able to finish in the office at around five thirty and not take any worries home with her. She still did much the same work, but in an unofficial capacity, and this suited her well. It made the job more interesting and she did not regret that she had turned down what looked like promotion. She now worked full-time with the help of another part-time secretary, a mild and unobtrusive middle-aged woman called Jenny Crow.

At first Belinda hoped that they might become real friends but Jenny, whose husband Richard taught technology at the high school and who had two meek and well-behaved teenage daughters, shied away from exchanging confidences and Belinda found that she could not be quite herself when she was in the office. She had to remember not to swear when her computer misbehaved or Mark Savage lost an important file and in conversation found herself talking in a bright voice and stressing the mundane and ordinary aspects of her life rather than talking about the sort of things she shared with Dinka.

She often thought that Jenny looked tired and pale but if she ever suggested that it was tough to run a home and work as well, Jenny shied off the subject by saying that Richard, her husband, shared the chores. This meant that any giggly 'all men are hopeless' conversations never got off the ground. Belinda had sometimes seen her and Richard on joint shopping expeditions in Sainsburys, Richard pushing the trolley and taking an active interest in the list in Jenny's hand, which was so far from her own experience of husbands that she realised that there was little common ground between them.

It was just as well, really, to keep work and home separate, but it meant that apart from Dinka, she had few women friends with whom to chew the fat. Working full-time excluded her from many of the village activities which relied on either retired or non-working women and since David's death her social life had withered away. There wasn't time, for one thing, she thought, as she unlocked the door of the office and stepped over the pile of post to switch off the alarm, and for another, she was too bloody tired.

By ten o'clock the same morning, Jess had finished mucking out the boxes and had ridden out on exercise with the first and second string of horses. Her ribs, bruised from her fall, ached miserably and her neck felt stiff. The cold didn't help.

Despite the physical work, her toes and fingers were freezing.

Mondays were always the same. After the matey, cheerful atmosphere of Saturday night, everyone on the yard was short-tempered and disinclined to chat. Now, halfway round on the hour's exercise with the third lot of horses, Carl had bawled out Moira for riding too close and allowing her horse to be kicked and she'd shouted back, sawing at the mouth of the young grey gelding she was riding, throwing him onto his hocks and then screaming as he skidded backwards across the lane. Jess kept her place at the rear behind Susan, who rode quietly and competently, and as they trotted the horses up the hill, she hunched her sore neck into her collar and pulled her scarf up higher round her ears.

This was routine stuff and although she rode with only half a mind, she was aware of the horse beneath her, how he was moving, the mood he was in. He was an experienced gelding, an eleven-year-old with the stable name of Buck, but he was idle in training and needed constant pushing to stride out properly. Ken put her up on him because he knew that she would do her job, not let him slop along as Moira would. This morning he was less sluggish than usual because of the cold, but he still did not walk out well, preferring to hurry along taking small steps, not using his quarters, not dropping his head onto the bit. Jess could feel his slackness, the lack of muscular effort, and she drove him forward, holding him between her hand and leg so that he did not move any faster, but took longer strides and was forced to use the long muscles of his back and neck.

She could do all this on autopilot, it was second nature to her, but she still derived satisfaction from making a horse move well. Up in front, Moira's horse had settled and she had managed to light a cigarette, which was strictly against rules, but she found riding out boring and repetitive: a mile up the lane between the dark, naked trees and the black hedges, the frozen grey fields rising on either side, and then the turn at the top of the hill for the loop round by the old railway line, where the rusty wire fences were strung with frayed plastic from the rubbish that the gypsies left behind. It was the same old route, day after day, and none of them enjoyed it, but it had to be done and for Jess it was always preferable to be on a horse than not.

This morning, as she booted Buck along, she was thinking about Izzy. As a general rule, Jess tried to avoid doing this. It was easier that way. She could convince herself then that everything was all right and would be all right in the future. If, for one moment, she allowed this confident nonchalance to slip, then the fear took hold. That was why she had to keep brave and bold and turn her back on her mother's remonstrations.

Why didn't Belinda see? Why didn't she understand that she had to do something great, something to be proud of, something that would make everyone sit up and take notice so that poor little Izzy had *something*, for God's sake? Jess didn't need to be *told* that she was all Izzy had got; it was exactly because of that that she wanted Izzy to be proud of her. She did not want her to have to apologise throughout her life for having a hopeless teenage mother who was stupid enough to get pregnant, and a yawning blank on her birth certificate where her father's name should be. Jess had nothing else to offer but her talent as a rider although, if she was honest, she couldn't pretend that she was racing only for Izzy. She wanted it just as much for herself. One day Izzy would appreciate what it was all about. One day Izzy would understand.

Then there was Izzy and the boy. Uncanny, it had been. She had looked that word up in a dictionary last night. It said 'weird' or 'supernatural'. It was weird, that's exactly what it was. Weird and inexplicable, an extraordinary co-incidence, that when the boy had stared at her from his pony and pushed back the brim of his cap with his hand, he could have been Izzy's double. Izzy's doppelgänger, Izzy's twin, Izzy's brother. Impossible, obviously, but weird enough to make Jess feel rattled and uneasy.

Perhaps it was just the similar glasses and the round face, and she had imagined the same set of the mouth, the same pinkish pale hair that she thought she glimpsed under his riding hat. The similarity had faded as soon as he opened his mouth. In fact, he hadn't seemed at all like Izzy after a minute or two. It was stupid of her to think so, children all looked alike in riding hats anyway, especially if they wore glasses.

They were nearly back now, filing onto the bridlepath that followed the river and came out on the lane near the stables. The brown water moved fast, swollen by the recent rain, reflecting the grey, sliding light of the glowering sky. Buck tripped on a frozen rut and Jess gave him a sharp reminder to pay attention. Up at the front of the line, Carl and Moira had resolved their differences and were chatting amicably, Carl turning in his saddle to talk to her over his shoulder, something about the drinking session they had had on Saturday night in the Cricketers. Susan joined in and for a moment Jess felt left out, but it had been her choice not to go along with them. She had never been a pub-going sort of girl anyway, and it wasn't only since having Izzy that she had opted out of the singles scene. She liked to joke, liked to fool about, but she wasn't a drinker and after a bit found it boring to watch everyone else getting hammered.

The horses reached the end of the bridlepath and turned out onto the lane. Anxious to get home where a feed was waiting for him, Buck woke up and started to jog, sidling sideways, and Jess spoke sharply to him, telling him to behave. Five minutes later she was jumping down in the yard, running the stirrups up the leathers and unsaddling, stamping her frozen feet on the ground.

She shut Buck's door and crossed the yard behind Moira. This morning Ken would be allocating rides for next Saturday's racing at Black Forest Lodge, down in Devon, and she wanted to be there to try and inveigle rides on some of the good horses, otherwise Carl would have his pick.

The girls kicked off their boots and shed their outdoor layers in the boot room before joining the others in the kitchen where Mary was standing at the Aga waiting for the huge kettle to boil. Susan was already there, making toast, while Lisa spread each slice thickly with butter before adding it to the mounting pile keeping warm on the lid of the hotplate. Ken was on the telephone, giving an enthusiastic account of a horse's progress, the form book open on the table in front of him, while Rhona was busy disentangling a nest of brightly coloured tail bandages heaped in a laundry basket, and turning each one into a neat, tight roll.

'What's that horse he's talking about?' asked Moira, mocking. 'That's not a horse I recognise.'

Ken finished the call and they all sat round the table, helping themselves to toast and biscuits, flicking through *The Racing Post* and chatting, while Mary passed round mugs of coffee and tea. Jess watched Ken from under her eyelashes. Any moment now he would casually reach for next week's entries and the discussion would begin.

Ken lit a cigarette, put on his glasses and turned over the papers on the table, looking for a biro. Without being asked, Mary passed him the entries book.

'Right,' he said. 'First race, one o'clock. Confined – we've no runners in that. Second race, one thirty. Restricted. I'm putting in Another Rose, Captain Jack and Fresh Angle. Carl, I'm putting you on Angle and you, Jess, on Rosie. OK? Tom can have Jack, who should be favourite. I'll not run any of them, mind, if we don't get the rain that's forecast for Wednesday.' Jess and Carl nodded. Jess was secretly pleased and tried hard not to smile at the thought of Carl getting Angle who was notoriously unreliable over the fences, while she had Rosie who was competent, if not the fastest.

'Men's open,' went on Ken. 'I'll double enter Jack and Fresh Angle. Wolf Run is entered and he'll be favourite by a long way. He's heading for Cheltenham, that horse.'

'The lads from Robert Taylor's yard were down the Cricketers on Saturday night,' Carl volunteered. 'They said Wolf Run's been having nosebleeds. He won't be going on Saturday and Robert's taking all his horses to Hursley Hambledon instead. He reckons the ground will be better there.'

Ken scratched his neck. This sort of local pub gossip was useful. Robert Taylor had one of the best yards in the West Country and it was always helpful to know where his horses were running – and to avoid them. Put your horse in the worst company and yourself in the best was one of Ken's sayings.

'In that case we'll run those horses in the men's open,' he said. Carl smirked at Jess. Captain Jack, a repeated winner, was a horse they both wanted to ride.

'Ladies' race.' Ken paused and looked at Jess. 'I want to run Silver Dollar, but she'll tail off in good company. The others will be too sharp for her, but I don't want to put her in the maiden. I'd rather she ran with more experienced horses. I'll want you to ride a careful race, Jess, nurse her round a bit. OK?'

Jess nodded. This made up for losing Jack to Tom. Silver Dollar, or Dolly as she was known in the stables, was a young hopeful, bought by Ken for a staggering sum at Ascot sales last year for a local builder who knew nothing whatever about horses. Left to his own devices, according to Ken, he'd have bought a kitchen table if it had four legs and anyone had told him that it ran well. By the end of the season Dolly should certainly have produced some wins and Jess hoped that they would be with her in ladies' races.

101

'Intermediate race. Jess, you can have Glen Chieftain. You'll be in with a chance there, girl, if you get your arse in gear. That leaves two divisions of the maiden race. I'm running Dawn Call and Fenny Princess. I'll decide later who I'll put up. Any preference, Carl?'

Carl shrugged. Both were young horses. Both had some potential. 'Makes no difference to me,' he said.

'That's it then,' said Ken. 'I'll triple enter everything, and we'll wait and see what the weather does.'

Jess and Carl nodded. This sort of uncertainty was routine. Horses and riders would not be decided until declarations were made on the course on the day.

Ken looked across at Jess. 'You had a telephone call this morning,' he said. 'Ted Dawlish, to say that he's running that mare of his on Saturday. Said she didn't have a proper outing last time and can go again. He wants to know if you'd like the ride. I told him you'd ring back.'

Jess nodded, trying to look nonchalant, aware of Mary glaring at her across the table. 'Yeah, OK. Thanks,' she said, and helped herself to another piece of toast to show that she didn't really care, one way or the other. It was better than she hoped – four rides and two of them on decent horses. She was especially pleased to get Dolly, and then Glennie in the intermediate, a ride which might easily have gone to Carl or Tom.

Rhona caught her eye, smiled and gave her a surreptitious thumbs-up. She was glad for Jess. Carl had been dragged before the stewards for excessive use of the whip when lazy Buck came back from a race with marks across his quarters, and Rhona had never forgiven him. Jess was a much more considerate jockey in her view and deserved some good rides.

'So,' said Mary, adjusting her reading glasses and looking down the list. 'That's seven runners, Ken. Two loads. I'll get Dave Pritchard, shall I?' Ken nodded. Dave was a local horse carrier who drove for the yard when they had more than one lorry of horses going racing. 'I'll sort out the colours.' Each of Ken's owners had nylon shirts or knitted jerseys and caps in their own racing colours and it was Mary's job to make sure that they were all present and correct on a race day.

'Everything will depend on the weather,' said Ken. 'With any luck the ground should be good to soft. We'll decide for definite who's going on Friday but we'll give them all a pipe-opener over the practice fences on Thursday.' He closed the book and took off his glasses and there was a general movement to get up. Susan began to stack the mugs in the dishwasher and Jess put the lid on the biscuit tin.

'Oh yes,' said Ken, as if he had just remembered something that would interest them all. 'You'll never guess who I heard from this morning. I didn't know he was back in the country, for a start.'

'Who was that then?' asked Carl.

'Johnnie Bearsden,' said Ken, casting an eye at Jess. 'He wants to keep a horse with me again.'

'Who's he?' asked Moira who hadn't been on the yard long enough to know.

'Friend of Jess's,' said Ken. 'Ask her.'

'Oh, leave off, Ken,' said Mary. 'God, you're a stirrer. He's just a bloke,' she said to Moira. 'Just a bloke who used to have a good horse here years back. An owner rider.'

Moira shrugged. 'So what?' she said to Ken.

'Nothing. Just a piece of news. Thought Jess would be interested, that's all.'

'Why should I be?' said Jess, putting on her coat, her face averted.

'How have we got room?' asked Rhona. 'We've no spare boxes at the moment. Not till Tommy gets moved into National Hunt next month.'

'He's not in a hurry. The horse is still in Ireland.'

'What horse is it? A good one?' asked Susan.

'Don't know,' said Ken, indicating the form book. 'I was just looking it up. It's won a couple of point-to-points there, but that doesn't mean much. Everything wins in Ireland, usually by arrangement.'

'Will this Johnnie bloke ride his own horse?' asked Moira.

'No. He's given up now. He's a family man these days,' said Mary.

'He was then,' said Ken. 'But that didn't stop him.' He leered across at Jess.

'That's it, is it?' said Moira, like a terrier smelling a rat. 'Our Jessy had the hots for him, did she?' She turned to grin at Jess but she had already gone.

'Oh, be quiet all of you,' said Mary from the other end of the table. 'That's enough of that. Hurry up and get out of the kitchen. I've got things to do.'

Belinda heard the news over the phone from Derek Farmer that morning.

Derek was a local auctioneer, and always full of chat and

gossip. He picked up news before anyone else, a bit like an Aborigine hearing a train coming two days before it arrives, a fact which Belinda had recently gleaned from a television programme on the Outback.

This morning he was as bluff as ever.

'Heard about Quatt Lodge?' he asked Belinda.

'It's been sold, hasn't it?' she said.

'Certainly has. But do you know who to? Old friend of your daughter's.'

'Who?' Even as she asked the question, Belinda felt she knew the answer.

'Johnnie Bearsden. The place was left to the six nephews and nieces of the old man. Apparently Johnnie's bought out his cousins' share to avoid the house going out of the family.'

'Has he? Oh.' Belinda felt confused and caught out.

'Thought you'd be interested,' said Derek in an irritating, knowing tone.

'Well, of course I am. Anyone would be, I mean. Anyone local, that is. Is he going to live there? With his family?'

'I presume so. He wouldn't have bought it otherwise, would he?'

'I don't know. I don't know anything about him. Not recently, I mean. Has he moved in already?'

'Not yet. It's rather gone to rack and ruin with the old man bedridden for so many years. Needs a small fortune spent on it, but I gather Johnnie's wife isn't short of a bob or two. Anyway, thought you'd be interested. Now, is that boss of yours about?'

'Yes, he is. Hold on a moment and I'll put you through.' That done, Belinda sat with her hands in her lap, gently swivelling on her office chair. So that was the explanation for the books in the jumble sale. She had guessed right that the old house was being cleared out, but not who was moving in. What would this news mean for Jess, and more importantly for Izzy?

Suddenly the whole edifice of security that she had tried to build around the little girl looked shaky. With Johnnie back, the gossip would start again and it wasn't fair. Belinda remembered what Izzy had said about the twins at school. It would be like that for her all the time and Belinda was not going to allow it. She felt a surge of anger and protectiveness. Poor little Izzy was not going to bear the brunt of it all. Not if she could help it. But what could she do?

Dinka would help. Clever, worldly-wise Dinka would know how to deal with Jess and the return of Johnnie. Very rarely did Belinda ever call Dinka at work, she was much too intimidated by the Sloaney girls who answered the telephone and demanded her business, but these were exceptional circumstances. The moment Jenny put on her coat to take some packets to the post office, Belinda picked up the telephone.

'Dinka,' she said when she was grudgingly put through. 'It's me. I need your help.'

'Belinda. What's happened?'

'Nothing. I mean, we're all fine, everybody's all right, but listen to this, Dinka, if you've got a moment, and tell me what to do.'

Dinka was a good listener. She heard Belinda's story without interrupting and then she said, 'Dearie me. So this explains those books surfacing at your jumble sale. We always knew, didn't we, that the subject of Izzy's father had the makings of a Norse saga. Before the longships, or whatever they're called, were even launched. Before we'd even thought of putting on our horned helmets!' Dinka chuckled. 'What exactly do you want to do? Confront this Johnnie person? Scrape some DNA off him? Force him to acknowledge Izzy with an announcement in the local paper?'

'No, of course not. I can't do that. I just want advice from you, given Jess's attitude. You see, the difference now is that Izzy is old enough to get wind of the speculation and gossip. That's what I want to prevent. Why should she, the innocent in all of this, be the one to suffer?'

'You could, of course, be blowing the whole thing out of proportion, you know. As I told you yesterday, illegitimacy is hardly a hot topic these days. I don't suppose anyone much gives a damn how many little bastards Johnnie Bearsden has spread around the country. Oh, sorry, I didn't mean it to sound like that.'

'But Dinka, of course people are interested. This is Dorset, not London. The country thrives on gossip, especially about someone like J. Bearsden who was always considered glamorous and exciting. Now he comes back to live in the big house and you can imagine how it will stir things up. Everyone will be riveted.'

'Dear, oh dear. What a sad lot you are, but I get your point. Really, I don't see that there's anything you can do. It's Jess who matters. It is how she handles it that counts.'

'That's what worries me. I have an awful feeling that the minute anyone puts any pressure on her, she'll flip. She's always denied that Johnnie is Izzy's father.'

'Well, maybe that's the truth. There's no evidence to the contrary, is there?'

'No, not really.' Belinda hesitated. 'It's always been an assumption, that's all, and I feel so strongly that she should face up to it and allow Izzy to know who her father is. If it *is* Johnnie, then he should be responsible for her in some way. I'm sure these things can be handled discreetly. He could pay for her education, for one thing, and contribute towards her maintenance. If he preferred it, I suppose she needn't know about him until she's eighteen, and then the decision about their future relationship would be up to them to sort out. It's this state of denial that Jess insists on that is so unfair. She seems to think that the whole problem will just go away if she does nothing, but of course it won't. It will be much more acute with Johnnie back in the frame.'

'Could you tackle him yourself, if you really can't talk to Jess?'

Belinda was horrified. 'Of course not! It would be insufferable interference. Jess would never forgive me.'

'Well, there isn't much else you can do. Sit tight, I suppose, and be there to pick up the pieces. Now, darling, I must dash. I'll ring later and find out how things are.'

Belinda put down the telephone feeling worse, if anything. Of course Dinka could not really help – what could anybody do or say? The problem of Izzy could not be so easily resolved. Nevertheless, Belinda made up her mind to find the right moment to talk to Jess, to have it out in the open. Perhaps tonight after Izzy had gone to bed.

As it turned out, the opportunity never presented itself

because when Belinda got home from work at half past five, she found Izzy alone in the cottage, and no sign of Jess.

'She went out somewhere,' said Izzy, not moving her eyes from the television. 'She said you'd be back to look after me, Granny.'

'Where? Where has she gone?' asked Belinda in a tight voice.

'I don't know. Just somewhere.'

'And she left you on your own?'

'I don't mind. I didn't want to go with her. Please don't talk, Granny. I want to watch this. The dinosaur is going to eat that man's head off . . .'

Belinda felt so angry that she had to go and stand outside the kitchen door in the dark and biting cold to avoid exploding. Sometimes, really, she could kill her daughter.

Chapter Five

Earlier that same afternoon, high up on a bleak Dorset hill, further south than the more gentle woods and curves of the Blackmore Vale, the slate-grey clouds were darkening in a glowering sky. The solid mass was underlit on the horizon to the west by the last of the February sun which pierced the gloom with shafts of lurid yellow. It was bitterly cold but the wind had gone and now the stillness hung as if frozen over the farm buildings below. The sound of sheep and the call of a pheasant seemed to scatter and bounce like pebbles thrown on an icy pond, each voice clear and distinct and sharp-edged as it echoed up from the dark valley.

The two Dawlish men sat side by side in silence in the cab of their battered truck. Both held binoculars and were studying the horizon with intent, while a pair of nervy black and white collies whined from the rear. Down the hill in front of them a track curved through the turf and, below, where the ground levelled into the valley bottom, were four homemade brush fences. It was here that they trained their horses. By a freak of nature the valley escaped frost and when the ground was too hard all over the county they were still able to gallop at home.

'Here she comes now,' said the older man to his son, as a horse appeared over the hill. 'Going nicely.'

Pete Dawlish grunted, watching intently as the little mare flew down the hill towards the fences and took the first with hardly a check in her stride. The second went the same way but at the third she tried to swerve out to the left in the direction of the track which led down to the yard and had to be pulled back on course. She met the fence wrong and jumped it clumsily, but regained her momentum and pace over the fourth, before streaking away over the hill.

'She should have been ready for that,' said Pete with some satisfaction in his voice. 'The lass isn't as bloody good as she thinks.'

'She's good for a maid,' countered his father. 'The mare goes well for her, and you know yourself, she's not easy.'

They lapsed back into silence, waiting for the pair to reappear and watched intently as they came back into view and sped down the hill for a second time.

'She can gallop all right,' said Mr Dawlish. 'Look how she eats up the ground. Like her mother.' This time there were no mistakes and the jumping was fluent and assured. The little horse was so keen and full of running that it was with reluctance that she pulled up on the far side, swishing her tail in impatient circles and sidestepping coquettishly.

Ted Dawlish turned on the engine and the truck bumped slowly down to meet horse and rider.

Pete wound down his window. 'Well?' he said with a mocking leer. 'Good enough for you, is she?'

Jess leaned down to stroke the fine-skinned shoulder beneath her. 'She's got some engine,' she said, ignoring the sneering tone of voice. 'She powered away up the hill. I don't think I've ever sat on anything so keen.'

Ted nodded. It was what he expected to hear. He took care how he bred his horses and this mare, although she was small and fine, had a big heart and ability to match. Her dam had been a grand sort and won eighteen Points before they retired her. Flying Fancy, or Fancy, as they called this wilful little chestnut offspring of hers, had the same stamp.

'That first time out,' he said, 'she was green, like. She'll learn. She's a fast learner, but she's got a bit of tempera-ment. She's a nervy sort. She's worth taking carefully. I don't want her spoiled.'

Despite herself, Jess warmed towards the gruff, unsmiling man. Anyone who took the trouble to understand their animals went up in her estimation.

'You're right,' she said. 'You need to pick her races. Start her gently. I don't want her to have another bad experi-ence. Not with me, she won't. Not if I can help it.'

'That was a shite race she ran,' said Pete sourly. 'We don't want another one like that.'

'I'm not making excuses,' said Jess defensively. 'She wasn't ready to run and that's the truth and you know it. She'll be better next time out. I'd like to school her again on Thursday, if that's OK. I'll come over after work. She needs to have confidence in me. From what I hear she wasn't the easiest to qualify with the hounds.'

Pete Dawlish grinned. The mare had been a menace and the tough little ex-jockey who had ridden her had come home early every time, swearing and red-faced, after Fancy had thrown him about in the saddle for three hours, fizzing with wild excitement.

'You should have hunted the socks off her,' Jess went on. 'Kept her out until she'd settled. That's what Ken does with his youngsters.' Pulling up her sleeve she looked at her watch. 'I'll walk her round for ten minutes and then I must get on home.' She allowed the fidgeting mare to move away and started to circle her on a loose rein.

Ted Dawlish put the truck into gear. Pete lit a cigarette and threw the empty packet onto the floor to join the three or four inches of litter in the cab. 'Cheek, she's got, telling us what we should have done. Come on, Dad,' he grumbled, 'get a bleeding move on. My feet are frozen.' He drew on his cigarette and looked away out of the window, before asking, 'Are you letting the lass have the rides all season?'

'I don't know, do I? Let's see how it goes. There's no one else as good as her who'd want to take her on as she is.'

'Yeah, that's as maybe, but it's not what I asked you. Give Fancy a few more outings and there'll be others who'll be glad for the chance. We could get Nick Martin lined up, for one. Area champion he was, last year. We should book him for the last couple of outings.'

'I don't know as I want her having more than four runs. She should be turned away to mature. We don't want to spoil her, not while her bones are still soft. That's a class mare, that is.'

Pete sighed. This was what he was up against all the time with his dad. It was the same with the horses, with the farm, with the business. The old man was so bloody cautious and in Pete's view you didn't get anywhere unless you stuck your neck out and went for it. Some risks were worth taking.

'Well, don't go giving her any promises,' he cautioned. 'That lass is too big for her bloody boots already.'

'She's all right. Ken Andrews rates her. Says he'd trust her with any of his horses.'

'Yeah,' said Pete. 'That's it, isn't it, with all these bloody girls. Taking care is what they're all about. We don't want her taking fucking care. We want her out there to win!'

'You know what he means,' retorted the old man. 'We want the mare in one piece at the end of the season.'

'She's insured, isn't she? We pay enough bloody insurance.'

Ted did not answer. While he was around, things would be done his way.

The truck bumped through the metal gate and into the yard. Lights were already glowing in the low farmhouse tucked into the side of the hill. Nita, his quiet little wife, would be frying the bacon for supper and the big brown teapot would be hot on the Rayburn. He parked the truck and let the collies out of the back. They swarmed joyfully against his legs, knowing it was time for their one meal of the day.

'Put the lights on in the stable,' he told Pete gruffly, 'and stay and help the maid with the horse.'

His son grunted and shambled across to the old stone building where the two brood mares were already in and pulling at hay nets. Fancy's bed had been put down for the night and her rugs thrown over the manger. Pete snapped on the light and busied himself heaving a bale of hay into the back of the truck. The three or four young horses who wintered on the hill, their coats grown thick and woolly and caked with mud to protect them from the weather, would be milling round the gate, cold and hungry. If the old man thought he was hanging around to wait on the girl, he'd got another think coming.

Ted Dawlish collected the scraps which his wife left in the old dairy – cold porridge, old mashed potato, bacon fat – and divided it between tin bowls. The collies danced round him as he added a bit of dog meal and put the bowls down in the wire-fronted shed.

He heard the sound of the mare's hooves as he turned to go inside and he hastened his step. He didn't want to talk to the lass more than he had to. They had already said all that needed saying. More words would be wasted breath.

As Jess jumped down in the yard she heard the back door scrape shut. She didn't care if there was no one about. She would rug up the mare for the night and get off home. It was already nearly dark and unless the weather changed she had doubts about racing at the weekend. Once the frost got into the ground it took days to thaw, but looking up at the sky she saw that it had clouded over and only a few stars winked through the gaps. Perhaps a change was on the way.

The collies' metal bowls clattered on the concrete as they nosed them round their run, licking out the last traces of food as Jess led Fancy into her box. She was a waspish sort, laying back her ears as Jess undid her girth and turning her back on her when she threw the rugs over her quarters. Jess talked to her all the time and when she had finished she found the end of a packet of mints in her pocket and offered her one. The neat, sharp ears went forward and the fine nostrils explored the outstretched hand before delicately picking up the little white ring and crunching it between her teeth. Jess put a slow hand up to stroke her neck and the lovely head turned, looking for more.

'There, girlie. There. See, we can be friends, you know,' but the mare jerked away, eyeing her suspiciously.

Jess looked at her watch. When she got back to her car she would ring home on her mobile telephone and check on Izzy. She hadn't liked leaving her this afternoon but Izzy had been adamant that she didn't want to come and it would have been a long, cold wait for her in the car.

It was her mother who answered the telephone and immediately Jess could tell from her voice that she was angry. Oh, shit. It would be about leaving Izzy alone. Well, there was nothing she could do about it now.

'I'm on my way,' she said. 'I've been schooling that young horse I rode on Saturday. I'll be home in twenty minutes.'

She turned off her telephone and started down the long drive to the road, her headlights sliding across the silver trunks of the beech trees which lined the way. The light had gone now and the line of hills to right and left were deep purple shapes against the darker sky. Halfway she met the headlights of Pete Dawlish's truck coming in the other direction. They pulled up nose to nose and Jess realised that he was going to force her to reverse a long way to a gateway in order to let him pass. She raised a hand as he went by and he grinned through his window at her. Really, he was a horrible man and if it wasn't for the mare, she'd keep well clear of him.

The wild little horse was worth it, she was sure of that. There was something about the way she moved and how she felt to sit on that convinced Jess she was something out of the ordinary. She wasn't big, with the raw strength of some of the horses she rode at Ken's, but she had a toughness, a whiplash economy of movement, and a spirit that suggested she would stay galloping until she dropped. She flew her fences with a natural athleticism, but it was more than that. She jumped as though she loved it.

Her temperament was going to be the problem. She was such a firecracker that unless they could calm her down before her races, she would be worn out before the start. Experience would help but not until she had notched up a fair few runs and had the hang of racing. Maybe not before next season. In her next race she would be mad with excitement, perhaps even more so than the first time. Meanwhile Jess was going to have to ride her right, ask the right questions at the right time and help to concentrate that fretful energy into her performance. It wasn't going to be easy.

All the way home she thought about the chestnut mare and not until she turned into the drive of Rosebay Cottage did she remember Johnnie Bearsden.

When she walked into the kitchen, Belinda was sliding fish cakes onto plates for supper and Izzy was leaning on the kitchen table, drawing on yesterday's newspaper. Snowy barked joyfully and Belinda looked up as the door opened and looked down again as quickly. Jess caught the avoiding glance and saw it as confirmation that her mother was angry with her. In that one moment, all the exhilaration of riding the mare left her, and she suddenly felt cross and tired. Ignoring her mother, she dropped a kiss onto the top of Izzy's bent head.

'Hi, Izzo. What are you doing?' She laughed when she saw that the line-up of stick-thin models on the front page now sported moustaches and beards.

'I've made hairy ladies,' said Izzy, looking up, beaming.

'Yeah. I see beards are big this year!'

Belinda pointedly ignored them and Jess slung her bag on a chair and went to warm her hands on the top of the Rayburn. The hostility emanating from her mother was almost tangible. She shot her a look.

'What's the matter?' she asked, preferring to provoke a row than be subdued by this silent resentment. 'You're obviously in a mood.'

Belinda glared at her and made a face towards Izzy.

'What?' said Jess, deliberately not understanding. 'What's the matter? What have I done now?'

'Nothing's the matter!' hissed Belinda. 'Sit down, Izzy,' she said in a different, normal voice. 'Your supper's ready.'

Izzy moved herself slowly from one end of the table to the other where three places were laid. Belinda put a plate in front of her.

'Fish cakes,' said Izzy dreamily. 'It's funny that fishes get made into cakes. Water babies must eat fish cakes, mustn't they, Mummy?'

Belinda put two more plates on the table and sat down herself, only to get up to fetch napkins from a drawer behind Jess.

'I could have passed those,' said Jess impatiently, but

Belinda ignored her and instead started a bright conversation with Izzy about school and what she had eaten for lunch.

'Oh, for God's sake!' said Jess loudly. She sat down and began to eat, pulling the newspaper across to her plate and engrossing herself in reading the front page. Silence fell. Only once did Izzy look up from mashing tomato ketchup into her fish cake, turning it a synthetic pink She glanced between her mother and grandmother for a moment, her glasses and solemn little face lending her a knowing air. Whatever it was she was thinking was evidently not worth telling for she dropped her eyes again and continued pressing her fork into her food.

There was something about this level look that irritated Jess. It was as if the child was judging her.

'Don't mess about with your food like that,' she said sharply. 'Get on with eating it.'

'I like it pink,' said Izzy, adding, 'You shouldn't be reading anyway. Granny says.'

'Don't be cheeky,' snapped Jess. 'Don't you dare tell me what to do.'

Izzy flinched as if she had been hit. Her face took on a closed, preoccupied look and she dutifully began to shovel pink mash into her mouth. Belinda threw a furious glance at Jess. They continued their meal in silence while the atmosphere in the kitchen seethed with resentment and dislike. Even the sound of their knives and forks on the plates sounded unnecessarily sharp and aggressive.

When they had finished eating, Jess sent Izzy upstairs to get into her pyjamas and the two women faced one another over the table.

'You are the absolute limit, you know that, Jess?' burst out Belinda. 'I will not have rows in front of Izzy!'

'Why do you pick one, then?' countered Jess. 'You've been spitting mad since I came through the door!'

'And with reason! How dare you go off and leave Izzy like that? It's utterly irresponsible!'

'Oh, for fuck's sake, Mum! She didn't want to come with me and I knew you would be back straight after work. The Holloways were in next door. She could have gone round there if there was an emergency.'

'Jess! They're both over eighty and stone deaf. It's just not good enough. Besides, she said you told her to stay where she was.'

'She was watching the television, Mum. I told her to stay put until you got home. She couldn't possibly have come to any harm. She wasn't likely to start rewiring the house, or something, was she?'

'Look, Jess, I'm not arguing with you about this. I'm telling you that it's not to happen again. Not in this house.' As soon as she said it, Belinda realised her mistake.

Jess's voice altered instantly. 'Fine,' she said coldly, tossing her head. 'Izzy and I can go. We'll move out if you feel like that.'

This change of tactics left Belinda helpless and pleading. 'Don't be ridiculous, Jess. You know I don't want that. My only concern in this is Izzy. You know very well that she is best off here.'

'But what you really mean is that I don't care about her. That's it, isn't it?'

'No, I'm not saying that. Stop twisting my words. I'm

saying that in this instance you were wrong and irresponsible. I have every right to tell you that. You live under my roof and she's my granddaughter.'

'Well, as I said, we can move if you don't like it,' said Jess stubbornly. 'Ken has a caravan on the yard we can have. He's always telling me.'

'Stop it, Jess. Stop it. This is your home. It's Izzy's home.'

'I can't stay here if you treat me like a child, telling me what to do, interfering in everything.'

'That's not fair! I don't do that!'

'Yes, you do! You should get your own life, not spend your whole time poking around in mine!'

'Jess!' The injustice of her attack took Belinda's breath away. 'Give me one example. I make the greatest effort not to interfere.'

'All right,' said Jess in a triumphant tone. 'This, for example.' She reached across to where Izzy had been drawing and picked up the book which had been lying beneath the newspaper. With a flourish she slammed *The Water Babies* down in front of Belinda. 'Explain this!'

Belinda looked at the faded cover and her mind went blank. She was cornered. Jess had outmanoeuvred her.

'What do you mean?' she said, to give herself time. 'It's the book Izzy bought at the jumble sale.'

'I know that,' said Jess. 'What I want to know is why you cut out the front page. The page with a certain name on it.'

'I-I . . .' faltered Belinda and then rallied enough to say, 'Jess, this is irrelevant. It's got absolutely nothing to do with you going off and leaving Izzy at home on her own. You're just trying to get out of admitting that you were wrong.'

'All right, what do you want me to say? I know that in an ideal world I shouldn't have left her. I wouldn't have done if it had seemed dangerous or something. It seemed better at the time to leave her here than drag her out with me.'

'Why did you have to go at all? What is more important than Izzy and her welfare?'

'Mum, I had to. I had to go and ride that horse.'

'You didn't *have* to. You chose to.'

'It's my job, riding horses. It's not just for me. I wasn't just doing what I wanted to do. You know that.'

Belinda fell silent. The argument was going too deep now, into her general disapproval of Jess's choice of lifestyle, into her racing for a living, and she did not have the stomach for that particular fight. Her heart was thumping in her chest and her hands were shaking.

Jess sniffed loudly, an ugly hawking noise, and said in a determined tone, 'You still haven't explained why you cut out the page.'

'Oh, Jess, you know why,' said Belinda quietly.

'Yes, I do, and I'm warning you, Mum, if you start the whole thing up again, with your hints and disapproval about Johnnie Bearsden, I'm leaving. I'm taking Izzy and going. Now he's back, I want that clear. I told you before, and this is the last time I'm saying it, Johnnie Bearsden is not Izzy's father, and you have no right to go around behind my back as if he is.'

Belinda stared at her daughter. Jess's fine skin was rosy with emotion. Two bright spots burned on her cheeks. So she has heard the news, she thought. At least I don't have to tell her or wait on tenterhooks for her to find out. But if Johnnie really isn't Izzy's father, why in God's name can't she say who is and end all the gossip once and for all? Belinda sighed. Wearily she rested her hands on her forehead. More than anything she hated these arguments with Jess. They left her feeling exhausted and wrung out and infinitely depressed. But she did feel that Jess had come as near as she ever would to admitting that she was wrong to leave Izzy. Belinda did not believe that she would do it again.

'All right, Jess. I admit I did cut the page out. I thought that when you saw his name there it would spark something off, that you would accuse me of something, and I couldn't face it. It seemed the right thing to do at the time. A pre-emptive strike, I suppose. I'm tired, Jess, and I can't stand any more of this. You know how I feel and you've made your own feelings clear, which I suppose is a good thing. Better to get things out in the open, I suppose. But I've had enough. We must both just let this go now.'

What pointless gibberings these were and she was aware all the time of Jess's hostility. But Jess remained silent and when Belinda eventually stood up, rubbing a hand wearily across her eyes, Jess said unexpectedly and in a deliberately offhand voice, 'I'll do the washing-up. Go and sit down if you're tired.'

Belinda recognised the awkwardly disguised truce and went gratefully. She slumped in the armchair by the fire, too weary to even read the paper or see what was on television. Not long afterwards Izzy reappeared in her pyjamas and old dressing gown, carrying her hairbrush. She climbed onto Belinda's lap, sucking her thumb while her grandmother tried to untangle the finely spun hair, the colour of the flesh of a ripe peach, pink and gold in the firelight. She was quiet but Belinda sensed that she was alert, as if invisible antennae were searching for signals, reading the atmosphere. She kept glancing at the open kitchen door from where she could hear the sounds of washing-up – but only the gentle swish of water and clink of plates, the radio playing quietly, nothing furious. She leaned back on Belinda's chest and, twisting round, looked up into her face.

'It was quite all right, you know, Granny. It was quite all right for Mummy to leave me on my own. I *asked* her to. I didn't want to go with her. Now she'll be cross with me.'

Belinda's heart moved. What sort of burden had she and Jess unconsciously laid on the child?

'Of course she won't be cross, Izzy. It wasn't your fault. It's nothing to do with you.'

'It is. It is, Granny. It's all to do with me.'

Belinda didn't know how to reply because of course Izzy was right.

'Well, it is and it isn't. It certainly isn't your *fault*, darling. Now, do you want a story?'

Izzy trotted out to the kitchen to collect *The Water Babies*. What a lot of bother that wretched book had caused.

Tom spent a cold evening out with his ewes. He had only two left to lamb and although they were both old girls who had produced healthy twins year after year, he still

125

liked to keep an eye on them, which was just as well, as it turned out. The five acres of land on which he kept his sheep was not ideal but he had picked it up relatively cheaply, re-fenced it, brought in mains water and rigged up a corrugated shelter. The trouble was that it could only be approached down a long tussocky track and, like all the vale, it was inclined to get waterlogged when the weather was relentlessly wet. It was a useful place to turn out a resting horse or two in the summer and because it represented his first foray into land acquisition, his first step towards owning his own farm, Tom was fond of the lonely spot, tucked between a secretive stream and a large wood which offered protection from the west winds.

This evening, as he turned off the engine of his old Land Rover and got out, the bitter cold seemed to have abated. The sky had clouded over and he was sure the temperature had risen as darkness fell. It was a black night and whistling up his old lurcher, Meg, he set off with a torch across the field. Meg moved away to silently work along the edge of the wood and a moment later Tom heard the sound of deer crashing through the trees. Meg would not go far. She was old and arthritic and preferred to spend her days sleeping by the stove or in the cab, the killer instinct of her youth long dimmed.

He walked to the end of the field shining his torch from side to side but he couldn't see the sheep. As the temperature had risen, the wind had increased and the roaring in the trees made it difficult to hear, but as he got to the bottom end he saw them, fleeing this way and that across the range of his torch. White bodies flashed across the beam, bobbing and frantic, lambs scudding between the criss-crossing stick legs of the ewes who, with heads thrown back and wild eyes, rushed and bunched along the fence. He saw what was driving them then, two streaks of brown and white flashing amongst the sheep, snapping and nipping in an ecstasy of excitement.

Tom started to yell and the dogs instantly dropped back, turning to look at him apprehensively. Both sank to the ground and lay panting, pink tongues lolling. He reached the first, a spaniel, and his fury made him lash out with his boot and catch the dog a glancing blow on its ribs. It yelped and rolled over and he caught it by its collar and dragged it to its feet, swearing under his breath all the time. With his free hand he reached into the pocket of his coat and pulled out a tangle of binder twine and looped a length through the collar. Dragging the dog behind him he tried to catch its companion but it shied away and lay down again further off, watching him nervously. Tom pulled the dog to the fence and tied it to a post.

His sheep were bunched up, trembling, in the corner of the field. He ran the torch over them, looking for telltale signs, ripped ears, bloodied noses, torn wool, but they seemed all right, just terrified, with heaving sides and trampling feet, the lambs all mixed up amongst them, bleating piteously. He tried to count heads but in the dark it was impossible to tell if there were any missing or if his pregnant ewes were amongst the bobbing flock. He would just have to hope that while he searched the field for any injured sheep the others would sort themselves out, and that when they had calmed down, the lambs would find their mothers.

He untied the spaniel and it trotted obediently to heel while the other followed at a safe distance as he methodically swept the field with his torch, walking backwards and forwards until he found one of the old ewes laid up near the shelter, giving birth to twins. One tiny creature was already struggling to free itself from the bloody birth sac at her feet, while the little dark nose of its twin was laid neatly on its pointed feet, halfway out of its mother's rear end.

He tied up the dog again, fetched a sack and rubbed the lamb all over before helping it up onto its feet. By now the second had slipped out and the ewe was nosing it with a mixture of curiosity and maternal pride. Before long both babies were standing on each side of their mother and had found her full and drooping udder amongst the matted wool.

Thank goodness for that, thought Tom, picking up his torch again. Meg had returned and was eyeing the strange dogs suspiciously. Tom made a second attempt to catch the other dog but again it ducked away and lay down, keeping its distance and whining nervously.

The second pregnant ewe was nowhere to be seen. Tom began to walk the field again, this time along the edge of the stream where the bank dropped quite steeply away. He had not gone far before he found her. She had managed to get herself down into the stream and had somehow got her head stuck in the sheep netting. Her body was still warm but she was dead, drowned probably. Working as best as he could in the dark and standing with his feet in the icy water, Tom felt inside her and carefully drew out her two lambs. The first was dead, but the second was still breathing. He tucked the slimy little body inside his coat, struggled up the bank and went back to the Land Rover.

He wrapped the lamb in an old coat and nestled it beside Meg on the passenger seat before dragging the captive spaniel into the back and tying it tightly amongst the sacks of sheep nuts. The other dog he would leave to find its own way home. Without its companion it wouldn't bother the sheep again.

He bumped down the track to the road, his hands frozen, unfeeling lumps on the wheel. The lamb's eyes were closed and it was hard to tell if it was dead or alive, but it was worth trying to save. Meg was sniffing it with curiosity and then began to lick its blunt little furry face. He would try to get it to feed from a bottle when he got home and tomorrow set about finding it an adoptive mother. The loss of the ewe and the other lamb was galling. She had probably got into the stream to get away from the dogs and he shook his head in anger. It wasn't entirely the dogs' fault. It was a strong instinct, to worry sheep, and at least they hadn't actually harmed them as far as he could tell. He hoped he wouldn't find any trampled lambs tomorrow. It was the owners he blamed, who allowed two dogs to roam together in stock country at lambing time. He had had trouble with dogs before but that was when he had sheep close to a village with a footpath crossing the field; he had not expected trouble in this remote location. He wondered who the dogs belonged to. When he got back he would see if he could find a collar tag.

He felt weary and cold and wondered what Jess was doing and if he could persuade her to come over for the evening. He remembered that she had been schooling the Dawlishes' lunatic chestnut mare and hoped that it had gone well. He was not going to tell her the gossip that he had picked up from the farrier this morning, that Pete Dawlish had tried to book Nick Martin to ride at the South Dorset point-to-point at Milborne St Andrew in three weeks' time because he hadn't liked the way Jess had ridden.

The farrier, a great Goliath of a man who was as gentle as a girl with the nervous young horses Tom was breaking in, had shaken his head. 'A right bastard, he is,' he had said, blowing on his frozen hands. 'Jess doesn't want to take any notice. Everyone knows he's a bastard.' But Tom knew that she would mind. Girls were like that. They took criticism to heart and behaved as if they were mortally offended, whereas male jockeys returned the abuse and got on with it. Racing was a tough business not suited to the thin-skinned.

He pulled up outside his dark cottage and carried the lamb tenderly inside. The old solid fuel Aga stood in the corner, and after Tom had rubbed the limp little bundle with an old towel, he wrapped it up, noting that it was a ewe lamb, and laid it in a cardboard box filled with straw, which he put in the plate oven. Later he would make up a bottle and see if he could get her to feed. Meg had already jumped up onto her place in the armchair by the stove and was watching him with gentle eyes, clouded with age.

Now for the dog. Tom went back outside and untied it from the back of the Land Rover. It jumped down willingly and came rushing inside, full of energy and curiosity. Tom perched on the edge of the Meg-occupied chair and held the dog between his hands. It was young, he could see that now in the light of the kitchen. A beautiful spaniel bitch probably not more than eighteen months old. Her broad head was prettily marked in liver and white and her coat was silky and fine. She was a fit dog, lean and well muscled and she looked up at Tom adoringly as he ran his hands over her back. Her muzzle was clean and there were no bloody marks on her anywhere, so with any luck she had not actually attacked his sheep, although worrying them as she had been was a serious enough offence. When he found out who owned her he would have some strong words to exchange, as well as the bill for the poor old ewe and her lamb – and the one in the oven, if it did not survive.

The bitch was wearing a rolled leather collar and a tag engraved with a name and a telephone number and what looked like a post code. He unbuckled the collar and the spaniel, happy to be free, ran round the kitchen, sniffing excitedly while Meg looked on disdainfully, her elegant paws crossed in front of her. Tom held the collar under the light. The name on the tag was Bearsden. Bloody hell, he thought. I don't believe it. Johnnie fucking Bearsden.

As he made up a bottle for the lamb, Tom considered his options. He could telephone the police and make a complaint, but at this time of the evening the nearest manned police station was miles away and anything less than homicide would get short shrift. That left ringing the number on the dog's collar.

Maybe it wasn't Johnnie Bearsden at all. There could be other Bearsdens in the area. But the name made him think of Jess. She had never told him anything about Izzy's father but when he got back from his year in the United States and found her heavily pregnant, the local talk had been that Johnnie was responsible. Or had it been his mother who had put that idea in his head? If it was her, then the rumour would have originated with Belinda, who he knew believed Johnnie was the father.

Up until then, Jess had been a friend, a mate, someone with whom he had grown up. They had ridden together in Pony Club teams, fooled about and danced at teenage discos – snogged probably, he couldn't really remember. Then when he came back he found her large-bellied and defiant and so stroppy that it was almost laughable. He could see that she was making things hard for herself; her attitude alienated a lot of people who might otherwise have been prepared to offer her a bit of support.

Tom couldn't help but admire her dogged independence and toughness and when Izzy was born, he visited her in Yeovil hospital in the hot maternity ward and found her sitting cross-legged on her bed, red-faced, grumbling about the soppiness of the other mothers and determinedly offhand about the tiny scrap wrapped in a cellular blanket in a plastic crib beside her bed.

'Don't look,' she said. 'It's hideous! A miniature, wrinkly Winston Churchill. It's really embarrassing. Don't bother to try and think of anything nice to say.'

He had leaned over Izzy and marvelled at the tiny creased wrists the thickness of his thumb and minute hands, the little cross-patch face and strange unfocused gaze. Then Jess had scrambled down the bed to join him and her long hair had tumbled forward and between the two curtains of hair he had glimpsed her expression and he was done for. He fell in love at that moment because he saw the truth of what she really felt and the sudden revelation changed his understanding of her for ever.

When Izzy was two, Tom asked Jess to marry him. She turned him down flat, but not unkindly, and they had drifted on like this ever since, with the unspoken understanding that Tom loved Jess more than she loved him, but also that they were promised to each other and that marriage at some time in the future was a possibility.

The problem he had with Johnnie Bearsden, he thought now as he gently coaxed the lamb to feed, was that Jess had probably loved Johnnie in a way that she would never love him – a sort of starry-eyed worship, a teenage thing really but flattering and wonderful, he imagined, to be on the receiving end. Not that Johnnie seemed to take much notice at the time. In the Pony Club days of their youth he was so busy being smooth and charming right across the board that Tom didn't think Jess had been singled out for any special attention. Tom had liked Johnnie, too. He was easy-going and good company in that rather self-satisfied, smart army officer style. Tom had wondered how bright he was, deplored his choice of red or canary coloured trousers, but admired his horsemanship. Then his own life had taken a different direction and he went to work in America, followed by university, and he hadn't thought about Johnnie much since.

Until this evening. Bearsden was an uncommon enough name to make him wonder. He put the lamb back in the oven and fried himself bacon and eggs for supper. When he sat down to eat, the spaniel bitch slid out from under the table and laid her head on his knee. Meg looked up and whined from her chair. 'Don't worry,' Tom told her. 'She's not staying.' He rested his hand on the broad head. 'You'll have to go back, my girl,' he said sternly to the spaniel. 'Back home. I don't want them thinking I've stolen you.'

When he had finished eating, he picked up the collar from the arm of the chair and went to the telephone. He dialled the number and waited, listening to it ring. Finally, just as he was about to put down the receiver, it was picked up at the other end. Silence.

'Hello?' he said. 'Hello?'

''Allo?' came a faint, nervous reply.

The voice was female and foreign and not at all what Tom had expected.

'Izzy,' Belinda said at breakfast time as she poured cereal into a bowl and peeled an apple to share with her grand-daughter. 'Would you like to come with me to see your great-grandparents? I thought we might go on Friday after-noon and come back on Sunday. It's ages since we've been to Suffolk, isn't it, and they would love to see you.'

Izzy looked up, her spoon halfway to her mouth. 'What about Mummy?' she said. 'Will she be coming too?'

'No, she won't. She'll have to go to work, Izzy. You know that. She goes racing every weekend from now until June.'

Izzy pondered on this information, stirring her spoon thoughtfully in the milk in her bowl.

'All right,' she said finally.

'Well, don't sound so thrilled,' said Belinda, amused by

the lack of enthusiasm. 'I thought you'd be pleased. You love it at Polders End, don't you? You'll be able to feed the ducks and take Ernie out for a walk.' Ernie was her parents' very ancient Norfolk terrier. It was scraping the barrel a bit, she realised, to offer him as an inducement to Izzy. He had a confirmed retrieving habit and dropped sticks or balls at the feet of his victims and then trembled with anticipation until the object was thrown for him and he hurtled after it, only to bring it back and repeat the performance. He was exhausting and impossible to ignore. The ducks were nothing much out of the ordinary either, just mallards and a few coots that gathered on a muddy slope by the village pond.

'I like the fish and chips,' said Izzy thoughtfully. It had become part of the Polders End experience to have a Saturday fish and chip supper from the shop in Bury St Edmunds.

'Well, we can do that, and the Greats will be so pleased to see you.' Belinda handed Izzy another quarter of apple. She knew in her heart that the little girl must find it dull in the dark thatched cottage where time seemed to tick by so slowly and the old people shuffled about on sticks and shouted alarmingly at one another, but that was too bad. It wouldn't hurt Izzy just for the weekend and, anyway, she believed that children, however young, should have an understanding of what it meant to be old.

'Come along,' she said briskly. 'Eat up or we'll be late for school.'

She went to the window where she kept a small mirror on the sill and began to put on her make-up. A cheery pink lipstick went on first and then with wide open stare she drew a brown smudge of eyeliner and brushed on mascara. That was her face seen to. She smiled brightly at herself in the glass and then let the smile go and saw the lines of her mouth droop. What a misery she looked like that. She experimented with a slight half-smile. That's what I ought to aim for, she thought, and wondered if it was possible to train herself to keep it permanently in place. On second thoughts, fixed like that, it made her look slightly demented, or like a woman caught by the camera on *Songs of Praise* who hoped to appear uplifted.

In the corner of the glass she glimpsed Izzy drooping over her breakfast. She seemed so dejected that Belinda forgot about her own appearance and turned round.

'What's the matter, darling?' she asked. 'Why so mis?'

Izzy lifted large grey eyes welling with tears behind her glasses.

Belinda went swiftly to her side. 'Oh, Izzy. What is it, darling?'

'If we go away, Mummy will be on her own. I don't want her to be all on her own.'

'Oh, Izzy! Silly thing! No, she won't be. She'll have Snowy and probably Tom will come to stay. I know he would, if he thought Mummy was lonely.'

Izzy considered this, but still did not look cheered.

'Does Mummy know we love her?' she asked finally.

'Izzy! What a question! Of course she does!'

The heavy tears gathered and brimmed over to trickle down Izzy's bunched up cheeks. She cried quite beautifully, thought Belinda. No snuffling or red nose, just effortless, sliding tears. Belinda caught her up in her arms but Izzy pulled herself free and resolutely put a spoonful of corn-flakes into her mouth. Her resistance to comfort was touching and Belinda let her go and squatted beside her chair, stroking the shoulder of her red school sweatshirt.

'Don't be sad about Mummy. She'll be fine here. You know she will.' She was on the point of mentioning how Jess would be far too busy racing to miss them but stopped herself. Perhaps this was partly the reason for Izzy's distress.

Izzy said nothing but continued spooning up her break-fast and then wiped a hand across her face, got up and took her bowl to the sink. Her sturdy little legs, the rather long school skirt slightly caught up behind, the averted face still wet with tears, wrenched at Belinda's heart and suddenly reminded her of Jess at about the same age. She remembered how she had gone upstairs to kiss her good-night and found her crying silently in bed. There was nothing wrong, Jess had tried to explain, but her heart felt heavy and she was just sad. Belinda had sat on the bed and taken her in her arms but could not uncover any reason for her sudden unhappiness. Later it came to her that Jess had reached an age when she was aware of the possibility and the arbitrariness of human suffering. Perhaps it was the same with Izzy. Much more likely, of course, was that this anxiety stemmed from the row she had had with Jess the night before. But for now there was no time to ponder on questions about life and the human condition. She must be brisk and chivvy Izzy along or they would be late.

'Cheer up, darling, and go and get ready for school,' she

said brightly as Izzy trailed from the room. 'And no more worrying about Mummy!'

At least now, in February, the mornings were light. Looking out of the window as she washed up the breakfast things she could see that the sky looked high and pale. Old Mr Holloway from next door had been out already to stoke his bonfire and a thin line of very white smoke drifted from between the trees. Perhaps it would be a nice day – proper spring day to cheer them all up.

'Come on, Iz,' she called through the door. 'Where are you? Get your coat and run Snowy round the field. Have you packed your bag?' Izzy's school reading book had to be searched for each morning. It had a habit of sliding behind cushions on the sofa, or under a chair or Izzy's bed, or lost amongst the muddle of papers on the kitchen table.

Izzy appeared at the door, her book in her hand. 'Good girl. Snowy next. Put your boots on.' But Izzy was not a child to be hurried. She took her time over everything, sometimes seeming deliberately slow. It was one of the things that irritated Jess who was always so quick and who saw Izzy's slowness as a form of defiance. Of course, thought Belinda as she helped Izzy into her coat and pushed her feet into her rubber boots, if she was part of a proper family, with several children all growing up together, there would be no one to chivvy her along and she would have to learn to hurry up a bit.

Izzy rested a hand on Belinda's back as she bent over her boots, making little effort to help herself although she obliged by standing first on one leg and then the other, dreamily twisting a lock of hair round her finger, the tears gone and her face vacant of expression.

'Go on, darling. Buck up, or we'll be late. Don't let Snowy roll in the fox poo again. Quick now, off you go.' Izzy went obediently, Snowy trotting alongside. Belinda fetched her own coat and went out to feed the chickens on the boiled potato peelings and scraps which she cooked overnight. She saw Izzy open the field gate and stump off along the fence. I wish she wasn't alone so much, she thought, struck by the solitary little figure. I must remember to tell Jess to invite friends home after school. Now the evenings were getting lighter they would have time to take Bonnet out, and having a pony was one of the things that would be in Izzy's favour in the eyes of the other children.

The hens bustled self-importantly round her legs as she emptied the bucket of mash. 'There,' she told them. 'Lucky girls.' She glanced at her watch. It seemed as if she was always racing the clock. There was just time to change her shoes, round up Izzy and go.

Ten minutes later, sitting in her car in the drive with Izzy belted into the seat behind her, she turned the ignition key. The engine whirred and then wheezed into silence. She tried again. This time there was even less of a response.

'Damn, damn, damn!' she said. 'Bloody thing! Sorry, Iz, but really, this is the last straw. What the hell do we do now?'

Chapter Six

'This is a waste of time,' said Belinda. 'It's not going to start. It must be the battery or something. I'll have to telephone the garage. You might as well come inside with me, Izzy. Leave your stuff in the car.'

Together they went back to the cottage where Snowy guiltily got off the sofa and greeted them as rapturously as if they had been gone all day and not five minutes.

Belinda hurried to the telephone and dialled the number of the garage and was relieved when her call was answered by a woman. She was glad that she didn't have to explain her predicament to Victor. It would seem too much like asking a favour, and embarrassing after his telephone call. She said who she was and what had happened. The woman listened in silence and then said in a voice full of doubt, 'I'll have to go and ask Mr Bradford. They're that busy in the workshop this morning, I don't know as he'll be able to help you. Not at once, anyway. Don't you belong to the AA?'

'No,' said Belinda, thinking, if I did, I'd have called them, wouldn't I?

The woman put down the telephone and Belinda heard her walk away and the sound of a door opening. There was a lot of background noise and Belinda imagined the television churning out the morning's news from its stand on the wall of the shop. She stood drumming her fingers impatiently. Victor will come to the telephone, she thought. He'll take the opportunity to talk to me, but she was wrong, because after a few minutes the woman came back on the line. She was breathing heavily.

'He'll send someone as soon as he can,' she said. 'He said to hang on. He's got a lad out on a job, but when he gets back, he'll send him right over.'

'Thank you. Please thank him from me. I'll just wait then.'

'Does he know where to come?' asked the woman and for a fraction of a moment Belinda wondered whether this was a leading question.

'No, I don't think so. He's never been here before,' she said. 'I'd better give you some directions. It's not far, but we live well outside the village.'

When she had rung off she was aware of Izzy standing beside her, looking up anxiously.

'Is it going to be all right, Granny? I mustn't be late for school.'

'Don't worry, Iz. The garage will send someone to help us. It won't be your fault if you're a bit late. I'll come in and tell your teacher, if you like. Look, in a minute you could go and stand by the window and tell me when you see the garage man coming. I'm going to put the kettle on and have a cup of coffee.'

She waited for the water to boil and was standing with a mug of coffee in her hand wondering how to fill in the unexpected time she now had on her hands. The mornings were always such a rush but now she couldn't think of anything to do.

'There's a van coming, Gran,' called Izzy from the sitting room. 'I think it's from the garage. It's coming very slowly up the lane.' Belinda took her mug to the window.

'Thank goodness,' she said. 'That was quick, wasn't it!'

Izzy began to wave as the white van turned into the drive and Snowy jumped at the window, barking enthusiastically.

'Oh, no,' said Belinda, catching a glimpse of the driver. 'It's Victor.'

'Who's Victor?' said Izzy, looking up at her. 'Granny, your face has gone pink.'

'No it hasn't,' said Belinda hastily. 'It's the hot coffee. Come on, let's go out and meet him. At this rate you'll hardly be late at all.'

At lunchtime, Tom drove to Ken Taylor's yard to pick up Jess. He had telephoned earlier to suggest that he take her out to lunch.

'I've got something to celebrate,' he told her on his mobile. 'I sold those beef calves this morning, and got a better price than I'd hoped for. Let me take you for a steak at the Bird in Hand. I've got some news for you too.'

I know what that will be, thought Jess after she had rung off. Yet another person wants to be the first to inform me that Johnnie Bearsden is back, and then she felt bad at thinking that of Tom. However, as they drove away together and she pulled her hair free from her woolly hat and scrabbled in her bag for her brush, she sensed that there was something coming. There was a sort of buzzing in the atmosphere between them and she knew that Tom was about to broach a touchy or difficult subject.

To begin with they talked about the weather, the most absorbing of subjects for those who race ride, and how the warm spring sunshine was thawing out the ground by the hour.

'Ken reckons it will be raining by tomorrow,' said Jess. 'Two days of rain is what we need before the weekend. That will soften everything up nicely.'

'So it will,' agreed Tom. There was a moment's silence before he went on, 'I had an extraordinary time last night,' he said, not looking at her, concentrating on the road ahead. 'I wanted to telephone you when I got back, but I thought it was too late. I did try your mobile, in fact, but it was switched off.'

'What?' said Jess. 'What do you mean? What happened?' She looked across at him, seeking clues from his face.

'Well, it's a bit of a long story and I want to hear how you got on schooling that horse.'

'Fine. Fine. It was good, but I'll tell you about that later. I want to know what you were up to first.'

'Well, it began with the sheep. I went up to check them yesterday evening – you know I still had those last two ewes to lamb – and when I got there I found a couple of dogs creating merry hell with them. They had the sheep running and were really getting going, working into a frenzy. I reckon I turned up just in time.'

'Bloody hell,' said Jess. 'Whose dogs were they? What was the damage? Did you lose any lambs?'

'I'm coming to that. It was too dark really to see, but I

caught one of the dogs, a spaniel bitch. I couldn't get the other, and then I checked round the field and found one of the ewes had gone down into the stream – you know the place where we put the netting across in the summer when they were getting out – and she had managed to get caught up and drowned.'

'Bloody hell,' said Jess again, shaking her head.

'One of her lambs was dead but the other was just about still breathing. Anyway, I took it home with me and put it in the plate oven and it seems as if it might agree to live. She's taken two bottles of milk today and started to hurtle round the kitchen. Later on I'll see if I can get one of the other ewes to adopt her.'

'What about the dogs? Did you tell the police?'

'I'm coming to that. Look, here we are. I'll finish telling you inside. What time have you got to be back?'

'Ken's given me an extra half an hour, so we don't have to hurry.'

They trooped into the popular village pub on the main road to Salisbury. 'I've booked a table,' said Tom. 'You get such a mob in here, the food's so good.'

'It's just as well I've got Dinka's posh jumper on under this,' said Jess, peeling off her holey old sweater covered in hay seeds. Underneath was the sleek grey cashmere.

'You look lovely,' said Tom. 'As always.' And he was right because when Jess walked through the crowded pub to go to the Ladies, the men leaning on the bar, the hardcore locals, all turned their heads to watch her in her tight jodhpurs which showed off her long legs, and with her mane of shiny brown hair swinging down her back.

'Well?' she said when she came back and picked up her glass of elderflower cordial. 'Go on.'

'Yes, well, when I got back I dealt with the lamb and had a better look at the dog and noticed that its collar had a tag engraved with a name, telephone number and a post code.'

'Yeah? What name?'

'Bearsden,' said Tom watching Jess's face. Her jaw tensed for a moment and a flush of colour crept up her cheeks.

She looked down at her glass and twiddled the stem before saying, 'So?'

'I rang the number.'

'And? Come on, Tom, get a bloody move on with this story. You're going to tell me it was Johnnie's dog, aren't you?' Her voice had already taken on a defensive tone.

'Not quite. A girl answered the telephone. A foreign girl. In fact, she could hardly speak any English. I told her what had happened and she just said, "Sorreee, I no understand." Eventually I got it across that I had one of her dogs and had a very serious complaint to make and she started to cry.'

'Huh,' Jess snorted. 'How irresponsible can you get.'

'I told her that I would bring the dog back and asked her where she was and it turned out to be Quatt Lodge and that she's a sort of au pair, some kind of keeper for the Bearsden brats. Did you know the Bearsdens have moved in, or are about to?'

'Yeah. Funnily enough, a number of people have drawn it to my attention,' said Jess drily. 'I'm frankly sick of the subject. Johnnie's going to keep a horse at the yard, what's more. So what happened next?'

'I took the dog round like I'd promised and at first I thought the house was empty. It was in total darkness with all the ground-floor shutters closed. I've always thought it's a horrible gloomy old place with all those yew trees round it and miles from anywhere. Then I saw one little light at the very top of the house, and it turned out that this girl lives in the attic. She's got a sort of flat up there. Anyway, I rang the front doorbell for ages but she didn't answer and then I went round and thumped on the back door and she still didn't come and so I rang the telephone number again on my mobile. Eventually, she answered and I told her I was standing outside with the dog and would she please open the door, and only then did she come downstairs.

'The lights went on in the kitchen and then I heard chains rattling and the door opened a crack and this terrified face looked out. When she saw that I really did have the dog with me, she had to open up. To cut a long story short, it turns out she's from the Ukraine and has only been in the country for six weeks. Two weeks ago she was dumped at Quatt Lodge so that there's someone to let the tradesmen in – builders, decorators and painters and so on – and she's terrified of everything, the country, the dark, being alone in the house, the dogs. Everything. There's a gamekeeper who sees to the dogs during the day and she's supposed to take them out last thing but she was too scared to go with them last night. She heard a scream, she said, so she ran back and bolted herself into the house.'

'How pathetic,' said Jess contemptuously. 'A scream? I expect it was a fox or an owl. What sort of use is she?'

'Jess, be a bit more sympathetic. The poor girl's lived in a high-rise block of flats in a city all her life.'

'You seem to have learned a lot about her.'

'Well, I couldn't just dump the dog and go, not with her in that state. I only stood on the step. She wouldn't ask me in. I told her I'd come back in the daytime and speak to the keeper about the dogs and leave a bill for the sheep.'

'What did she look like, this girl?' asked Jess suspiciously.

'Pretty, actually. Dyed blonde hair, but a sweet little face. Not like a shot putter or one of those tractor driver types you associate with Ukrainian women.'

'Hardly. They're all top models now. Had the other dog showed up?'

'Yes, I found it lurking around outside. I shut them both in the kennels and that was that.'

'So have you been round again today? Been to comfort pretty little Olga from the Volga?' Jess's tone was sarcastic.

'Ludmylla, actually. No, I haven't. I wondered if you'd come with me.'

'Me? Why? It's nothing to do with me.'

'Well, I thought it might be nice for Ludmylla, you know, to meet another girl. She's obviously terribly homesick and lonely . . .' Tom's voice trailed off. He could see from Jess's face that this was a vain hope. The Bearsden connection ruled out any chance of sympathetic interest from Jess.

'Well, fascinating as I'm sure she is, I can't, Tom. Not today, anyway. I mustn't be late for picking Izzy up from school. Mum and I had a terrible row yesterday because I left Iz at home on her own for about three minutes while I went over to ride the Dawlish mare.'

'We could take her with us. Go round after we collect her from school.'

'Tom, do you mind? Give me a break!' Jess's voice had an indignant ring. 'I don't want anything to do with the Bearsdens. You can deal with this on your own.'

'OK, Jess. It was only a suggestion and I just wanted to tell you what had happened. I didn't want you to think I was keeping it from you.'

'Fine. That's fine,' said Jess, in a why-should-I-care sort of voice.

Tom groaned inwardly. This had gone worse than he had anticipated. He was thankful that at that moment their steaks arrived with piles of crispy thin chips, and suddenly Jess reached across and took his hand.

'Thanks, Tom,' she said, more reasonably. 'I'm kind of horribly interested in all this, of course I am, but I don't want to get involved. OK?'

'Sure,' said Tom, squeezing her hand, grateful that she seemed friendly again.

'I'm schooling that horse again on Thursday,' she went on. 'The mare. I'd hoped you'd come and watch. I can't stand Pete Dawlish, although the old man's all right, and having you there would lend a bit of moral support and you could look after Izzy while I rode.'

Tom took a mouthful of steak and chewed thoughtfully. Of course he would go. He was glad that Jess had asked him, but at the back of his mind was the thought that it was always like this. He would do whatever Jess wanted.

'Yeah, OK. I'll collect Izzy from school if you like and we can all go straight on.'

Jess rewarded him with a dazzling smile. 'The mare's good, you know, Tom. Mad, but really talented. I've just got to crack the temperament thing. I've got to work out how to gain her confidence and get her to listen to me and trust me. Maybe then she'll calm down.'

'Don't let her break your neck in the process.'

'Don't you start. You sound like Mum and Jo and Mary. I've got this feeling about her, Tom, that she's going to win races. She's got a really special quality of gutsiness and speed and jumping ability. If I back off riding her now, I won't get the chance again.'

Tom fell silent. There was nothing much he could say, especially after what he had heard from the farrier about Pete Dawlish preferring another jockey. He saw no point in telling Jess. He wanted things to go right for her and he knew how passionately she felt, so why be discouraging? Nothing anyone said would put her off anyway.

'Yes,' he said. 'I understand. I'll help you all I can.'

In the end Belinda did not have to speak to Izzy's teacher because, despite everything, she was not late for school. 'I came straightaway,' Victor said. 'Before I started the other job. You'd have had a long wait otherwise.'

'Thank you so much,' she said, genuinely grateful. 'Here's my horrible car. I don't know what's wrong with it. I'm afraid I'm like my father whose idea of problem-solving is to get out in a temper and kick a wheel.'

'I see,' said Victor. He smiled and Belinda looked at him properly for the first time. He was as tall and big as she remembered, his solid-looking body filled his old blue overalls and underneath she saw that he wore a checked flannel shirt. He had a broad face, rather high-coloured, and thick, bushy greying eyebrows which overhung very blue eyes. When he smiled his face crinkled and he looked amused and good-natured.

'We'd better have a look then.'

She followed him over to her car and he opened the bonnet and slowly and methodically poked about inside and then clipped on jump leads and connected them to the battery in the van. With this transferred charge her engine leapt into life.

'Keep it running,' he instructed as he removed the leads. 'Flat battery, that's all the trouble is. Call in at the garage on your way past and we'll test it for you. You probably need a new one. Are you ready to go now?'

'Yes, yes. Hop in, Izzy. I'll just go and lock the door. Thank you so much!' Belinda could hear herself twittering. She really was grateful and because she had rejected Victor's invitation, she felt even more indebted. He was so sensible and matter-of-fact, too, there was no need for awkwardness or embarrassment.

'I'll follow you down the lane,' he said, getting back into the van. 'Just in case.'

'Thank you, thank you,' called Belinda again, running up the path, locking the door and then having to repeat the procedure because she had not noticed that Snowy was in the garden. Shooing him inside, she locked up again, ran back and hopped into the driver's seat, inadvertently turning on the windscreen wipers instead of the indicator. Fool, fool, she told herself under her breath, full of dread that she might stall the engine and require another jump-start.

She managed to drive fairly competently down the narrow lane to the crossroads and then turned left to the road to Bishops Barton. Someone had been muck-spreading and there was a build-up of wet dung and straw on the road and a strong agricultural smell wafted through the window.

'I'm not late, am I, Granny?' asked Izzy from the back. 'He was a nice man to help us, wasn't he?'

'Very, very nice,' agreed Belinda, 'and no, you're not going to be late at all. Look, here are all the children still crossing the road with Mrs Vickery.' They stopped as the almost square figure of the lollipop lady stepped into the road. She was sheathed in white and yellow and had very frizzy blonde hair, on top of which her black cap looked about to spring into the air. She held her lollipop aloft and beamed at the little troupe of children and mothers who crossed in front of her.

'She hits the naughty boys with her stick,' Izzy informed Belinda. 'When they push and don't do what she says.'

'Good for her,' said Belinda. 'Serves them right.'

She pulled up outside the school in a line of cars disgorging children. Proper country cars, she thought, all filthy dirty with dogs in the back, and then waved at Victor as he went past in the van.

'There you are, Izzbug. In you go. Have you got your school bag and your book? I can't come in with you because I don't dare turn the engine off.' She turned to kiss Izzy's pink, round face, but she was already struggling to open the door and didn't look back. Out on the pavement she gave the door a mighty slam and set off at once without saying goodbye, through the gate in the chain-link fence and into the milling playground. Belinda watched her go, small, solid, determined, not looking right or left, *The Water Babies* clutched tight under one arm, her school bag in the other hand, her striped hat pulled well down.

I hope she's all right, she thought, remembering the twins and their taunts. She imagined Izzy's day stretching out in front of her. Belinda could remember so vividly what it had felt like, when school seemed like a long grey road, lit by occasional sun-filled patches when there was art or music and movement, but mostly strewn with awful trials to be endured, like PE and spelling tests and the terrifying reciting of tables. Of course, school wasn't like that any more, she told herself. Nowadays it was all child-centred activities, whatever that meant, but it probably still felt the same. Children probably still had that same sense of powerlessness and helplessness in a world controlled by confusing, contradictory adults.

She swung out into the road and drove to the garage. Outside the workshop she could see Victor talking to two of his young mechanics in blue overalls. He looked over and waved. She turned off the engine and got out.

'This won't take too long,' he said, coming over. 'Kevin will check your battery and if necessary we can fit you a new one in fifteen minutes or so.'

'Thank you so much,' she said again.

'See, it won't hold the charge,' he said when Kevin sat in the driver's seat and tried, unsuccessfully, to restart the engine. 'That's what the trouble will be. Now come into the office and wait in there. Would you like a cup of coffee?'

She would rather have stayed outside in the warm, watery sunshine, but declining the offer seemed churlish. She didn't want any more coffee, she was already awash, but Victor had gone to fill the kettle in the washroom across the passage. She looked round the office which was neat and orderly. There were no photographs of the late wife to be seen and no tits and bums posters either. She watched his back through the open door. She tried to remember if she had ever seen him without the woolly hat but didn't think she had, so she couldn't picture what his hair was like, or even if he had any, but judging from his eyebrows it would be silvery grey. When he came back he had already put milk in both mugs and although she took hers black, Belinda smiled gratefully. He had nice hands, too, she noticed, big and brown and square with neat, clean nails.

'Now,' he said, passing her the coffee and sitting down opposite, behind his tidy desk. He smiled. 'This might seem like taking advantage, but do you think you might reconsider going out with me one night? I told you I would keep trying.'

Belinda smiled back. It must have been a combination of the spring sunshine which had lifted her spirits and her gratitude at being rescued that made her say, 'I can hardly say no, can I?' and because that sounded rude, which she hadn't intended at all, she added, 'Yes, please, I'd really like to.' Somewhere in her head she heard Dinka cheer her on.

'How about one night this week? I'd better strike while the iron is hot, hadn't I? Before you change your mind.'

'A drink?' said Belinda. 'Why don't we go for a drink one evening?'

'How about Thursday?'

Belinda thought hard. She was quite capable of saying yes and then remembering some reason why she couldn't and she didn't want to do that to Victor.

'Thursday would be lovely, although I go to Pilates straight from work, so it would have to be late,' she said. 'Pilates,' she explained, seeing his mystified face, 'is a sort of exercise class.'

'Oh, I see. I've never heard of it. I'll come and collect you, shall I? Eight thirty?'

'Lovely, Victor. Thank you very much.'

'I said yes, Dinka!' said Belinda that evening on the telephone to her friend. 'I can hardly believe it now, but I did, and I've been regretting it all day!'

'For heaven's sake, why?' asked Dinka. 'Saying yes to a drink is hardly a lifetime commitment, is it?'

'No, of course it's not, but I don't know that I want to start all this sort of thing up again – you know, going out with a man.'

'Why ever not?' asked Dinka whose worst nightmare was the thought of life without one.

'I suppose after James . . .'

'Belinda, that was years ago. One doesn't have to adopt the recovery position on a permanent basis, you know. A bad man experience needn't be a terminal condition.'

'But I'm perfectly happy as I am, I don't need the *disturbance* that a man causes.'

Dinka sighed. 'Then don't go out with him again. Make it only once.'

'I can't do that. Not after he was so kind this morning.'

'That's his job, mending cars. Rescuing breakdowns.'

'He was nicer, more helpful than he need have been.'

'Oh, Belinda!' said Dinka. 'Then just go, for heaven's sake, but make it clear you only want to be friends.'

'Yes, I could try that,' said Belinda doubtfully. 'But things always turn out to be more complicated, don't they? I mean, to begin with James was only being kind to me because of David.'

'Hmm,' said Dinka who had always felt that James Redpath had been an adventurer, a man who sought opportunities with most of the women he met.

'I suppose I could just be busy all the time.'

'What developments have there been on the Johnnie Bearsden front? That was your crisis of yesterday, if you remember.'

'Oh, that,' said Belinda, as if it was long ago. 'When I got home Jess and I had a furious row about her leaving Izzy on her own and somehow the Johnnie thing took a bit of a back seat. I'm still desperately worried about Izzy and the effect it may have on her, but Jess has said that she will not have the subject discussed, so that's that. She threatened to leave if I as much as mentioned his name.'

'Maybe that wouldn't be such a bad thing,' suggested Dinka.

'What? Jess leaving?' asked Belinda, aghast.

'Yes. In the long run it might be for the best.'

'Dinka!' said Belinda, horrified. 'How can you say that? It would be disastrous!'

'Hmm,' said Dinka again, thoughtfully. She often

wondered whose need was the greatest, Jess's or Belinda's, with Izzy caught in the middle. If she wasn't careful, Belinda could become one of those dangerous, smothering types of mothers, whose children were never allowed to grow up or grow away, because to do so would reveal the emptiness of their own lives.

'Anyway,' said Belinda, 'your advice was right. There doesn't seem to be anything I can do apart from being here to pick up the pieces and act as a sort of buffer. It's a bit nerve-wracking, playing a waiting game, but I really don't want to precipitate a crisis. But, Dinka, enough of us. Tell me how you are, and how is Javier?'

'Playing up,' said Dinka shortly. 'Being quite restless and naughty. I think when the weather is better I will bring him down to you for the weekend. I need to get him away from his friends in London.'

'That would be lovely,' said Belinda, trying to sound enthusiastic. Last spring when Dinka had brought Javier for a visit, he had been disappointed that it was so cold. He said there would be mimosa flowering in the gardens in Spain and had sulked when he was taken on a walk and got stuck in his new designer trainers in a muddy gateway.

After she had rung off, Belinda sat for a moment and thought about her friend and the conversation that they had just had. Their lives had taken such different paths that it was impossible to imagine being in the other's shoes. Dinka doesn't understand how I feel about Izzy, she thought. How could I expect her to? Just as I can't understand what she sees in Javier. Well, obviously I *can*, but I would find him much more trouble than he was worth.

In both their cases, it was love, of course, that made the difference. For a moment Belinda wondered whether it was wrong of her to assume that maternal or grandmotherly love superseded all others, but how could it be otherwise when it was the only truly unselfish love that she had ever experienced? When she thought she was head over heels in love with James Redpath it was all about how he made her feel, she could see that now. Suddenly she was this blessed person, much superior to her ordinary self, a person who was loved by a man – a shit, as it turned out, but there you are; that was all it took to make her deliriously happy and the world to be transformed into a quite different place. Whereas what she felt for her three children and for Izzy was something quite other. It had nothing to do with how she felt, which was mainly anxious and often irritated, but it was always totally and utterly *devoted*. The only thing that maternal love asked in return was that the offspring should be happy and safe.

Of course, there were mothers who did not experience this flood of maternal feeling, those that battered and neglected and abandoned babies in skips or on doorsteps, but surely these were aberrations, creatures whose own lives had been warped by circumstances that prevented them from being normal. It was true that she had questioned exactly how unselfish Jess was, but she never doubted for a moment that she loved Izzy completely, in her way.

No wonder Dinka did not understand.

On Wednesday, the rain came as forecast in great grey curtains that swept across the fields from the west. Water swilled in gutters and poured from downpipes and flowed in eddies across Ken's yard into the brimming drains. Work went on as usual, the horses ducking their unwilling heads into the wind and coming back from exercise with their coats dark and steaming.

There was schooling to be done and Ken, sitting in his Land Rover, took three lots out to his practice fences behind the house to watch them jump. Jess, on Dolly, who hated the weather and rounded her back and refused to go forward, rode alongside Carl on Dawn Call. Behind them came Susan on Glennie. They rode across the field, shoulders hunched, and showed the horses the first fence to remind them what they were to be asked to do. Circling round in a working canter they brought them into it for a second time and drove them on. Dolly's ears pricked and she took off when Jess gave her the signal, but jumped too big and lost ground on landing while Glennie went ahead. At the second fence Dolly jumped low and fast and made up what she had lost and at the third she was a stride in front. They circled for a second time and by now her blood was up and she forgot the rain in her face and flew all the fences, clean and sweet. The third time round they had been instructed to press on and extend into a gallop, meeting the first fence side by side, the riders sitting deep, encouraging their horses to stretch out, aware even over practice fences of the desire to be first.

Pulling up when they had finished, Jess leaned down to stroke Dolly's neck. Ken wound down his window and shouted across, 'Not much to worry about there. Feel all right, did they?' The three riders nodded and waved and began to walk back across the way they had come, except this time their horses were strung up and on their toes, swinging their quarters, tossing their heads, oblivious of the weather. The galloping and jumping had put fire in their hot thoroughbred blood.

The practice had gone so well that Jess felt a smile creep into the corners of her mouth and she hardly noticed the driving rain, the water dripping off the rim of her hat and the mud in the gateway. The burst of speed had sent pure physical excitement bubbling inside her like a spring and she was brimming with energy and happiness. Jumping down in the yard, she led Dolly into her box before fetching buckets of warm water to wash her down. An hour's exercise on the automatic horse-walker would be her lot for the day, while Jess would go back down to the fences with the second string. Later, Tom would be coming to ride out the horses he would race on Saturday and Ken had told her he wanted her to school upside, ride her horse alongside his and jump shoulder to shoulder.

This was when she most admired Tom, when he was sitting on a racehorse, his long legs hooked into short stirrups, his natural balance and innate understanding of horses lending him an easy grace so that the horse became relaxed and happy under him. Small, light horses looked more substantial, gangly youngsters more coordinated, lazy horses woke up, and nervous, frightened horses gained confidence. He had what Ken called 'soft' hands, so that what passed between him and the horse along the length of the reins was an understanding, not domination or a battle of wills. Strong-pulling horses relaxed their jaws and became easier to stop, and horses that would not accept the bit lowered their heads and became compliant and cooperative.

It was something you were born with, Jess thought. You either had it or you didn't, and although almost anyone could become a competent rider, natural-born horsemen like Tom were few and far between. He would have some advice about the Dawlish mare, she knew. He would watch how she moved and then he would have some suggestions to make. Perhaps a different noseband or different bit would help steady her. Tom would know.

As Jess led Dolly back out into the rain to the horse-walker, she heard a car come into the yard. As if on cue, it was Tom in his old Land Rover. She stopped and waved as he got out but he was looking for something in the back and shrugging on his coat, and did not see her.

Jess moved on thoughtfully. It was funny that sometimes when you had a glimpse of someone and they did not know you were watching, a moment of revelation could take place. It was as if in that tiny space of time you saw them clearly and objectively, like the concentrated, reduced view from the wrong end of a telescope, and then your own feelings for them came rushing at you, nearly knocking you sideways, taking your breath away by their unexpectedness.

I do love him, she thought. I'm not just fond of him. It's something much more than that.

'Look where you're going!' said Moira, coming the other way with a barrow of hay, and the moment was lost.

What Jess did not realise was that Tom had in fact seen her as he drove into the yard. He saw her stop and turn in his direction as she led a grey mare through the driving rain in the direction of the horse-walker. He saw a rather vacant expression on her face, not even a welcoming one, and immediately turned his back, reaching for his coat, to avoid having to acknowledge that he had seen her. It was an instinctive ducking aside. He needed to compose himself, get a grip, so that he could be quite certain that his reaction would not betray him.

He felt so thoroughly confused by the events of the morning that he had not even worked out for himself how he felt or what difference it made to him and Jess. Only an hour ago he had been sitting in the kitchen at Quatt Lodge drinking a cup of coffee with Ludmylla. He had gone round as he said he would, to speak to the gamekeeper about the spaniels. He found him, a taciturn Yorkshire man, cleaning out a coach house round the back of the house. Despite the rain, he was heaving out old pheasant coops, nothing more than a pile of broken wood and tangled chicken wire, and chucking them into the back of his truck. Tom introduced himself and gave him a hand with the last one or two, before broaching the subject of the dogs and his sheep. The man eyed him suspiciously, his hard face giving nothing away under the brim of his cap.

'It's that bluddy useless girl,' he said shortly. 'She's no bluddy use at all.'

Tom said nothing. It wasn't his business. All he wanted was his compensation and an assurance it would not happen again.

'And the oother one,' the man went on. 'Thinks she knows it all, but I tell you, she's bluddy ignorant.'

'What other one?' asked Tom.

'Boss's wife. The American. Pig ignorant, she is. Calls it 'unting.'

'That's what they say in America. What we call shooting, they call hunting.'

The man took out a tobacco pouch and a packet of cigarette papers. Tom watched as the thick, cracked fingers deftly rolled a slim white tube. 'He's all right. She's a pain in the arse. She'll ruin them dogs.' He put the unlit cigarette in his mouth. The thin paper stuck to his fat, red lower lip.

Tom shrugged. 'Maybe, but what I need to know is that it won't happen again. I lost a ewe and a lamb.'

'I'll keep an eye on the boogers,' the man promised. 'I'll tek them hoome with me of a night. They'll not get out agen.'

'Whatever,' said Tom. 'Just as long as I don't see them anywhere near my ewes. Once they've got a taste for sheep-worrying you can never trust them.'

'I'll not tell ye agen, I'll see to them.' The gamekeeper turned away, the conversation over, and got into the cab of his truck. He drove off without looking back and Tom was left in the rain to make his way to the house and look for Ludmylla.

He found her in the kitchen, a small, dark room, mopping the floor in a half-hearted fashion. There was a television perched on the dresser and as she mopped she gazed, transfixed, at the screen, from which came occasional bursts of game-show laughter. Now he had a proper view of her, Tom could see that she was in her twenties, small and slight, her dead-looking, daffodil blonde hair yanked up into a

163

ponytail. She was wearing jeans and a sweater and very high-heeled boots and every now and then took a drag from a cigarette left smoking in a saucer on the table. She jumped when Tom rang the old ship's bell by the door and looked round guiltily.

Tom stood in the door and took off his boots. He intended to go inside, out of the rain, and make sure that he made himself understood. In his pocket was the envelope containing the short note he had written, explaining what had happened and including a bill for the ewe and the lamb. It had taken him a long time to write. He had screwed up and discarded all his 'Dear Johnnie, I'm not sure you will remember me . . .' versions and in the end settled on an impersonal, formal tone, not referring to any previous acquaintance. It was less complicated that way.

Ludmylla turned off the television and stood looking at him, mop in hand. She had an unhealthy-looking yellowish skin and a gold stud in her nose, which at first Tom thought was a large spot.

'Can I come in?' he asked, stepping over the doorstep in his socks.

'Yes. Come in. You want coffee?'

'Yeah. Great. Look,' he held out the cheap brown envelope which had got damp in his pocket and was curling at the edges, 'please give this to Mr or Mrs Bearsden.'

'Major,' she corrected. 'He want to be called Major.'

'OK, then,' said Tom. 'Major.'

The girl took the envelope and put it on the dresser where there was already a pile of unopened post.

'She come today,' she said. 'Mrs. She come today, with

children. It half-term.' She took a drag on her cigarette.

'Oh, well, that's good,' said Tom. 'I should get paid, then.'

'No, not good. Not good for me,' she said. 'More work for me.'

'Kids are OK, are they?' asked Tom as she filled two mugs with water from the kettle. 'I'll have mine black, please.' Ludmylla heaped spoonfuls of sugar in her own and topped it up with milk.

'Kids OK, but have too much. Too much stuff and parents they are like this.' She made a screwing action with her down-turned thumb.

'It's the same with all children today. They all have whatever they want,' said Tom, not really thinking, just mouthing something he had heard other people say. After he had said it, he thought of Izzy. It wasn't true of her. She wasn't spoiled, that was for sure. He remembered her pleasure in the old-fashioned books she had got at the jumble sale.

'How many children are there?' he asked.

'Boy, nine years. He called Mikey. Twin girls, four years old, Alice and Alexandra.'

'So you have to look after them?' asked Tom. 'That's your job, is it?'

'There is another girl, Kerry. Australian. She is nanny. I am au pair.'

'Blimey,' said Tom. 'A bit labour-intensive, aren't they, these children?'

Ludmylla turned to look at him, uncomprehending. 'My English very bad.'

'No, it's not. Not at all. Better than I thought the other night.'

Ludmylla laughed. 'I was very frightened.'

'Well, sorry, but I had to bring the dog back.'

'No, no. You very kind.'

'What did you do? Back in Ukraine?'

'I am student. I am mathematics, but no work in my country.'

'Yeah. So I've heard.' Tom drained his mug and got up. 'I'd better get on. Got a lot to do this morning.' He paused on his way to the door. 'What do you do all day, stuck here?'

'Piano. I play piano,' said Ludmylla. She opened a door out of the kitchen and showed Tom a long dark passage. God, it was a gloomy house. She pointed. 'Piano there. In big room.'

'Really? I'd love to hear you.'

'Come,' said Ludmylla.

'Well,' said Tom, hesitating. He ought to be off if he was riding out at Ken's before lunch, but she had gone, disappearing through a door further down the corridor.

As he hesitated in the kitchen, rippling piano music swelled towards him, a wonderful surge of sound that stopped the words in his mouth. The music soared and swooped and, mesmerised, he followed it down the passage and stood in the door.

It was a big, high-ceilinged, closed-up room. The furniture was draped with sheets except for a grand piano at which the girl sat with her back to him in her cheap acrylic jumper with its sparkly pattern across her thin shoulders and her coarse, yellow hair gleaming under the electric light. Her hands hovered and dashed over the keys while her high-heeled boots worked at the pedals.

It was so unexpected that this scrap of a girl with her clumsy English and her ugly, cheap clothes could produce such a sound. It was miraculous and Tom was ashamed at how easy it had been to feel superior and patronising when he had known so little about her. The music filled the room, he could feel its reverberations through his socked feet, and then as quickly and as unexpectedly as it had started, it finished. The hands stopped and fell into Ludmylla's lap and she sat for a moment, her tarty boots dangling, not quite touching the floor.

'That was amazing!' said Tom. 'You are a fantastic pianist.'

Ludmylla got up and shrugged. 'I was at Conservatoire for two years.'

'What were you playing? It was so grand, so . . .' Words failed Tom.

'Rachmaninov.' Ludmylla closed the lid of the piano. 'I finish now.'

'And I must go.' Tom followed her back down the passage to the kitchen and went to the door to put on his boots. 'Here,' he said, turning back. 'Have you got a piece of paper handy? I'll give you my telephone number. If you need to, you can give me a ring.'

Ludmylla handed him a pad and a biro and when he gave it back she stood looking at what he had written. 'OK,' she said, dismissively.

'Right, I'm off.' Tom turned to make a farewell gesture but she had already closed the kitchen door and he heard the television turned back up.

Weird, he thought, a weird experience. He could hear

Meg barking from the Land Rover and when he turned the corner out of the kitchen courtyard into the drive, he saw that a car had pulled up. It was a glossy estate car and out of it was climbing a tall woman with very thick curly brown hair, wearing a large brimmed waterproof hat. She turned to glance at him before opening the rear door and ducking inside again to release two small girls from child seats. She turned back to him.

'Hi,' she said in a light, sing-song American accent. 'I'm Karen Bearsden. Can I help you?'

Tom groaned inwardly. Now he would have to go through it all again, just when he wanted to make a quick getaway.

'I've left a note,' he said, 'explaining.'

'OK. Fine.' She mistook him for some sort of tradesman, he assumed. She turned away again to shut the car doors. 'Hurry, you two,' she said. 'Run in out of the rain.' The two dark-haired little girls trotted away, the hoods of their sweat-shirts pulled over their heads, each clutching pink plastic handbags.

The woman looked towards the coach houses. 'You'll get soaked,' she yelled, and Tom turned in the same direction and saw a very large blonde woman and a boy come across the yard, hatless and coatless. The young woman was laughing and gave Tom a bold, appraising look as she went past. She bent to get something out of the car and he saw, above the top of her low-cut jeans, a lacy G-string cutting across her great backside. Tom realised that she was Australian from something she said to the boy, and when he turned to look at him – he was dawdling about, scuffing gravel into puddles, not bothering about getting wet – he saw Izzy's double standing there, glasses glinting with rain, tangerine hair flattened with dark streaks.

As he drove away, one thing was clear to Tom. Jess couldn't go on denying it any more. Not with that evidence trotting around on two legs not more than five miles away. Jesus, he thought, it will all come out now. He wondered how much Jess already knew, whether she realised that Johnnie's son was such a dead ringer for Iz. Poor old Jess, he thought sadly. Poor little Izzy. It was one hell of a can of worms waiting to be opened.

By the time he reached Ken's, he had made up his mind. He would say nothing to Jess. It was better to let things take their own course without him putting his oar in. He was going to keep his mouth shut. When the whole thing blew up he would be there to do what he could.

Seeing Jess in Ken's yard upset him unexpectedly. Because of what he had just discovered, he felt as if he had lost something, as if she had moved further away, out of his reach. Pretending he had not seen her, he turned to collect his wet coat and his helmet from the back of the Land Rover and when he got out, she and the horse had gone.

Chapter Seven

Thursday was the turning point in Belinda's week. She thought of the working week as a landscape. From Monday to Wednesday was a long uphill stretch, with the summit reached when she closed down her computer on Wednesday evening. Thursday was definitely over the top and going downhill, and by the time she went to her Pilates class on Thursday evening, she was positively free-wheeling towards the weekend.

Thursday evenings were one of the occasions when she insisted on getting away from the office promptly in order to drive across to the other side of the town to the high school sports centre. Because she was older than her two bosses, and not intimidated by them, she found it easy to be quite firm about such things and had trained them not to bring her work to be done much after five o'clock.

At first it seemed strangely perverse to lie flat on her back on the dusty floor while gentle whale-type music drifted over her, especially as the temptation was strong to go straight home after a long day at work, but she had discovered that at the end of the session she felt better, physically and mentally, and so she forced herself to make the effort.

'Now scan through your whole body,' said Xanthe, the

dreamy-voiced instructor to the fifteen women prone on mats on the floor, 'and let go of any tension. Let it float right away. Gently roll your head first to one side, and now to the other, roll your chin onto your chest, make that double chin and enjoy the stretch in the back of your neck. Now let your shoulders relax down your back and feel yourself floating away.'

Belinda felt so relaxed after all of this that it was an effort to move onto her side and struggle to her feet to begin the proper business of the class. Xanthe, at least, was a perfect advertisement for her art. Her body was sensational, Belinda thought, strong and lean and supple, with high, round buttocks and a proper womanly chest, and as she demonstrated each move she flexed and arched her back like a cat.

The class was a mixed bag A good cross-section of women in terms of age and size rolled and strained on the mats, and although it was not supposed to be competitive, Belinda had to place herself somewhere in the bottom half of the ability range. Wearing an old pair of Jo's jogging trousers and a T-shirt and with her hair tied back in a band, she looked far from glamorous and it was hard to concentrate on the swan dive position when on either side of her two rather stout middle-aged women were beached, face down and struggling to heave their extensive frontages off the mat. We're more like sea cows than swans, she thought, but I suppose we all nurse the secret hope that we'll turn into Xanthe if we try hard enough, and it struck her how it was always women who attended these self-improvement classes. Men either didn't bother, being quite content with themselves as they were, or did show-off, sweaty exercise in gyms, in tight shorts. Women seemed to be more humble about themselves. She couldn't imagine Victor doing anything like this in order to keep in shape.

'Don't try this next exercise if you have trouble with your neck or lower back or knee pain,' advised Xanthe, demonstrating an upper leg lift and stretch combined with raising her torso in an elegant arch. 'Navel to spine,' she commanded. 'Tighten those pelvic muscles. Breathe IN, two, three, four, five, and OUT, two, three, four, five.' Fifteen women strained and heaved, faces contorted with effort and concentration. 'Let those shoulders relax. Rest when you need to. Let's have eight more of those. *Lift*, one, two, three, four.'

Bloody hell, thought Belinda, wondering if she could cheat just a little. Out of the corner of her eye she could see that Shirley, sixty if she was a day, with tinny-coloured red hair, was lasting the course, so she felt she had to too.

'Last one, now,' said Xanthe. '*Lift*, one two, three, four and *rest*. Well done, ladies!'

Belinda and Shirley exchanged grimaces. Agony, but worth it, their expressions seemed to say. Belinda knew that Shirley was a hairdresser in the town, in a salon full of teenage girls who considered her well past it. It was important to keep trim and fit if only to keep them in their place, even though many of her regulars were in their eighties, Sherborne being the sort of town it was. The old dears saw her as young, bless them, she'd told Belinda.

An hour later, the cheerful group of women crossed to their cars in the wet, dark car park, calling goodnight to one another. Waiting to back out of her space, Belinda watched as elderly, genteel Pat reversed her small car into the rear end of Monica the librarian's Fiesta.

Driving home, she went through in her mind what she had yet to do before Victor came to collect her. She would have a scant half-hour in which to change, turn round and go out again and she wanted to telephone her mother and confirm the weekend visit and she must ask Jess what arrangements she had made for Izzy for the forthcoming half-term. Just the thought of going somewhere with a man made her wonder whether she shouldn't give herself some sort of overhaul, or a refit, like dockyards gave old liners. Her hair could do with another colour rinse and she hadn't bothered with a manicure for months. Oh, well, it was too late now.

As she was passing through Bishops Barton, past the garage on the left, she noticed that the lights were still on in the office although the forecourt and the petrol pumps were closed. Was Victor there, she wondered, working late and passing the time before he would come to take her out? Although it was only half past seven, the village was already in darkness. It had stopped raining at last but the road was still streaming with wet. The car park of the Coach and Horses was nearly empty. No one would want to be out on a dismal February night. She turned into the lane to home and a fox crossed in front of her, a big red dog fox, quite unhurried as he slipped into the opposite hedge. A travelling fox out looking for a vixen.

She longed to be home. She hoped Jess had lit the fire and that supper would be ready. She would hardly have time to gobble hers before she had to go out again and she felt hollow with hunger. When it was Jess's turn to prepare the evening meal, as it was tonight, it was always sausages or a chicken pie bought from the butchers in Sharston. Jess couldn't be bothered with cooking. Izzy would have had hers early and now be bathed and tucked up in bed waiting for Belinda to kiss her goodnight. The curtains would be drawn against the night and all would be safe and secure in the little cottage on the ridge, like a tight little ship out on a dark sea.

Of course, she might have known it would not be like that. There were no welcoming lights as she pulled off the lane and Jess's car was gone. Even Snowy appeared to be out and the cottage was eerily quiet. Belinda fumbled for her key and let herself in and began putting on lights and drawing curtains. Jess had left no note and Belinda could not think where they could all be at this time of night. She glanced at the kitchen clock. It was quarter to eight and Jess still had Izzy out somewhere and she had school tomorrow and then the long drive to Suffolk. Really, it was too bad of her, especially after the last time they had argued over Izzy.

She felt fired with indignation as she bustled about, still in her coat, deciding not to bother to light the fire, pulling wet clothes out of the washing machine and draping them on the clothes dryer in front of the Rayburn. It's always up to me, she thought, to do everything in this place. Jo is quite right when she complains that Jess behaves as if she's a teenager. She should know what it's like to run a home. Just this once she could have been in at a reasonable time and done some of the things I have to do, night after night. It's far too late to have Izzy out.

She slammed cupboard doors and clattered saucepans and stirred a tin of baked beans on the stove. Jess was supposed to have bought bread and the last straw was to find that the bin was empty. She felt tired and dispirited by self-pity.

Taking the saucepan and a spoon upstairs with her, she started to change in her cold bedroom, eating beans as she went. She would have liked to have had a bath but there wasn't time and deciding that clean jeans and a black sweater would be suitably casual and understated for her date with Victor, she pulled them on and added a pretty Moroccan necklace that Jo had brought her back from a holiday and her best black boots with a bit of a heel which was meant to make legs look longer.

She was in the bathroom putting on her face when she heard a car arrive outside. She paused, mascara brush in hand, to listen. God, I hope it's not Victor come early, she thought, but then heard Izzy calling to Snowy and the back door bang. She felt another wave of anger and jabbed herself in the eye with a smudge of black. Damn. She heard Izzy's feet clattering up the stairs in a great hurry and then she was at the door of the bathroom, eyes shining, her face pink. She grabbed at Belinda's hand, shouting, 'Granny, I saw Mummy ride the naughty horse. I went with Tom and I saw his lambs and one is wearing another one's coat so its mummy won't know it's not her proper baby, and we had a pizza to eat at his house.'

Despite her burning disapproval, Belinda could not help but share in her excitement. 'That's lovely, Izzy,' she managed. 'Although it's very late for you to be out.'

'Late doesn't matter,' said Izzy loftily, following her back into her bedroom where Belinda took her best coat out of her wardrobe and squirted herself with scent.

'Me, too!' said Izzy, and Belinda sprayed a little behind each of her round, pink, cold little ears.

'Get your pyjamas on,' she said. 'It's too late for a bath tonight.' She started down the stairs and went into the kitchen where Jess was emptying supermarket bags onto the table.

'You might have left a note!' she said. 'I was worried. I couldn't think where you were. It's very late for Izzy on a school night.'

'Oh, don't start,' said Jess dismissively. 'She's had a lovely time.' She delved into a bag and brought out a loaf which she dumped on the table in front of her mother. 'Sorry if you were waiting for this. Is that why you're cross?'

'I'm not cross. Well, yes, I am. I'm going out tonight and I could have done with some supper before I go. It's supposed to be your night to cook.' She sounded selfish and grudging now, when she should be glad that being with Jess had made Izzy so happy, but it was hard to swap one mood for another, and her state of indignation had already worked up a good head of steam.

'I didn't know that, did I? You never said you were going anywhere. I've got half a pizza here for you, too,' said Jess. Belinda saw she had put a box on the table.

'I'm in a hurry. I've already warmed up some beans,' she said, and then felt ungracious and added, 'but thank you all the same.'

'Where are you going?' Jess was cheerful. Belinda could feel her good mood and for some contrary reason it made her feel more irritable.

'Out for a drink. With a friend.'

'Who? Good thing you've had something to eat then. Don't want you getting pissed!'

'Oh, ha, ha.'

'Who did you say?'

'I didn't. He's called Victor Bradford. He owns the garage in Bishops Barton.'

'Mum! You didn't tell me! What's this about?'

'What do you mean, "about"? It isn't "about" anything.'

'Going out with a man? For a drink? What am I supposed to think!'

Belinda felt distinctly unamused. She couldn't stand any teasing tonight. 'Oh, shut up, Jess. You're always telling me to get a life.'

'Oooh, Mrs Grumpy!' Jess pulled a mocking face.

Izzy appeared in her pyjamas, carrying *The Water Babies*, and pushed Belinda to sit down at the table and then wormed her way onto her lap, twisting round to show that her hands and face were washed.

'I had a lovely, lovely time, Granny, and I saw the orphan lamb in his coat, and I saw Mummy on the horse go round and round and Tom said she would win a race if she stayed on her feet.'

Belinda looked across at Jess. That was why she was radiating good humour. 'It went well, did it? That horse that gave you a fall last time?' It was impossible to be cross for long.

'Really, really well,' said Jess. 'Tom reckons she's got quite a bit of talent. He suggests I try her in an Australian nose-band which will stop her opening her mouth and might mean I don't get run away with.'

'Well, I'm glad to hear it.'

'Granny, where are you going?' said Izzy, noticing that she was wearing her coat.

'Out for a drink, darling. With a friend.'

'What sort of drink, Granny? Is it gin? Because in *The Water Babies* the Queen of the River has to coax little children from the gutters and turn women from the gin-shop door. It *says*, Granny.' Izzy bent her head to find the page, while Jess and Belinda burst out laughing.

Waiting by the front door for Victor, Belinda nervously adjusted her hair and put on fresh lipstick. The moment she heard a car draw up she shot out, pulling the door closed behind her. The cottage was in no state to receive a visitor and, anyway, she wanted to keep the whole of this evening on neutral territory.

Victor was in the process of reversing into the space beside the cottage ready to turn back out onto the lane and Belinda waited for him to finish the manoeuvre, realising as she did so that she had stepped off the hard drive and into the mud which squished softly up the side of her boots. Hastily, she tried to wipe them in the long grass. The interior of Victor's car was sure to be immaculate.

He leaned over to open the passenger door and as the light in the car came on she saw that he was not wearing the hat and that his hair was indeed silver, close cropped and thick.

'Thank you,' she said, and slid in the door, noticing before the light went out that her boots were filthy.

'Oh dear, I'm sorry. I stepped in the mud. Your lovely clean car!'

Victor glanced down and laughed. 'A bit of mud won't hurt. Where would you like to go? Somewhere quiet or somewhere noisy?'

'Somewhere in-between? You know what I mean, not all jukeboxes and not deathly silent.'

'What about the Fox at Anstley? That's not too far, is it?'

'Lovely,' said Belinda. She was glad because there would be no one she knew drinking there on a Thursday evening. She sat back and closed her eyes for a moment. It felt like an achievement just to have got out of the house. When she opened them she looked slyly in the dark at Victor's profile and his large hands on the wheel. His bulk filled the driver's seat and his head nearly brushed the roof. His size was reassuring, she thought. It made him seem solid and dependable, and he drove well, slowly and smoothly down the tiny dark lanes which gleamed wet in the headlights.

'Now,' he said, as they paused to turn onto the main road. 'How about you telling me a bit about yourself?'

On Friday, Belinda took the afternoon off, leaving Jenny in charge, and she and Izzy set out for Suffolk. The weather had turned mild and damp and it was a gloomy sort of day, with a low grey sky which blotted out the horizon. Although the days were getting markedly longer now that spring was creeping on, this afternoon there was very little light. From the ridge the vale below was transformed into a silver void, all the hedges and trees swallowed up and the circling hills smudged into obscurity.

Izzy sat in the back with her bag beside her and *The Water Babies* on her lap. As the time to leave had got closer, she had helped Belinda pack the box of provisions for her great-grandparents. There was a jar of local honey from the farm in Peaceful Lane, organic bacon and sausages from the farmers' market, leeks from the garden and two cakes from the WI stall in Sherborne. Belinda had also found her mother a spring jacket from a charity shop in a bright, showerproof poplin and had made up her mind to try and bin the old school raincoat which she herself had worn as a teenager, and which her mother could see nothing wrong with.

'It's just so ancient, Ma. It's almost green with age. You look one stop from being a bag lady.'

'Years of wear in it yet,' retorted her mother. 'It will see me out, at any rate.' In fact, thought Belinda, she was really a bag lady already, with a larder hung with plastic bags stuffed full of other plastic bags, or pieces of string saved from a lifetime of parcels, used Christmas wrapping paper, milk bottle tops, carefully opened envelopes which would have a label stuck over the address and be used again.

In many ways her parents represented the very best of a long-vanished England, guided as they had always been by a Fabian sense of duty and responsibility to others. Greed and ostentation and consumerism, the me-centred, self-obsession of society was anathema to them. Their lives had been upright, frugal, hard-working, all totally admirable, but these were also chilly and unlovable traits in some ways. Unforgiving towards weakness and self-indulgence, they had been aloof and unsympathetic as parents and Belinda and her brothers had grown up as secretive and deceiving teenagers.

Belinda, who had not shone academically and therefore felt a failure in their eyes, had seen marriage as an escape, which it had proved to be. Since then she had spent no more than a night or two under their roof but as the years went by, feelings softened on both sides and these days she could see and understand the sort of people they were and allow her affection for them to run clear of the old restraints.

Even so, she had dreaded telling them that Jess was pregnant. Her mother's condemnation of 'silly girls' who 'got into trouble' when she herself was growing up still rang in her ears. For all she knew, her mother would recommend adoption for the baby or a home for unmarried mothers for Jess, or incarceration in a Magdalen laundry if such a thing had still existed.

When it came to it, however, her parents had been marvellously understanding and supportive of Jess, and Belinda had been left wondering how it was she had grown up terrified of the stigma of illegitimacy. Had her parents' attitudes changed or had she misjudged them? She would almost rather have cast herself under a bus than have had to tell them that she was pregnant. She supposed now that they would have been sensible and kind, but how was it that she hadn't known that? How could she have misjudged them so dramatically?

In fact it was their clear-eyed and objective advice that was most helpful in those early days when she was so upset and at her wits' end with Jess. They had been far more use than the rest of the family. Jo had been furious and Charlie deeply embarrassed and David's mother, who was a wobbling, sentimental creature, wept down the telephone at the thought of the fatherless baby. Perhaps for the first time, Belinda had valued her parents' unswerving common sense and tough pragmatism. She wondered now whether she might have the opportunity to tell them about her current fears for Izzy. In a way, it seemed unfair to burden them with something they could do nothing about, but it would be a relief to share her worries with them.

They were devoted to Izzy and treated her kindly and firmly. Their lack of mobility and deafness, their slightly disconcerting and eccentric habits, the non sequiturs and rambling, often repeated stories, which Belinda found sad and alarming, Izzy took in her stride. 'You've said that already, Great-Gran,' she would say. 'You've told us that story,' and Belinda's mother would look over her glasses and say, 'Have I? I don't remember a thing these days!' and go blithely on.

A long drive stretched ahead. Belinda planned to stop on the M25 and have something to eat and hoped they would be in Suffolk by seven thirty.

'Do you want a tape, Izzy?' she asked and slotted *The Secret Garden* into the cassette player. With Izzy entertained, she could think about Victor and allow herself to smile and feel a little lift of spirits. The evening had passed so much better than she had expected and she wanted to go through it all in her mind and file it safely away while she had the chance.

The pub had been half full and they had found a corner

table next to the roaring fire. Victor helped her off with her coat and then disappeared to get them both whiskies. He had approved of her choice.

'I thought you'd be a woman who liked a proper drink,' he said with a laugh. Belinda laughed too.

'Is it that obvious?'

He had given her arm a squeeze to show that he was joking. She looked at him standing at the bar and saw how the barmaid seemed to know him and laughed at something he said. He was wearing a dark pair of trousers and a navy sweater over an open-necked checked shirt. He looked like a man who wore clothes that he was comfortable in and wasn't too bothered with his appearance.

'You said you only had time to grab something to eat,' he said, coming back to the table with the drinks. 'Would you like to eat here?'

'Isn't it too late?'

'No. They know me. They'll do us a bar snack, if you'd like one.'

'Actually, I do still feel a bit hungry. What about you?'

Victor passed her a menu and she choose a hot roast beef baguette and Victor said he would have the same with chips.

The food had been a good idea. They ate and talked and laughed and Belinda found out that Victor had been born and bred in Bishops Barton and had a huge family in the area, although his two daughters, one married, the other living with a boyfriend, had moved away.

He had gone to the village primary school and then to the grammar school in Sherborne and straight into his father's little business which had grown into the garage he still ran today.

His wife, whom he had married at nineteen, had died two years ago of cancer after a long and dreadful illness, and now, said Victor, he felt it was time to start living again.

'But you can't be lonely,' said Belinda. 'Not with your enormous family all around you.'

'Ah,' said Victor, looking at her with his very blue eyes. 'There's a different sort of loneliness, isn't there?' and Belinda said she knew what he meant.

They stayed in the pub until closing time when Victor took her arm across the dark car park and opened the passenger door for her, and all the way home Belinda wondered if he would try to kiss her and if she would mind and decided that she would be very disappointed if he didn't.

When they pulled in beside the cottage, it was in darkness although Jess had thought to leave the light on outside the back door, and Belinda turned to Victor to say, 'That was a lovely evening. I really enjoyed it.'

She felt Victor's arm move behind her shoulders and he said, 'Oh, Belinda, come here, woman,' and then he kissed her, gently at first and then hard and hungrily on the mouth. 'I've been longing to do that all evening,' he said when they broke apart. 'I can't pretend I asked you out just because I was lonely. The truth is I fancy you rotten. There, I've told you now.' He looked across at her in the darkness.

'You do?' said Belinda, taken aback. 'Really?'

'Don't sound so surprised. You're a lovely looking woman. I've had my eye on you for some time.'

'Victor!' Belinda was about to start on a self-deprecating

denial and then remembered Dinka. 'Thank you for the compliment,' she said instead. Victor took her hand in his, which felt very large and warm and dry and they sat for a moment in silence. She had forgotten how tender it could be, to hold hands with a man in the dark.

'I'd better go,' she said at last. 'We've both got to work tomorrow.'

'Yes,' he said, and got out to go round the car and open her door. 'Can we do this again?'

'Yes, please. Why not? Here,' she scrabbled in her bag for a pen and a bit of paper. 'This is my email address at work.'

'Email, eh?' He looked at the paper in his hand and then folded it and put it in his pocket.

He hadn't tried to kiss her again but went with her to the back door, behind which Snowy was barking furiously.

'Hush, Snowy! It's me! Shut up, stupid dog. You'll wake everyone up!' and she had turned and kissed him hastily on the cheek.

It was dark long before they arrived at her parents' Suffolk village and turned into the no-through lane to Polders End. Izzy was asleep, the traces of her hamburger smeared round her mouth. Glancing at her in the driver's mirror, Belinda felt guilty that she had fed her another fast food meal, but it couldn't be helped. At the same time a slight feeling of dread started to edge into her heart as she negotiated the speed bumps in the lane. It was how she always felt on coming home, a sense of her independent self diminishing and shrinking away under her parents' level scrutiny. In a moment she would be as uncertain as she had been as a teenager. It was ridiculous in a woman of fifty. Her neck felt stiff from driving and her head swam from the onslaught of car headlights against which she had battled since it got dark.

She mustered a bright voice. 'Wake up, Iz. We've arrived.'

Jess was relieved that Izzy and her mother had gone. She and Snowy stayed with Tom on Friday night and he cooked steaks while she took a long hot bath. When she came down, wearing one of his old flannel shirts and with her hair wet, they ate in front of the fire in amicable silence.

It was a relief to be on their own. The last week or so her mother had been tetchy and difficult and she was glad that she would be out of the way when she went racing tomorrow. It was so wearing having to deal with the constant disapproval, even if it was mostly of the silent and martyred variety.

With the flames lighting the walls of Tom's untidy sitting room, she felt snug and contented curled up on the sofa with Snowy beside her while Tom cleaned first his racing boots and then hers. She watched him bending over under his wild mop of hair, the planes of his angular face lit golden. He had been quieter than usual, she thought, and wondered if there was something worrying him. She caught him looking at her once or twice in a way that slightly unnerved her.

'What's wrong?' she asked.

'Nothing that I know of,' he replied lightly but she nevertheless sensed that something between them was shifting.

'You seem a bit quiet.'

'I'm fine, fine. Just tired. Lambing is always knackering. I keep promising myself I won't do it again next year.'

He finished the boots and sat staring into the fire. Jess watched him for a moment and yawned. He looked across at her.

'Tired?' he asked.

She nodded and stood up slowly. Her tall shadow loomed on the wall behind as she unbuttoned the borrowed shirt and let it fall to the floor. Tom watched as she stroked her hands down the curves of her body, caressing her breasts, sliding down her hips, moving across her smooth flat belly towards the dark mass of hair between her legs. Reaching out, he pulled her towards him and then down to straddle his knees.

'Jess, Jess!' he whispered urgently while Snowy whined disapprovingly from the sofa.

Chapter Eight

Saturday started slowly at Polders End although Belinda's parents woke early. She heard them clattering about, dropping a walking stick, banging a cupboard door, calling the dog. Whatever time was it? She reached for her watch and saw that it was a quarter to six and just starting to get light.

She lay for a while, absorbing the familiar shapes of the spare room. Somehow it combined feeling unused with a sense of being overcrowded. The bed was uncomfortable, with a lumpy mattress, and made up with the old linen sheets her mother had had since she first married. The tall mahogany wardrobe was full of clothes, not worn for years but too good to throw away. The overcoat her father wore to funerals was there and his old bowler hat on the shelf above, and a moth-eaten ginger fur cape that she couldn't remember her mother ever wearing. The drawers of the chest were the same, filled with the flotsam and jetsam of their lives – a silver-backed brush set embellished with her mother's initials, a china pot of hairpins, a flat cardboard box containing white linen handkerchiefs, never used. Postcards, envelopes full of foreign stamps, books of newspaper cuttings, old theatre programmes. So much stuff! How ruthless she would have to be when the time came to clear it out. Her brothers with their busy, efficient wives wouldn't want any of what they would think of as rubbish. Where would it end? Car boot sales, charity shops, blowing about on the council waste site? Two lives, sixty years of marriage, picked over, fragmented and dispersed.

She heard her father go to the bathroom next to her room and then a long splashing stream of urine. It seemed that he no longer bothered to close the door. It was as if the edges of his life were unravelling.

She had noticed the same thing last night. There were stains on the front of her mother's jumper and her skirt hung like an empty sack from her shrunken bottom. The bread that was put on the table for supper had a blue fuzz of mould which she saw her father peer at and then brush off with his hand. As they muddled about putting ham and cheese on the table and refusing all her offers of help, they bickered quite viciously in loud voices.

'I told you we needed more mustard. It was the one thing I told you when you asked.'

'Well, I don't remember. Why didn't you write it down on the list?'

'Because I *told* you. You asked if there was anything and I told you. Does everything have to be done in triplicate?'

'Don't worry about the mustard,' Belinda said. 'We don't want anything to eat anyway because we ate on the way here.' But there was no stopping them.

Her father looked unkempt. His coarse white hair had got out of control and wedges of it sprung from either side of his high, bony forehead like a divided tidal wave. If his face had been jollier he could have been Coco the Clown with a string concealed inside his jacket, a tug on which would shoot his hair suddenly upwards to make the children laugh.

They both had new hearing aids, designed to be discreet and comfortable, but they seemed not to have mastered how to control them without taking the pieces out of their ears and worrying at the tiny devices with stiff fingers.

'Great-Gran, why have you got flowerpots on the floor?' Izzy had asked last night, stepping over one sited in the middle of the sitting room.

'Flowerpots?' asked Belinda's mother, perplexed, staring at the orange plastic pots, placed upside down at random. 'Oh, *those* flowerpots! No, don't touch them!' She knocked one aside with her stick and revealed a small hard dog turd. 'That's your father's idea,' she told Belinda. 'It prevents us treading in them.'

'Mother!' cried Belinda, horrified. 'Whatever is the matter with the dog? Is he incontinent?'

'Oh, no, poor Ernie. It's not his fault. It's only when we drop off and don't let him out at night. Jenny will clear them up when she comes on Tuesday.'

God almighty, thought Belinda. How long will Jenny, the cheerful home help, put up with that?

Later on, as they sat together in the untidy sitting room and her parents dozed through the late news on television, she noticed two bowls of white, sweet-smelling hyacinths on the table. Her father had brought them on from bulbs in his greenhouse, and on the floor beside her mother's chair was a folded newspaper with a completed crossword on the back page. These were acute reminders of the people her parents had once been. The fierce intellect was intact, if a bit askew, but it seemed to Belinda that in old age some personality traits had become defined to the point of eccentricity, while a sense of themselves in relation to others seemed to have diminished. Their lives had narrowed, she thought, and, as with children, small things now featured large because these were what filled their lives and affected them most.

From downstairs came the sound of the radio, turned up very loud and not properly tuned in. Belinda lay for a bit longer with her eyes closed but then gave up and threw a warm shawl over her nightdress and went downstairs to make a cup of tea. She found her mother pottering about in the kitchen in her old quilted dressing gown, putting together some sort of concoction of fat and seeds for the bird table. A pan of grey porridge bubbled slowly on the stove.

'Oh, there you are,' said her mother. 'We didn't wake you up, did we? I am afraid we keep very uncivilised hours these days.'

'Don't worry, Ma. I was awake anyway. It's nice to have the opportunity to talk to you,' said Belinda. She put a tea bag in a mug and put the kettle on to boil. 'How are you both? I mean, really, how are you?'

'We are very well, you can see that,' said Charlotte briskly. 'Well, of course we're ancient and so we have all the usual complaints. Arthritis, and my hip is going again and your father has trouble with his waterworks, and we're both as deaf as posts. What we find hardest is being so useless. I've had to give up all my voluntary work which I miss. I used to feel I was contributing when I helped with lunches at the day centre and Meals on Wheels.'

Belinda nodded. It had been a source of amusement to herself and her brothers that even in her eighties, their mother talked about 'poor old things', some of whom were considerably younger and more robust than she was. Her career of serving the community came to an end when one wet day she tripped over her umbrella and fell through an old person's front door carrying a shepherd's pie and jam roly-poly and broke her hip.

'But can you really cope with everything? I mean, Father isn't much help, is he? There's all the shopping and cooking, and this house to run.'

Charlotte looked at her over her glasses. 'Cope? That's such a silly modern word. We manage. We're all right. Far better off than some. We have friends in the village who keep an eye on us. We've just lived too long, that's all. Past our "use by" date. Anyway, we don't believe in resources being wasted on old people like us.' This was familiar territory and Belinda changed the subject before they got onto biodegradable coffins and composting.

'What are you doing making fat balls at six in the morning?'

'I have to catch the post. They have to have hardened by the time the postman comes at nine. I should really have done it last night.'

'The *postman*?'

'He hangs them up for me. In the tree. I won't let your father on the stepladder since his fall.'

'I see. What an obliging postman.'

'Oh, he is. He takes your father's letters too, when he can't get to the postbox in the winter.'

'What letters?'

'To the Prime Minister, or Prince Charles or our MP. Those sort of letters. I tell him that they don't want to be bothered with the rantings of a foolish old man, but that doesn't stop him.'

'What are they about?' Belinda remembered thinking that the outside world was losing its interest for her parents. How wrong she was.

'Everything. Asylum seekers. He's terribly keen on asylum seekers, but for every one in, he wants to deport one of our undesirables. Disposable nappies are another of his things. I tell him that we shall need them soon but he still wants to get them banned. It's something to do with landfill sites. Traffic through the village, the lack of sports in school, fluoride in tap water, oh, the list goes on and on. There's very little he doesn't feel strongly about. Listen. He's at it now.' She paused and held up a hand and Belinda heard the slow and irregular *tap-tap* of a typewriter coming from the sitting room.

'Goodness,' she said. 'At this hour?'

'It's because of all the news he listens to,' explained her mother. 'He has it on all day on the radio and it gets him worked up. And *Thought for the Day*. That particularly aggravates him. He's always writing to *Thought for the Day*.'

'I suppose it keeps his brain alert,' said Belinda.

'Don't be patronising!' said Charlotte. 'His brain is still fine. It's his judgement that's gone. He still feels he can make a difference.'

'It was you who said he was an old fool,' reminded Belinda. There was an acrid smell of burning and she turned to whip the porridge saucepan off the heat.

Her mother looked at it. 'Did I put that on?' she asked.

'I suppose so. I certainly didn't.'

'That's the trouble. I can remember exactly what happened in nineteen sixty-three, for instance. I could give you the names of every child in the school, but what I did ten minutes ago is instantly forgotten. Gone without trace.'

'Everyone says that. About growing old. It happens to me, too. I find myself standing on the landing wondering what on earth I've gone upstairs for. You're not going to eat this now, are you? Burnt porridge is truly disgusting.'

'We can't waste it.'

'Do you want a cup of tea? Look, come and sit down with me for a moment. I want to talk to you before Izzy wakes up.'

Together they sat at the kitchen table. Belinda remembered the cloth from when she had been a child. It was East European, made of thick uneven threads in woven blue and yellow squares. It had probably been brought back from one of their family camper van trips to Poland or Yugoslavia, in the days when no one else she knew went to communist countries but spent their holidays in sensible resorts in Italy or Switzerland. She had so wished to be normal in those days that the van was agony to her. She had longed for an ordinary family saloon, like a Rover or a Riley, and holidays in hotels.

Her mother sat opposite her, her thin, white hair secured to the side with a childish clip, her old, papery skin still pink and healthy looking, her eyes bright behind her spectacles.

'It's about Jess and Izzy,' Belinda said, looking at her mother's hands. They were so familiar but, if asked, she could not have described them. The fingers were crooked with arthritis, the nails clipped short, the backs freckled with age and threaded with twisting veins like thick blue worms. Her mother wore only a wedding ring, a plain gold band, thin with age. Both hands rested on the tablecloth and with a shock Belinda realised that they were the master copies of her own, distorted by age but the same broad palms and short, inelegant fingers. Capable, strong, working hands. As she looked at them, the thought came into her head that they would, before too long, be folded over her mother's lifeless chest, that after a lifetime of busyness and gainful occupation, that would be their final position and she was horribly struck with sadness. I must tell her that I love her, she thought. I never have, not properly, and she reached out and took one of the hands in her own. Her mother looked surprised but did not try to withdraw it.

'So what's this about Jess and Izzy?' she asked.

'I'm so worried about them.'

'What now? I thought last night that Izzy was well. She's grown and seems happy at school.'

'It's nothing like that.'

'What then?'

'The man I'm pretty sure is her father is back on the scene. Jess, as you know, won't talk about it, but everyone else will, and I'm distraught about the effect it will have on Izzy.'

'But we don't know, do we, who her father is?'

'No, not for certain, but Johnnie Bearsden has always been the likely candidate and he's moving in about five miles away from us. He's married with a family, I don't know how many children, and an American wife. It's an impossible situation because Jess won't have it even mentioned, she still denies it flatly, and yet I know his coming back will revive all the speculation there was when she was first pregnant.'

'Why don't you believe her?' asked her mother calmly.

Belinda considered. 'Because she's obviously covering up. I don't even know if Johnnie's aware of Izzy's existence. He'd left the Army and moved to America – his wife is American – by the time Jess told us she was pregnant and this is the first time he's reappeared.'

'I think you should accept her word.'

'But what about Izzy? She's already being called names at school, and I can't bear it for her. More than anything else I want to protect her from being hurt and confused, and maybe from feeling that she was a mistake and that she wasn't wanted.'

'I understand that, but I don't think it's your business, Belinda. It's a matter between Jess and Izzy and nobody else, apart from the father, of course. Jess will be obliged to tell Izzy the truth eventually but when is a matter for them only. It really isn't your business.'

'You make it sound as if I'm meddling,' cried Belinda, 'when all I want to do is protect Izzy.'

'I don't think you can do that,' said her mother. 'Children can't be protected like that. I know from experience how cruel they can be to one another. Fat children get bullied, so do ugly or stupid or slow children, children with red hair, children with eczema, children with birthmarks. Their protection has to come from within, from the confidence they have been given by those who love them. That's our job in all of this. To make Izzy feel that it is fine to be exactly who she is, not to raise all these questions about who she might be.'

'She was called a bastard at school last week.'

'Well, is that all? Really, Belinda. How old-fashioned you are. These days the child from a normal, conventional family with both a father and a mother living under the same roof is an exception. It's lamentable but true. Izzy's unconventional parentage won't raise an eyebrow at school and I'm sure the word wasn't used with any awareness of its true meaning.'

'Do you really think that?'

'I do.'

Belinda paused and then changed tack. 'But why should Johnnie Bearsden get away scot-free? Ruining Jess's life, wrecking her chances to do anything, and not contributing a penny to Izzy's upkeep and then moving back into the neighbourhood to upset everything.'

'But Jess says he's not the father. How can you give him that responsibility if she doesn't?'

'Well, I can't, I realise that. That's why it is so impossible – so impossible to help.'

'Belinda, dear.' Her mother laid her other hand on top of Belinda's. 'You know what I really think? I think that you should cultivate a little distance from all of this. After David's death you had to be everything to the children, and you made a splendid job of it.' She paused and Belinda looked at her, surprised. She couldn't remember when her mother had ever told her this before. Jo and Charlie, maybe, were made a splendid job of, but then Charlie had been a sunny, easy boy and Jo was born practically middle-aged and sensible. Jess had been a disaster.

'I mean it. Dad and I were terribly aware of what a burden it was on you, and if anyone has sacrificed their life, it's you.'

'Me? They *were* my life! I didn't have anything else to sacrifice, Mum. I didn't have a job. The children were my life. The children and David.'

'Exactly. That's what I mean. Now you're continuing this level of involvement with Izzy. I don't think you should. Jess is a perfectly adequate mother and as far as one can tell, Izzy hasn't suffered.'

'But she's missed so much. She hasn't had a normal upbringing. Any stability she has is because I've provided a home for her. Jess was so young and, frankly, hopeless, completely irresponsible . . .' Belinda was aware of a note of self-pity creeping into her voice and she fought down tears which were gathering behind her eyes. Suddenly she felt angry. Angry with David for dying and leaving her, angry with Jess, angry with her mother for giving her the wrong sort of sympathy, angry with her father for tap-tapping his stupid old man's ravings next door in the sitting room surrounded by the flowerpots hiding dog turds. The only person she did not feel angry with was Izzy.

Her mother went on, 'Jess is her mother and Izzy adores her, quite uncritically, as children do. I think you should encourage that, and go on being loving and supportive, but perhaps take a little less on yourself. If you withdraw a bit, I think you would find that Jess would take more responsibility.'

Belinda removed her hand from under her mother's. 'I don't think you understand,' she said. 'It's me that keeps the whole house of cards standing. If I withdraw, as you call it, the whole lot comes down, and the one who will suffer is Izzy.' You wouldn't understand, she thought angrily, because you were selfish as a mother. You were so engrossed in your bloody school that your own children were pushed to the side. We didn't feel important to you. Even as she thought this, Belinda knew it wasn't true. She and her brothers had always been central in both their parents' busy lives but from a very early age they had been encouraged to be independent. They were never fussed over. That was it, and she supposed she was, by nature, a fusser. For her it was an inevitable accompaniment to loving and caring for someone, and yet both her mother and Dinka had suggested that she was at fault.

She got up, feeling hurt and defensive. Seizing the porridge saucepan, she scraped the contents into the bin.

'You're not eating that,' she said irritably. 'I'll make you some more.'

Her mother sat on at the table, saying nothing, and as Belinda put the pan to soak and looked for the oats, she was suddenly aware of the stillness and vulnerability of the frail figure, the shoulders rounded with age, the back of the head revealing the pink of the scalp where her hair had thinned.

We just make what we can of things, she thought. All of us. Bound together like links in a chain. Upstairs, Izzy was still innocently asleep, Jess was already at work with a day's racing in front of her, driven by God knew what, she herself muddled along in the middle, burdened by love, trying to make sense of it, trying to do her best, while her mother drew inexorably towards the end of her life. Belinda put down the packet of oats and went back to the table. She laid a hand on her mother's shoulder.

'Thank you,' she said gently. 'Thank you.'

Her mother started, drawn back from wherever her mind had slipped to.

'Whatever for?' she asked.

'Oh, you know,' said Belinda lightly. How inadequate I am, she thought, at expressing what I would like to say. All the years of restraint and reserve render me inarticulate.

She was glad that at that moment the door opened and Izzy appeared in her pyjamas, carrying her book.

'Hello, darling,' Belinda said. 'You're up early. Did you sleep well?'

'I slept like a dead pig,' said Izzy.

'Like what?' Belinda laughed.

'Like a dead pig. That's how Tom slept when he was a little chimney sweep. Have you seen my book, Great-Granny?' She put it on the table and opened the pages, to show off the colour plates.

'Goodness,' said Charlotte, adjusting her glasses. 'How well I remember *The Water Babies*.'

'Have you got a red petticoat and a dimity bedgown?' asked Izzy, looking up at her hopefully. 'Only that's what the very old lady wears – look, the nicest old woman Tom had ever seen.'

'Slightly before my time, Isobel. There weren't child chimney sweeps even when I was your age.'

'Not in the olden days?'

'Izzy, do you want porridge?'

'Yes, please, Granny,' said Izzy, still hanging over her book. 'I'm almost clemmed with hunger and drought.'

'It doesn't look a very promising sort of day,' said Belinda, looking out of the kitchen window at the garden. It had the untidy, wrecked look of February. The grass of the lawn was grey and trampled after the winter and the only colour came from the crocuses under the trees. They were Belinda's least favourite spring flowers, poking out so close to the brown earth, their yellows, purples and whites reminding her of discarded crisp or cigarette packets.

The hedge between Polders End and the cottage next door had grown tall and bushy, blocking out the light, and the whole garden had an air of increased seclusion and neglect as if it had slipped out of control and was developing wayward ideas of its own. A little flattened path was worn across the grass to the bird table where a gang of starlings were quarrelling raucously.

It's all coming to an end, she thought sadly, and then round the corner of the house trotted Ernie with a yellow ball in his mouth. He caught sight of her through the kitchen window and, fixing her with a look full of intent, dropped the ball in a meaningful way. He looked from his ball to her. Come on, he seemed to say. Do something useful for once.

*

The same grey weather hung over the Devon hills beyond Exeter. Standing on a rise of ground near the start of the point-to-point course, Tom couldn't see to the far side where the land fell away, and the low cloud pressed down, obscuring the track, which emerged again in the distance as a thread of white rails after the bend.

It had been a good day so far. Jess, on Another Rose, had been third in the restricted, a race for horses that had never won anything other than a maiden or a hunt race, and Tom had won a hotly contested men's open on Captain Jack. Dolly had run a textbook race in the ladies and had come in an easy second. For once, Ken showed his delight. 'She wouldn't have blown out a candle afterwards,' he said. 'She'll win next time out,' and her owner, a great, burly man, had cried and kissed Jess so effusively that she blushed.

Jess also rode in the intermediate, for horses who had never won an open race, and in which winners of hunt, maiden or restricted races carried a weight penalty. Jess had hoped to win on Glennie but she was passed at the last by Tom riding a top point-to-pointer for a local Devon farmer. In this, its first season, the horse had already won his novice and confined races under another leading jockey, Tim Barnes, who had had a fall and broken his shoulder in an earlier race, and Tom had been asked to pick up the ride. If the horse continued winning, he was a potential Cheltenham entry, bound for the foxhunter chase at the famous March meeting. Glennie was simply outclassed.

Now, in the second division of the maiden race, the last race of the day, Jess went down to the start early on Fancy, the Dawlishes' little chestnut mare. Tom stayed with her in the paddock, adjusting the new rubber noseband which held her mouth shut, helping the Dawlish men saddle up, trying to keep the sweating mare steady as she spun in circles and foamed at the mouth. He gave Jess a leg up and before she had time to settle her toes in the irons, the mare was leaping to the side.

'Don't do that!' Jess cried to Pete, who was jabbing at her mouth. 'Let her have her head!'

Tom jammed Jess's offside toe into the stirrup and managed to check the girth before Fancy danced sideways out of the paddock, her tail lifted like a plume, her head thrown up and her eyes wild. With her mouth held closed by the noseband she had less opportunity to evade the bit and Jess managed to set off in a slow canter down the course towards the start.

'Jess!' Tom shouted after her, ducking under the rails and running out onto the track. 'Jess! Good luck!' but she didn't hear him. The wind was in her ears and all she was aware of was the thud of the oiled hooves on the soft turf and the rhythmic snorting breath of the mare. The noseband was bothering her, holding her back, stopping the flight that she wanted to take, and she shook her head from side to side. Gobbets of foam flew from her mouth and all the time Jess stroked her neck and talked to her softly. Eventually, she slowed her into a trot and Fancy floated along, her neck flexed, her ears flicking back and forth to the sound of Jess's voice.

Out across the course where it was quiet and away from the crowds, Jess took her up to look at the first fence. The ground in front had been cut up deep by the preceding races and Jess decided that she would get onto the inside rail and stay there, avoiding the worst of the going towards the middle of the fence. She let Fancy take in the unfamiliar white plastic wings and the orange ground rail. The tight-packed black brush twigs that made up the jump were the same as those she schooled over at home.

'Look,' Jess told her. 'This is what we are going to be jumping in a minute.'

Across the course she could hear the drifting sound of the horn and the mare began to tremble. Fancy would remember that sound from the misty mornings of the previous autumn when she had behaved so badly out qualifying with the South Dorset hounds. The tips of her little ears nearly met as she stood rooted to the spot watching the sixteen other runners make their way up the track behind the scarlet splash of the huntsman's coat. Jess sat still, letting her look, talking quietly to try and keep her calm, but it was no use. As the first of the runners arrived at the start it seemed as if a coiled spring had been released and Fancy shot up in the air and pawed out with her front feet, snaking her neck, and Jess was nearly unseated.

'Bloody hell, Jess! What's that you're on?' asked one of the other jockeys, keeping out of her way as the mare struck out with a hind leg. 'That needs putting in a tin, that does. It's a bloody maniac!'

Jess did not answer. She had to concentrate on what she was doing, and try to sit still. Tom had told her that the more she tried to fight Fancy, the worse she would be. 'Let her have her head. Keep her at the back, out of the way of the others but let her behave as badly as she wants for a minute or two. I think she'll work through it. It won't last long and then you can ask her to listen to you.'

It was scary, though, perched on top of that volcano of unpredictable muscle and bone, knowing that you had little control and that there was not much common sense or self-preserving instinct to save you. The natural reaction was to try and temper the lunacy, as she had done the first time she had ridden her, but Tom was right, she must sit tight, give Fancy a long rein, let her burn herself out.

The other riders had problems of their own. This was the worst moment, milling about near the starter, trying to concentrate their young horses on what they were doing, all the while sick with awareness of the dangers of the race ahead.

Jess kept well away from the starting line and after a minute or two Fancy stopped leaping and lunging and agreed to walk in a circle, still trembling, but more controllable. Jess was able to take up a bit more rein and push her a little so that she lowered her head onto the bit. This was better than last time, much better, but when the starter dropped his flag and they were off, she was right at the back and made a slow start, trailing off behind the others.

'What sort of bloody start was that?' growled Pete Dawlish, looking through binoculars from the rails by the first fence. 'She's got left right behind. That's no bloody use!'

'It doesn't matter,' said his father. 'She'll make it up. It's keeping the mare upright that counts.' He narrowed his eyes, watching the horses coming towards them, the leaders in a close bunch in front, going much too fast. As they got closer they could hear the jockeys swearing at each other, trying to keep their horses straight at the fence, trying to take each other's ground. They flashed over and were gone and then came the line of stragglers, with Jess and Fancy bringing up the rear. The noseband's helping a bit, thought Tom, she's not getting run away with this time, but as they approached he could see that she was still going too fast. She practically hurdled the fence, frantic to catch up the other horses and jumping dangerously low, sending chunks of twigs into the air as she ploughed through the top foot of the stiff brush. Tom caught a glimpse of Jess's face, tense and pale behind her goggles. She's not enjoying it, he thought. She's got no confidence, not when she jumps like that. Unless she can get her to pick up, she knows they'll crash sooner or later.

Fancy ran on, still too fast, and had overtaken the back runners by the time she reached the second fence. She made a terrible mess of that as well, jumping low and right-handed, only just saving herself from coming right down by scrabbling along the ground on landing. Jess was lucky to stay on board.

'Jesus!' said Tom. It was agonising to watch and the three men stood in silence, the Dawlishes with their binoculars trained on the mare and Tom squinting into the distance.

The third fence was on the bend before a long pull uphill to the fourth and then the runners were in open country and out of sight until the track curved back round at the top end of the course.

The space between the second and third jumps seemed to give Jess the opportunity to gain a bit of control and

Fancy met the third in the middle of the back group of horses and, for the first time, jumped beautifully, and ran on, working her way up through the pack on the inside rail. She jumped the fourth, the open ditch, brilliantly, standing right off and bringing herself alongside the leader of the back runners. 'That's more like it!' said Mr Dawlish. 'She's settled now.'

She was gone then, swallowed up by the cloud and the curve of the land. By the time she reappeared, she was well in front of the last group of horses, the blue of the Dawlish colours like a blob of bright paint against the backdrop of grey fields and paler grey sky. They watched her jump the second open ditch out on her own and then steadily close the gap on the leading horses who were going much more slowly now. The early burst of speed had taken it out of them and Tom watched as the bright chestnut mare came racing down the hill behind them, eating up the distance, Jess crouched over her shoulder, still and balanced, not interfering. At the next fence she caught the last of them and started to move up on the inside rail.

Tom watched her meet each dark line of fence and flow over and he began to relax. She's found her stride, he thought. She's not hurrying, just hunting round. He could tell that Jess and the mare had started to enjoy themselves. They were coming back past the start now, for a second time, and Jess seemed to be putting on the pressure and Fancy was carving through the other horses. She was lying fifth and contesting for fourth place as she met the third last fence, the fence at which he and the Dawlish men were standing.

Tom could hardly bear to watch. How would the mare react when she was pushed? There was a chance she would get a place, even win, if she carried on as well as she was going now. What happened next, he couldn't be sure, but something went horribly wrong. The horse nearest them took off too close, got right under the fence, couldn't make it and came crashing to the ground, landing on its side with its legs straight out. Fancy skewed in mid-air to avoid a collision, pecked on landing, skidded along the ground on her knees while Jess shot out over her neck. For a moment Tom couldn't see what had happened to her as other horses flashed past.

'Oh, Jesus!' he said, ducking under the rails.

'Fucking hell!' said Pete, watching the mare, who got up, shaking her sides, her reins dangling over her head. Then Tom saw Jess was back on her feet, the seat of her breeches stained grass green and that she had caught the mare's rein and was shouting something. The jump steward, looking nervously over his shoulder, hurried towards her and then gave her a hasty leg up. For a moment she was slung over the saddle like a sack as Fancy started away, but she kicked her leg over and, without finding the stirrup irons, set off at a gallop after the other horses.

Tom and the Dawlish men dropped back and watched her go. At least she's all right, thought Tom, his heart racing. When she reached the second last fence she was still without her stirrups and Tom held his breath, but she jumped it neatly and set off for the last, well behind the front five horses who had already cantered past the post, but still in sixth place.

209

The crowd, who had been told over the loudspeaker that she had fallen and remounted, gave her a ragged cheer as she cantered over the finishing line and old Mr Dawlish set off to lead her in.

Tom blew out through his mouth. 'Phew! That was bad luck. They were going so well.'

Pete Dawlish stopped to light a cigarette. 'Aye,' he said drily. Tom could tell he was not satisfied.

'There was nothing she could have done. She was brought down. You saw!' he persisted.

'She could have kept out of trouble, couldn't she?' said Pete.

'Of course she couldn't. Not then, anyway.'

'She'd got plenty of room. There was no need to jump so close.'

'Oh bollocks!' retorted Tom. 'That other horse went across her!' He shut up then. There was no point in arguing. They would never agree.

When he caught up with Jess, coming out of the weighing room carrying her saddle, he wondered what mood she would be in, but she turned to him and he saw that despite a swelling black eye, she looked happy.

'Wasn't that bloody marvellous?' she said, her face still hot and red and splattered with mud. 'Bloody, fucking marvellous! After those first two fences, she jumped like a stag. She was a dream, Tom. She went like a dream!'

Back in the lorry park, Rhona squatted on the grass beside Fenny Princess, whom Carl had ridden in the first division of the maiden race. In the end, Dawn Call had been withdrawn because Ken hadn't been entirely happy with a very slight puffiness Rhona had noticed down the tendon of her near foreleg after her Thursday workout. She was completely sound but he thought the ground was a touch hard and he didn't want to risk a promising young horse, especially before her bones were set and strong.

Rhona worked fast, smearing the lower part of Princess's legs with a thick white cooling paste and then wrapping them in brown paper before Moira, who was at the mare's head, handed her the thick, rolled bandages to go on top. The big brown mare had been sponged down and her coat was shining and seal-like, still steaming from exertion and excitement. Carl had done as he was told and pulled her up when he felt she had done enough, and Ken was happy with the way she had jumped the first eight fences and how she had settled in company on this her second outing.

But she was fired up now and wheeled about and cow-kicked with alternate hind legs as Rhona worked and she had to move fast, crab-like, still squatting, to keep out of the way of the flying hooves. All the time she talked to the horse in a low, soothing voice, calling her a good girl, a clever girl, but the mare was wild from the excitement of the race and would not settle. Her nostrils were flared open and pulsing, lined with red, and her eyes ringed with white. The fine and beautiful head with the white star on the forehead was lifted, straining to hear the sounds of the race now in progress.

She spun round again and knocked over the plastic bucket and sponge that Rhona had been using, and Moira jumped out of the way and cursed and smacked her neck and called her a stupid cow.

'Don't do that!' snapped Rhona. 'Don't hit her! Get those plaits undone!'

Moira pulled a face and began picking at the rubber bands which held the mare's mane in tight little knots down her neck. She resented being told off and had already made remarks about Jess getting out of the work because she was riding. Rhona knew she was sour because Jess had won the prize for the best turned-out horse with Glennie. There was always a bit of competition amongst the yard girls to catch the eye of the judge in the paddock and Glennie had looked wonderful, his black coat gleaming, diamonds brushed on his quarters and his mane and tail beautifully plaited. Rhona was glad for Jess. She deserved it. She took no end of trouble with the horses that she was responsible for, while Moira was slapdash and careless and never bothered to plait a tail or make quarter marks.

Rhona would have liked to have watched the last race and tried to hear the commentary, but from the lorry park the voice over the loudspeaker was jumbled and indistinct and she could not catch the names of the runners, let alone how they were doing. Straightening up from the bandaging, she cast an eye over Princess as Moira worked away at her mane, concentrating on each tight knot.

It was at that moment, across the mare's back, that Rhona saw them, an awkward sandy-haired boy at that gawky age between being a child and a teenager, sauntering along behind a tall, good-looking couple who she presumed were his parents. She could see that they were threading their way between the horseboxes and coming to the lorry to talk to Ken who was sitting on a folding chair by the cab, eating a ham roll. One look was enough, and she didn't want Moira poking her nose in and winding up Jess about Johnnie Bearsden.

'OK, Moira,' she said briskly. 'Leave those plaits and start walking Princess round. Take her well up the far end away from the other horses. That'll help calm her down.'

Reluctantly, Moira yanked on the head collar rope and took Princess off in the opposite direction.

Mikey Bearsden was bored by the races. If his father had had a horse running, that would have been different. He would have liked to stand in the middle of the paddock with the other owners and everyone in the crowd watching. He was wearing the tweed jacket and flat cap his mother had bought him in London and because these were the sort of clothes his father wore, he felt properly grown-up.

It was boring, though, with his parents stopping every few minutes to talk to people; the same old thing, blah, blah, blah, with his dad telling everyone how nice it was to be back and that no, the pointer he had bought in Ireland had got a leg and wouldn't be coming over this season. Got a leg! It was such a silly thing to say. It wouldn't be any use without one, would it?

He had had two hot dogs and bought some toffee from a sweet stall and now he was feeling a bit sick as well as bored. He almost wished he had stayed at home with the twins but there was nothing to do there either.

The only good thing was having a bet. He had won two

pounds over the afternoon and when it was the last race but one, he put all his money on a big black horse called Bobsmyuncle. Greys or blacks were his preferred colours and he never backed a horse ridden by a girl, because in his view girls weren't as good at riding as men.

Anyway, he put his money on the horse and it was hopeless. It came in nearly last and so he was feeling fed up with that and then his parents wanted to go and look for someone his dad knew, who was going to train his horses. They trailed about in the lorry park until they found the horsebox and then there was more talking and he got bored and said he wanted a slash, as the boys at school called it, and he wandered off.

He was waiting outside the line of gents' Portaloos for one to become vacant when the door nearest him opened and out came a man he recognised. It was the man who had been round at the house with the letter about the sheep, which had annoyed his mother. They were face to face and Mikey knew that he recognised him because he gave him such a funny look and mumbled something. It wasn't hello or anything friendly like that, and the man's face had looked startled. As Mikey turned to close the door of the cabin, he saw him walk over to where a woman was waiting, a woman jockey wearing white breeches under her fleece jacket, and sort of hurry her away, but not before Mikey had time to recognise her as well. It was the woman who had been with the brat on the pony, the day he had been out riding. She had been unfriendly as well. What's their problem? he thought resentfully as he held his nose and peed into the smelly void. His mom was right. English people could be a pain in the ass.

Chapter Nine

The message Tom found on his answer machine when he got home on Saturday evening took him by surprise. He thought he was done with the matter of his sheep and the Bearsden dogs. He had imagined that he would get a cheque through the post and that would be that. He hadn't expected to hear the attractive female American voice saying, 'Hi. This is Karen Bearsden. Thank you for your note. Would you mind calling me back?'

It was tricky because he had Jess with him. He had come home on his own from the races to do the rounds of his stock and feed the horses in the yard behind the farmhouse and Jess had gone back in the lorry to finish off the day's work at Ken's. Now she was lying on the floor in front of his television set trying to get the video to work so that they could watch a recording of Fancy's race which she had bought on the course.

He listened to the message twice. It had been left half an hour earlier and he decided that Mrs Bearsden was going to have to wait for him to call her back. It wouldn't be particularly tactful to do it in front of Jess. He wanted to keep as wide a distance as possible between Jess and the Bearsdens. Seeing that boy again at the races had taken him aback; at least he had managed to steer Jess away so that a face to face encounter was avoided. Perhaps it showed a lack of courage on his part; maybe he should tell Jess about him and force the situation into the open. After all, the boy's resemblance to Izzy said clearer than words who her father was, and sooner or later Jess was going to have to face up to the fact that her 'secret' was public knowledge. But he shrank from the confrontation he knew this would provoke. Last night had been so wonderful. After a night like that he would do almost anything to keep things just as they were. But now bloody Johnnie Bearsden was back and that identikit child was popping up everywhere and he felt as if his relationship with Jess was on borrowed time.

He had never had any problem with Izzy's existence. In fact, he loved her. She was a smashing little girl. But the child he knew and loved was the fatherless Izzy. Izzy with a paid-up and local father was rather different. Bugger it, he thought gloomily. This afternoon he had been relieved to hear that Johnnie Bearsden's horse was out for the season because of an injury and was not going to appear on Ken's yard after all. He felt that at least this was one complication removed from their lives, for the moment anyway, but now Karen Bearsden was pestering him. Why couldn't she just pay up for his sheep and leave it be?

He saved the message and put down the receiver. Jess had managed to sort out her tape and now a group of racehorses whizzed backwards on the screen towards the start. 'Come on, Tom,' she said over her shoulder. 'Come and watch with me. God, we were lucky to get over the first fence. She hardly took off.' Obediently, Tom went to sit on the armchair behind her and she leaned her elbow on his knee and he coiled a hank of her thick brown hair round a finger. He could see the side of her face; her eye was now closed completely and a puffy blackberry stain was spreading across her cheekbone.

Why did everything have to be so complicated? he thought. He loved Jess and wanted to do everything he could for her and Izzy, but it wasn't enough. The life that they had carved out for themselves felt threatened by a huge disrupting force and people like the Bearsdens, with their money and power, would always come out on top. If decisions about Izzy ended up in court, they would win and get their way, whatever that might be.

Tom's spirits took such a dive as he sat there that he could not concentrate on the video of the race that Jess was so absorbed in. At the back of his mind, he realised he had nursed a hope that one day he would adopt Izzy and that the three of them would be a proper family. That hope felt completely crushed. He had a sudden vision of Izzy with a suitcase being shuttled between Rosebay Cottage and Quatt Lodge, from the cosiness of life with Jess and Belinda to the chilly gloom of the big house and the offhand care of a disenchanted au pair and a stepmother. This idea had such a melodramatic Victorian quality that he imagined Izzy in an oval sepia photograph wearing a pair of buttoned boots and a pinafore, clutching her copy of *The Water Babies*. Poor little Iz.

'Watch this,' said Jess, turning to look up at him with her one good eye. 'See how she moves up through the pack. I was thinking that since I'd got her this far and she was still upright and had settled a bit, I might just ask her for a bit more, and I did. Look here,' she pointed to the screen, 'and see, she listened, and watch how she responds! Now! See how deep she digs!'

For the first time ever, Tom felt impatient and at odds with Jess's enthusiasm. Why doesn't she realise that there are more important things going on here? he thought. He got up and watched the rest of the race standing, distancing himself from Jess's absorption in the tape. He saw the little mare corkscrew in mid-air and pitch onto her knees and Jess somersaulting over her neck. Maybe Jo is right, he thought. Maybe Jess is selfish.

In the kitchen he stoked up the Aga and put a pan of water on to boil. He would make them some pasta for supper. It was important to eat when they were both racing again tomorrow, even though he could not afford to satisfy his perpetual, gnawing hunger. He wouldn't do it again. Not another year of starvation to make the weight. He had had enough. In the corner the old washing machine churned away, milky coloured suds lapping against the porthole, filled with their muddy stocks and racing breeches which would have to dry overnight in front of the stove. The kitchen still smelled richly of the orphan lamb, which after a day on the bottle had been successfully adopted by a ewe who had lost one of her twins. Tom had skinned the dead baby and fastened its little fleece around his orphan and after sniffing it suspiciously, the ewe had allowed it to suckle. He wondered whether he could justify charging the Bearsdens for the dead twin. He had found it in the field the morning after the dogs had been worrying the sheep. It was hard to tell what it had died of but the chances were that it had been trampled or separated from its mother. He would tell the Bearsden woman when he telephoned her that there had been another casualty. After all, people like them could afford it.

The water came to the boil and he dumped in the pasta. He put some tomatoes and garlic to simmer in another pan and somewhere in the fridge there was a lump of cheese he could grate on top. Jess did not care what she ate. She'd had chips from a van at the racecourse and a bowl of soup in Ken's kitchen, but she would still be ravenous.

He stirred the pan, standing in his socked feet in Meg's round, furry dog bed, which was pushed up against the warm side of the Aga. He felt so hungry that his guts seemed twisted inside out and his head ached. You really had to want to race above everything else to put up with the pain, and he recognised that he had lost the edge. It had been a good day with a nice win and a couple of places but he did not care enough any more. The whole of this year he had found that he was happiest working on his young horses or out farming, looking after his stock. Before, when these had just been activities to support his racing career, it had been the other way around.

It happened to most race jockeys, this cooling off as the years went by. Falls, injuries, broken bones all took their toll as well as the relentless discipline of keeping fit and all the hours spent riding out and schooling. The weekends throughout the season were given over to hours of travelling to far-off point-to-points and although he loved the atmosphere and the beauty of the settings and the country crowd and the camaraderie of the sport, there came a time when the option of not going, of staying at home on a lovely spring Saturday, seemed infinitely appealing.

The passion has gone out of it for me, he thought, and then wondered if this was a temporary development because he was fed up and hungry and was reacting in a perverse way to Jess's enthusiasm. I don't know, he thought. I just don't know. I'll go on supporting Jess. Of course I will. It's where I stand in all of this that I'm not sure of. Although the sandy-haired boy had nothing to do with his feelings about racing, seeing him that afternoon had sent a tremor through the ground Tom stood on, and had shaken things enough to dislodge old certainties.

'Hey, Tom,' said Jess, coming into the kitchen and putting her arms round him. 'What's wrong?'

'Nothing. Why do you keep asking that?' he said with a suggestion of defensiveness in his voice.

She shrugged. 'I don't know. You just seem a bit odd. Subdued or something. You bloody shouldn't be. Not beating me and Glennie like that. You had the best ride of the day, you lucky sod.'

Tom managed a wan smile. 'Yeah. That was one hell of a horse. He'll go to Cheltenham all right.'

'You'll get the ride again, too, if Tim Barnes is stood down for a bit.'

'Maybe.' Tom turned away to stir the sauce. He was aware of Jess still standing there. It felt as if one side of his body was prickling with the sensation of her closeness.

'Tom, what is it?'

Deliberately Tom watched large red bubbles form on the surface of the sauce and then burst with a soft plop. He spoke without turning, his voice weighty with patience. 'Nothing. OK? I've got a bit of a headache, that's all, and I'm so bloody hungry I could eat this wooden spoon.' To change the subject, he slipped a question into the moment of silence which followed. 'Have you rung your mother? She'll want to know that you're not being laid out, won't she? Use my telephone if you want. Supper will be ready in a minute.'

'Yeah, OK.'

Jess knew there was something Tom wasn't telling her but she couldn't go on asking if he didn't want to talk about it. She knew what it felt like to be badgered. But to be kept at a distance by Tom was a new experience for her and it made her feel excluded. If there was something bothering Tom she wanted to know and it seemed to her that their closeness as friends and lovers gave her the right to expect the truth from him. His evasiveness made her feel suddenly deflated and rather hurt. Tom was supposed to be the steadfast one. She had grown to depend upon it.

As she lifted the telephone receiver she realised that she did not have her grandparents' telephone number with her. She paused for a moment, wondering what to do, and then noticed that there was a message for Tom.

'Tom,' she called through to the kitchen. 'You've got a message. Do you want me to listen?' but he was clattering about, draining the pasta. Jess pressed the playback button and Karen Bearsden's voice came down the line, sing-song and drawling. 'Hi. This is Karen Bearsden. Thank you for your note. Would you mind calling me back?' Jess put down the telephone. Was that what Tom was keeping from her?

Some sort of plot with the Bearsdens? If it was, he was quite right. She didn't want to know.

Tom appeared at the door with two plates, followed by Snowy and Meg, both sniffing the air hopefully.

'Here,' he said, passing one over. 'Did you get your mother?'

'No,' said Jess slowly, watching him. 'I don't have my grandparents' number. I'd forgotten that. I'll have to wait for her to ring me.'

On his way to sit down, Tom turned on the television and they ate their supper to the accompaniment of various fatuous game shows.

'It's always crap television on Saturday nights,' said Tom, but they were both glad that it gave them an excuse not to talk.

'She must be all right or we would have heard,' said Belinda to Jo on the telephone on Sunday morning. 'I've left a message on her mobile but she hasn't rung back. I can't remember where they are racing today. Somewhere more local, I think, like Larkhill or Badbury Rings. She was down in Devon yesterday at that Black Forest place.'

'It's typical that she can't be bothered to telephone,' said Jo. 'It's so thoughtless of her when she knows how you worry.'

'We've always had an understanding that no news is good news,' said Belinda. 'Which is fair enough, really.'

'Hmm,' said Jo. 'It suits *her*, I can see that. Less effort all round. Anyway, how are Gran and Grandpa? Give them my love.'

'They're all right, I suppose,' said Belinda. 'Just terribly old and frail, but there is still an indomitable will in evidence. There's no question of me being given a chance to alter their lives in any way. I'd like to try to get them more home help, for instance, or arrange to have some simple aids fitted, like rails for getting in and out of the bath, but they won't hear of it.'

'I'm sure there must be local authority agencies available to them. Don't they realise they have some rights in their old age? After all, they've both paid taxes all their lives.'

'They don't see it like that. They don't want to be a drain on resources, they say. It's madness, really, because if one of them slipped and had a fall, they'd be far more trouble to everyone.'

'Poor Mum. Everyone you have to deal with seems to be bloody-minded and obstinate. Is it just our family, or what?'

'We're probably no worse than most. At least it seems to have skipped a generation and gone straight from my parents to Jess!'

'It will be crisis management soon though, won't it? I mean, things aren't going to improve down there, are they?'

'No. They know that, in their hearts. But they're a battling generation. They went through the war, remember. They don't surrender!'

'What do they do all day? Time must seem to drag when they can't really get about any more.'

'Actually it doesn't. They're up at dawn but everything takes them so much longer and there are various points in the day when they have a snooze. Father writes letters most of the morning, takes the dog out, goes to the shop. Thank goodness there's still one in the village. Mother reads the newspaper from cover to cover, does the cooking, potters about a bit in the garden.'

'What sort of letters? Who can he have to write to? Most of his friends have kicked the bucket, haven't they?'

'They're not personal letters. Yesterday he wrote to *Thought for the Day*, which is his favourite recipient, apparently. He can't bear that Rabbi. You know the cosy, homosexual one who is always on about his mother? Father says he doesn't want to share his thoughts and doesn't see why he or anyone else should have to. They had a man on Saturday's programme with a cheerful, bouncy sort of voice, pondering on what would be Jesus Christ's favourite film, and that set him off, as you can imagine. His theory is that the BBC deliberately encourages ignorance and stupidity. You know, cultivating a mindless underclass like in *Brave New World*.

'Well, he may have a point!' Jo laughed.

'He bangs them all out on his old surgery typewriter in such a fury that the keys practically go through the paper and the page looks like a sheet of Braille.'

'What energy,' said Jo. 'I can't get round to writing to anyone, even my friends.'

'Different generation,' said Belinda. 'Letter-writing is an alien activity for you lot. Anyway, darling, it's nice to talk to you and love to Nick. I'll give everyone your love but I must go and get lunch underway. You know how it has to be on the table at one o'clock, and then I want to get off soon afterwards. It's an awful drive home at the best of times.'

224

'Yes, OK. Drive carefully. Love to Izzy.'

Belinda put the telephone down and went through to the kitchen.

'Let me scrape those potatoes,' she said, watching her mother's crooked fingers fumbling with the knife in the bowl of muddy water.

'I can do it,' said her mother. 'It's one thing I can do.'

'But it would be quicker for me. Why don't you sit and talk to me? We don't have much time together, do we?'

Her mother dropped the knife in the water and shuffled to the table where she sat down heavily.

'Everything is an effort,' she said. 'I have to hold on with one hand when I move about, as you see, so it all takes so long.'

'Yes,' said Belinda. She nearly said, poor you, but stopped herself. You couldn't commiserate with someone over the inevitable decline of old age. It was something that had to be accepted. Surely there was an accompanying mental change, a dampening of the fretting and chafing spirit? Perhaps a calming sort of wisdom came dropping like a balm with advancing years. It didn't seem necessarily to be the case, not with her father, anyway.

She finished the potatoes and opened the oven door to baste the chicken. A cloud of evil-smelling and greasy steam hit her face. The oven was filthy, stained brown with the cooked-on fat of years of roasts.

'I won't be remembered for my sparkling stove, will I?' Charlotte remarked. 'You won't be able to commend me for *that* at my funeral!'

'Hardly,' said Belinda, laughing.

'They do that now, you know,' her mother went on. 'Relatives and friends are invited to stand up and share a recollection of the deceased. I think it's extremely risky, myself, and I certainly don't want that sort of thing when I go.'

'No, all right,' said Belinda. She was used to these remarks and took them lightly. Death was not a taboo subject. 'At least, I promise not to mention the oven.'

'Thank you. I would be grateful. There aren't many of us left these days. I miss my friends. I think that's one of the hardest things. I often find myself with my hand reaching for the telephone and then remember that Sheila is dead, and Rosemary, and Betty. They all died last year. In fact, there really isn't anyone left to share things with. Well, there's you, of course, but I mean of my own generation.' Her face clouded with sadness. 'And, do you know, just lately I've missed my mother.'

'Your mother?' said Belinda, surprised. Her grandmother had been dead for thirty years.

'Yes. She was so wise, you see. A wonderful person. I seem to remember her more clearly than ever. Memories have begun to seem more real than the present.'

Belinda fell silent. This reaching back into the past seemed to accompany old age, when the future held nothing but death. Would she feel the same about her mother at the end of her own life? Would Jo and Jess remember and miss her when they themselves were old? She was so used to having her opinions dismissed that it was hard to imagine that they would ever come to respect her judgement.

'You must promise to telephone me, Ma,' she said, 'if

ever you want to talk. I don't suppose Dad is much company in that sort of way.' She realised that she wanted to feel that they were close, that they shared something exclusive. But her mother looked at her curiously.

'Well, I would always ring if I had something to say,' she said. 'But I don't believe in chat for chat's sake.'

Belinda felt snubbed. The passing of years did not necessarily mean a closing of the gap between parent and child, even if there was more understanding and sympathy.

'Well, in case, you know,' she said lamely. It was true, her mother had never been one to chat. There had never been cosy exchanges of confidences between them and she had in many ways been grateful for this distance. When she was growing up she had felt sorry for girls at school whose mothers had insisted brightly that they were their best friends. It had always seemed inappropriate to her. Best friends were best friends and mothers were something quite other.

Now as she busied herself making bread sauce and cutting up spring greens, she realised she hardly knew her mother as a person. She knew so little about what went on in her head compared, say, to how well she knew Dinka, or how well she felt she knew her own daughters. Time was running out, and she had a panicky feeling that she was in danger of losing something of herself, missing a chance to achieve some vital self-knowledge. But she did not know how to seek this understanding. With her mother it was like wandering in a maze, where every path was familiar but you never knew if you were getting near the centre.

Love is the thing, she thought suddenly, and leaving what

she was doing she went over to her mother and laid a hand on her shoulder. Her mother reached up and patted it with one of her own. This was as much as they could manage, although Belinda's heart felt full.

The next moment there were voices in the hall and Izzy and her great-grandfather were back from church and Ernie burst through the door carrying his ball which he dropped at Belinda's feet, fixed it with a stern eye and trembled with anticipation. Belinda gave it a sharp kick under the table and he shot after it. A second later he was back, a self-congratulatory smile on his face, to repeat the performance.

Izzy came in, carrying *The Water Babies*. Her cheeks were pink from the walk through the village. 'Great-Grandpa is going to have a beer,' she announced. 'He's going to drink strong ale to wash away his sorrows.'

'What?' laughed Charlotte.

'It's in the book,' said Izzy, putting it on the table. 'Look, he found the place.'

Later, when lunch was finished and washed up and Belinda had sorted out the fridge and talked her mother through the various meal options she had stowed away, it was time to leave. Izzy had to be chivvied to collect her things and pack her little bag. She had disappeared with her great-grandfather into his study and he had amused them both by writing out some rude limericks for her.

'There was a young man of Westphalia, who painted his arse like a dahlia,' chanted Izzy.

Westphalia, thought Belinda. Does such a place exist any more?

'That's it then, Ma,' she said, throwing her coat into the back of the car. 'I think I've got everything.' She turned to face her mother who was standing watching, wearing the new poplin raincoat. It was a mistake, Belinda saw now. The colour was too bright and hard and drained the life from her mother's pale face and white hair, making her look startlingly unlike herself, as if she was dressed up to represent someone else in a play. Belinda supposed she had put it on to please her and she felt touched.

'Shall we just take a turn round the garden?' she suggested. 'Before I go?' She took her mother's arm which felt as light as a stick resting on hers, and they walked round the little gravel paths, exclaiming at the celandines and clumps of snowdrops and the little wild cyclamen poking through the long grass on the bank. From the top of the apple tree came the lilt of a blackbird's song and they both stopped to listen. Belinda could see him quite clearly, his glossy head lifted and his bright yellow beak opening and shutting as he poured his lovely melody into the pale grey sky.

'A foretaste of heaven,' her mother said. 'Another spring, as perfect as ever it was.'

As they turned back, she squeezed Belinda's arm. 'Thank you for coming,' she said. 'We love seeing you, and dear Isobel. Our lives have got very dull. It's boring, you know, at our age. Boring.'

Belinda laughed. 'You sound like a teenager. We were never allowed to say we were bored when we were young, do you remember?'

Izzy came skipping out of the house. 'Granny, listen. "I

229

am a cow, and I do not like my Huddersfield!" Do you get it, Granny? Great-Grandpa told me. "I am a cow, and I do not like my Huddersfield!"'

'See,' remarked Charlotte. 'That's what I have to put up with.'

They were still laughing as Belinda put on her seat belt and turned to reverse out of the drive. At the last moment, as she turned back for a final wave, she saw that her mother's cheeks were wet with tears.

Tom did not feel the moment was right to telephone Karen Bearsden until Sunday evening. He had been racing at Larkhill, but left after the men's open race which he won for Ken on a good horse called Spiderman. It was a satisfactory victory against some quality horses and Ken and the owner were justifiably pleased.

He drove home along the busy road past Stonehenge where the great grey stones looked like beasts crouched in the winter pale grass, ringed by tourists. It was a mild afternoon and every now and then sunshine seeped through the grey sky and washed across a far hillside.

As he drove, he thought about Jess, who to her fury had not been allowed to ride. Her closed eye, just a bloodshot crack in a puffed-up purple cheek, did not get past the course doctor, despite her protestations, and she had spent the afternoon at Ken's lorry, helping to get the horses ready and then sponging them down and walking them round to cool off after their races. She was in an uncommunicative mood and he had kept his distance. What was the point of trying to talk to her if she just brushed him off? After his race he had shared a jumbo hot dog with Moira, and when they were laughing and wiping away the smeared mustard and ketchup, he had seen Jess give him the sort of look which could be loosely interpreted as a death threat. Oh, bollocks, he thought. Be like that.

The two girls spat at each other all the afternoon, arguing over a lost body brush, a weight cloth left in the paddock and who had eaten the ham roll with no mustard which Moira always wanted, until even Ken was roused enough to say, 'Cut it out, the pair of you! What's the matter with you? Give us a break, will you?'

The night before, he and Jess had been knackered, and although they had slept naked together in his bed, they did not touch but turned away to curl, back to back, into their own space. How could things be so different, when really nothing had happened between them? Tom could not answer his own question. They just seemed out of kilter in some way, as if they were facing each other on either end of a see-saw, rising and falling, joined together, but never meeting.

After he had done his evening rounds at home, checking his sheep, feeding his cattle and bedding down his three young horses for the night, he found himself in the kitchen with a slice of cheese on toast and a long evening in front of him. It was then he remembered the telephone message and thought he might as well get it over with.

He went through to his sitting room and dialled the number he had written on an envelope. After a short time, it was answered by the American voice which he recognised. It was a seductive, Southern voice, girlish and breathy.

'Hello,' he said. 'This is Tom Hodges. Returning your call.'

'Hi, Tom. Thanks for calling back.' She said his name as if she knew him, thought Tom, as if they were friends. 'The other day, you should have told me who you were. You know, that day in the rain.'

Who am I? thought Tom.

'Johnnie said he knew you from way back.'

'Oh, yes. A long time ago.' He must get to the point. 'I came round about the sheep. I'm sorry to say that your dogs are responsible for three of them – a ewe and two lambs. I found another dead lamb the next day.'

'Yeah. I'm real sorry about that. We haven't had these dogs long. They came with the keeper that Johnnie has hired and we're getting them trained for shooting. I'm real sorry. It's this girl I've got. She said you met her. Ludmylla. It was her fault. She let them out and then didn't stay with them, didn't watch them, and they went off hunting, I suppose. Johnnie was mad at her. Anyway, I'm going to write you a cheque, unless you would rather have the cash?'

'No, no. A cheque would be fine. I just want to know that it won't happen again.'

'No, Tom, it won't happen again. I promise you that. Our keeper has taken care of them. We don't have the dogs up at the house any more. Now I have something else to ask you.'

'You do?' Tom wondered what was coming.

'How about meeting me for lunch tomorrow? I can bring you your cheque, your blood money.'

'I don't have time for lunch.' It was the last thing Tom wanted.

'Everyone has to eat. An hour, that's all. No children, I promise. How about the White Horse in Bishops Barton?'

'Wrong direction for me,' said Tom and knew that he had thereby given the impression that he had accepted her invitation.

'OK. You suggest. I don't know your schedule.' She pronounced it skedule.

'Well, I'm riding out at Ken Andrews' in the morning. I've got a fencing job to finish near Shaftesbury in the afternoon. How about the Three Tuns in East Ditton? It's on my way.'

'The Three Tuns it is. A quarter of one?'

'OK. Will Johnnie be coming?' asked Tom in the moment when he might have said goodbye.

'Johnnie? No, not Johnnie, I'm afraid. He's already back in London.'

Tom rang off feeling dissatisfied with himself. Why had he allowed himself to be talked into meeting Karen? What was the point? He didn't want to know the Bearsdens, didn't want them in his life at all.

It was with some trepidation that he pulled into the Three Tuns at lunchtime on Monday. He was in his work clothes and pretty sure that he smelled of the stable and the farm. He glanced round the car park and spotted the Bearsden vehicle at once – it was the only sleek and expensive estate car there, and he noticed that it had a galloping horse mascot screwed onto the bonnet. A typical, classy touch.

He pushed open the door to the bar and Karen Bearsden was the first person he saw. She was sitting at a table by the fire, a glass of wine in front of her, turning over the pages of a Dorset tourist magazine. She was wearing blue jeans and brown boots and her thick, wiry dark hair was held back in a tortoiseshell slide. She didn't look like most people's idea of an American but was instantly recognisable to Tom who had lived in Kentucky. She had the polished, understated look of old money. She belonged to the sort of people he had worked for on the stud farm in Woodford County outside Lexington. Easy, confident people whose expectations of life would match those of a man like Johnnie Bearsden. At a glance he could see that they would be well suited.

'Hi there,' she said, noticing him. 'Glad you could make it. You want to get yourself a drink? I've already got one.'

'I'll have half of Badger, please,' Tom said to the barman, and took his glass to the table and sat opposite her. She turned away from him to snap open a flat leather bag and get out a chequebook that was larger than any he had ever seen before.

'Let's get this out the way,' she said. 'I'm going to give you a hundred and fifty. OK?'

'That's too much,' said Tom. 'That's more than they were worth. She was an old ewe.'

'Come on,' she said. 'Nuisance value, et cetera. I insist.' She wrote out the cheque in a large round hand. 'Tom Hodges, is that right?'

'Yes, that's right,' said Tom, made uncomfortable by this largesse.

She handed over the cheque. Tom saw that it was drawn from a private London bank best known for its grand clientele. He folded it over and put it in his pocket.

'Thanks,' he said and took a mouthful of beer.

'What are you going to have?' she asked. 'There seems to be a menu on that blackboard.'

'A ploughman's will do me,' said Tom, wanting to make as little of this lunch as possible.

'A ploughman's for a ploughman, is that right?' she asked. Her eyes were extremely blue with thick short lashes. You couldn't call her pretty, thought Tom. She was handsome, rather in the way that a horse or a greyhound can be, with a long bony face.

'Not quite. I'm not exactly a ploughman. More of a stockman.'

'Ah.' She turned to study the board. 'I think I'll have the lamb casserole, if that's not too tactless.' She laughed lightly and touched his hand. 'Would you mind putting our order at the bar?'

'Of course not,' said Tom, standing up.

When he sat down again, Karen had lit a cigarette. She looked at him thoughtfully.

'So,' she said. 'Johnnie tells me you were quite a horseman. Still are, obviously.'

'Does he? That's kind of him. What's he doing these days?'

'We have a travel business. Exclusive safari holidays tailored for the discerning traveller and we specialise in racing breaks – taking top people to top race meets round the world.'

'I see,' said Tom, thinking, typical, that would be right up Johnnie's street. His charm would be put to good use. 'Does that keep him in London?'

'Well, he obviously has to travel a lot, but the office is in London and we have a branch in Louisville, where my family comes from.'

'So are you down here much? At Quatt Lodge?'

'We intend to be. In the school holidays and at weekends, for shooting and riding. Which is what I wanted to speak to you about. We have a bit of fencing to be done and Johnnie wants to put in a small cross-country course for the children. You do that sort of thing, I think?'

'I do, yes, but I'm very busy at the moment. I couldn't take on anything like that.' Wouldn't want to was more like it, he thought.

'There's no hurry. Mikey has a pony down here. We keep it at Perrings livery yard while we're in London and he's at school. Eventually, Johnnie will want to keep a couple of hunters. At the moment he has two in Leicestershire but he intends to hunt with the Blackmore and Sparkford Vale.'

'Ah,' said Tom. The local hunt was a magnet for people who were brave enough to go across some of the biggest hedges in the country. 'Mikey is your son, I assume.'

'Yes. He's nine. He goes to a boarding school in Berkshire but he has a lot of exeat weekends which he'll spend down here in the country when the house is ready.' The carrot-haired boy, thought Tom.

They paused while their food arrived at the table and there was a bit of organising knives and forks and passing bread between them. Tom noticed that Karen's hands were slim and tanned, the nails free of polish and worn short. She had a chunky ring – stonking great diamonds, he guessed – on one finger and a gold signet ring with a family crest on another. A further touch of Johnnie's style.

'The thing is, what with us not being down here much and Johnnie having been away from the area for so long, Mikey doesn't have anyone to ride with. Do you know any pony-minded children?'

Tom made a surprised face. 'I'm not the one to ask. There must be lots of Pony Club mothers about the place.'

'Yes, I'm sure. We just haven't had the chance to start any social life yet.' She paused. 'There is one child that we've met out riding. A little girl, six or seven years old. Brown pony. I wonder if you know who she is. I ask, because Mikey said that he saw you with her mother at the point-to-point on Saturday.'

Tom looked up from buttering his bread. 'What?' he said.

'Mikey said that he met you on Saturday, at Black Forest Lodge. He remembered you from the other day. When you called round with the bill for your sheep.'

'Oh, right. I see. Yes, we did bump into each other, I think,' said Tom evasively.

'The point is that he said he saw the little girl's mother again. He said you were with her.'

'I can't think who that was,' said Tom. 'I was hanging around with a lot of people. You know how it is at the races.'

'So you don't know who she is? She can't live far from us if we met her out riding, can she?'

'No idea,' said Tom, shrugging. He felt as if he was being stuck, wriggling, on the point of a pin. 'As I said, I'm not really into the children thing. None of my friends have them yet.'

'Really?' Karen Bearsden narrowed her very blue eyes. Tom could not be sure whether she put particular emphasis on the word, or if it was just her accent that made it sound disbelieving.

'I can give you the name of the Pony Club secretary, if that would help,' he said, throwing out a red herring. 'She happens to be my sister.'

Karen smiled and leaned across to touch his hand again. 'I knew you would be the one to talk to,' she said. 'I knew you would help.'

Tom fished in his pocket for a pen and Karen produced a notebook. He wrote down his sister's name and telephone number, and then regretted it because it seemed like further, unnecessary involvement. He knew he could not prevent Karen Bearsden from identifying Izzy if she set her mind to it, but he did not want to help her.

As she put the piece of paper into her Filofax he noticed the determined set of her jaw and the fact that her dark hair, which was of the wilful and frizzy type, was threaded with white, like a sprinkling of springy silver coils. She was older than he had thought, older than Johnnie he would guess; the light, girlish voice was misleading. He had the impression that Karen Bearsden was a person to be reckoned with, more so than Johnnie, who had always seemed to him to be a lightweight.

'I don't know when we'll be down here again as a family,' she said. 'The Easter holidays, I expect, when we get back from skiing. We're having a lot of work done on the house at the moment, so I whizz to and fro, keeping an eye on things. The contractors need chivvying, I can tell you.' Out of politeness, Tom did his best to look interested.

'Perhaps you'll be able to come over and discuss the cross-country. I'll give you a call. Come and have supper with us.'

'I'm sorry, but I think I said I was very busy at the moment,' said Tom, quite rudely, he thought, but determined not to give way.

'Oh, I'm sure you could find the time. To give us some advice, at least,' Karen insisted with a smile. 'Johnnie would love to see you again.'

This seemed such a remote possibility that Tom found himself speechless. He had no skill at all at conversations that skidded along the slippery surface of obvious untruths.

He looked at his watch and Karen said, 'Of course, you have to go. I shall sit here for a moment and have a cup of coffee and a cigarette.' Tom felt he had been dismissed. He stood up, jogging the table with his knee and knocking a knife onto the floor. He stooped to pick it up.

'Well, thanks,' he said awkwardly. 'That was very nice.'

Karen laughed softly. 'Yes,' she said. 'It was. I'll look forward to the next time.'

As Tom left the bar, her words seemed more threatening than anything else. He was glad to get into his old Land Rover and slam the door. Meg unfolded herself from the passenger seat and licked his ear. He sat for a moment, his eyes moving over the familiar detritus of his trade: the tangled binder twine, the wire cutters, the claw hammer, the boxes of penicillin, the iodine spray, the litter of straw and sheep nuts and old racecards. Tucked into the shelf under the dashboard was a pink scarf belonging to Jess. He pulled it out and held it to his face. It smelled of her hair and skin. He wished he had never set eyes on Karen Bearsden.

Chapter Ten

Tom should have known that he wouldn't get away with it. He hadn't seen Moira's car in the car park, or realised that she was sitting in the snug bar of the Three Tuns having a lager and a basket of chips with Carl. She hadn't seen him either until she got up to go to the Ladies. As she crossed the lobby, she glanced through the open door of the saloon and saw Tom sitting with his back to her, having lunch with a good-looking dark-haired woman. They seemed to be deep in conversation.

'Heh,' she said, when she went back to Carl. 'Guess who's next door? Our Tom. Jess's lover boy, and he's with another woman.'

'Yeah?' said Carl, not really interested. 'Who would that be, then?'

'Smart-looking tart,' said Moira. 'Older type. Looks as though she'd know the score.'

Carl made a face. Moira was a vicious gossiper and he'd been on the receiving end of her mischief himself.

'Doesn't mean nothing,' he said. 'Any more than us being here together does.'

'Yeah, but there's one big difference. We're free agents, you and me. Jess reckons Tom's accounted for. I think she's wrong, mind. You shouldn't take a bloke for granted, like

241

she does. She might get a surprise one of these days.'

Carl drained his glass. It was an accepted fact that Moira was jealous of Jess. It had caused quite a bit of trouble on the yard over the last six months. Rhona, the head lass, had had to speak to her about it, but it hadn't done any good. Moira wouldn't take it from another girl. In the end Ken had had to have a word and Carl knew that more than anything he hated having to sort out his staff.

'Come on,' he said, getting up. 'We'd best be going.'

Moira halted to have another good look through the saloon door. The woman was sitting on her own now, smoking a cigarette and talking on a mobile telephone. Moira stopped Carl with a hand on his arm and pointed her out. 'That's her,' she said. Carl stared, despite himself, and had to admit that the woman was what he would class as posh totty. There was no sign of Tom, but as they went out to the car park they saw his old Land Rover turning onto the main road.

'Leaving separately,' said Moira. 'They don't want to be seen together.' She cast an assessing glance round the remaining cars. 'That'll be hers,' she said, pointing out the expensive estate car. 'Look, it's got one of those horse mascot things on the front.' Carl thought she was probably right. The other cars in the car park were the usual old beat-up locals or the grannymobiles which did the rounds of the local pubs at lunchtime.

'Come on,' he said. 'We've got those youngsters to work this afternoon.' Although they squabbled over rides, he liked Tom and he liked Jess and he didn't want to be party to Moira's speculations.

*

Jess knew that her mother disapproved of her arrangements for Izzy's half-term but there was nothing she could do about it. She had to work and she could not afford expensive childcare. She did what all working mothers of slender means have to resort to, made a cobbled together arrangement which was not ideal but would do.

Cheerful, friendly Lisa, who worked with her at Ken's yard and had two boys a bit older than Izzy, had made a suggestion. Her mum, Maureen, would help out with the three children in the mornings and then when she went to work as a carer at an old people's home after lunch, Lisa would be able to take over. She only worked part-time at Ken's, doing the tack cleaning and mucking-out. She loved horses but had never been a rider. Jess could come by her house and collect Izzy when she finished work. Her mum would be glad of the extra money, said Lisa. She was saving up to go on holiday to Turkey with her new partner, Ian. He needed the break because he was going through a bad divorce.

So that was it, and it would have to do. The fact that Izzy did not know Lisa's two boys, Ben and Darren, and that Maureen lived in a council house at the far end of Sharston with a garden full of rubbish was beside the point.

When Jess took Izzy to meet Maureen, she was tongue-tied and awkward, and frightened of the Alsatian dog which came bounding to meet them on the end of a chain.

'Quiet, Sheba!' called Maureen from the window, fag in mouth. 'Come in, love. She won't hurt you. Door's open.'

Maureen, soft and large in grey sweatpants and a pink sweater, took them into the sitting room which was very untidy, overflowing with newspapers and magazines and discarded clothes and full ashtrays. A vacuum cleaner stood abandoned in the middle of the floor and a large television set blared from the corner. Maureen picked up the controls and turned the volume down. 'Here,' she said, shifting a load from the black plastic sofa to the floor. 'Sit down, love. Cup of tea?' She was warm and friendly and kind, that was the most important thing.

Ian appeared from the kitchen, a big fat man with a heavy, red face, wearing a T-shirt and jeans. When he sat down, his stomach rested cosily on his knees like a small child. Jess had to nudge Izzy to stop her staring. 'Don't sit down, love,' Maureen told him. 'Put the kettle on and make us a cup of tea.' Obediently, he heaved himself back up onto his feet and shuffled out in his white socks and trainers.

'So what's your name, lovey? Izzy? That's a funny name. You'll be all right with your Auntie Maureen, won't you?' She leaned over and took Izzy's hand. Izzy looked terrified. It was only because of Maureen's harsh, smoker's voice, thought Jess, and because she doesn't know her. She'll soon feel at home.

'She'll get on fine with the boys. They're good little bleeders most of the time. They can play out the back when it's nice.' Through the kitchen window Jess could see a beaten-down patch of grass, a broken chain-link fence and an old car under a tarpaulin.

'Actually,' she said, 'Izzy likes to read and draw and things like that. She'll bring all her books and things with her.'

'That's lovely. She can do that here, at the table.' Maureen pushed aside a large arrangement of plastic rosebuds in a Grecian-style urn. 'Most days I get the boys a video down the shop in the village. You'll enjoy that, won't you, darlin'?'

Izzy nodded shyly.

'I'll send her with a packed lunch,' said Jess.

Maureen laughed. 'Don't you bother with that, love. I always do something for the boys, lunchtime, before I get off down the home. She can have whatever they have.'

'Thank you,' said Jess. 'Thank you very much. It really helps me out that she can come here. My mother will drop her off every morning on her way to work.' She glanced down at Izzy and saw the shut-off look on her face. She could at least try to look a bit interested, she thought. Maureen's doing her best to be kind.

She knew what Belinda would think. She would be horrified by the state of the house, by Maureen, by the live-in lover, by the sense of disorder. She would not want to leave Izzy there, but that was too bad. It was only for a week and it wouldn't do Izzy any harm. After all, most people lived like that – just managing, getting by.

'You'll be all right there, won't you, Iz?' she asked as they drove home, glancing in the driver's mirror to see Izzy's face. She was sitting on the back seat, her arms crossed over *The Water Babies*, holding it to her chest. She did not reply but Jess saw her avert her face to look out of the window and then nod her head.

It was a brave little gesture and it moved Jess. Shit, she thought. She could guess how much Izzy did not want to be left with Maureen's unknown boys and she wished that things could be arranged differently, but it was the best she could do. Somehow or other she would make it up to her.

*

As a general rule, Belinda did not hold with the modern preoccupation with the state of well-being. Feeling exhausted and stressed-out seemed to be a full-time occupation for some of the women she knew. Yes, life was often a grind, a treadmill, but one just had to get on with it as best one could and moaning was no help at all. She felt that she, more than any of her friends, had an excuse to be tired out – working full-time and with the extra burden of looking after Izzy, but at least she didn't have a husband to consider, and it seemed to her that it would be this extra requirement, on top of everything else, which would be the last straw.

Men of her age and acquaintance required such a complex support system, what with their unshakable belief that in their homes something called 'the wash' occurred regularly, their pant and sock collections were supervised, their shirts received the necessary ironing and folding, and their suits were taken to the cleaners. Their diet preferences had to be studied and certain foods avoided and others not allowed to run out. Her own marriage had fallen into this pattern and it had seemed perfectly right and natural back then, when she did not go out to work.

But things were more complicated than that. She had one friend who had to hurry home from work and hoover the sitting-room carpet before she took her coat off because her husband complained about the dog hairs. Another dreaded the end of the month when her husband made her go through all her purchase slips and tot up and account for her expenditure. Then there were the wives who had to entertain because their husbands wanted full social lives

246

and a crammed diary. Belinda did not think she would be capable of shopping and cooking for a dinner party, cleaning the house, doing flowers and setting the table. She could, possibly, accomplish all that, but would then rather whisk a bottle of wine off the table and go to bed early and leave her guests to entertain themselves.

There was no doubt that men were a lot of work and what exactly was the payback? Companionship, definitely, but could that always be relied upon? Only last week she had heard a dispiriting programme on *Weekend Woman's Hour* which claimed that while romantic love would almost certainly wane, so too, over the years, did companionable love, which was what most women settled for, anyway, thinking it could be relied upon.

It was all rather bleak, she thought as she drove into Sharston on Monday morning to drop Izzy off at Maureen's. Somehow she had lost sight of how nice and supportive men could be, and funny and good company, and how rewarding it was to make them happy and contented. Going out with Victor had reminded her of that and she felt a yearning to be treasured and cosseted in return. She thought of the sort of closeness she missed so much. A hug. God, she could do with a hug. And a shared joke, and holding hands, and an arm through which to hook her elbow. She remembered what it was like to lean against a man's chest, the texture of his sweater against her cheek, while his arms held her close. She missed these things more than she did the sex. She could do without that.

She supposed it was because she felt so tired this morning that her life seemed full of holes. The long drive home on

Sunday afternoon, the anxiety about her parents and the emotional wrench at leaving them, Jess's black eye and mood to match when they got back, and the slapdash arrangements for Izzy's half-term had all contributed to her feeling exhausted and wrung out.

Unsatisfactory telephone calls made last night to her brothers had not helped. They both remained at a determined distance from their parents' precarious situation. They'll ask for help if they need it, they told her. There's not much we can do. They seemed to imply that anything other than the occasional visit was beyond the call of duty. 'I don't know,' she said later to Dinka on the telephone. 'Sometimes I long to be eighty-five and happily ga-ga and living in a care home. I am sick of feeling that I have to keep everything afloat.'

'I know what you mean,' laughed Dinka, who had been recounting an impossible situation she was having to deal with at work. 'All our adult lives women have argued for independence but the older I get, the more attractive an arranged marriage to a lottery winner appears to be. We've taken a wrong turning at some point, haven't we, you and I? Slogging away day in day out and ending up in this bloody cul-de-sac!' She was joking, of course, but there was a little, bitter taste of the truth about her words.

When Belinda had collapsed into bed she had been unable to sleep. She had padded downstairs to make tea at two in the morning, haunted by the memory of her mother's tears.

She was awake at six as usual, searching for something to wear to work and disheartened by the sight of her drawn, tired and, frankly, old face. God, she thought, it would be nice to share all this with someone. Dinka's words came back to her and she realised how sick she was of shouldering it all on her own. David should have been there by her side, and if not David, then someone else. She yearned for a bit of cherishing and support. She had always loved that word 'cherish' from the marriage service. It was one of the promises couples made to one another and, in her view, the most important. To feel cherished must be the most wonderful thing in the world. She thought with envy of Dinka lying in Javier's strong, young arms. The reality might be a bit different, but at least she was half of a couple. She did not have to face the slings and arrows of outrageous fortune on her own.

Now, driving past the garage, Belinda inevitably thought of Victor. He seemed a strong, dependable sort of man. She remembered how he had pulled her towards him in the car and she was glad that he had got on with kissing her without fumbling or asking her permission, or saying that he was sorry afterwards. She remembered what it had felt like to sit in the dark with her hand in his. I hope he telephones, she thought. In fact, if he doesn't, I might ring him myself.

'Izzy!' she said, suddenly braking. 'Damn! I must be daydreaming. I nearly forgot that I'm taking you to Lisa's mother's. Silly me. I've gone past the Sharston turning. We'll have to do a detour.'

Belinda's reaction to leaving Izzy with Maureen was just as Jess had predicted. She was appalled. Really, she thought as she drove away, she wouldn't have left a bicycle in the care of such a household. Izzy had hung back and cast desperate looks in her direction, and must have seen the dismay on her face.

There was nothing wrong with Maureen; in fact, she seemed a very pleasant woman, but the state of the house and the sight of Ian sitting at the kitchen table in a vest, plodding his way through a pile of toast, were something quite else. Lisa's boys came rushing down the stairs to stare with interest at Izzy, and Belinda did not like the look of them, either. Their heads were so closely shaved that there was only the merest suggestion that they were not, in fact, bald, and the older one wore a gold hoop earring and trousers with the crotch somewhere just above his knees.

Belinda had no option but to leave Izzy but she drew Maureen to one side and gave her her work telephone number with instructions to ring her if Izzy was at all distressed. Bugger work, she would just come right back and collect her. This evening she would tell Jess how strongly she objected to the arrangement, how unsuitable it was, and insist that something better was provided for the remainder of the week. Surely Jess could think of someone else, some other mother from Izzy's school, or a respectable, older woman in the village who would look after her.

She remembered her mother's advice, that she should endeavour to be less involved, but what was she supposed to do? Stand back and see Izzy bullied by those two little thugs? Abandoned in that awful house with that dreadful slob of a man in a vest, with tattoos up his fat arms? For all Jess knew he was a child abuser. The papers were full of situations like that, and she always wondered how the family of the child could have let it happen.

She thought about Izzy all day and watched the clock,

wondering whether the hours were dragging for her, and then feeling relief when she saw it was time for Jess to collect her. She telephoned Jess's mobile to check that Izzy was all right, but it was switched off and she couldn't frame the words to leave a coherent message.

The afternoon passed so slowly it felt as if she was walking through deep water. The sleepless night caught up with her and she longed to drop her head on her desk and close her eyes. About every half-hour she checked her email in vain to see if she had a message from Victor. At last it was time to start tidying her work and to close the office for the day. She drove home fast, steeling herself for the forthcoming confrontation with Jess but when she pulled into the drive, the lights were on and she could see the bright glimmer of the fire already lit.

She opened the kitchen door, and fending off Snowy's delirious welcome, saw Izzy kneeling on a chair at the kitchen table. She turned to beam at Belinda.

'Hello, Granny. I had a lovely time and Ben showed me how to draw cars, and we had a video and More-Ian cooked us chips.'

Jess was washing something at the sink. 'Izzy calls them Ian and More-Ian,' she explained. 'What's the matter? You've got your pained face on.'

'Oh, Jess,' said Belinda wearily. She sat down opposite Izzy. 'So you really had a nice time, darling?'

Izzy looked up again from drawing short fat cars with spindly wheels. 'I had a lovely, lovely time and tomorrow I'm going again, and Ben said school is shite and he showed me Chinese burns on Darren and they did fight all day.'

'Oh dear,' said Jess, amused. 'Your granny won't let you go again if you tell her that.'

Belinda shot her a glance but the truth was that Izzy's happy chatter had thoroughly taken the wind out of her sails.

'I'm glad you enjoyed it,' she said, getting up and kissing her on the top of her head, which she noticed smelled strongly of frying. 'I was thinking about you all day.'

'I've done supper,' said Jess. 'It's only ham salad and baked potatoes.'

'It sounds great,' said Belinda, softening towards her. 'I've got to go out again later to the village hall meeting.' It was the last thing she wanted to do.

'Poor old Mum,' said Jess. 'It must take it out of you, being a do-gooder.'

'Mrs Doasyouwouldbedoneby!' said Izzy, not looking up. 'She was the nicest fairy in the world. She's in *The Water Babies*, Granny, and that's who you are.'

Belinda could have wept.

'Anyway,' said Izzy, with satisfaction, putting the top on her felt tip pen. 'Ben and Darren liked Great-Grandpa's rhyme. The one about the arse.'

Tom got the text message from Moira in the afternoon when he was busy hammering in fence posts round a renovated farmhouse outside Shaftesbury. Until six months ago it had been a dairy farm, in the same family for generations, but falling milk prices had driven old Mr Harris out, the herd was dispersed, the land parcelled off and the farmhouse sold to a London restaurant owner, who was currently embracing country life with the fervour of the recently converted. The smart post and rail fencing and newly hung gates had provided a winter of work for Tom and he was not complaining. The next thing Antonio wanted was to take up hunting and he had asked Tom to look for a horse for him.

It was enjoyable work which was physically demanding but also required full concentration and Tom was glad of that. He didn't want to spend the afternoon thinking about Karen Bearsden. He was sure that he had landed himself into something which was going to spiral out of control although he could not guess in what direction. The last thing he wanted was to be disloyal to Jess, and yet that was exactly what this felt like.

He swung his sledgehammer rhythmically, aiming carefully so as not to split the post, and stopping every now and then to wipe his brow and straighten his back. From where he was working, high up on the hill, there was a wonderful view across the whole of the Blackmore Vale. It was a pale, mild sort of day and the milky light washed across the rolling distance, melting the far-off woods into a soft blue haze. The villages and farms and the intricate patchwork of fields were silvered over by the sliding light so that they looked illusive and insubstantial, as if at any moment all might float away. Close at hand, the bare, black fastness of the blackthorn hedge was alive with the bustle and song of birds and Tom noticed that the vicious thorny twigs were tipped with tiny red points of new growth. Under the hedge, on the sunny side, there were wild daffodils with their delicate stems and pretty little slender yellow trumpets, and crowns of primroses shone through the matted winter grass.

Tom could remember jumping this hedge out hunting in the winter. In fact the ground was still cut up where the horses had landed on the other side. It was a terrific fence, made more ferocious back then by a brimming ditch and deep mud. Only three or four of them had jumped it, and as a result he had got a good price for the brave, young horse he was riding. He had sold him on a week later, to hunt in Leicestershire.

This afternoon the still air seemed to tremble with the bleating of sheep and new lambs. Tom could see them dotted over the hillsides and watched for a moment as a shepherd crossed a field below on his quad bike, his black and white collie balancing behind him. Sheep and lambs looked so easy, thought Tom, skipping about in the spring fields, but they were bloody hard work. He would have to take a couple of days this week to ring and number his own lambs, worm the ewes and trim their feet.

Thinking about his sheep brought him back to the ewe he had lost and then back to the Bearsdens. Shit, he thought, why did I have to get involved? Feeling a deep sense of unease, he shouldered the sledgehammer to start work again and then, from the pocket of his jacket which he'd hung on a fence post, he heard his mobile telephone signal the arrival of a text message.

'Who's yr grl frnd?' he read. What did that mean? He looked at the number and then realised that the message was from Moira. Oh God, he could do without this. She must have seen him with Karen. That really fucked things up nicely. Moira would make the most of it and the first person she'd tell would be Jess.

The village hall meeting dragged on. It was held in the beamed sitting room of Eileen and Colin Busby's thatched cottage, and once the committee had sunk into the comfortable chairs round the fire, it seemed as if they wanted to make a night of it. Eileen moved amongst them, her large and imposing bosom like a bolster, as she distributed cups of milky coffee and homemade biscuits. There was a diversion when mild Janice Green asked if she could have decaffeinated, and then fearing that she was being a nuisance said that just a glass of water would be fine and she would get it herself.

Eileen managed to make a gala performance of announcing that she had only sparkling bottled water to offer, then found she hadn't, then went back to the kitchen and returned with a glass containing ice and lemon as well as water and fussed about with a coaster to put it on.

'Oh, please,' Janice, mortified with embarrassment, kept saying, 'you shouldn't have.'

Bloody hell, thought Belinda crossly. It's only a bloody glass of tap water, for God's sake. Can't we just get on with the meeting?

The evening dragged on. Reports were given and minuted on the usual topics that seemed to Belinda to come up meeting after meeting: the leaking roof, the dripping hot tap in the kitchen, the servicing of the boiler, the scale of charges for rental. Round and round they went, over the same old ground, until Belinda thought she would scream.

Much as she liked and valued Eileen, she was one of those people who jump on conversations as if onto a horse, and gallop off on them in a direction of their choice. A discussion on who should be responsible for putting out the bins after a function at the hall was turned by Eileen into a discourse on how much thinner and less durable the council rubbish bags had become. A comment from someone on the condition of the china kept for village functions became a lengthy discussion on the best route to the new Marks and Spencers on the Bournemouth ring road. A suggestion that the roof should be checked by a local builder blew into a full-scale account of the problem Eileen and Colin had had with the thatchers while they were away on holiday in Spain, and then swerved into the question of whether Brittany ferries still ran their service from Plymouth to Santander.

At last, at half past ten, kindly Richard White, the chairman, brought the meeting to a close and Belinda heaved herself out of her chair, desperate to get home, have a bath and go to bed. She was not going to offer to help wash up.

'Are you all right, Belinda?' asked Eileen as she handed her her coat at the door. 'You seem a bit quiet tonight.'

'Do I?' She knew it was a gentle rebuke, that she had not made enough effort to be bright and chatty. 'I had a busy weekend. I was in Suffolk with my parents.'

'Oh, I see. How are they? Old people are such an anxiety!' Eileen did not stop for an answer. 'Colin said he saw you on Thursday evening. At the Fox? They have the Rotary meeting there every month.'

'Oh really?' Belinda's heart sank. There was no use denying it. 'Yes, I was there. Having a drink with a friend.'

'Victor Bradshaw, Colin said.'

'Yes, that's right,' said Belinda, thinking, thank you very much and fuck off, Colin.

'Well, that was nice for you, although I've heard he's quite a one for the ladies.'

'Really?' Belinda forced a bright laugh. 'Well, I wouldn't know anything about that. Now I must go. Sorry. I'm rather tired, that's all. You know what Mondays are like.'

She saw that Eileen was about to launch into an unrelated topic and so said a hasty goodnight and bolted down the path to her car. Of course she doesn't know what Mondays are like, she thought as she drove away. She's never had to do a day's work in her life, and what did she mean by her remark about Victor? Memories of James Redpath came forcing their way back into her mind. Not another one, she thought. Not another charmer. I couldn't face it.

When she opened the back door, there was no sign of Jess. The sitting room was in darkness and the fire had burned to a few glowing embers but the television was on and then she saw that Jess was curled up on the sofa.

'Hi,' she said, without looking up. 'How was the meeting?'

'Don't ask,' said Belinda. 'Did Izzy go to bed all right?'

'Yeah, of course. Why shouldn't she? By the way, you had a telephone call from your boyfriend.'

'What?' Belinda paused halfway to straighten the chair cushions and pick the newspaper off the floor.

'Your garage man. Hannibal Lecter or whatever his name is.'

'Victor?'

'That's the one. He said will you give him a ring tomorrow. Something about Friday night.'

'Oh,' said Belinda. 'Oh, thank you.'

'You're welcome,' said Jess, getting up and turning off the television. 'There's never anything on but crap,' she said. 'I'm going to bed. Goodnight.'

If Belinda had not been thinking about Victor she might have noticed that Jess had been crying.

Up in her room Jess looked at her face in the mirror. The bruising was really black now, but at least her eye had opened a bit and she could see a little through the slit between the lids. It looked much worse than it felt. Her other eye was red, too, as was her face, which looked hot and swollen. She hated to cry and hardly ever did, but tonight was an exception. The row she had had with Tom was unexpected and bitter and she found it hard to get hold of exactly what it had been about. It was like trying to grasp something slippery and unseen under water. You knew it was there, could feel it, but could not get enough of a grip to bring it to the surface.

She had been pissed off with him ever since he had told her about going to Quatt Lodge and meeting the Ludmylla girl, but she knew that none of that was his fault. Then there was the message on his answer machine. That wasn't his fault either, but it felt as if he was conniving behind her back. Then she'd heard from Moira that he had been in the pub with another woman. They had schooled horses together all that morning and he hadn't said a word about it. It had made her feel such a fool, and Moira had loved every moment of it.

When he had telephoned her tonight to ask if she would come and help him with his sheep tomorrow afternoon after work, she had let him have it.

'What the fuck are you playing at?' she had demanded. He had hedged and that made her madder than ever. It was the one thing that annoyed her about him. He would never come straight out with things if he thought he could avoid giving offence. Too often this seemed like weakness. When she found out that it was Karen Bearsden he'd been having lunch with she had been even angrier.

'I can't understand you,' she cried. 'You know how I feel about all of that, about them. All right, their bloody dogs worried your sheep, but that doesn't mean you have to start seeing the woman in secret!'

'Don't be ridiculous!' Tom shouted back. 'I'm not seeing her! For God's sake, Jess. I met her for lunch in the public bar of the Three Tuns. That's hardly a hanging offence.'

'Why? Why did you?'

'Because she asked me!' said Tom. 'She was very insistent and I couldn't get out of it!'

'Oh fuck off!' snarled Jess. 'You are so pathetic! Why didn't you tell her that you couldn't? Tell her where she could put her bloody lunch? You must have wanted to go!'

'I did not! I didn't want to at all!'

'Then why did you?'

This went on and on, and none of Tom's protests convinced Jess that he wasn't sucking up to the Bearsdens behind her back. She did not really believe that Tom was interested in Karen, but his lunch with her felt like treachery and she still smarted from her humiliation in front of Moira.

She had put the telephone down on him in the end and then sat hugging her knees on the sofa and bawled. Tom, of all people, she thought, wallowing in her misery. She'd thought she could depend on Tom.

When the telephone rang again she was certain it was him calling back to try and make it up, but it was her mother's lover boy, or whatever he was, sounding keen and then disappointed to find Belinda was out. Whatever was her mother thinking of? Wasn't life complicated enough already, and why on earth did she want a boyfriend at her age? The disaster she had had with the first one should have put her off for life.

Tom was feeling equally miserable. Jess was utterly impossible when she was in one of these moods and there had been nothing he could say to convince her that none of this had been his fault. Of course, with the advantage of hindsight, he would have come clean and told her that he was meeting Karen Bearsden. He had had the opportunity while they were riding together in the morning, but the reason he hadn't done so was because he knew it would upset her. In trying to avoid that, he had made things much worse.

The way she put it made him sound weak and easily pushed around, and he feared there was a bit of truth in that. With three bossy sisters and a domineering mother he had always found it easier to acquiesce, and Karen Bearsden had been similarly controlling. He had regretted agreeing to meet her at the time and even more so now, but he could not see that it was such a major offence on his part.

He put on his coat and boots and called to Meg and went out to the yard to check on his horses. The sky had cleared and there was a bright sprinkling of stars and a sliver of new moon, but Tom did not notice. He filled buckets and straightened rugs automatically, feeling miserable and preoccupied. Just when he had imagined that things were going so well between him and Jess, this ridiculous argument cropped up out of nowhere and he was buggered if he knew how to make things better. He hated hurting Jess and because she had made him feel guilty, he needed to justify what he had done, but it did not make him feel any better. It did not cheer him up to tell himself that she was irrational and obstinate and made no effort to see things from his point of view.

As he worked, faithful old Meg trotted backwards and forwards at his heels, touching his hand now and then with her long nose, but Tom was oblivious to her attempts to comfort him.

'So,' said Belinda on the telephone to Dinka, 'contrary to what I said to you, I'm going out with Victor again. I telephoned him from work and said yes, I would go on Friday. He's collecting me at seven o'clock and we're going to a concert in Sherborne Abbey and then afterwards to dinner. It's our first proper date, really. Last time was only for a quick drink in a pub.'

'You must have liked him then. Good first impressions are terribly important.'

'Yes, I do like him. I really do. I've struggled since not to think about him too much.'

'Don't get carried away,' said Dinka sternly. 'One moment I'm pleading with you to go out and the next I'm advising you to put on the brakes. Emotionally, at least.'

Belinda knew that Dinka was thinking of James Redpath and the brief road she had taken between euphoria and despair as their relationship had run its course.

'I've already been spotted with him by someone from the village and warned that he's a ladies' man.'

'Is he?'

'I don't know. He was happily married for years, or so he says. I've no idea what he's been up to since. He's sort of skilful with women. That's the right word. I think he probably likes women's company and he knows how to deal with things. I told you he kissed me?'

'I should bloody well hope he did. It would have been a very bad sign if he hadn't. You don't want a man who thinks of you like his sister or, even worse, his mother, and some do, I can assure you!'

'I'm in my usual state now,' confessed Belinda. 'Getting nervous about going out. I mean, he seemed keen and everything and he gave me some nice compliments, but I just hope it goes well. Now I have to decide what to wear to this concert which will be full of Dorset's grandes dames. I don't want to look like a relic from a bygone age and it's so long since I've had to dress for a man.'

'Don't go overboard,' advised Dinka. 'He obviously likes you as you are. Natural looking. Don't be tempted by the sequins and slit to the navel option.'

'I wouldn't do that, anyway. Not for Sherborne Abbey!'

'Well, good luck. I shall want a blow by blow account. By the way, I don't think I told you that I'm going into hospital for a few days,' said Dinka, changing the subject. 'I'm having a bit of surgery, a little discreet nip and tuck while Javier is away in Spain visiting his family.'

'Oh, Dinka, why? You're so lovely as you are! Why put yourself through it?'

'Don't start. It's worth every penny.'

'But I read yesterday in the newspaper that lots of these clinics face prosecution from dissatisfied customers. Cosmetic surgeons are eight times more likely to be sued than other surgeons. Aren't they all struck-off doctors, or the sort that have created their own qualifications? You know, they've swum a width of the swimming pool, got the certificate, and then spent the afternoon at the kitchen table with the Tippex and a John Bull printing set.'

'Don't be ridiculous, Belinda. I am going to the top man in Harley Street. I'll be in for three days and then have a week off work. By the time Javier comes home I shall be looking ten years younger.'

Eventually you won't, thought Belinda. Eventually, it will catch up with you.

'Anyway,' went on Dinka, 'at least I'm honest about it. I don't pretend that it's just the enhancing effect of the new lipstick I'm wearing when I appear wrinkle-free, with my forehead dragged back behind my ears.'

'No, you're horribly honest, I'll give you that,' agreed Belinda.

'So think of me. When you're under your lover, I'll be under the knife,' said Dinka.

'Please! It's our second date!'

'Well, don't waste time. It's been clinically proven that sex is good for you, and you must be getting very rusty indeed.'

Yes, I must, thought Belinda when she rang off. It was one of the things that worried her. Was she really up for it? She wouldn't know until she tried.

On Thursday afternoon when Jess collected Izzy from Maureen's, she stopped off at the little supermarket in Sharston to get something for supper. Izzy was full of what she and Ben and Darren had been doing, which seemed to be mostly watching videos and then throwing stones at the glass of an old cold frame at the bottom of More-Ian's garden.

'Darren doesn't like girls,' she confided to Jess as they parked the car and walked hand in hand to the shop. 'There's a big girl called Kelly in his class and she sits on the boys and kisses them for punishment. Darren says it's disgusting!'

'Yuk! I expect it is,' said Jess. 'He likes you though, doesn't he?'

'Yes, but I'm little.'

'I see. What shall we have for supper? I can never think of anything. How about chops? I could do lamb chops. What else do we need? Potatoes, lav rolls, bread, Marmite,' she read off the list that Belinda had stuck to the fridge. 'Don't pull my arm, Iz! What do you want?'

'Look, Mummy! It's Mikey! There's Mikey and his mummy!'

Bearing down on them from the opposite direction was a tall, dark woman pushing a full trolley of shopping, followed by two little girls and an older boy slouching along behind, wearing a baseball cap.

Jess had only a second to take in the scene. It was the boy she focused on. Even with his cap pulled low and his face averted, she recognised him instantly. Izzy's double was coming towards them. His cap covered his distinctive hair, but the likeness between the two children was still striking. Even his slow, dragging, reluctant walk was the same.

Jess swallowed her panic and turned to look at the woman who was tall and slim, wearing jeans and polished brown boots and a suede jacket. Her wiry dark hair was held back in a slide and she was wearing dark glasses.

Shit, she thought, hoping that they had not been seen and wondering if there was any chance of escape, but the woman pulled up alongside and pushed the glasses to the top of her head. She looked hard at Izzy and then at Jess. There was a moment's pause. Time seemed frozen as Jess waited. She heard the splutter of a motorbike on the road and the bang of a car door. A pigeon clattered noisily on a rooftop.

'Hi,' said the woman. 'I've been wanting to meet you.' She had a soft American accent, girlish and gentle and not what Jess had expected.

'Have you?' said Jess, not trusting her own voice.

'Hello, Mikey,' said Izzy shyly.

'Hi,' he said in a bored tone, unwrapping a sweet from his pocket and putting it in his mouth.

'Goodness, that's quite a black eye you have there,' Karen said with a smile. She seemed perfectly at ease while Jess's heart was beating so rapidly she could hardly speak. 'Is this your little girl? I met her out riding last week.'

'Yes,' said Jess. 'She said.'

'I'm Karen Bearsden,' the woman went on. 'We've come to live at Quatt Lodge, and I've been hoping Mikey might meet other children to ride with.'

'Izzy doesn't go out on her own. She's too little,' said Jess. She felt more confident now. The woman's completely normal manner made it easier to be the same. 'Why doesn't he join the Pony Club? Look, I'm sorry, but I'm in an awful rush.' She made to move on, but Karen stopped her.

'She can some over and ride with us then,' she said. It sounded less like an invitation than a command. 'What's your name, darling?' she addressed Izzy.

'Isobel,' said Izzy clearly, looking up, her little face bright as a daisy.

'Isobel what?' said Karen.

'Isobel Haddon,' said Izzy. 'And this is my mummy. Her name is Jess.'

'Jess Haddon?' said Karen. 'Why, isn't that a coincidence! Johnnie and I were talking about you the other weekend.'

'Really?' said Jess in a stony voice.

'Yeah. We saw your name on the racecard at Black Forest Lodge. He said you worked at the same yard where we intend to keep some horses. He said he knows you from way back.'

'Yes,' said Jess evasively. 'Not that well. I looked after his horse for a while, that's all.'

'He spoke very fondly of you,' said Karen, smiling pleasantly. Jess saw she had powerfully white and even American teeth.

'Well, that was nice of him, but if you don't mind . . .'

'Yes, you're in a hurry. I must let you go. Nice to meet you, Jess. Nice to meet you, Isobel. How old are you, by the way?'

'Six but nearly seven,' said Izzy. Mikey turned away in disgust.

'You'd like to come over and ride, wouldn't you?' said Karen.

Izzy nodded politely.

'Well, we must arrange it, mustn't we, Jess? Hope that eye gets better!'

'Thanks. Come on, Izzy,' said Jess and pulled her by the hand.

As the two families parted, she heard Mikey say crossly, 'Mom! What did you say *that* for! She's six. She's only a baby. I don't want to go riding with a baby!'

Izzy looked up at Jess, her face clouded over with disappointment. 'Did you hear he said I'm a baby, Mummy? I'm not a baby, am I? Six isn't a baby!'

Jess squeezed her hand. 'No, of course it's not. He's a horrid little boy and you don't need to have anything to do with him.'

Chapter Eleven

It was a relief to Jess that Belinda had not noticed she was upset the other night. She did not want to have to explain that she had had a row with Tom. She did not want to talk to anyone about it. On the yard she kept out of Moira's way, ignored her smirks and got on with her work, managing to be busy when Tom turned up to ride so that she did not have to speak to him. It was hard to know how to extricate herself from the position she had put herself in by slamming down the telephone. She told herself that the next move should be his, she would wait for him to say he was sorry.

She constantly checked her telephone for messages and when she knew he was on the yard she made sure that she was out of the way but that he could find her if he wanted. This made her feel nervy and on edge and she longed to restore normality between them but was too stubborn to take the first step herself. It was a stupid way to behave, and she knew it. She missed Tom already and wished that they could just rewind what had happened like a tape, and start afresh. The biggest difficulty was that when she talked to him again, the subject of Karen Bearsden would have to come up and that brought her back to her need to forget that the Bearsdens existed.

As she mucked out, her mind was free to range over what had happened. The scene in the supermarket car park, her feeling of being cornered, the wretched boy in the baseball cap and Karen's insistent questions went round and round her head. What was the woman playing at? What was her game? Much as she needed to be secretive, Jess longed to be able to talk it over with someone in a dispassionate way, to pick over the possible explanations until her mind was clear, instead of the muddle of tangled possibilities and dead ends that confused her now.

Her only recourse was to forget it all, blank out what had happened, believe that the Bearsdens would disappear as suddenly as they had forced themselves back into her life, but she knew she was deluding herself. Things might go quiet for a week or two. They would return to London at the end of half-term, the boy would go back to school, but they would be back.

This was such a horrible certainty that she could do nothing but shove it to the back of her mind and think instead about the coming weekend's racing. Ken had decided which horses he would run and she had five reasonable rides to look forward to. Saturday's meeting was at Barbary Castle in a sweep of the Marlborough Downs, a wide open course, freezing when the weather was miserable and glorious when the sun shone. Sunday was at Badbury Rings, where the course was in the lee of a great ancient earthworks on the Dorset hills. With any luck, on the day, she might pick up some extra rides at both meetings.

This afternoon she was leaving Izzy an extra hour or two with Lisa while she went to work Fancy at the Dawlishes'.

The little mare had been stiff after her fall but was ready to start schooling again and Jess wanted to make sure that she would have the ride on her next outing. She felt convinced that Fancy had it in her to win a race this season and Jess wanted it to be with her. It had to be. She had to prove that she could get on a horse as green and as problematic as Fancy and get her right, and win. That would show them, her mother and her sister and Mary, and the bloody Bearsden woman, and Tom and Iz, and everyone else, that she was good. That Jess Haddon had what it took. That she was worth something.

This is what she would concentrate on and leave the rest of it well alone. Let Tom find the way to put things right between them. The Bearsdens could bugger off. She wasn't going to let any of them get in her way.

However, as she was going out of the kitchen after the staff coffee break, Mary called her back to deliver a bombshell.

'Jess, can I keep you a minute? I want to check some paperwork in the injury book. Can you remember the date you broke your collar bone last year?'

Jess stayed, surprised, as the others trooped out. All that had been dealt with long ago. She stood by the kitchen table while Mary fiddled about with a cardboard file of papers. Then when they were alone she looked up, directly into Jess's face, and instantly Jess knew that this was about something else. Mary's tone changed to confidential.

'Sit down, Jess,' she said. 'There's something I think you should know.'

Jess watched her mouth with its pink lipstick dried into

tiny, powdery lines of colour and wondered what was coming.

'What?' she said, sitting down, her heart thumping. 'What is it?'

'I had a telephone call yesterday,' said Mary, looking down and straightening the pages of the *Racing Post*. 'Rather a peculiar call. It was from Karen Bearsden, Johnnie's wife.'

Jess's mouth went dry. She felt the blood rushing to her face.

'Yeah?' she said, trying to sound nonchalant.

'She was asking a lot of questions about you, Jess. Personal questions. About Izzy and so on. She asked who Izzy's father was.'

Jess swallowed hard, furious now. 'Of all the bloody cheek! What the hell has it to do with her?'

'She said that she had met you and that you were very offhand.'

'What did you say?'

'I said I didn't think that there was one.'

'But what did she ring you for? It can't have been just to discuss me.'

'She was giving me an update on the horses they want to keep here. It will be next season now, but they intend to bring some over from America where her family are big in bloodstock, apparently.'

'I see,' said Jess bitterly. 'They would be, wouldn't they? They'd have to be big in something. And I just cropped up, did I, in the conversation?'

'Something like that,' said Mary evasively.

'There's more, Mary, isn't there? You're not telling me it all.'

'Well, she annoyed me, actually.'

'Why?'

'I wasn't going to tell you this, Jess, but she said that if they placed the horses here, with us, she and Johnnie would want to be reassured that you had nothing to do with them, either on the yard or racing. She said your attitude made you unsuitable – or words to that effect.'

Jess felt her mouth drop open. 'Why? What the hell have I done?'

'Well, owners can always say who they want to ride their horses in races, as you know, but we've never had anyone try to dictate how we run the yard before. It sounded like a bargain. You know – you'll get our horses if you let us call the shots.'

'What did you say?' Jess knew how important a big owner could be to a small yard.

Mary faltered. 'Oh, just that Ken and I would have to discuss it, but that we had absolute confidence in you. Something like that.' She looked at Jess. 'What have you done to put her back up? Jess, you mustn't take this wrong, but you haven't been seeing anything of Johnnie, have you?'

'What?' Jess cried. 'No, I bloody haven't, Mary! I know what you mean and it's absolutely not true. I don't want anything to do with any of the bloody family!'

'The feeling is mutual, then,' said Mary drily.

'Yeah, well, that's fine by me. But when I met Mrs Bearsden for the first time a day ago, she didn't even know who I was, and when she found out, she was all over me like a rash. Izzy must go and ride with her boy, all that sort of thing. Next thing, she turns on me. Why?'

Mary shrugged. 'I'm not in a position to know,' she said. 'I've only told you this because it needed some sort of explanation. I thought you might be able to give me one, but you obviously can't. I shall have to tell Ken, but I won't mention it to anyone else. You don't want this sort of thing being talked about.'

Jess looked at her and knew what she meant. When owners warned someone off their horses, word soon got round the racing fraternity and it never looked good.

'Right,' she said, in a pinched, tight voice. 'Thanks, Mary, but I'm not going to let her do this to me. I'm going to have it out with Mrs Johnnie Bearsden. I'm not having her going around bad-mouthing me like that.'

'I shouldn't do that, Jess. It's all a long way off. It's next season we're talking about. Just let it be. I expect it will all have blown over by then.' Mary did not want trouble, Jess could see that. She did not want to offend a prospective owner.

Jess stood up. 'OK,' she said, 'but I need to do something. I need to think about it but I'm going to find out what's behind all this.' She reached behind her head and rewound the band which held her hair back. Her face was red and defiant as she pulled on her coat and went out.

Mary sighed and took off her glasses and put them into their case. Jess was so stubborn, pig-headed even. It was obvious to her what the cause of the trouble was. Mrs Bearsden had got wind of the old rumours, had found out about Izzy, done some sums and she did not like the conclusion she had come to. That was it. Plain as a pikestaff. Mary didn't think it was fair, that was why she had warned Jess. After all, the poor girl had been left holding the baby, literally in this case, and life for a single mother was hard enough. She didn't see why she should go on taking the flak. But why didn't Jess just tell the truth about Izzy's father? They would all support her. After all, she had been with them since she had left school as a gangly teenager, tongue-tied and awkward and only at ease on a horse.

Mary remembered how pretty and fresh and young she had been with her delicate colouring and long hair. No wonder she had caught Johnnie Bearsden's eye. He had been quite a player back then, with a wife and child in London, dashing backwards and forwards in his fast car, often with a brother army officer. Johnnie had made a lot of Jess because she looked after his winning mare, Daisy Belle, who, thanks to her efforts, often collected the best turned-out prize in the paddock before the race. He had liked having his horse led up by such a pretty girl. It had all seemed innocent enough at the time, and at the end of the season Johnnie had sold the horse, left the Army and gone with his wife to America and that had been that. Except that Jess was pregnant.

Mary sighed. From then on Jess would say nothing. Just like today. It would have been so much easier if she had come clean from the start. Everything could have been sorted out and Izzy would know who her father was. After all, these days it happened all the time. There was little stigma attached to an illegitimate child. Still, there was nothing she could do about it. Jess, as usual, would go her own way.

On Thursday morning, Tom went to a farm sale. It was the eighth dairy farm to have gone out of business in the Blackmore Vale in the last few months and the stock and the milking parlour were being auctioned on the farm. It was sad to see the old stone barns and yards redundant after hundreds of years. Thomas Hardy would have known this farm, maybe walked these fields on his way home to Sturminster Newton. Vale of the Little Dairies, he called it.

The talk amongst the local farmers was gloomy. A fine herd was going under the hammer and each cow was known by name and nature to the cowman, Ron, who stood in the makeshift ring and showed off his animals as they were herded through the cattle crush by the auctioneer's men. He had probably calved each one, thought Tom, leaning on the rails, and their mothers and grandmothers, and now they were all going. According to the man standing next to him, a crooked old farmer who looked so generally green and mossy that he might have been growing out of the ground, Ron had got another job as head herdsman on a farm a few villages away, and a cottage with it, so at least he would still be able to go on with the work he loved. He was one of the lucky ones.

Tom watched Ron as he moved a cow around the ring so that the bidders could get a good view of her. He was a tall, angular man with a grizzled beard and the face of a saint, wearing a baseball cap and green overalls. He was slow-moving and gentle, hardly raising his voice, and each animal, distressed by the throng of people and the noise, became calm and reassured by his familiar presence as he placed a guiding hand on her rump.

Bidding was brisk and, as with all things, one man's loss was another's gain. There were several farmers Tom recognised at the ringside, restocking after a TB cull, and they were fortunate to have the opportunity to buy into this quality herd.

Tom was interested in picking up a few bull calves to rear and sell on, but the bidding rose out of his price range. He watched for a bit and then went for a cup of tea and a bacon roll at the mobile catering van in the yard. He did not recognise the two men in front of him in the queue but they were obviously farmers, in their battered green waxed coats and working trousers. One wore a woollen hat and the other a flat cap and both had the fresh, red complexion of men who work outdoors in all weathers. Their wives were with them, making an outing of it. Both were sturdy women, dressed like their husbands in working clothes and unfashionable rubber boots, who probably took an equal share in the farmwork. They were marking prices in their catalogues, keeping a sharp eye on the bidding and enjoying the chance of a get-together and a gossip. Farming could be a lonely business and with the local cattle markets closed, farm sales provided a rare opportunity to catch up with neighbours and friends.

They are an endangered species, these small farmers, Tom thought, as he took his plastic mug and roll and went to sit on some bales in the Dutch barn. They're like the Eskimos or the American Indians, struggling to maintain a way of life in a changed and alien world. Only the adaptable would survive and the countryside would never be the same again. Agribusiness was taking over, with land a commodity like any other in a share portfolio, or parcelled off and farmed as a hobby by Londoners. It wouldn't be sweated over and cursed and loved in the old way, and it wouldn't shape men any more, as these people had been shaped.

'Cheer up,' said a voice. 'You've got a face like a wet weekend!'

Tom looked up to see Pete Dawlish in a check woollen jacket and woollen hat standing in front of him.

'Oh, hi,' he said unenthusiastically. 'How's things?'

'All right,' said Pete, sitting down next to him and stretching out his trunk-like legs in dirty work jeans. 'What are you here for, then?'

'Thought I might pick up a few calves, but they're going for more than I wanted to pay.'

'Oh, aye.'

'And you?'

'This and that,' said Pete evasively. It was all right to ask other people their business but not to divulge your own.

'How's the mare?' asked Tom.

'Looking well. That uppity lass of yours is giving her a pipe-opener this evening. We've got her entered at Cothelstone a week Saturday. Dad wants it to be her last race this season.'

Lass of mine! thought Tom. 'What she needs,' he said on an impulse, 'is to school upside another horse. That's what blows her mind at the moment, having something galloping and jumping next to her. She's so inexperienced, she gets distracted and makes mistakes. You should ask Ken Andrews if you can bring her over to his practice jumps and school her with some other horses.'

'Yeah?' said Pete, pulling a face.

'He'd charge a bit for the use of the fences, but it would be worth it. Look, I've got his number here in my phone. Give him a ring now. I'm going over there this afternoon to school that good mare of Mrs Toynbee's. Your mare could go alongside.' Ah, he thought. Jess won't be able to avoid me now.

Pete Dawlish was not a man to be hurried. 'I'll have to ask Dad,' he said. 'The old bugger will have something to say about it.'

'Is he here?'

'Yeah, he's watching the bidding.'

'Go and ask him. I'll be here for ten minutes or so, finishing this.' Tom indicated his roll. 'Then I'm off.'

Pete Dawlish stood up. 'I don't know. She's a bugger to load in the trailer. Gets right sweated up. She struck out and caught Dad on the knee last time.'

'Then all the more reason to box her up and take her over. It's all good experience for her.'

'Yeah.' Pete Dawlish shrugged. He did not want to accept advice, but what Tom said made sense. 'All right,' he said, 'I'll go and ask Dad. I'll be back in a minute.'

Tom watched as he lumbered off towards the sale ring, then sat and finished his roll, enjoying the weak sunshine. Opposite, the stock doves jostled on the tiled ridge of the roof of the old cow byre. Was he right to have interfered? Would Jess be even more annoyed with him? But his suggestion had been genuine. It was exactly what the little mare needed before her next race.

A few minutes later Pete was back, his large red face impassive. He stood in front of Tom and nodded his head.

'Yeah,' he said. 'He'll give Ken a ring. We've done it before, mind. Taken our horses over there to school.' He didn't want Tom to get the impression that they had been influenced by his advice. Tom stood up and wiped his mouth with the back of his hand.

'OK,' he said. 'I'll be seeing you.'

'Aye.'

As Tom walked back to his Land Rover, he was glad he had done something to break the impasse with Jess without it seeming so. It was stupid to let it go on any longer. He got in the cab, pushing Meg off his jacket, and was turning on the engine when his telephone rang.

'Hello?'

'Is that Tom?'

'Yeah. Ludmylla?' He recognised the hesitating, foreign accent.

'Tom, I telephone you because I lose the dogs again. I am very worried by this.'

'When? When did you lose them?' Shit, thought Tom, looking at his watch. He could do without this.

'Just now. I go to feed them, but they run out through the door. They will not come back to me.'

'Where is everybody else? Where is Mrs Bearsden?'

'She has gone back to London today.'

'What about the gamekeeper? He was going to look after the dogs, wasn't he?'

'Mrs Bearsden says he collects them this afternoon, but now I lose them.'

'Shit! Well, where are they now? Did you see where they went?'

'They are not far away, in wood. I hear them.'

'Can't you catch them? They'll come if you call.'

'They will not come. They run from me and I do not like to enter the wood.'

'Shit!' said Tom again.

There was nothing else for it. 'OK, I'll have to come round now. I'm not that far away. It will take me about fifteen minutes.'

'Please come quick.'

'I'm on my way. Go outside and call them again, Ludmylla. Rattle their bowls!'

'I do not understand! What is "rattle bowls"?'

'OK. I'm coming.'

As he drove, swinging his Land Rover along the twisting lanes between the high hedges, aware that at any moment he might meet a stock wagon coming the other way en route for the farm sale, he felt annoyed with himself for a second time for getting involved with the Bearsden set-up. It was stupid of him to have given the girl his telephone number. He couldn't remember now why he had done it, except that at the time she had seemed pathetic and alone and in need of a friend and he had been moved by her wonderful piano playing. Well, he would give her short shrift this time. He was too busy to go buggering off on these mercy missions, and it was annoying that the bloody Bearsdens, with all their money and swank, couldn't be more responsible about their dogs.

It was in this mood that he turned off by the gatehouse for Quatt Lodge and drove too fast down the drive. To the right and left, the high iron railings enclosed the old deer park where considerable tree-cutting was taking place. The old oaks were undergoing radical surgery and piles of timber were stacked all along the edge of the fence. Johnnie and his wife were already making their mark on the neglected old place where little had been done for the last fifty years. Ahead of him, the house was encircled by the great, gloomy yews but when he drew up in the stable yard he could see that the builders had now got scaffolding up against the south front and that part of the roof had been stripped, ready to be re-tiled. A row of skips was parked on the front gravel and it was clear that extensive work was under way, although this morning there was no sign of any activity.

He got out and banged the door. Ludmylla was nowhere to be seen but in the stable yard one of the doors stood open and he saw that inside there were old-fashioned loose boxes. He stood in the doorway and was struck by the lost grandeur of the old days when this whole yard would have been full of hunters and five or six grooms would have been employed. The loose boxes were partitioned by tongue-and-groove oak boards and topped by iron rails. The floor was cobbled and a continuous oak manger ran along the far wall. Tom would give anything to have such a yard, but it would never be used again for its original purpose, even with Bearsden money. Those days were gone. Now there was one incompetent foreign girl left in charge.

The dogs had obviously been kennelled in the furthest box – there were two dog beds and water bowls, and two feed bowls were upset on the ground in the passage outside, amongst scattered dog biscuits which Meg was collecting. He supposed that the girl had opened the door to put down the bowls and perhaps the dogs had jumped up and she had lost her nerve.

He went back outside and set off round the corner where the garden ended and the park began. The first pheasant covert was only a few hundred yards away and judging by the explosions of birds clattering into the air from every direction, the dogs were in there and working hard amongst the trees. He started to whistle and yell and after a moment or two the first spaniel appeared and ran to meet him, wagging her tail joyfully, soon to be followed by the second. Bloody hell, he thought in exasperation, it would have taken someone only half competent to get them back. Where was the wretched girl?

'Come on, you,' he said, as Meg greeted the two repro-bates with disdain. The two dogs slunk towards Tom, stom-achs lowered to the ground, in abject, slavering apology. At least he had them now, and they followed him obediently back to the stables where he shut them in.

There was still no sign of Ludmylla so he went to the back door and looked through the kitchen window. To his surprise he saw her sitting at the table smoking a cigarette, staring into space. He knocked on the glass and she looked up, startled, and got up to open the door.

'Oh, Tom,' she said. 'You have the dogs?'

'Yes,' he said. 'I've shut them back in the stables. Look,

Ludmylla, I can't go on doing this. You've got to look after them properly.' His voice was perfectly reasonable but to his dismay her narrow brown eyes filled with tears which quickly brimmed over and trickled down her cheeks. Theatrically, she threw herself back onto the chair and sank her head onto her arms on the table. Tom found himself looking down at the cocoa-coloured roots of her yellow hair.

Jesus, he thought. How do I keep landing myself in situations like this?

'Look,' he said, in a pleading voice, 'everything is all right. The dogs are shut up safely. Just don't let them out again. That's all.'

'It is not only the dogs,' wailed Ludmylla in a stifled voice. 'It is everything.' She looked up and her sharp little face was scarlet with emotion. 'I do not like it here. I am not happy.'

'Why do you stay then? Go home if you don't like it.'

'I have to stay. I need money. There is no money in my country. My family needs money.'

Oh, God, thought Tom. I'm going to hear about a sick mother and a drunken father and all the hungry brothers and sisters needing an education. He felt his sympathies were being manipulated.

'My child. I need money for my child.'

'Child?' said Tom, surprised. He hadn't expected that.

'Yes. My little angel. She is six years old. She lives with my mother.'

'I see. Well, how long are you here for? In England, I mean?'

'Two years. I save much money.'

'Two years? Without seeing your little girl? That's a bit hard, isn't it?'

Ludmylla shrugged. 'I must. We need money. We must live.' She sniffed and wiped her nose on the sleeve of her sweater.

'What about your husband?'

'No husband,' said Ludmylla.

Oh, God, thought Tom. Not another one. He felt stumped.

'What do you want to do, then? Get another job? Leave the Bearsdens?'

'No! No!' said Ludmylla. 'This is good job. Good money, but I do not like this house. I do not like it here on my own.'

Tom couldn't see what he could do to help. 'Have you told Mrs Bearsden that you don't like it, that you would rather be in London?'

Ludmylla shrugged dismissively. 'It is my job. She tells me she wants me here. I must stay. Later it will be better. She get me a car and sometimes children and nanny are with me. Mrs Bearsden is a kind lady. I do not complain.'

'Oh, I see.' Tom felt relieved. It had been almost automatic to cast Karen into the role of exploiter, and for Ludmylla's sake he was glad to find this wasn't true.

'You will be able to get out a bit then.' It was a silly thing to say. Where the hell was she supposed to go, stuck in the country miles from anywhere, and knowing no one? 'You could come to a pub skittles night, if you like. We play a lot of skittles round here. It would be a way of meeting people.'

'Skittles, what is this?' she asked.

285

Tom found himself giving a demonstration, trying to explain the principles of the game. Ludmylla shook her head in total bewilderment and they both laughed.

'You'll have to come and see for yourself,' said Tom. 'We've got a match next Wednesday. There's a league, you see, in the Blackmore Vale. We're playing at the pub in Bishops Barton. I could come and pick you up.'

'Yes?' Ludmylla looked doubtful. She made a face. 'OK,' she said without much enthusiasm, shrugging her thin shoulders.

God, thought Tom. He was only trying to be kind and from her manner you would have thought it was the other way round.

'I'll telephone you on Tuesday evening. OK? To check that you still want to come.'

'OK,' she said again.

'Anyway,' said Tom. Seeing that she had cheered up a bit he felt it was safe to mention the spaniels again. 'What's happened to the keeper? He told me he was going to look after the dogs.'

'He had to go to a funeral. In Yorkshire. His father die. He returns today.'

'I see. Well, you won't have to look after them for much longer then.'

'No,' said Ludmylla, lighting another cigarette, and drawing deeply on it. 'Thank you, Tom, for coming. It is a big help.' She narrowed her eyes. 'You have a girlfriend?' she asked.

'Yes,' said Tom firmly. 'Yes, I do.' This was one thing he wanted to make absolutely clear. He didn't want any more grief from Jess, any more accusations of duplicity. 'I have to go now. I will telephone you on Tuesday evening.'

At that moment, as if on cue, the telephone in the kitchen rang and they both looked at it and laughed. Ludmylla picked it up and listened. Tom could hear a female voice on the other end.

'No,' said Ludmylla. 'Mrs Bearsden is not here. She gone back to London. Who is it speaking, please? She tell me to write down all names.'

Tom hesitated, wanting to catch her eye to mouth goodbye, but she was busy with a biro and a pad, trying to make sense of the caller's name which was being spelled out for her. As he hovered, waiting to go, he could not helping seeing that she had written 'Jessica Hadden' with much crossing out. When she put down the receiver he said, 'It's spelled with an "o", not an "e".'

'What?' Ludmylla did not understand.

'Haddon,' said Tom. 'Look, like this.' All the time he was thinking, with deep unease, bloody hell, what does Jess want with Karen Bearsden?

When Ken Andrews came across the yard to tell Jess that he had had Dawlish on the telephone and that they were bringing Fancy over to school upside another horse, she stopped what she was doing and leaned on her pitchfork, squinting into the pale February sunshine. 'OK,' she said. 'That's good. It's what she needs and saves me the trek over to their farm.'

'Tom will go out with you on Cinders. She needs a

practice jump before her race on Saturday. Mrs Toynbee's going to come over to watch.'

'Oh,' said Jess, thinking instead of Tom. It would mean having to face him again. She knew it would have to happen sooner or later, but she needed to prepare herself, to work out how to handle it. And what Mary had told her that morning was still churning round in her mind and what came to her as she went back to mucking out was that she wanted to tell Tom, to share it all with him, to ask him to help her. She could understood now how Karen Bearsden had pressurised him to meet her for lunch. She could see how it would happen. Kind, nice Tom, who did his best to accommodate people, would not have it in him to hold out against a determined woman like that.

When she had telephoned Quatt Lodge that morning, determined to confront Karen Bearsden, she had been ready to do battle. She had nerved herself for it and then that foreign girl had told her that Mrs Bearsden was in London. She did not want to telephone London herself and risk having to talk to Johnnie, and neither did she want Karen Bearsden to have her telephone number and to ring her back. She needed to be in control of the moment when they spoke again. Jess wasn't good with words, and if she was not prepared, a sharp and confident person like Karen Bearsden would get the better of her and tie her in knots.

She had never been articulate. Her feelings got stuck somewhere in her chest and she could never say what she felt. She had always had to depend on those she knew well, and those she loved, to understand and to interpret her clumsy and awkward expressions, especially of affection. She knew, for instance, that she should tell Iz how much she loved her. And her mother. She loved Belinda and was so bloody grateful to her, but she did not know how to show it. Her awkwardness about expressing her feelings was like a blocked drain, and her way of dealing with it, this feeling of emotional congestion, was to ride and gallop and jump and race. She had done it when her dad had died and left them helpless and bereft, she had done it when her mother was pathetically in love with a terrible man, she had done it until the life of her unborn and unwanted baby was at risk, and she would do it again now. She would pit herself against Tom this afternoon and ride that little mare as if nothing else mattered. She would go on to gallop and jump and show Karen Bearsden what courage was all about. It was her against the lot of them, and she couldn't see any other way.

She finished mucking out and attacked the stable floor with the yard broom, and as she did so, an idea suddenly came to her. She stopped what she was doing and leaned on the handle. How stupid she had been. Now she saw it all. She saw what it was that was troubling Karen Bearsden and she saw with sudden clarity exactly how high the stakes would be.

The practice session in the afternoon turned out to be Tom's masterstroke. Fancy came out of the Dawlishes' rattling old trailer like a rabbit out of a trap and it had taken Jess ten minutes of walking round to calm her down. She was cantering in circles when Tom joined her on Cinders, with

Carl as a third on Glennie, and the little mare's bright coat was already black with sweat.

She rushed the first couple of fences, fighting for her head and throwing herself over, maddened that she was being held back to keep her place behind the more experienced horses, but gradually she settled. They finished jumping side by side, three abreast, and she was taking off when Jess told her and spreading over the fences, outjumping both the others at the last.

When they pulled up by Ken's truck where Mrs Toynbee and the Dawlish men stood watching, everyone looked pleased.

'Well ridden, Tom,' said old Mrs Toynbee, perched regally on her shooting stick. 'That was lovely, and that's a talented little mare, too, that you're on, Jess. Still a bit green, but you rode her beautifully. How is she bred?' She turned to Ted Dawlish while Jess flushed with pleasure. Mrs Toynbee was one of those grand old ladies who wasn't in the least bit grand with anybody. She and Ted Dawlish began an animated conversation and Jess saw him pass her his hip flask for a nip of something to keep out the cold.

Rhona, who had also been watching, came to walk beside her back to the yard. She patted Fancy's neck and looked up at Jess.

'She's right, the old girl. You did ride well. The mare is starting to trust you, isn't she? She'll be a grand little horse one day as long as they don't let some bloody man spoil her.'

'Thanks, Rhona.' Jess smiled gratefully. She was aware that Rhona, who was not very good at relationships outside work, was a sort of ally, and just at the moment it was important to her to have her support.

Her success was enough to thaw her mood. Later, as they washed the horses down, she told Tom in a rush about Karen Bearsden, and he was glad for the opportunity to heal the stupid rift between them.

As they were talking, heads together, the yard hose splashing noisily between them, Moira came out of the feed room behind them and they both started. They hadn't realised that she was in there, measuring out the afternoon feeds. How much had she heard? The habitual radio was blaring pop music as usual so with any luck their words had been drowned, but Tom didn't like the way she smirked as she went past.

Driving home from Pilates on Thursday evening Belinda went through in her mind what she wanted to do before Victor came to collect her tomorrow night. She had a box of the Ravioli hair colourant amongst her shopping in the back of the car and she would apply it tonight and give herself a manicure too. She still hadn't decided what to wear and if he was going to pick her up from the cottage, she would have to ask him in and offer him a drink and that meant she must wash the kitchen floor and tidy the sitting room. Flowers, too. She must have some jugs of daffodils about the place, and kick Snowy's smelly old bed into the washroom. Like the hair dye, it was all part of an attempt to disguise reality. Or perhaps to enhance it.

Her thoughts turned to Dinka who was being admitted this evening to a London clinic and was perhaps at this moment lying in a white hospital bed thinking nervously about tomorrow when her face would be mapped out with a felt tip pen and the surgeon would pick up his scalpel and make the first incision. It was too horrible to think about. No man was worth it.

Treacherously, she suddenly had a vision of Javier at home in Barcelona, sitting at a pavement cafe with a group of his young friends. Sunshine flooded the scene and the delicate scent of mimosa hung in the air. One of the girls, a dark-haired beauty, was flirting with Javier, tossing her gleaming hair and showing off her smooth, taut stomach beneath her cropped T-shirt. I must stop this at once, thought Belinda. It seemed like disloyalty to even picture such a scene. Poor Dinka. How she must torture herself with similar imaginings.

Her thoughts shifted to her parents. She must go and see them again soon and bully her brothers to do the same so that they established a rota of regular visits. She would have to organise it or it would never get done and she would have to keep pestering Tony and Leo to remind them of their commitment or they would get out of it the first time anything else came up.

It wasn't just that her mother and father needed a watchful eye kept on them; Belinda recognised a longing in herself to achieve a closeness with them, to have the time to sit and talk and absorb something of their spirit before it was too late. I need to know them, she thought, in this quiet lull in their lives and before there is some sort of crisis to be dealt with. I need time and peace just to be with them.

Fat chance of that, she thought as she pulled off the lane beside the cottage and saw that Tom's Land Rover was parked next to Jess's old car. With a shock, she realised that she couldn't remember anything of the last fifteen minutes of the drive home. It was frightening to think how often she drove like an automaton, with her mind engaged elsewhere.

The lights were on in the cottage, the curtains undrawn. Belinda felt relieved that it was Jess's turn to do supper, but when she opened the back door and repelled Snowy's delirious onslaught, Jess and Tom were sitting opposite one another at the kitchen table and there was no sign of any meal in progress. Taking in the scene, she felt instinctively that she had interrupted something important and from their faces she guessed this was a crisis meeting. Oh, no, she thought. What now?

Chapter Twelve

It was Tom who told her, while Jess sat looking blotchily furious.

'Jess has got something fairly heavy to sort out with Karen Bearsden,' he said. 'Apparently she's doing her best to get her jocked off Ken's horses.'

Jess nodded, stabbing at the tablecloth with a fork, like a cross child.

'Stop that, Jess!' said Belinda automatically. 'What do you mean? What has she done?' She sat down next to Jess while Tom recounted the conversation Jess had had with Mary. When he finished, Belinda sat thinking for a moment, trying to make sense of it, and like Mary came to the obvious conclusion that Johnnie's wife had heard the rumours about her husband and Jess.

'So?' she said, not trusting herself to say more.

'Jess tried to telephone her this morning but she had already gone back to London, so we're deciding what to do next.'

Belinda noticed the 'we'. Tom was not usually so presumptuous. Jess threw him a grateful glance. They were obviously in this together.

'I'm going to see her,' Jess said. 'We've decided that it's

best to have it out face to face. I'm not having her ruining my reputation just when I'm starting to get good rides.'

Belinda stared at her daughter in complete incomprehension. Was Jess's outrage all about racing and nothing at all to do with Izzy?

'Tom has got to know the Ukrainian girl who's been dumped at Quatt Lodge to look after the place while the Bearsdens are in London. She's going to let me know when Karen's coming down again, and I'm going round to see her. To confront her. We think that's the best way. To take her by surprise. I'm not going to let her do this. She won't get away with it.' Jess spoke in a determined rush.

'I see,' said Belinda. She took a deep breath. 'But Jess, hasn't all this got something to do with Izzy?'

There was a moment's pause before Jess looked straight at her mother. 'Yes,' she said slowly. 'Of course it has. It has everything to do with her.'

By the time Belinda opened the front door to Victor on Friday evening she was feeling almost hysterical. She had been delayed in the office, waiting for an important fax to come through, and when at last she got home there was no sign of Jess, although Izzy was in the sitting room watching television. Dropping a kiss on her head, Belinda began to rush round, tidying up.

'Where's Mummy?' she asked as she rolled balls of newspaper and made a wigwam of kindling in the hearth. She must light a fire. It made the room look less shabby and more homely. She was aware of how badly she wanted to go to the loo and how there never seemed to be time. I work faster on a full bladder, she thought, like most women.

'She's feeding Bonnet,' said Izzy, not taking her eyes off the screen. 'Why are you in such a hurry, Granny?'

'Because I'm going out tonight, darling, and I have a friend coming to collect me and I want everything to look nice.'

'Why?'

Belinda rather wondered that herself. 'Never mind about why. Pick up all those books, please.'

'Who? Who's coming?' asked Izzy, poking at her books with her foot, but not picking them up.

'Mr Bradford. The kind man from the garage. Do you remember?'

Izzy nodded. 'Has your car broken again?' she asked.

'No, it hasn't, thank goodness.'

'Then why is he coming?' persisted Izzy, lying on her bean bag and twiddling a corkscrew of hair, her eyes still on the screen. She was watching something entirely unsuitable on the regional news about a serial rapist who struck in a multi-storey car park in Portsmouth.

'Turn that off at *once*, Iz!' said Belinda, removing the considerable layer of dust on the sideboard with the sleeve of her jumper. 'Stop asking questions, darling. If you look in the shopping bags on the kitchen table you'll find some nibbly bits. Could you put them in a bowl for me?'

'Why are you giving the garage man nibbly bits?' asked Izzy, genuinely interested now and rolling off the bean bag. She trotted through to the kitchen, galvanised into action by the prospect of something novel to eat. Belinda switched on table lamps, shoved some supermarket tulips into a pretty pottery jug, and hid a jumble of detritus behind the curtains. She consulted her watch. She did not have time to wash the kitchen floor and really, she thought, a man would hardly notice anyway.

'And get me out a lemon, please,' she called to Izzy. 'And put the bottle of tonic in the fridge, there's a good girl.'

'But why, Granny?' asked Izzy, appearing at the door with a packet of Ultra Cheesie Morsels in her hand. 'He has lots of crisps in his garage. Boxes and boxes of them. Mummy buys them from his shop sometimes.'

'Yes, well, that doesn't mean that he won't like these, does it?' Izzy began to open the packet with her teeth. 'No, darling, don't put them in that plastic bowl. Find the pretty one Aunt Jo-Jo gave me from Italy.'

Goodness, she thought, stopping to survey the room, I need a drink. She searched in the sideboard for the few cut glass tumblers that had not been chipped or cracked over the years. She found two and polished them on a tea towel. They were heavy and solid in her hand and made her think of David because he had always used them for his whisky. He had expensive taste and liked to drink Glenmorangie and she could never smell the delicious, flowers-and-toffee scent of the malt without thinking of him. Poor, dear David. She wondered if he was watching her now and what he would be thinking, seeing her racing about getting ready to entertain another man. Even after all these years it made her feel slightly uncomfortable. She put the glasses on a little painted tray, and then went and got the bottle of gin out of the larder.

'Izzy, get me the ice, darling. I'm going to have a drink.'

Izzy trotted off to the freezer and came back with an ice tray.

'Can I have a drink too, Granny? Can I have some of your fizzy water?'

'Tonic? Yes, I suppose so.'

Izzy knelt on a stool at the table and sniffed deeply and appreciatively at the open gin bottle. Belinda filled her own glass with a good slug of gin and then added a bit more. She needed it. She gave Izzy a glass of fizzing tonic and added a slice of lemon.

'Now, Iz, I'm going up to have a bath. When Mummy comes in, remind her about my visitor. Tell her I don't want any mess.'

'OK,' said Izzy, dreamily, tracing her finger round the top of the bottle. 'Can I have some gin too?'

'Certainly not! Mrs Doasyouwouldbedoneby would *not* approve!'

'But you're having one,' pointed out Izzy, 'and you're always saying how lovely it is.'

Belinda was running her bath when she remembered Dinka, so she turned off the taps and went through to her bedroom, naked – Jess must have borrowed her dressing gown from the back of the bathroom door and all the towels seemed to have vanished. She sat on her bed, found the piece of paper on which she had written the telephone number of the clinic and dialled. A thickly accented foreign nurse answered and Belinda had difficulty getting her to understand that she would like to speak to Miss Inkster. Eventually she was put through and a weak, faint voice answered.

'Dinka? How are you? Did it go all right?'

'Dreadful. I'm feeling dreadful. Fucking awful, thank you, darling.'

'Oh, dear. Is it very sore?'

'Yes, but I've got some lovely painkillers. I'll be all right.'

She's so brave, thought Belinda, suddenly catching sight of herself in the glass on her dressing table. She sat up straighter, but there was not much improvement. Her body still looked like a landslide.

'But it all went all right, did it? No complications? When do they say you will feel better?' She turned a little on one hip and pressed her breasts together between her arms in a top-shelf magazine pose. Did that look any better? Any more seductive? Unfortunately, no. She looked foolish and old. Any undressing she might do in the future would have to take place in the dark or under a duvet.

'It went beautifully, Mr Benzir said, and I'll feel better in a day or two,' croaked Dinka. 'I'm all bandaged up. They won't let me see how I look for a few days.'

'Oh, Dinka! Well, I'll ring tomorrow. Have you got everything you need?'

'Yes, thank you, darling. I just want to sleep. You're out tonight, aren't you, with lover boy?'

'How clever of you to remember. Yes, I am, but I'm not feeling like it,' said Belinda, crossing her legs and pouting, one hand behind her head, rumpling her hair, and watching herself in the glass. Definitely more Hogarth than Renoir.

'Ring me tomorrow,' said Dinka sleepily.

'And I have a new instalment of the Jess and Johnnie Bearsden saga for you.'

'I can't wait. Tell me all tomorrow. Lots of love.'

Belinda stopped posing, put down the telephone and looked at herself in the glass again. 'Dear, oh dear,' she said out loud. She found a towel and went back to the bathroom to have her bath, with a big dollop of basil and bergamot essence in the water and her gin on the side. This was almost as good as it got, she thought, lying in the foam. She would settle for the bath and the drink and do without the man and the date.

She thought about what Jess had told her in the kitchen the night before. Was it, at last, the long-awaited admission? A crack in the armour plating? It had sounded like it at first, but Jess's manner was so strange, still so defiant and angry towards Karen who, after all, was the woman she had wronged. Belinda couldn't make it out, especially when Jess went on, 'I know what you're thinking, Mum, but you're wrong. Like you have always been.'

Belinda had looked across at Tom who just shrugged. He was not aware of all the facts either, it seemed.

'Your riding aside,' Belinda had said carefully, choosing her words, 'what does this confrontation with Karen Bearsden have to do with Izzy? You've just said that it has everything to do with her, but you won't say what, and what I want to know, what I really care about, is how it will affect her.'

'Why should it affect her?' Jess said shortly. 'It doesn't change anything for her, really.'

Belinda stared at her daughter, uncomprehending. It did not make any sense and yet she felt almost relieved that at least Jess was reacting, doing *something*, rather than just pretending that the situation did not exist. It felt as if there was a softening of the position that she had maintained for so many years and it seemed entirely in character that it was only a threat to her riding that made her take any action.

'Well,' Belinda said resignedly, 'if you won't tell me, there's nothing I can do to help, is there?'

'Mum, please!' said Jess, turning away with the familiar, cornered look on her face. In a moment she would become hostile, so Belinda did not respond but sat on at the table, still in her coat, pulling her gloves through her fingers in a distracted fashion.

'Where is Izzy?' she asked finally with a sigh.

'Having a bath. I'm going to do supper in a minute. Or rather Tom is. He's promised us spag bol.'

Long-suffering Tom, thought Belinda. That's really his trouble. He's too nice and those sort of men always get taken for granted.

'Let's have a glass of wine, shall we, Tom?' she had said, smiling at him. 'There's a bottle of plonk in the larder. If you open it, I'll go and get Izzy out of her bath.'

'OK,' he had said, looking relieved. He had obviously been dreading a scene.

Belinda glanced at her watch on the side of the bath. She had only fifteen minutes to get ready for Victor. She hauled herself out of the water and, wearing a towel, went through to her bedroom and started to pull clothes out of her wardrobe. She had worried about what to wear ever since Victor had asked her out. Her better clothes were to do with looking neat and smart at work, and the rest were old things she wore at home. She wanted to look young and stylish and although she had trawled through the piles of discarded garments in the corner of Jess's room, she had come to the conclusion that Jess was worse dressed than she was.

In the end she had decided on Dinka's black polo neck and a long brown knitted skirt she'd got from Oxfam. With her good black boots she looked perfectly all right, but boring. It was an inoffensive, please-ignore-me sort of outfit, designed to blend into any background and be instantly forgettable. She wanted to do better than that. What would Dinka wear? This was not a helpful line of enquiry when she considered Dinka's wardrobe and budget, but she needed a dose of Dinka's flair. She would wear a belt slung low on her hips, or a wonderful scarf knotted round her shoulders. Belinda rummaged through her drawers and found a gold link belt which just made her look like a chained barrel when she looped it round her waist. She threw it on her bed and then tried a belt like a narrow black rope, which changed her into a lumpy parcel.

What she needed was a bit of glamour. She slapped on an extra coat of lipstick to brighten things up a bit, but even then saw little improvement. Her red lips seemed to emphasise her weary eyes and made her think of an exhausted old slapper of a barmaid. Sometimes you have to accept that you look tired and dull, she thought, and unfortunately this was one of those occasions. An extra squirt of perfume would have to suffice, and then she spotted a little fur tippet that Jo had given her, lurking in the back of her wardrobe. She twisted it round her neck and the soft grey fur next to her face made her look instantly prettier. It was frivolous and fun and made her feel better. She had never worn it before but then she had not had a man to impress. It would have to do.

When she went downstairs, she found Jess in the kitchen cooking Izzy fish fingers. The door to the sitting room was open and the whole ground floor of the cottage smelled of frying.

'Jess, you might have shut the door!' said Belinda, rushing through to close it, but it was too late now. Jess looked at her and shook her head as if she was dealing with a mental retard.

'For goodness sake, Mum, chill. Whatever's that you're wearing? Is it road-kill or something Snowy brought in?' She laughed at her own wit and Belinda could have hit her.

'You look lovely, Granny,' said Izzy kindly. 'Like Little Grey Rabbit.'

Belinda kissed her and then rushed through the hall to put a clean towel in the downstairs cloakroom, which was as usual a muddle of coats and boots, the basin smeared, the soap a small grey-grained lump and the lavatory in need of a clean. 'Bloody hell!' she said aloud and started frantic wiping and polishing. She was on her hands and knees with her head in the pan, wielding the lavatory brush, when she heard Snowy start to bark furiously.

Damn, that would be Victor. She looked at her face in the glass above the basin, and under the harsh, unforgiving light saw a dishevelled, agitated woman with too bright lipstick. The fur tippet had shed a circle of silver hairs round the neck of her black sweater and she went to open the door smelling, she thought, more of something that dealt with the U-bend than Chanel.

*

'Come on, Iz,' said Jess, as the door closed on Belinda and Victor. She could still hear her mother's voice, chattering brightly. The poor man was having a struggle to get a word in edgeways. 'Finish your supper. We're going out.'

'Going out, Mummy? Where are we going?'

'We're going to meet someone Tom knows. A girl who comes from another country and she's a bit lonely because she doesn't have any friends here. Tom's coming round to collect us in a minute.'

'Good,' said Izzy, who loved an outing. She wiped her chin with her hand and carried her plate to the sink. 'Can Snowy come?'

'Yes, I should think so, although he will have to stay in the Land Rover with Meg.' She glanced out of the window. 'Here's Tom now. Go and get your coat on.'

Izzy sat happily between Tom and Jess on the front seat of the cab, with Snowy panting hot dog breath down her neck from the back. She was busy telling Tom about Ben and Darren. 'Ben says I can tell the twins at school that they are arse'oles. Arse'oles is a rude thing, worse than bottoms or pants. So I'm going to,' she finished in a satisfied tone.

'I see,' said Tom. 'They deserve it, do they? These twins?'

'Yes, they bother me. They call me names.' She screwed up her face in thought and then finished, 'I can't remember now, but bad ones.'

'Well, they do deserve it then,' agreed Tom, looking over her head at Jess, but she was staring out of the window. 'What's all this about?' he asked her.

She shrugged dismissively. 'Kids' stuff, that's all. They're Carina Westland's snotty boys.'

'Oh.' Tom accepted her answer. He didn't want to push anything with Jess at the moment.

It had been her suggestion that they go to see Ludmylla and that they take Izzy too. Tom had raised his eyebrows at that. Jess had met the Bearsden boy. She must know what Ludmylla's reaction to Izzy would be, and yet she seemed to want to set up the situation, as if it would somehow strengthen her hand.

Izzy continued to chat happily, her hands clasped round her fat little knees, her feet dangling off the floor of the Land Rover. She was excited to be going out late, almost past her bedtime, and she only fell silent as they turned in by the gatehouse and started up the long drive.

'Look, Izzy. Deer,' said Jess, and in the darkening park they saw the ghostly gleam of the pale-coloured hinds grazing on the long grass, and a stag lifted his head to gaze across at them, his antlers a black fretwork against the sky.

The house looked as gloomy as ever, the only light coming from a room on the top floor, but Ludmylla was expecting them and when they drew into the courtyard at the back they could see that the kitchen was lit up and there was the flicker of a television. They climbed out of the Land Rover and banged the doors shut. Tom went and tapped on the window and Ludmylla called, questioning, from inside.

'It's me, Tom,' he said. 'Open up.' A chain rattled and then the door opened and Jess saw a thin-faced girl of about her own age, with peroxided hair and wearing very tight jeans.

'Come,' she said, holding the door open.

In the kitchen the two women looked at each other

awkwardly as if now that they had come together they could not remember why.

'This is Jess, Ludmylla,' said Tom. 'And this is Izzy,' but Ludmylla was already staring at Izzy with a mixture of surprise and amusement.

'My God,' she said. 'What is this? A twin? She is your girl?' she asked Jess.

'Yes,' said Jess. 'Her name is Isobel and she is six.'

'And a quarter,' said Izzy shyly, pulling at Jess's hand.

'Why she so like the other one?' asked Ludmylla, passing round a packet of cigarettes. She interrupted herself to ask Tom, 'You brought me cigarettes? Like you said?'

Tom put four packets on the table.

'Why do you think?' asked Jess quietly. 'You can guess, can't you?'

Ludmylla shrugged and grinned. She didn't care. She knelt down beside shy Izzy and said, 'I have a girl too. Same age as you. Katya. I love her very much. Look, I show you photo.' She reached for an envelope from the dresser and took out two photographs of a pretty little fair-haired girl sitting with her ankles crossed and her hands in her lap. Izzy looked with interest.

'This hair,' said Ludmylla, touching Izzy's head. 'It is amazing. The other one has it too. A coincidence, no?' She looked at Jess again and laughed.

Izzy looked doubtfully from face to face, and Ludmylla bent to kiss her. 'Look,' she said. 'I make special cookies when I hear you come to visit. Like I make at home for Katya.' She put a plate on the table and Izzy gazed longingly at the star-shaped white-iced biscuits which smelled of cinnamon. 'Take one,' urged Ludmylla. 'Try. You want coffee? Tea?'

When they were all sitting round the kitchen table, Jess said, 'Tom tells me that you're coming to skittles on Wednesday night. That's great. You'll enjoy it.'

'Yes,' said Ludmylla, still looking at Izzy and blowing out cigarette smoke. 'I hope.'

'What I want to know,' went on Jess 'is all about the Bearsdens. I used to know Johnnie quite well.'

Ludmylla turned to her, then glanced back at Izzy. 'I think this is so.'

'But I don't know Mrs B.'

'No.' Ludmylla laughed again. 'What you want to know? Look, I understand. It is the same with me. A married man. My Katya, you understand?'

Tom sat rooted to his chair. This was a side of Jess he had never seen. He could hardly believe that she was revealing so much in such a direct way to a girl she had only just met. The pair of them were smirking and whispering like old cronies. Thank goodness Izzy was munching her way through the plate of biscuits and not apparently listening to a word.

'Come on, Iz,' he said, getting up. 'There's a piano through here. Shall we go and see if we can play a tune?'

'I don't know, Jess,' he said later as they sat beside the fire in Rosebay Cottage eating toasted cheese and Izzy was upstairs in bed. 'What was all that about? What are you trying to do?'

'What do you mean?'

'All that girlie confessional stuff. I've never heard you like that before.'

'Are you mad?' said Jess with her mouth full. 'What did I confess? Bugger all. I might have hinted, but that's all. I need Ludmylla on my side, don't I? You said that. I need to know how things are with those bloody Bearsdens and she wouldn't have told me otherwise.'

Tom considered. So it was all tactics. Jess, whom he had always thought was so straight and open, was playing a tactical game.

He sighed. 'I don't understand what you're up to, frankly.'

'Don't try,' said Jess shortly. 'Look! What are all those bits of china in the hearth? It looks like pieces of Mum's best bowl. Do you think she's been throwing things at her boyfriend?'

When Belinda woke, early as usual, she lay for a while relishing the fact that it was Saturday morning and she did not have to get up. Outside, it was beginning to get light and over the last day or two she had noticed that the garden birds were starting to get the dawn chorus going again, like an orchestra reassembling after a break. She could hear them now, a blackbird and a thrush, probably perched on the ridge of the roof, and the myriad chattering of sparrows on the telephone line outside her window. A dog barked from the farm further along the lane and as she listened she realised that the whole vale below was trembling with the sound of sheep, the plaintive piping of the lambs and the answering reassurance of the ewes' deeper voices.

It was a luxury to be able to lie in peace and think about

last night. The evening had not exactly got off to a good start although her first impression of Victor, when she opened the door, was how attractive he looked, tall and broad and slightly pink in the face from a fresh shave. He was wearing a tweed jacket and a blue shirt and tie, and his hair was so good for a man of his age, thick and short and straightforward, not bouffant like a game-show host or artfully arranged to cover a bald patch.

'Victor,' she cried. 'Come in.' She was still brushing nervously at her black pullover. 'This wretched fur has moulted all over me! I look as if I'm losing all my hair!' Oh no, she thought instantly. Fool, fool! How could she be so stupid when she knew that his wife had died of cancer? 'You must come and meet my daughter,' she said brightly when she had handed him his drink, and she took him into the kitchen and introduced him to Jess and Izzy. Neither exactly rose to the occasion. Izzy smiled with her mouth full of a Dracula mix of fish fingers and ketchup, and Jess merely said, 'Oh, hi,' in an offhand voice and offered no further attempt at conversation. Snowy, meanwhile, made a persistent and thorough examination of his trouser legs.

'Naughty boy,' scolded Belinda, pulling him away. 'I expect he can smell your dog.'

'I don't have a dog,' said Victor. Jess snorted.

Belinda extricated him immediately and firmly closed the door to the kitchen. She had already told him a little about Jess and Izzy, but before she could stop herself she began again on a long and rambling explanation. Once started, she felt she had to finish although it kept taking her into territory she wished to avoid, like the subject of Izzy's father.

'So Jess is the daughter who races,' said Victor, looking with interest at the many photographs of her in action ranged round the sitting room. 'It's a grand, old-fashioned sport, point-to-pointing. I enjoy a day at the races myself now and then.'

'Do you? I don't go often because I find it too nerve-wracking to watch her.'

'I can see that. From a mother's point of view. But it's quite something to have a daughter like that. It's a tough life and you have to work damn hard, I know that much. You must be very proud of her.'

'No, I'm not. Well, I don't mean I'm not proud, but I want her to stop. I think it's madness when she has Izzy.'

Victor considered for a moment. 'Maybe, but I still think it's great. My daughters don't get off their arses for anything very much, as far as I can see.'

Belinda offered him the bowl of Ultra Cheesie Morsels which she had been pressing on him at intervals and took one herself. When she put it in her mouth, it was so vile it stopped her in her tracks. It tasted of cardboard and was covered in a strange lurid dust which reeked so horribly of chemicals that it could well have been a toxic by-product of the nuclear waste industry. In fact, she noticed an orange glow had already developed on Victor's lips and at the corners of his mouth.

'These are disgusting!' she cried. 'Please don't eat them!'

'They're not at all disgusting,' he said politely.

'But they are,' she insisted, and snatched up the bowl which somehow slipped through her fingers and dropped onto the rug, spilling the contents over their feet. 'Please don't!' she cried as he stooped to help her pick up the glowing orange tubes, and she scrabbled about on the carpet between his well-polished brown shoes. She finished collecting the scattered bits into the bowl and turned to toss them into the fire – but the bowl shot out of her hand and smashed into the side of the fireplace.

They both stood looking at the pieces in astonishment and then at each other. Belinda clasped her hand over her mouth in dismay before bursting into laughter.

'What am I *doing*? You'll think I'm completely deranged. I am so sorry. I don't know why I feel so nervous about this evening.' There, she thought. I've said it. Now he knows.

'Come here, lass.' Victor pulled her towards him. 'What have you got to feel nervous about?'

She found herself leaning against the front of his jacket and then put her arms round him, laying her hands flat against the prickly tweed of his back. His body felt like a large, tight drum and it was comforting to stand there for a moment in his arms. He was quite different to hold than James Redpath, who had been tall but very slim. Victor was more like a stout tree. Gently, he lifted her chin with one finger and looked at her face. She felt girlish and confused.

'You're lovely,' he said simply, before letting her go.

Victor drained his glass and looked at his watch and said that perhaps it was time to go. He asked to use the lavatory – he called it the toilet, she remembered – and as he left the room she saw with horror that the back of his smart, dark trousers was liberally dusted with Snowy's short white hairs. The naughty dog must have got up on the sofa after she had vacuumed it.

'Victor!' she cried. 'Your trousers!'

'What about them?' he said, surprised.

'Dog hairs. It's that wretched Snowy. I'm afraid he sits on the furniture when I'm out as a sort of protest at being left behind.'

Victor was good-natured enough to say that it didn't matter at all and began to brush at the hairs with his hand. She fetched a clothes brush and set about his trousers in a determined way. It was so absurd that they both began to laugh again. 'We'll remember this,' he said to her over his shoulder. 'The second time we went out. You throwing china and then going at me with the clothes brush! Literally!'

On the way into Sherborne Belinda felt so exhausted that she hardly spoke but Victor chatted on regardless about holidays and the problem of going away if one was single. She'd had too much gin and her head felt thick and her thoughts slow, but unless she concentrated she got the whirlies, like she had felt as a child sitting in a spinning teacup on a fairground ride.

Thank goodness that the concert sobered her up a bit and sitting quietly gave her a rest from having to make conversation. During the interval Victor disappeared for ages trying to get them coffee from a stall set up at the back of the abbey. There were many people she knew in the audience and she confided to her friend Caroline Davis, who sat down next to her for a chat, that she was tight. They giggled together and Caroline gave her two extra-strong mints from her handbag.

'It's nerves, Caroline, that's what's to blame. I mean, I'm out with a *man*.'

'You seem to have lost him, though,' said Caroline, looking about. 'Where is he, this man of yours? I think you're on a phantom date, myself. Like a phantom pregnancy.'

'If he is, he's a very solid, large phantom. Oh goodness, here he comes.'

Caroline stood up hastily and Belinda introduced her to Victor who was carrying two full polystyrene mugs and couldn't shake hands. She felt rather proud of him. He looked fit, to use Jess's terminology, and his manners were so easy and friendly. He stood and chatted to Caroline for some minutes. Suddenly what Eileen Busby had said flashed into Belinda's mind. Was he really a ladies' man? He could give that impression, she thought, seeing him twinkling down at pretty, blonde Caroline. She said goodbye and, catching Belinda's eye over Victor's head as he sat down, gave her a wink and a thumbs-up.

The second half of the concert was wonderful with music by Strauss and Mozart. Belinda studied the programme notes and learned that the characters and the arias they sang appeared somewhat deranged. Donna Anna is descending into dementia, she read, after everything she has gone through, which seemed to be attempted rape and her father's murder, until she enters into a slightly surreal, eerily peaceful mode. How appropriate, thought Belinda. Almost exactly how I feel.

The Strauss was all about the wilder shores of love. The surprisingly chirpy notes told her that *Guntram* shows what can happen when a woman gets her man. 'Freihild, in *"Fass'ich sie bang"*,' she read, 'gives full, glorious voice to the boundless rapture she feels at being rescued by a knight in shining armour, and Salome's final scene shocks with an ecstasy that seems both unworldly and carnal.' She saw Victor was studying his programme. 'Racy stuff, eh?' he whispered, giving her a nudge, and she nodded, amused, and indicated the largely elderly and staid audience on either side who were listening to such unlikely-sounding material with rapt expressions.

When the concert came to an end, with many curtain calls for the charming red-haired soprano, she followed Victor's broad back through the throng of people beneath the magical beauty of the fan-vaulted roof of the abbey, and out into the chilly dark.

Sherborne was transformed on a Friday night. The pensioners and their walking frames and wonkily parked vehicles and fat dogs on leads were gone and the streets were overflowing with noisy young people spilling out of the brightly lit pubs and roaring down Cheap Street in souped-up cars. Belinda remembered that Shirley from Pilates had told her that one Monday morning she had gone to work to find that a Vauxhall Nova with a big grafted-on exhaust pipe had gone through the salon window in the early hours and come to rest amongst the basins and styling stations. Almost like a modern art installation, Shirley said. It probably could have won the Turner prize.

'I've booked us a late dinner at Plover Manor,' Victor said as he held the door of his car open for her to get in. 'Is that all right?'

'Victor,' said Belinda, in quite genuine delight. 'How lovely.'

Later, looking about the attractively lit and comfortable dining room, it was easy to think that this was how life should be, peaceful and well-managed and insulated from the turbulence and uncertainties of the outside world. Their fellow diners looked comfortably off and middle-aged. This is how I imagine David and I might have been at this stage of our lives, thought Belinda. After a lifetime of hard work and bringing up a family, we should have been able, at last, to reap the benefits of good husbandry. She was sure that there was a reassuring parable in the Bible about it. Either to do with vineyards or wise virgins, or talents, she felt too befuddled to remember which. Instead, here she was with a man she hardly knew, on what Dinka had referred to as a bonking opportunity, and wondering whether she would eventually go to bed with him and what it would be like. Since it was common knowledge that men thought about sex virtually nonstop, she supposed that the same thought must have occurred to Victor.

She looked at him across the table, at his large square hands breaking open a roll, at his very blue eyes behind the glasses he had put on to read the wine list and decided he would be good at it. He gave the impression of managing most things competently and naturally, without any fuss. She remembered the elaborate courtship she had enjoyed with James before he got her into bed and how, on reflection, it seemed more about his own good opinion of himself as a seducer than it did about any feelings he might have had for her. She didn't think Victor would be like that. She hoped not. She could not go through that again.

She felt perfectly in control of the situation when they

pulled into the space beside Rosebay Cottage and she leaned over and kissed his cheek. 'That was a lovely evening,' she said. 'Jess and Tom are back, I see. Would you like to come in and have a coffee?'

Victor looked across at her and took her right hand and put it on his thigh and laid his own on top. She turned hers over so that she could lace her fingers into his.

'And I'm sorry about throwing the china round the room. I'm surprised that you didn't take fright and do a runner!'

Victor nodded. 'It would take more than that to scare me off. Yes, I'd like a cup of coffee. Thank you. I'll come in for a minute or two.'

When Belinda opened the sitting-room door, Tom and Jess were slumped together watching television. Tom looked over the back of the sofa and disentangled himself to get up.

'Hi, Mum,' said Jess, without moving, her eyes on the screen. 'How was the hot date?'

'Lovely,' said Belinda. 'I've got the hot date with me, in fact.'

'Oh, shit!' Jess looked hastily over her shoulder. 'Sorry, Mum. Sorry, um . . .' She grinned across at Victor. She had obviously forgotten his name but he seemed unconcerned. He pulled Belinda into a playful bear hug.

'Hot date, eh?' he said with a laugh. 'Hello, Tom.' She might have guessed they would know one another. It seemed that Victor had sold petrol to the Hodges and looked after their vehicles for years.

'Real? Instant? Decaff?' she asked, going through to the kitchen to fill the kettle. Jess stood up and stretched, yawning, showing inches of smooth white belly.

'Not for me, thank you, Mum. I'm off to bed. I'm knackered. Night, um . . . Night, Tom.'

'I'm off too,' Tom said. 'No coffee for me, thank you, Belinda. I'll see you tomorrow, Jess. Have you got an early start?'

'Same as usual,' said Jess. 'I'll be at the yard at seven. I'll see you on the course.'

So it was only Belinda and Victor who sat by the embers of the fire with mugs of coffee. Belinda had turned off the television and apart from Snowy's snores and the sound of the log hissing in the grate, silence settled comfortably about them. The room seemed altered by Victor being there, thought Belinda. It wasn't just that he took up physical space, with his bulk on the sofa, his long legs stretched out in front of him and his looming shadow on the wall. It was more that having him there made her feel as if she herself was more substantial. She had so often sat on her own, with Izzy gone up to bed and Jess out somewhere, and been conscious that the emptiness of the room made her feel that she was too slight and inadequate to fill it and as if she was losing the battle for possession of the space. She sometimes felt so thin and bloodless and transparent that she wondered if someone coming in might think the room was empty. Victor, on the other hand, radiated such a vitality that his presence seemed to reach into the very corners. Even sitting here quietly, she felt surrounded by a comforting sense of life rather than enveloped by the dusty dark of the shadows.

James had never made her feel like this. He had hated the cottage and had never wanted to spend any time there, as if it was an unworthy backdrop for his love affair.

'It's been a grand evening,' said Victor, putting down his mug beside his seat. 'Come and sit over here, lass.'

Belinda moved to sit beside him on the sofa, knowing perfectly well what was coming next. She put a hand on his thigh and turned towards him, sure that he would kiss her.

'Look at us,' she whispered. 'At our age. Grandparents. And the young ones have left us to it!'

'What's age got to do with anything?' asked Victor. 'Anyway, the years haven't touched you.'

'That's a lovely thing to say. Not true, but nice.'

'Ssshhh. God, woman, do you never stop talking?'

Much later Belinda turned off the lights in the kitchen and went upstairs. She cleaned off her make-up and got into bed. She felt really tired but she wanted to go over each detail of the evening and file it away in her memory, as if, at some point, she would need it as evidence. Although it had started out badly she would be able to tell Dinka that it had ended really rather well.

Chapter Thirteen

Jess did not have to wait long before she could put her decision to confront Karen Bearsden into action. On Wednesday evening she and Tom collected Ludmylla as promised and took her to the Coach and Horses in Bishops Barton where there was a Hunt League skittles match.

It was a jolly, beer-drinking affair, supported by many local people as a cheap and sociable evening out with a bit of a competition as well, which some took more seriously than others. Girls' teams, lads' teams, mixed teams, old and young competed and Ken Andrews' yard had, by tradition, always put together a scratch side. Rhona, Carl, Jess, Moira, Susan, Lisa, if she could get a babysitter, joined up with Tony, the yard farrier, and Tom. There was joshing humour and exchange of local gossip and Ludmylla caused considerable interest in her spray-on jeans and high heels.

In the ladies' cloakroom Ludmylla turned to Jess and said, 'I forget to tell you. Mrs Bearsden comes down on Saturday evening. She has meeting with builder on Sunday morning.'

Jess drew her to one side, conscious of Rhona and Lisa in the lavatory cubicles next door. 'What time?' she said in a low voice. 'Did she say?'

'I not know. Saturday is night off for me but she say in the evening.' She opened her eyes very wide. 'You want me to telephone when she arrives?'

'Yes,' said Jess, looking about her, still anxious not to be overheard. 'Do that, Ludmylla, if you don't mind. Don't tell her, though. Or anyone else. OK?' She put her finger to her lips to indicate secrecy.

'I understand. I not say nothing.'

'Thanks. Come on, then.' Jess steered her back towards the bar. 'Come and meet people. That's what you're here for.'

After Jess had introduced her to all the single, local men, Ludmylla was soon leaning on the bar, smoking, with a line of lagers in front of her, the centre of a lot of attention. She'll be all right, thought Jess. She's a survivor.

She also proved to be a dab hand at skittles, sending the ball dead straight down the alley to accompanying cheers and appreciative remarks about the neatness of her arse viewed from behind.

'Just watch yourself, Dave,' large Kelly Adams warned her boyfriend, a tractor driver on a nearby estate. 'I know what you're thinking!'

'Me?' exclaimed Dave in mock indignation. 'I'm just enjoying the view, that's all.'

'So what's all this about?' asked Rhona as she and Jess waited at the bar to buy drinks. She indicated Ludmylla.

'Someone Tom's discovered,' said Jess. 'Johnnie Bearsden's au pair, as it happens.'

Rhona raised her eyebrows. 'Why?' she asked.

'Why what?'

322

'Why is she tagging along with you two?'

Jess shrugged. 'She's lonely. Doesn't know anyone. Tom's just being kind, you know him.'

'Ah.' Rhona looked at her. 'That's it then, is it?'

'Yeah. Why?'

Rhona looked down the bar to catch the eye of the barmaid. 'Just something Mary said. Something about Johnnie Bearsden's wife.'

Jess glared at her fiercely. 'Mary promised me—'

'Cool it, Jess. I won't tell anyone, you know that. Mary can't keep that sort of thing from me. Not after all the years I've been working for her and Ken. She knows I won't tell anyone else and I am as angry as you are about it. I've never heard of anything so bloody stupid. I'm just surprised to see the au pair with you, that's all.'

'She's all right,' said Jess. 'She can't help who she works for.'

Rhona looked thoughtful.

'What's the matter, Rhone?'

Rhona shrugged. 'Nothing. Just watch your back, girl. That's all.'

It's because they're so different, thought Jess, looking past Rhona to Ludmylla, surrounded by men and blowing smoke seductively into their faces. Chalk and cheese. Rhona had made no special effort for the evening out except to change into a clean pair of boots and jeans, her plain, honest face devoid of make-up behind her round glasses, and her hair, thick, clumpy and straight, cut by Lisa in the tack room. Jess was tempted to say something to Rhona, to the effect that Ludmylla was on her side, but she thought better of it. The less people knew the better. Still, it was a comfort to feel that Rhona was indignant on her behalf.

Rhona, for her part, was never one to trespass into other people's lives. She felt she had said quite enough and now brought the conversation to a close by shouting to the barmaid who was serving a bunch of young farmers at the other end of the bar. They were big, hefty, red-faced lads, grouped like a herd of jostling roaring bullocks and passing the brimming beer tankards over their heads to their mates at the back of the room.

'Come on, what are you doing, serving all that lot first?' Rhona yelled. 'We've been stood here for hours.'

The barmaid glanced at her and laughed. They were old friends.

'It's always the men get served first with you, Patsy! If it's balls that count, Jess and I here have got far more than any of those tossers!' Laughter drowned Patsy's reply.

By the end of the evening, Ludmylla was playing the piano in the bar, and although Dorset drinking songs were not in her repertoire, she could play all the old Beatles numbers by ear and everyone could sing along to those, even if the words ran out after the second line.

It was handsome Ivan Davis who hung around at closing time and appeared to have decided to take her back to Quatt Lodge in his pick-up truck. Ivan was a slow man whose thoughts passed across his face like clouds across the sun. Tom often waited for him to speak, thinking that a sentence was forming and on its way, only to see the moment pass and to realise that any words Ivan might have been summoning had slipped away again unspoken. He was on his own since his marriage to a flashy Birmingham girl broke up last summer. Now he had Ludmylla clasped in his arms. She trilled her fingers in a wave to where Tom and Jess were sitting.

'I go with Ivan,' she called. 'OK?' The drinkers at the bar cat-called and bellowed in delight and Ivan, grinning, propelled Ludmylla out of the door in front of him.

'She'll have him for breakfast,' said Jess.

Tom laughed. 'I don't think he'll object. There's no language barrier because they've both got about the same grasp of English. They'll get on fine.'

On the way home, Jess told Tom what she had learned from Ludmylla. 'So it's this Saturday,' she said. 'I'm going to have it out with Karen this Saturday.'

'Can't I come with you?' he asked. 'I'd wait outside. I'd just like to be there.'

'No thanks, Tom. I'd rather be on my own, if you don't mind.'

They lapsed into silence and Jess wondered if Tom was hurt. She hoped not. Dear Tom. She couldn't tell him how much depended on how she handled this meeting. She had to do it on her own. She couldn't tell anyone else, not even her mother. She had let Belinda think that it was all about the threat posed to her racing, but of course it was much more than that. At the very heart of it was Izzy. Izzy and her future. Izzy depended on her. Jess felt quite sick at the thought of what she had to do, breaking the years of silence, but there was no other way.

*

In the meantime, it was horses that occupied her mind. On Thursday morning, during the coffee break when everyone was gathered in Ken's kitchen and he was studying the entries for Saturday's racing, the telephone rang, as it did incessantly, and Mary answered it and passed the receiver across to Jess.

'It's Ted,' she said. 'Ted Dawlish, for you.'

'Ooooer!' mocked Moira. 'Jessie baby, it's for you!'

Jess picked up the telephone and turned her back on the table.

'Hi,' she said. 'Yeah. Yeah. OK. Which race? All right. Yeah. I'll see you. Bye.' She turned back to Mary and handed her the telephone.

'So?' said Ken, looking up from the form guide, his glasses on the end of his nose. 'What did the old bugger want?'

'He wants me to ride Fancy again on Sunday. The maiden race at Bratton Down.' She was aware of Moira whispering something to Carl.

'What?' Jess said, turning on her. 'What did you say?'

'Nothing,' said Moira airily. 'Just that that's not what I heard.'

'What do you mean?'

'I heard, down the Cricketers, that Pete Dawlish has booked Nick Martin to ride. Said he wanted to give the mare a better chance of getting some form this season.' She smiled sweetly. 'But I must have heard wrong, mustn't I?'

Jess glared at her. 'Who did you hear that from?'

Moira shrugged. 'I don't know. I can't remember exactly. Someone from Robert Taylor's yard.'

Jess swung round to Rhona and Susan. Carl had already slunk out. 'Did you hear this?'

Rhona stood up, impassive. 'I wasn't there. Cool it, Jess. It's just yard gossip. You know what a loud-mouthed, ignorant arse Pete Dawlish is. Who cares what he says anyway? It's his dad that makes the decisions.'

'He wouldn't have asked you to ride, would he,' said Ken, 'not if what Moira said is true? Now stop this messing around. You've got a good ride on Saturday, Jess. Dolly stands a fair chance in the ladies' race. You concentrate on that, and stop all this faffing around about Dawlish's mare. It's me you work for, remember.' Jess flushed angrily. She opened her mouth to say something but Mary suddenly banged the lid of the biscuit tin.

'That's enough!' she said. 'Shut up, all of you. Go outside and get on with your work. I've had enough of the whole lot of you.'

Belinda's week passed in a similar rush. She was busy at work and diverted by emails from Victor which had started to arrive on Monday morning. They began rather formally but soon became warmer and Belinda responded briefly to each one. She did not want to encourage virtual sex or whatever it was that people did on the internet, but it made a change to be on the receiving end of admiring and appreciative remarks and an email correspondence of this sort was something new to her. She found it far easier than dealing with telephone calls, especially at work, and she could respond when she had time to think what she was going to say. The short messages which zipped backwards and forwards between their computers, sometimes four or five times a day, were fun and light-hearted.

It was easy to be mildly flirtatious and she began to feel absurdly happy when she saw the New Mail sign appear in her Inbox. She took the trouble to hide her pleasure from Jenny Crow, tapping away industriously across the room, but wondered how she could fail to notice the change in the atmosphere. Belinda felt something lighten within herself, like when the first warm day seems to herald the arrival of spring, or a glass of quickly gulped champagne sends its bubbles racing through the blood.

Things moved forward far more quickly than when she had last embarked on a relationship. She had had to wait by the telephone, evening after evening, for a call from James Redpath, who was never a very reliable communicator, and it had all been prolonged and agonising, those early days of their affair. Now, with Victor, things were fairly rattling along.

'What are you doing for lunch?' he emailed one bright morning when the sunshine through the mullioned windows of the office danced with dust specks and sent shimmering golden pools across her desk.

'Sandwich,' she sent back. 'No time for more.'

'Where?' he replied. 'Can I join you? I'll bring the sandwiches. Garage best.'

'Cheese and pickle?' she sent back. 'Sherborne Castle car park? 13.00?'

'I'll be there.'

When she pulled up, his car was already parked and he got out and came to her door.

'Have you got time to walk a bit? We could go over to that bench on the other side of the lake.' He was wearing work clothes – jeans, blue sweater, a check shirt and a thick padded jacket. He did not look anything other than a working man and Belinda was glad. She remembered James and his carefully chosen wardrobe in which every item shrieked class. It seemed so pretentious and self-conscious compared to Victor's ordinariness.

Although the sun was bright, the wind was cold and the banks of yellow daffodils nodded and danced and the water on the lake was a mass of dark and silvery wavelets. Coots scooted importantly among the reeds at the water's edge and a flotilla of little white ducks bobbed further out. Victor carried a supermarket bag in one hand and with the other reached for Belinda's.

'You're cold,' he said and tucked it in the crook of his arm. 'How much time have you got?'

'Fifty minutes. Not a second more, I'm afraid.'

When they reached the seat, they sat for a moment on the cracked white paint and leaned back to feel the sun on their faces. Victor put the bag down at his feet and turned to Belinda and kissed her. She closed her eyes and the bright light glowed through her closed lids. His face was cold and sandpapery and his mouth tasted of peppermint. She found the way into his padded jacket and under the thick wool of his sweater to where she could feel the warmth of his body through his shirt.

When they drew apart, Victor kept his arm round her and she laid her head on his chest. She felt cocooned and comforted.

329

'Here, lass,' he said. 'You'd better have something to eat,' and he reached down and unpacked the sandwiches. They were nothing special but they tasted delicious, eaten like that, looking out over the lake.

'Sorry it's not anything better,' he said, 'but I didn't have the time. I just had to grab what was in the shop. I've got some apple juice in a carton here. It's not much of a picnic.'

'It's perfect,' said Belinda.

When they had finished, he filled the bag with the rubbish and then kissed her again, this time reaching under her coat and touching her breasts. With the greatest difficulty Belinda screwed her head to the side to check the time.

'Victor,' she said, 'I'll have to go. I'd far rather sit here and snog, as Jess would say. I don't want to go, but I really must.'

They had to hurry then, hand in hand back to their cars and as they walked she told him that she was worried about Dinka and was thinking of going to see her on Saturday.

'I'll drive you if you like,' he said at once. 'I ought to go and see my daughter. The one who lives at Blackheath and is breaking up with her husband. I could drop you off and go on.'

'That would be wonderful. Do you really mean it?'

He looked at her and laughed. 'I wouldn't offer if I didn't.'

When she told Jess, she could see that she was annoyed.

'Why do you need to rush off to see Dinka? She's not exactly dying, is she?' Jess snapped.

'I'm sorry, Jess,' Belinda said firmly, determined not to weaken and agree to look after Izzy while Jess was racing, 'but I've got the offer of a lift from Victor and I would like to see her. She sounded rather down on the telephone.'

'Humph. If there's one person who can look after themselves, it's Dinka,' retorted Jess. 'Anyway, what's all this with the boyfriend? Are you having an affair or something?' She spat out the word with such venom that Belinda started and blushed.

'No, I'm not, and even if I was, it would be my business,' she retorted.

'Yeah, well, remember the last time,' and Jess went out, slamming the door.

Belinda looked after her, stung by her reaction. She remembered how Jess had behaved when she was going out with James, hostile and silent, resenting that her mother should so clearly be in love with someone other than her father. Perhaps she shouldn't go after all. It would mean that Izzy spent the day at the races, being looked after by whoever was around the horsebox, which was not at all a satisfactory arrangement.

'Don't be ridiculous, lass,' said Victor when she telephoned him that evening to say she wasn't sure that she could go. 'You can't let that great girl of yours bully you like that. Tell her you're going and that's that. It will do you good to have a proper day out. Me, too, come to that.'

Then there was Izzy. The following morning when Belinda was dropping her off at school, there was a tap on her car window as she was pulling away and she turned to see Carina Westland bending down and looking in at her. She was wearing a fur hat and a wax coat and her long thin nose was red from the cold.

Belinda leaned over and opened the door. 'Hello, Carina. How are you?'

'Oh, fine, fine, but could I just have a little word?'

Belinda stared at her, wondering what was coming. Her face was very solemn and concerned as if she had bad news to impart.

'Can I get in a moment?' she asked. 'It's fucking cold out here.'

'Yes, of course.' The grander you were, the more you swore, thought Belinda. Carina climbed in and Belinda saw that she was wearing breeches and long boots.

'Actually, it's about Izzy,' she said, settling herself into the passenger seat. 'I suppose I should speak to Jess, but she never drops her off, does she?'

'Well, no,' said Belinda, already feeling defensive. 'She goes to work before seven.'

'Yes, I know. The thing is, I'm just a little bit concerned that Izzy seems to be using really awful language. The boys say she swears at them all the time in the playground. You know, not just children's stuff, but really foul-mouthed.'

'What sort of thing?' Belinda demanded.

'Well . . .' Carina hesitated. 'Yesterday she called them fucking arseholes and cocksuckers. Several times. Not very nice, is it, from a six-year-old? I just thought you and Jess should know. I mean, I don't know where she could be picking up that kind of language but perhaps you could tell her that it isn't on. Rupert,' she went on, referring to her husband, 'thought the school should be told. He was fucking furious, actually.'

'I see,' said Belinda coldly. 'Well, Carina, of course I will tell Izzy that I never want her to talk like that again, but perhaps at the same time you could tell your boys not to call her a little bastard.' She looked at her watch. 'You'll have to hop out, I'm afraid, because I'll be late for work otherwise.'

She was shaking as she drove into Sherborne, half with rage and half with laughter. It would be those appalling boys of Lisa's who had taught Izzy the words and she was shocked to learn that Izzy had remembered and used them. All the same, she thought, good for little Iz. Good for Iz. She had glanced in her rear view mirror and seen Carina stalk back to her Range Rover, tall and skinny like a wading bird, her fur hat like a tuft on her head.

Thank goodness it was Jenny Crow's day off and she could telephone Victor and recount the conversation as soon as she got into the office. He roared with laughter when she told him. 'It's awful, though, Victor,' she said. 'That sort of language from such an innocent little thing. She shouldn't be mixing with rough boys like Ben and Darren. She thought they were wonderful and look what a bad influence they've been already.'

'Oh, come on. You make it sound as though she's well on the way to selling crack out of the front room. She's just learning to stand up for herself, that's all. You should be glad. It's a tough old world out there.'

When Belinda set off to London with Victor on Saturday morning, she hoped she might have the opportunity to ask him a question which she had put off until she felt she knew him better. A long car journey seemed the ideal time. It would be easier to talk to his profile as he concentrated on the road ahead than it would to face him across a pub table, for instance.

They dropped Izzy off at Ken's yard on the way, and while Belinda took her into the kitchen to say good morning to Mary, Victor got out of his car and had a walk round the boxes. Over the stable doors beautiful, alert thoroughbred heads looked out, some nodding and weaving impatiently, ears pricked, every one sensing the charge in the air on a racing morning. Ken's enormous blue lorry stood with the ramp down, ready to load, and from the tack room came the blare of Lisa's pop music as she put the final polish on the racing kit that would be needed, and folded rugs and leg bandages into the tin travelling trunk. Jess waved to him as she wheeled a barrow across the yard and then Belinda reappeared, hurrying from the back door of the farmhouse. She spotted Jess, waved and did a thumbs-up before joining Victor.

'Right,' she said. 'Shall we go? Jess can't bear me making a fuss and wishing her luck and everything and Izzy is happy helping Mary with the picnic in the kitchen.'

They went back to Victor's car and as they drove out of the yard he said, 'It's a good set-up, isn't it? A well-run place. You can tell that just from a quick look round.'

'I suppose so,' said Belinda. 'I've never really thought about it. I suppose I've always been so anti Jess working here. It seemed as if she was throwing her life away when she left school and went straight into racing.'

'Ah, well, I did the same thing, so I wouldn't be one to judge. Went straight to work, I mean. I'd be proud of her if I was you. I've told you about Heather, haven't I?'

'Only a bit,' said Belinda, remembering that Heather was the daughter he was going to visit.

'She's thirty-four and has two smashing little boys of five

and three but she wants to separate from Martin. They've been married eight years but she says she doesn't love him any more, and when I press her, all she'll say is that he's *boring*. Can you believe it? I mean, they lived together for three years before they got married. You'd think she would have discovered how boring he was by then. It breaks my heart to think of the children having to go through a divorce but she says that it's better to do it now when they are really too young to be affected.'

'Our children's generation seem to class being bored as an act of mental cruelty,' said Belinda. 'I don't know what we taught them to expect from life, but somewhere along the line they've picked up the idea that they have a right to always feel happy and fulfilled and, well, not bored.'

'Martin is as confused as I am,' said Victor. 'He's still living there, in the house, but is banned from all but the spare bedroom and his study. They've decided that it's a waste of money for him to move out and pay rent somewhere and Heather thinks he should share the childcare. I just can't understand it, how they can carry on like that. I'd like to knock their heads together.'

'So what will you do today? Take the boys out somewhere?'

'Yes. I promised I'd have them out for the day while Heather and Martin re-organise the house for this separate living arrangement. Poor little chaps. Heather believes that they should be told everything. I don't know what they make of it all. The last time I spoke to the older one, he said that he couldn't go and get her to speak to me on the telephone because he wasn't allowed to interrupt her "me-time"! Have you ever heard anything like it? Me-time! I reckon it's her that's the boring one!'

'Husbands seem to get chucked out a lot these days,' said Belinda. 'Marriage doesn't appear to suit young women. If it's not all romance and roses, they want a divorce.'

'You're right there,' agreed Victor. 'You see it happening all the time. Whereas men seem to prefer to be married.'

'Perhaps there should be a sort of Battersea Dogs Home for stray and unwanted husbands,' said Belinda. 'A holding centre where girls and women looking for a man could walk round and chose one to take home. There they would all be, lined up, trying to look their most appealing. Long-haired, short-haired and rough-coated, large and small, short and long legs, pure-bred and mongrel. They would have to have descriptive labels, you know, like "good with children", "needs lots of exercise", "not to be trusted off the lead" and so on. They could be taken home for a two-week trial period and if they weren't suitable, they could be sent back.' They both laughed.

'What would my label say?'

'Oh, reliable and trustworthy, I think. Something like "this lovely man deserves a good home. No fault of his own that he needs rehousing".' Goodness, she thought, what have I said? It sounded horribly arch, but when she dared to look across at Victor, he was laughing.

'Actually, Victor, that leads me to what I wanted to ask you. You might think it's cheek, but I feel I need to know. Have you had a lot of, well, relationships since your wife died?'

Victor glanced at her. 'You've heard then?' he said.

'Heard what? No, I haven't heard anything.'

'I thought you might have done. In a small place like Bishops Barton, word gets round. I did have an affair, as it happens, just a few months after Sally died. Angie was a nice woman. Lived in Bournemouth. I met her by answering an ad in the *Blackmore Vale* magazine. Trouble was, I knew it wasn't right from the start, that we weren't really suited, but I was lonely and so was she, and I wanted to be with a woman again. I felt as if I was half dead myself, at that point, and having an affair seemed to prove otherwise.'

'So what happened?' asked Belinda. She felt as if she was holding her breath.

'Eventually I had to break it off. I realised Angie was getting carried away with it all. Making plans. Wanting to move in with me and put her house on the market. Thinking that we had a long-term relationship. In the end I had to tell her the truth.'

Oh, God, thought Belinda. Did all men behave like this? Were middle-aged women always so deluded? She could not bear to go through a similar thing again.

'I see. How did she take it?' As if she couldn't guess.

'Not well. She said that I had misled her, taken advantage of her, that sort of thing. She was right in a way. I suppose I had, but I couldn't let it go on any longer.'

They lapsed into silence. Belinda looked out of the window, thinking about James. She had been like Angie, hopeful, in love, blind to the truth, willing to believe his propaganda.

Victor looked across at her. 'Don't go quiet on me,' he

said. 'I never felt about her like I do about you. Not for a minute.'

Belinda gave a wry smile. She had heard that before.

The point-to-point course at Barbury Castle was a chilly place to pass Saturday afternoon. It was a typical early March day, with blustery winds and high white clouds in a cobalt blue sky. Everything was sharp and bright, except where the soft piles of cloud banked on the horizon and drew colour from the distant downs, turning both a soft, hazy blue. As the wind rippled over the course, the long grass fairly glittered in the sunshine and, as the sun disappeared behind a cloud, deep shadows raced in a line across the wide fields, only to be banished a second later by another burst of brightness.

The wind still had a cutting edge to it but the side of Ken's lorry, parked amongst the horseboxes at the bottom end of the course, was hot to touch, and Ken and his staff took the chance to lean against it and feel the warmth creep through to their backs as they studied their racecards. Tom had one ride, on Cinders, and Carl had two, on Glennie and Captain Jack, while Jess, who had been scouting round for extra rides to no avail, had Dolly, as planned, in the ladies' race.

Mrs Toynbee shakily mounted the steep steps into the living accommodation of the horsebox handed up by Ken, and sat for a while on the horse blanket that covered the bench seat. She chatted to Tom about the race to come. Her rough little terrier whined from outside where he had been tied by his lead to the bumper of her ancient car. She gratefully accepted a ham roll and a glass of whisky and tapped Tom sternly on the leg.

'Just take good care of her, Tom,' she said in a voice that spoke from another generation. 'You know what needs to be done. Get a proper start, that's all I ask. There are some good horses here today and they will set a hot pace so don't mind pulling up if you think she's done enough.' She smiled at him, her old face criss-crossed by wrinkles but her eyes a pale sparkling blue behind the smeary lenses of her plastic spectacles. 'Now, if you would be so kind as to help me down I am going to put some money on the next race.'

The four horses, plaited and immaculate, were waiting in the lorry, the three youngsters tossing their heads and shifting their feet, snatching at the ropes of their head collars and straining to see out of the window. They knew where they were and the excitement of racing had already made them on edge and nervy, keyed up with the sort of energy which would send them leaping down the ramp when they were unboxed, eager to be part of the action.

The exception was the experienced Captain Jack who, according to Lisa, had been there, done it and got the T-shirt many times over. He stood with his eyes closed and a drooping bottom lip, like a seaside donkey, making the most of the chance to rest. Izzy had been allowed to stroke his nose and even help Lisa put on his Velcro leg bandages.

Now she knelt on the bench seat in the cab, wide-eyed at the generous picnic supplied by Mary, and bent over her pad, drawing with a felt tip pen.

'Look, Mummy,' she said as Jess climbed up into the lorry

to collect her bag of racing kit. 'These are water babies and they're going racing on seahorses.'

'Great,' said Jess, without looking, rummaging in her bag to check she had a hair net. She was annoyed that she had not managed to pick up any other rides. Two good horses had gone to another girl jockey who was less experienced but whose father had bought her a first-rate pointer to start her racing career and on whom she had notched up eight wins and earned a name for herself.

Still, she had her ride on Dolly to look forward to, and she felt confident that the grey mare would earn a place at least. Her owner, Mr Dare, a big, bluff builder from Bournemouth, was parked alongside in his new Range Rover and was more nervous than she was. 'Just the pair of you come home safe and sound,' he said over and over again.

It was time to get Cinders ready for Tom, who had already gone down to the official tent to weigh out. The big brown mare came swinging down the ramp of the lorry, head up, ears pricked, and Jess spent a moment oiling her hooves so they shone glossy and black, and brushing out the bottom of her tail to fan above her black hocks. She looked wonderful. Her deep brown coat shone, her mane was neatly plaited and sewn into hard little rosettes along her neck. Using a body brush and a mane comb, and working against the lie of the hair, Jess put the finishing touches to her grooming by creating a chequer pattern on her gleaming quarters.

'There,' she said to Rhona, who was tying Cinders' number band on her arm, ready to lead her round the paddock before the race. 'One smart horse.'

'Sure is,' said Rhona, shooting Jess a sympathetic smile. She knew how much she would have loved to have the ride herself. 'Mrs Toynbee will be pleased.'

The old lady was already on her way down to the paddock, well bundled up against the cold wind, her arm lightly tucked through Ken's. He would take care of her, escort her into the ring to watch Tom mount and keep her well out of the way of the other, nervous horses, and then find her the best place from which to watch the race. They had been doing this for years and Mrs Toynbee's field glasses, which she held to her eyes with a shaking, liver-spotted hand, fluttered with racecourse badges going back decades.

Jess put her head back into the lorry. Lisa was taking a break, sitting with Izzy, a mug of coffee in one hand and a ham roll in the other.

'Are you coming to watch?' she asked. Lisa shook her head. She could never bear seeing Ken's horses race. 'Just tell me when it's over,' she said. 'Izzy and I'll stay put, won't we, Iz?'

Izzy looked up and nodded. 'I just want to see you, Mummy. Not the other horses.'

'It's Tom riding. Don't you want to see Tom?'

Izzy stalled, torn between loyalty to Tom and the pleasure of being with Lisa and the picnic and Captain Jack, who was still asleep, his nose twitching.

'Oh, stay then,' said Jess impatiently, jumping down the lorry steps and making off to where she could see the start and most of the course from the rails.

The good weather had brought out the crowds and race-goers

swarmed around the paddock and the trade tents, which were bucking and banging cheerfully in the wind. Paper cups and litter from the fast food trailers bowled along the grass, and every now and then a tweed cap or a lady's hat was lifted off a head and spun along the ground before being retrieved and jammed back on again. As she passed the bookies, Jess could see that Cinders was favourite, although there were eight other runners and some proven horses in the race.

The horses were going down to the start, their jockeys standing up in their stirrups and trying to hold them in a steady canter, while the wind lifted their tails and fluttered their number cloths. Jess spotted Rhona coming from the paddock, folding Cinders' paddock rug over her arm, and caught up with her to find a place from where they could watch the race together.

'Cinders won best turned-out horse for you,' said Rhona, looking pleased. 'Mrs Toynbee was right chuffed.'

'Oh no,' said Jess, half pleased, half not. 'That's always unlucky for me. Whenever I win in the paddock, the horse runs a crap race.'

'Don't say that,' said Rhona, touching the wood of the rails. 'Not today, it won't. Not Cinders.'

They worked their way through the crowd to find a good place. The start was far away to the left and they could see the horses circling in the distance, waiting for the starter to get them in a semblance of a line and lower his flag. Mrs Toynbee's colours, red and gold with a gold cap, were easy to pick out and as they watched, the flag dropped and the bunch of horses suddenly surged forward and were off, galloping towards the first fence.

'He's made a good start,' said Rhona, 'Look, he's tucked in behind the front runners on the inside.'

Jess screwed up her eyes into the sun, focusing on nothing but the big brown mare. She saw her meet the first fence and fly over. It was always a relief to get the first one safely out of the way. The leading four now pushed ahead, the pace being set too fast by someone who could not hold his horse. Tom trailed behind them, Cinders galloping easily along the inside rail and taking the next two fences on her own, jumping smoothly and economically, just as if she was practising at home.

Jess fixed her eyes on the gold cap, admiring how Tom hardly moved in the saddle, seeing that he was not asking anything of Cinders so early in the race. When the time came she would have plenty left in reserve.

The runners were reaching the bend now, which would bring them over the next fence and past where the two girls stood along the crowded rails. There was a sudden gasp as one of the front horses made a bad mistake and fell, but Cinders was far enough behind to keep out of trouble and galloped safely on, still taking it easy, by the look of it.

'Tom's just hunting round,' said Rhona. 'Cinders is enjoying every moment.'

'I hope he hasn't let the leaders get too far away from him,' said Jess anxiously. 'He's got a long way to make up to get back into the frame.'

'Tom knows what he's doing,' said Rhona. 'He hasn't started yet.'

They watched in silence as the group of horses ran down the far side of the course towards the open ditch, their colours bright against the green turf and the brilliant sky. Again Tom and Cinders jumped on their own, lengths behind the front runners and well in front of those bringing up the rear. The sun went in as the horses reached the top of the course and it was several long minutes before they re-emerged on the bend at the end of the back straight. Jess and Rhona waited in tense silence, straining their eyes into the distance.

'Now will you look at that,' said Rhona as the first horses reappeared. 'I'd say he's moved up twenty lengths since they went out of sight.'

As the group galloped down the hill to pass the start for the second time, Cinders was eating up the ground on the inside. Steadily she overhauled first one horse and then another in an impressive display of speed. The commentator picked up her name and the crowd stirred with excitement. There were four more fences to go and Jess held her breath as the big mare took up a position to challenge the two leaders. Neck and neck, they took each fence and there was little between them as they raced for the second last.

Now Tom had begun to ride hard. Head down, arms and legs working, he was giving his best to the brown mare and asking her to do the same. This was when young horses could make mistakes and Jess could hardly bear to watch, but Cinders stood right off and took the fence very fast and low and jumped well into the lead. She was a length or two ahead at the last and galloped to the finish a clear winner, still fresh and full of running, her lovely head up and her ears pricked as if she knew she was a champion in the making.

Jess and Rhona clasped one another in excitement.

'And he never lifted his whip!' cried Rhona, who hated to see horses finish with stripes across their quarters. She ducked under the rails and ran down the course to lead them in.

Tom hoisted Izzy onto his shoulders so that she could see better.

'Gosh, Iz,' he said. 'What did you have for lunch? A concrete sandwich?'

Izzy laughed and held on to his hair.

'Ouch! Don't scalp me! Can you see your mum? She's easy to spot on a grey horse. Dolly's the only grey in the race.'

'I can see her! I can see her!' shouted Izzy, pointing as the horses thundered over the brow of the hill in the second circuit of the ladies' race. 'She's still in front! She's still winning!'

Yes, thought Tom, Jess was following Ken's instructions to the letter, taking Dolly to the front and staying there all the way round, making all the going and taking the faster, inside track. The grey mare had set a cracking pace and was still flying, getting the stride right and jumping confidently, and Jess was riding her beautifully, judging the fences perfectly and not making any mistakes. It was a copybook round and Tom felt a silly great smile split his face. He hung on to Izzy's ankles to stop her kicking him in excitement.

At the second to last fence after the bend to the final straight and the winning post, Dolly was five or six lengths ahead and the crowd was roaring its approval. A pretty jockey and a grey mare always caught the punters' eye and it would be a popular win.

Tom saw Dolly leap into the air over the fence and then something went horribly wrong. As she landed a hind leg crumpled beneath her and the next moment she was skidding along the ground on her belly, Jess still on top. The crowd gasped and Tom saw Jess tip herself out of the saddle and onto her feet, still holding the reins. Dolly was on her side now, thrashing her legs, trying to get up, and then there was a rush as other horses jumped round her. The next glimpse Tom got, Jess was sitting on the mare's head, keeping her on the ground. Tom could see Jess's mouth was open and realised that she was screaming for help.

He dropped Izzy with such a rush that the little girl stumbled to her knees.

'Stay there!' he shouted at her and started to run, but he could hear Izzy scream too, high and terrified, and he ran back to her.

'Mummy's all right!' he cried. 'You saw! Mummy's all right!' He frantically searched the crowd for someone he knew, but all faces were turned to watch the finish. Then he spotted a woman he recognised, a farmer's wife from Stur, and dashed over to her. He grasped her arm and the woman looked round, surprised. He pulled Izzy forward.

'Can you look after this little girl? Just for a while. Her mother's horse has just come down.' He indicated the fence where there were now screens erected around the fallen mare. The woman's comfortable, round face looked shocked, and she nodded.

'Which lorry?' she asked. 'I'll take her to the lorry.'

'Ken Andrews'!' shouted Tom as he ran. 'Ask anyone!'

As he ducked under the rails, he could still hear Izzy's wailing. He turned for one last look and saw that the woman had knelt to talk to her, holding her by the hand, but Izzy was pulling away, her face contorted with panic.

Shit, he thought as he ran. She shouldn't be here. She shouldn't have seen what happened like that, but he had to get to Jess. It was Jess who needed him.

Even though he ran as fast as he could, weaving through the milling crowd and then along the course, by the time he got to the fence it was all over. The vet was getting to his feet and Jess was standing forlorn, holding an empty bridle, the saddle hooked over her arm. The grey mound stretched on the ground was Dolly, lovely Dolly.

Jess turned a tragic face as white as paper when he called her name. 'Her leg went,' she said in a small voice. 'I heard it go like a pistol shot as she took off. It just snapped like a twig!'

The grey-haired vet looked troubled. It was a horrible job, to have to shoot a beautiful young horse. 'There must have been a weakness in the bone from an old injury,' he said. 'Maybe a star fracture that gave way. It's a miserable business. It can happen. I've seen it before.' He turned to Jess. 'You were lucky not to have been injured. Lucky it went like that. She won't have felt anything, you know. She wasn't in any pain.'

Then Rhona was there, tears streaking her anguished face, and Ken and Mr Dare, also in tears, wiping his big, red face with the back of his hand. 'She was going so well,' he blubbed. 'She would have won. She was going so well!'

Tom saw Jess turn and walk away from them, her face expressionless, Dolly's saddle and bridle in her arms. He ran to join her. Together, in silence but united in misery, they started back towards the lorry.

Nobody remembered Izzy.

It was Ken who suggested that Tom take Jess and Izzy home.

'We'll manage all right tonight,' he said. 'Have the evening off. We'll see you tomorrow for Cothelstone. Business as usual. And Jess,' he added kindly. 'There was nothing you could have done. It was a freak accident. You were riding a grand race. You would have won, no doubt of that.'

Izzy had been delivered back to the box by the woman in whose care Tom had so urgently thrust her, her face still scarlet and congested with tears, her breath coming in gasps. Tom knelt beside her, taking her hand, and tried to explain why he had run off and left her, but she was unresponsive. She looked away and said nothing, ignoring her mother. Everyone was too occupied with their own feelings and the need to talk through the horror and drama of what had happened to take any more notice of her.

They had all cried except Jess. Lisa wailed, tears streaming down her blotchy face, Rhona too, even Ken had to wipe the corner of his eye. There was nothing worse than losing a horse, he said, nothing got to him more. No one could bear to look at the empty space in the lorry where Dolly's head collar still hung by its rope and her rug and surcingle, neatly folded by Lisa, were lying over the partition.

The fact that Captain Jack romped across the line to win

the men's open for Carl did not relieve the gloom.

Away from everybody, Jess cried silently on the way home, turning her head to look, unseeing, out of the window, the tears sliding down to drop in dark patches on her jeans. Tom said nothing, just touched her knee in sympathy. It was better to let it out, all that pent-up emotion. He glanced at Izzy in the back. She was sitting between Meg and Snowy, holding Snowy's one black ear to her solemn down-turned mouth. It was her favourite ear, he had heard her say, with its own special smell, quite different from its opposite number, which was white.

Poor Iz, thought Tom. It had been awful leaving her like that. Perhaps he shouldn't have done it, but his first reaction had been to get to Jess. He wondered now what had gone through the little girl's mind when he had left her screaming. She must have seen that Jess was all right and she wasn't old enough, surely, to realise that the horse had been fatally injured.

Dolly's death was a miserable affair, but it happened in racing. It was the downside of a brave and dangerous sport. They all knew that, everyone did, everyone who had anything to do with steeplechasing. You had to accept that it could happen. The one thing he was glad of was that Moira wasn't there today. Her snide comments would have been the last straw.

All the same, after what she had been through, Tom was surprised when Jess sniffed, wiped her face on her sleeve and said, 'Can you babysit tonight, Tom? I've forgotten to ask you.' He had not expected her to still want to face Karen Bearsden.

'I'd rather come with you,' he said, not wanting to think of her going on her own.

'No thanks, Tom, I'll be all right. I need to do it. I'm not going to put it off. Funnily enough, what happened today makes me feel stronger, somehow. You know, racing costs a lot one way and another and I'm not going to let that woman screw it up for me.'

When they got out of the Land Rover at Rosebay Cottage, Jess told Izzy she must go and feed Bonnet straightaway and Izzy whined, saying that she was too tired and that her legs ached. Jess snapped at her, telling her not to be a baby, and gave her a sharp push across the yard.

'Come on, I'll help you, Iz,' said Tom, conscious of having something to make up for. 'Poor Bonnet's hungry. She'll be wondering where you are with her tea.'

Together they filled a hay net, Izzy painfully slowly, but at last it was done and Tom helped her tie it on the gate where the old brown pony was stamping her feet impatiently.

The cottage seemed strangely empty and quiet without Belinda, as though it was holding its breath and waiting for life to begin again. There didn't seem to be anything for supper so Tom made a list and he and Izzy went into Sharston to do some shopping while Jess had a bath, lying in six inches of foam with the radio turned up.

By the time they returned from their shopping expedition, she was dressed in clean jeans and sweater and Tom could tell she was on edge, watching the clock and waiting for Ludmylla's call. Eventually, she told him she could bear it no longer and that perhaps Ludmylla had forgotten and that she was going to call her mobile. He heard Ludmylla answer and gathered that Karen had not yet arrived but that she would contact Jess, as promised, when she did.

The call came about eight o'clock. Jess had been unable to eat the steak Tom had cooked. 'I'll have it when I get back,' she said, pushing her plate away.

'Where are you going, Mummy?' Izzy whined. 'I don't want you to go out.' It was unlike her to be clinging, thought Tom. She must be tired. He noticed that she had dark smudges under her eyes and her face was so pale it was the colour of lemonade.

'Tom's staying here with you,' said Jess shortly, collecting her mobile telephone and keys. 'I won't be long.'

'But where are you going?' persisted Izzy.

'Come on, Iz,' Tom said. 'Let's do the washing up and then we'll watch your video, shall we? *A Hundred and One Dalmatians*. You love that.'

Izzy allowed herself to look mollified. She had worked out that it was already well past her bedtime.

Jess gave her a kiss. 'Bye, Iz,' she said. 'Sorry I was cross with you. I'll come up and kiss you when I get in.' She looked across at Tom. 'Wish me luck,' she said, raising a fist in a show of mock aggression.

Jess drove as quietly as possible into the courtyard at the back of Quatt Lodge. The moon was bright and she had turned off her headlights coming down the drive because she did not want Karen alerted that she had a visitor. For once the lights were on all over the house and she could see that Ludmylla was in the kitchen waiting for her, her

351

face anxiously against the glass, trying to see out into the dark.

The kitchen door was ajar and Jess opened it cautiously. Ludmylla had the television on, turned down low, and she gestured to Jess to enter, holding a finger to her lips and indicating that Karen was somewhere down the passage that led from the kitchen to the main part of the house.

Jess stepped in and although she could feel her heart thumping she was not afraid. Above the television she could hear Karen's voice. It floated down the passage, sounding as though she was speaking to someone on the telephone. Jess heard her saying goodbye and then there was silence. Jess nodded to Ludmylla, who went to the door and called in a loud voice, 'Mrs Bearsden! Mrs Bearsden! There is some person here to see you.'

Karen appeared in the doorway, holding a pad and biro in one hand, looking startled. She had pushed her glasses to the top of her head, and her wiry hair was held back in a clip. She was wearing well-cut jeans and looked tall and slim.

She recognised Jess and her expression changed. 'Oh,' she said in her soft voice. 'It's you.'

'A surprise,' said Jess.

'Oh no, not really,' said Karen evenly. 'I was kind of expecting you. Did Ludmylla tell you I was here? Why don't you come through and we can have a little chat.'

Chapter Fourteen

'So why were you expecting me?' asked Jess.

Karen Bearsden had led her into a room that she clearly used as an office. A computer and printer stood on a large workmanlike desk which was spread with papers and files. A neat stack of document boxes was piled on the floor, the top one open, the metal clip holding down a sheaf of bills.

'House restoration,' she said, indicating the paperwork and ignoring Jess's question. 'It's proving to be a nightmare. A full-time job. This place is grade two listed, you see, which makes things much more difficult.' She moved across the room to switch on a table lamp. 'Why don't we sit down? We might as well be comfortable. Would you like a cup of coffee? A drink?'

'No thank you,' said Jess stiffly. She was aware that Karen was working to regain control of the situation; she'd been caught off guard, whatever she said.

Karen indicated a battered leather armchair on one side of the fireplace. The hearth was black and empty and the room had an unloved, impersonal atmosphere. Jess guessed that it must once have been the old man's business room. One of the walls was lined with wooden painted cupboards and shelves, numbered alphabetically, and it was free of any sort of decoration, although squares of unfaded paint on the walls indicated where pictures had once hung.

Karen sat opposite her on a matching chair. A tartan rug was thrown over the back where the old leather had split. She straightened the rug, grimacing. 'Horrible old stuff,' she said, 'but we have to live with it right now.' She turned back to Jess, a small, social smile lifting the corners of her mouth. 'So, you asked me how I knew you would come. I'll tell you. I tried the friendly, direct approach, inviting your little girl round, if you remember, but I could see that you were hostile. I guessed that you would always be like that. However, I reckoned that you and I had to sort this thing out sooner rather than later, and one sure way of getting your attention was through your racing.' She paused, looking at Jess shrewdly. 'I knew you wouldn't ignore what I said to Mary Andrews about you. I guessed, rightly it seems, that it would get you on line, so I was expecting a visit or a telephone call.'

Jess shifted uneasily in her chair. This was what she had been frightened of, that somehow Karen would outsmart her. Her notion that she would catch her unawares was now in pieces. She felt as if she had been drawn into a trap of her own making. But she had to go on now, say what she had come to say.

'What you said to Mary was outrageous,' she began, in an indignant tone. 'I don't know what you're up to, but I won't let you mess up my racing.'

Karen laughed softly and shook her head, as if Jess was so wide of the mark that it was absurd. 'Oh, come, Jess,' she said. 'Frankly, I'm not interested in your racing. There's rather more at stake here than that, isn't there?'

Of course there was. Jess regretted her opening salvo and realised that it made her seem childish and impetuous, but to talk of anything but her career was to break six years of silence and she did not know how to do it. No other living person, not Tom, not her mother, had managed to make her talk about Izzy, until now, and she wasn't sure she could find the right words to express what for so long had been sealed over.

She was unnerved by Karen's clever smoothness. She felt she would be outmanoeuvred and left empty-handed and foolish. Keep quiet, she told herself. Let Karen do the talking. She has more to lose than me.

'The situation,' said Karen, lowering her eyes and pointing the toe of her polished boot, 'as I see it, is this. Coming face to face with your daughter was a shock, to say the least. I'd probably heard your name in the past when Johnnie kept horses down here and I might even have heard that you had a child. I'm not sure, exactly, because of course it would have been of no interest to me. Why should it have been?' She looked up, her eyes very blue and direct.

Jess sat perfectly still but the quickened breathing pounding her chest gave away her agitation. She had no idea where this conversation was heading. It was like waiting to be attacked but not knowing from which direction the blows would come.

'Now that we have come to live here and I've met you and Isobel, that has all changed.'

Jess sat on, her face blank.

'As I say, I was very shocked when I first saw your little

girl. I thought I must be mistaken, that it was just an extraordinary coincidence, but then, after a second meeting, that time in the car park, and a little research on my part, I realised the truth. From your reaction I saw that you knew it, too. It was unavoidable, wasn't it? The similarity is extraordinary. And so unlucky. It's the hair colour, skin tone, eyes, everything. Even mannerisms. I realised that it could not be passed off as a chance likeness.' Karen smoothed the legs of her jeans over her long thighs. She betrayed so little emotion that she could have been talking about some minor inconvenience in her life.

'I also found out about you, Jess. I needed to know how you had handled things, what you had told people, and I guessed it hadn't been easy for you.' Karen smiled gently at her. 'What I found,' she went on, 'was that you had given nothing whatever away and although there was obviously a lot of speculation, nobody knew for certain who had fathered Izzy. I admire that. It shows strength of character.'

Oh no you don't, thought Jess, narrowing her eyes. You're trying to soften me up. I can see your game. There was a pause while Karen looked at her, waiting for her to respond. Jess let it go a long moment before saying truculently, 'Yeah. So?'

Karen laughed softly as if Jess's gruffness amused her. 'We've clearly got to find a way out of this bizarre situation. I intend to make this place a home for the family and we will be here more and more often. Having you and your child living a stone's throw away and sharing, to some extent, our social circle, particularly the horse world, which Johnnie will want to get back into, is not going to be possible.

I don't want Mikey to have to contend with gossip and rumour, and I'm sure you feel the same way about your little girl.

'One of the things I discovered about you, Jess, and forgive me for speaking frankly here, is that you have nothing much to offer other than your experience with horses. That's correct, isn't it? You live with your mother on what I assume is a small income. You must have given the future some thought. After all, the career span of point-to-point jockeys is fairly short, isn't it, and if you were going to make the grade, you would have done it by now. Forgive me, but I think it's important to be straight with you. I've talked to your boyfriend, as I expect you know, and the impression I got from Mary Andrews was that he would like to marry you but that his prospects aren't so great either. He'll never have the capital to have any real future in farming. He'll certainly never own his own farm, will he?'

Jess was sitting up straight now, her face flushed and angry. 'How dare you!' she burst out. 'How dare you be so bloody patronising! How do you know what either of us wants to do with our lives?'

'Jess,' Karen interrupted her gently. 'I'm being realistic, not patronising. Just hear me out, will you?' She stood up and went to her desk and sorted through some papers. 'Ah, here it is.' She had a folder in her hand as she sat down again. 'I'm prepared to make you an offer, Jess. Not that I have to, of course, but because I feel it would be to our mutual advantage. I am prepared to help you, with or without Tom, with the rent of a farm in North Yorkshire. As it happens, an American friend of mine has an estate up there and is looking for a tenant for one of the hill farms. There's a pleasant small farmhouse,' and she flicked through the papers to look for a colour photograph, 'and some good stone barns. I imagine they would convert into a useful sort of yard for horses. The whole thing would provide the opportunity for a fresh start for you. And for Isobel, of course. There's a good primary school in the village. Here,' she said, passing over the file. 'Have a look.'

Jess stared at her in disbelief. 'Wait a minute,' she said slowly. 'Are you trying to buy me out? Get rid of me and Izzy? Have us transported?'

Karen chuckled softly. 'That's a silly way to look at it, Jess. What I am proposing is the chance to lead a better life. Away from here, granted, but that is to our mutual advantage, isn't it?'

A silence fell between the two women. Jess could hear Ludmylla's television in the background, the bursts of laughter of a sitcom. She found it hard to believe that she was here, with Karen, having this conversation.

'I need to think about this,' she said finally. 'I need to work out the implications.'

'Sure,' said Karen. 'Although I can't allow you too long, I'm afraid. I would like to put this into action as soon as possible. For obvious reasons. I'd like you away certainly before the summer vacation.' She smiled. 'That sounds terrible, but you will appreciate what I mean. It would be better for both our sakes.' She leaned across to hand Jess the folder, and then stood up as if an interview was over.

'There's one thing,' said Jess slowly, staring at the folder in her hand, 'that I must ask you.'

'Ask away,' said Karen, unperturbed.

'It's about Johnnie,' said Jess, looking up. She thought she saw Karen stiffen and tense. 'I don't get it, you see. I don't get Johnnie's position in all of this.'

'Johnnie's position?' repeated Karen, giving her head a little sideways jerk as if she was surprised by what Jess had just said. Jess saw that she was stalling and realised that she had moved onto ground that Karen had skilfully avoided.

'Yes,' said Jess deliberately, as if she had come to the whole point of the discussion, 'because that makes all the difference, doesn't it?'

Karen looked down at her, her eyebrows arched, her easy, confident manner quite changed. She was as poised and alert as a snake about to strike.

'I would guess, from the offer you've made and the fact that you are so keen to get me and Izzy out of the way, that Johnnie doesn't know.' Her gaze didn't waver as she looked up at Karen. 'Is that it?' she said. 'Johnnie doesn't know the truth? Johnnie doesn't know that Mikey is not his son?'

It was a great relief to Belinda to see Dinka come to the door of her garden flat, smiling and dressed in a pair of tight jeans and cashmere sweater. She had a scarf wrapped round her face and wore dark glasses but when she took them off, the scars were hardly visible, the flesh around her mouth and eyes only a little bruised and puffy.

'See,' she said triumphantly. 'Worth all the pain. I'll be looking fab by Friday and ten years younger, which makes Javier my junior by only five years!'

'You certainly look much better than I imagined,' said Belinda. 'I thought you'd have a face like a bit of darning.'

'Wait until you see me with the full slap. I haven't worn any make-up for a week and I still don't look too bad, do I? I'll look sensational with a little cosmetic enhancement. Ready for a drink, darling? I've got champagne in the fridge and then I'll feel strong enough to go round the corner to El Pirata's for lunch. How about it? There's so much we need to talk about. Did I tell you that Javier has telephoned every day? He has, the sweetheart. Very loving. And I'm longing to hear about your man. What's his name? Something very dated and *Boys' Own* – oh yes, *Victor*! It's so clever of you to find a man who actually does something useful. I mean, I long to have a plumber lover, or a painter and decorator. Even a window cleaner,' she added, rubbing at a pane of the French windows with her sleeve. 'Javier is too pretty to even change a lightbulb!' The bright March sun streamed in, showing every smear on the glass and tiny motes of dust danced in the wide shaft as it hit the polished floor.

'Dinka, he's not my lover! I've only been out with him a few times and on the way here he told me that he preyed on lonely women!'

'What? He can't have done!'

Belinda recounted the conversation and when she had finished, Dinka said, 'Oh really, Belinda. For heaven's sake, don't get all tight-arsed about what sounds to me a perfectly acceptable means of dealing with grief. He was honest about it, and it's a well-known fact that sex can be wonderfully therapeutic. The woman must have been exceptionally stupid not to realise that he could not possibly have been ready to get into something heavy so soon after his wife died. Now come on, I want to celebrate. We need to drink to my new face and your new man,' and she swept into the kitchen, shouting instructions to Belinda to get out the champagne flutes.

Belinda fetched them from the cabinet in the sitting room and then stood in the kitchen door, one in each hand, and glimpsed the inside of Belinda's fridge which contained three bottles of champagne, a bottle of vodka and a lemon. We're a different species, she thought, Dinka and me.

'Don't you eat anything, Dinka?' she asked. 'Can you really live on drink and a lemon?'

Dinka laughed. 'Oh, Javier does food, darling. I don't. I can't bear having it lying around in the kitchen. I've lost half a stone since the operation. Isn't it wonderful?' She pressed her hands flat to her stomach and looked down at its concave surface appreciatively. 'Two birds with one stone, or half a one!' She opened the bottle with a flourish and the cork shot up like a little grenade to hit the ceiling and a waterfall of champagne poured in a cream foam out of the neck of the bottle. Dinka's eyes sparkled. 'Oh, yum,' she said. 'I haven't had a drop for a week. Now come on, I want to hear all about Jess. I must be episodes behind in the saga!'

Belinda felt at a loss to know where to begin. It all seemed so far removed from Dinka in her smart little flat with its empty fridge and slate and steel surfaces. How could she expect her to be interested? Dinka stood there waiting, leaning against her hand-crafted French oak cupboard, her glass to her lips.

'Oh, Dinka,' she said. 'Do you really want to hear? It's such a long story.'

'Of course I do,' said Dinka staunchly. 'I shall hang on every word.'

Later, driving home with Victor, Belinda felt almost as if she had been away on holiday. She and Dinka had enjoyed a long lunch and talked and laughed and everything that had been worrying her seemed to be put back in its proper place within the whole scheme of things. That was what was so wonderful about old friends, she thought. It did not matter how different their lives might be, the old point of contact could always be found and then away they went, their conversation ranging like a scatter-gun, dipping in and out of each other's lives, sharing, comparing, supporting. There was no one like Dinka for putting her straight, and she hoped that Dinka, in turn, felt equally nourished and restored by seeing her.

'I'm not going to let you bring him in,' she said to Belinda when Victor rang the doorbell in the evening. 'I want to meet him when I'm at my glorious best, not looking like a punchbag. Just pull the door to behind you.'

'So how was your day?' Belinda asked as they stopped and started through the London traffic. It had begun to rain and the road was black and greasy and the city lights smeared the dark evening with colour.

'Well, I didn't get anywhere with Heather. No nearer finding out what it's all about, so I can't see how I can help. She's determined to go through with it. To be honest I thought there must be someone else involved, but it seems there isn't. She says she wants to be on her own. That she and Martin have nothing in common. Nothing in common, I said, except the boys. Don't they count? She wouldn't have that. No way. Said I was trying to make her feel guilty.'

Belinda sighed in sympathy. 'God, it's difficult, isn't it? You think life will be easier and less complicated when your children are grown up, but often the problems are worse, in a way. They seem more intractable. You can do so little to help when things go wrong. I think all families are the same. I don't know any that haven't been through the mill in some way and those that say they haven't must be lying.' After she had said it, she realised that it hadn't been a very cheering little speech, except in a 'we're all in the same boat' kind of way.

She thought of Dinka in her chic little flat, with no family to speak of, and wondered whether she was happier. Definitely less anguished, she thought, and far better preserved, but she did not envy her. Dinka seemed to have more than made up for the lack of family worries by throwing in her lot with Javier. Perhaps worrying is just part of the human condition, she thought. If our lives are soft and easy, as ours are, free of hunger and war and plague, we find other things to destroy our happiness. Divorce and drugs and anorexia and doomed relationships.

'When we were growing up,' said Victor, 'our parents were rebuilding their lives after the war and the generation before were sent to die in the trenches. What a flabby, self-indulgent lot we are by comparison. We're the first to have come through with having it soft and it shows in our children, I reckon. It makes me mad when I hear the lads I employ talking about being stressed out. What do they know about stress?'

'But we do put ourselves through it on their behalf, don't we? All day I've been worrying about Jess racing. You know, in the back of my mind. Checking the time, thinking that I would have heard by now if there'd been an accident.'

'Of course you would, but you have to let the lass do what she wants. Live her own life. You can't be forever trying to stop her.'

'That's what Dinka keeps telling me, and of course I know it, but it's Izzy that's the worry. Being without a father. If anything happened to Jess, what sort of life would it be for Izzy?'

'You don't want to think like that, worrying about things which most likely will never happen.'

'I need to chill, you mean. That's what Jess is always saying.'

'Something like that. Now let's stop talking about our children. When we get out of London, shall we stop for a bite of supper?' He looked across at her as the traffic came to a stop in front of them, and slid a hand onto her knee.

'That would be lovely,' said Belinda, thinking, life's such a switchback ride. Up one minute, down the next, and only a moment of plain sailing in between. She wondered if there was a philosopher somewhere who had come to the conclusion that the only way to get through life was to do one's best and stick to the people one loved.

*

'I don't think that's any of your business,' said Karen coldly.
Jess could see a tiny twitch at the corner of her mouth. 'It
is absolutely nothing to do with you.'

'Well, it is in a way. You see, I have had six years of people
speculating that Johnnie is the father of my child. Ironic,
isn't it? Then you turn up here, and lo and behold, your
eldest is the spitting image of Izzy. It won't be long before
everybody notices, and jumps to the same conclusion, and
so you want me out of the way, and I can see why. If I
refuse to go quietly, we'll just have to sit it out, you and me.
I'm used to it by now, but it will be harder on you, and
tough for Izzy and Mikey. And Johnnie, of course. Especially
for Johnnie, because he will know one thing for sure, that
he isn't Izzy's father. I had a silly crush on him, I admit, but
we never had an affair. He was married, you remember.'

It was Karen who now looked rattled. Her mouth set, she
was breathing through her nose in quick, audible snorts. She
went back to the desk and drummed her fingers on some
papers before looking up and saying, 'OK. Cards on the table.
I admit it. Johnnie doesn't know and I don't want him to
find out. For the obvious reasons and some else besides. So
you're right, I guess, that it's worth it to me to make you
this offer. Eventually, I suppose, the truth may have to come
out, but not now. Now is very much the wrong time.'

It was Jess's turn to smile. 'You thought I'd grab at it,
didn't you? You thought because you are rich and I am not,
that you had power over me. You thought I'd be grateful.
Well, I'm not.' She let the folder drop to the floor with a
clatter and the typewritten sheets and a page of photographs
spilled onto the worn rug. 'I'm not even going to bother to

show this stuff to Tom. He doesn't have to be bought to marry me. He doesn't have to have a farm dangled under his nose like a carrot. You'll have to think again, Mrs Bearsden.'

Karen made a gesture of impatience and began to walk up and down the room. 'You're being pig-headed,' she said, clasping both her hands into fists in front of her and talking slowly and deliberately as if she had to get a simple point across to someone of limited intelligence. 'My suggestion does not amount to paying you off, as you put it. It is simply that I have it within my means to ease both of us out of this awkward situation. That's what money is, a facilitator. Nothing more. You would be mad not to accept. It's a great chance for all three of you.'

'How very kind of you to think of us,' said Jess coldly.

Karen narrowed her eyes. She did not like to be mocked. 'You're a fool if you turn it down,' she said. 'More stupid than I thought.'

Jess stood up. 'Then I'll go,' she said. 'If I'm that stupid there's not much point in talking to me. You don't owe me anything and neither does Johnnie and I don't want to be "facilitated" by you. In fact, I don't want anything to do with any of you and I never did from the beginning of all this. If later on in her life Izzy wants to know more about herself, because one day she'll have to know the truth, I shall tell her where to find her half-brother.'

Karen took up a defensive position by the door. 'You're not going yet,' she said softly. 'We haven't finished. You've been exceedingly awkward and unpleasant but I am prepared to give you the benefit of the doubt. I don't think, Jess, that you are the sort of malicious person who sets out to deliberately wreck a family. You said you were once fond of Johnnie. Well, he's just the same, a nice, decent man, and I'm certain that you don't want to be responsible for ruining everything for him, not to mention the children.'

'Let me out,' said Jess, standing by the door. Karen did not move. 'If you don't, I'll hit you.'

'Are you threatening me?' said Karen.

'I said let me out!'

'I'll see you don't ride again,' said Karen quietly. 'For the Andrews or anyone else.'

'Fuck off! You can't stop me.'

The two women glared at each other like cats squaring for a spat. Karen was the first to give ground. She turned away and held a hand to her head in a gesture of despair. 'I'm sorry, Jess. I apologise. That was a dumb thing to say. Of course I can't stop you and I wouldn't try. I give you my word. Although we can't keep our horses at Ken Andrews' yard if you are still there. You can see that. If you refuse to go away, we shall have to avoid all possibility of our children meeting.'

'We? Why "we"? Why should it matter to me? I'm used to gossip about Izzy. People will be only too pleased to see that they were right all along. Only you, me and Johnnie will know the truth.'

Karen said nothing, standing in the middle of the room holding her head in both hands. Suddenly she looked over to Jess and said, 'I've a question for you, too, Jess.'

'What?'

'It's something that puzzles me,' said Karen. 'Why have

you never told the truth? It can't have been easy to keep a secret like that. You've kept it long after it was necessary, and I just wonder why. You seem not to mind my husband's name being bandied about as Izzy's father. Why? You haven't even told your family. Why?'

Jess's face was empty of expression. 'What's it to you? It's none of your business.'

'Ah,' said Karen thoughtfully, watching her shrewdly. 'I thought you must have a good reason and now I can guess what it is.' She paused and then said in a changed voice, rather gentle and conciliatory, 'There's a lot of dangerous territory between us, isn't there? A lot of unexploded bombs. Tell me, did you love him?'

'Did you?'

'I adored him. The love of my life. I'd have left Johnnie for him. I guess you felt the same.'

'No,' said Jess, her face a frozen mask. 'I hated him.'

When Belinda was dropped off by Victor at eleven thirty on Saturday night, lights were on all over Rosebay Cottage and Tom's Land Rover was parked outside.

'Goodness. They're still up,' she said, gathering her bag and gloves. 'Tom and Jess are usually in bed by nine o'clock when they're racing the next day.'

'Where are they going tomorrow?' asked Victor.

'Let me think. Somewhere in Devon. One of those little country courses which Jess loves.'

'Let's go racing together one day,' said Victor. 'It's a long time since I've been to a point-to-point. I'd enjoy seeing Jess ride.'

'Would you? I told you I hate it, but it would be different if I was with you.' It would too, she thought. Victor was such a safe and reassuring man to be with. She looked across at him and smiled. 'Thank you so much for today. It was wonderful to have a lift with you. And thank you for the dinner.'

'No, thank *you*,' said Victor. He turned in his seat and kissed her. She kissed him back and had they not been in his car outside her house with Snowy barking like a maniac inside, it could well have led to something more exciting. As it was, she broke away, and turned to get out. He came round to hold the door for her in an old-fashioned and gentlemanly way.

'Tomorrow?' he said. 'What are you doing tomorrow?'

'Oh, I shall have a quiet day here,' said Belinda. 'You know, church in the morning and then doing all the chores before the week begins. Boring stuff like the ironing. And I'll be looking after Izzy, of course.' She paused. 'Why don't you come to lunch? I always cook on Sunday, even if it's only for Izzy and me. Please do. I'll get my jobs done in the morning and we could go for a walk in the afternoon if it's another nice day.'

Victor kissed her again. 'That would be very nice,' he said. 'I always find Sundays the worst day.'

Belinda wondered about this as she went to let herself in at the back door. Men aren't good on their own, she thought. Not like most women, who could somehow cling to domestic routines and find things to do to occupy empty lives. Does he just want to be with me because he's lonely and needy or was it real, the affection he said he felt and which she could not help but respond to? I wish I could be sure, she thought. He seems such a good, solid man, but I expect that's how Angie saw him, too.

When she opened the back door she found Tom in the kitchen, trying to damp down Snowy's enthusiastic welcome.

'Hello, Tom,' she said. 'You're up late. Where's Jess? How did it go today?' She threw her coat over a chair and went to put the kettle on the Rayburn.

'Jess is out,' said Tom. 'I'm getting a bit worried about her.'

'Out?' Belinda stopped short and turned round, the kettle in her hand. 'Where?'

'She went to meet Karen Bearsden. You know, we told you about it the other evening. She went over to Quatt Lodge about eight o'clock. She's not back yet.'

Belinda looked at him, trying to work out whether his anxiety was justified. 'Why don't you ring her mobile?' she asked.

'I have. It's switched off and then I tried Ludmylla's, but she's gone to the pub with Ivan. She said Jess was still there when she left.'

'You could always ring the house if you're really worried.'

'I don't want to do that yet. Jess would be furious, wouldn't she?'

'Yes,' said Belinda, 'she would. Well, we'll just have to wait. I don't suppose she'll be much longer. They can't have that much to talk about. It's not a social call, after all. Do you want a cup of tea? I'm going to make one. How was the racing? Was Izzy all right? Did she enjoy it?'

'No,' said Tom slowly. 'We had a bloody awful day. Ken lost a horse.'

370

'What do you mean? A horse was killed?'

'Yes,' said Tom miserably.

'Who with?' asked Belinda, searching his face. 'Who was riding?' Even as she asked, she knew the answer. 'Oh, no! Not with Jess? Oh, no!' She sat down at the table. 'What happened?'

Slowly, Tom recounted the events, trying to play down the drama and leaving out all reference to Izzy, but Belinda was quick to say, 'What about Izzy? Where was she? Who was with her when this happened?'

'She was with me,' said Tom. 'We were watching the race together.'

'Oh, no,' said Belinda again. 'How awful. What did she see? Did she see it happen?'

'She couldn't have seen much,' said Tom. 'It was all over quickly.'

Belinda searched his face. 'How was she afterwards? Did it upset her?'

'She was all right,' said Tom, trying to be truthful but not to alarm. 'Just a bit quiet that's all. A bit whiny.'

Belinda frowned. 'Poor Iz. She shouldn't have been there. I've always said it's not right. I shouldn't have let her go.' She rubbed her forehead with a hand and Tom thought she looked tired and old. He couldn't think of anything to say. He could see that she was right in a way. Izzy shouldn't have been there. He regretted it himself.

'I know you're shielding someone,' said Karen, 'but I can't work out who or why.'

'I don't have to tell you. You can guess as much as you

like,' said Jess. I can just leave, she thought. I can just get up and walk out of here, but she did not move to go, feeling as if she was held by the thread of a connection between them. I want to tell someone, she thought. That's what it is. After all these years, it would be such a relief. She has as much to lose as I have. She has a terrible secret, too. She'll know what it feels like.

Karen looked at her for a moment and then leaned across to touch her arm. 'I'll tell you what happened to me,' she said softly. 'There's no reason why you shouldn't know. I was in love with him long before I met and married Johnnie. For the first year or so, I had high hopes that we would get engaged, and then gradually it dawned on me that he would never marry me. That was hard, I can tell you. I was nearly thirty, with two or three disastrous affairs in the past, and it felt like the end of the world to me. There was quite a bit of pressure from my family to settle down. I was due to inherit from my grandfather, but only on the condition that I was married and had a family. He had this fear, you see, that I might end up an old maid and leave his hard-won fortune to a cats' home.

'So I settled for Johnnie. You know him and so I don't have to tell you that he is charming and kind and utterly eligible. My family welcomed him with open arms, the perfect English gentleman, and he was more than willing to marry me. A man like Johnnie, who is all style and no substance, needs to marry money and I fitted the bill very nicely.

'We started trying for a baby almost at once and as the years went by and nothing happened, I became increasingly anxious. I'm an only child, and if I didn't produce a baby, my father's younger brother stood to inherit. I know money isn't everything but we had grown used to it, Johnnie and I, and our travel business, well, it's more of a hobby than anything else. It gave Johnnie something to do when he came out of the Army but we certainly couldn't live as we were used to on the proceeds.

'Then, after a chance meeting with Mikey's father, our affair started up again and I was pregnant within two months. Wonderful! Mikey was born and all was well and Johnnie was as thrilled as I was. My grandfather died and I inherited his estate and that was that.

'We've got along very well ever since. The twins were born with the help of IVF and here we are, a happy family. You can see what would happen if Johnnie got wind of this. It would upset everything. It's not the easiest thing, you know, being a kept man, and I've had to be careful to go gently with him. He has not the slightest suspicion about Mikey and neither has anyone else. So, Jess, there is a lot in the balance here, and I find myself in the awkward position of depending on you. Now, how about you being honest with me?'

Jess closed her eyes and swallowed. She knew that Karen had been truthful, she could tell that, and she felt obliged to be the same, but it was a strange and frightening sensation, to be revisiting events which she had concealed for so long.

She shrugged in an attempt to appear nonchalant. 'What do you want me to tell you? He was down here in Dorset, something or other to do with the Army. My mum met him first, and you know what he was like. It wasn't long before he was hanging around her. She'd been on her own for ages and she kind of fell into his arms. It was disgusting to watch, I can tell you.'

'Your *mother*?'

'Yes. She wasn't bad looking then. She was completely pathetic about him. I don't know for sure what he felt about her, but it didn't stop him leching after me. He was always at it, coming round before Mum got home from work, trying to catch me on my own. I was only eighteen and I suppose I was flattered, I don't know, but I sort of fended him off, and then he took to parking in the lane, stopping me on my way home from the stables, and one day it just happened. Only once, I swear. I was disgusted with him and with myself. It felt as though I'd slept with my father.

'Next thing I was pregnant. I didn't tell him for a bit, hoping it was a mistake, but then he said he was going abroad and I was dead frightened about what I was going to do and so I told him. That was that. He sent me some money to get rid of the baby, buggered off to Serbia or somewhere, ditched Mum and got killed.'

Karen shook her head. 'My God,' she said softly. 'You poor kid.'

Jess shrugged. 'I thought I would get rid of the baby but then, I don't know why, I just couldn't do it. I left it so long that I had to go through with it. Mum was so beside herself about James that she didn't take much notice of me, and although I eventually had to tell her I was pregnant, I just couldn't tell her who the father was. It was too awful, for her and for me. It seemed like the worst thing to have done because she was so in love with him. I've never told her. In a way, Johnnie provided a useful smokescreen because Mum has always thought he was the father; even when I denied it was him, she didn't believe me.'

'Oh my goodness,' said Karen again. 'You poor, poor kid. What a secret. Do you ever intend to tell her?'

'Izzy will have to know one day and I suppose Mum will find out then. I've sort of banked on the passage of time making things easier. She had such an awful time of it with Dad dying and getting lumbered with us children on her own and no money. Not Jo so much, because she was born one of nature's prefects, or Charlie, who just got on with his life, but I was definitely a headache. I still am, come to that.'

Karen moved to touch Jess's arm. 'Don't say that,' she said. 'You've protected her all this time. You've kept the secret to protect her.'

Jess shrugged and pulled a face, She felt awkward talking about herself like this.

'Oh Jess, thank you for telling me. I was never under any illusion about the sort of man James was, so it doesn't hurt me to hear your story, but I can imagine what it cost you to tell me.'

'Yeah, well. It's a relief to have told someone,' said Jess gruffly. 'It feels like opening a window and letting in some fresh air.'

Karen nodded. 'What are we going to do?' she asked in a regretful, quiet voice. 'We both behaved badly, both did something we're ashamed of, but ever since then we've done the best we can to make things all right.'

'Yeah,' said Jess, thinking, she's completely different. Completely different from the cold bitch I took her for.

'Well, what about the farm?' said Karen, picking up the papers from the floor and putting them back in the folder. 'It still might be the answer.'

Jess allowed the folder to be put into her hand. 'I don't know,' she said. 'I don't know. I need to think about it. I don't know that I can take Izzy away from Mum. She loves her so much, you see.'

Chapter Fifteen

Ken's yard on Sunday morning was one of business as usual and Tom noticed at once that he had moved the horses around so that Dolly's box had a new occupant, a young horse that had come to him to be broken in. It was a relief to see an alert and inquisitive head looking over the door.

Lisa was having a day off so it was Rhona who was busy supervising the loading of the lorry, checking and double-checking the kit, making sure that all the racing colours were folded neatly into an old trunk, counting in the bridles and saddles and surcingles. Carl was filling plastic drums with water from the yard hose, and Jess was with Moira and Susan in the stables where they were putting the finishing touches to the plaiting of manes. All the boxes had been mucked out and set fair and before they left they would hay up and feed the horses left on the yard.

Ken came out of the house patting his pockets, checking he had his mobile telephone and his cigarettes. 'Five minutes, girls,' he called. 'Then we'll load up. Morning, Tom. All right?'

'Yeah,' said Tom. 'How's Cinders this morning?'

'Mary's got the magnetic boot on her hock. She must have given it a bang. It swelled up last night, but she's sound and fresh as a daisy. She'd like to be coming with us today and doing the whole thing all over again.'

'Good,' said Tom. After a race it was always an anxiety that the horse would be fit the following morning.

'Right you are, Jess. Let's have Princess on first,' called Ken, and Jess led out the bay mare in her rug and the padded travel boots and walked with her up the ramp.

'Hi, Tom,' she called as she went by.

They were all busy then, loading the horses and making a final check. Mary came to the back door and called to Carl to come and collect the picnic and then everyone climbed up into the lorry. 'See you there!' called Ken and drove slowly out of the yard, leaving Jess and Tom who were travelling separately in the Land Rover, watching them go.

'OK?' said Tom to Jess. He had sensed at once that she was different this morning. Quieter, calmer.

'Yeah. I'll get my kit out of my car.'

Tom was glad of the opportunity to be alone with Jess. She had come back from Quatt Lodge in such a peculiar mood last night, breezed into the kitchen where he and Belinda had sat waiting, drinking tea and eating biscuits. After the tragedy of Dolly he had expected that she would be depressed and morose, but she was the opposite. In fact she was almost elated, but in an odd nervy way, like an overdone child whose mother predicts it will all end in tears.

He and Belinda had looked at her expectantly but she had laughed and said, 'It was fine, actually. Karen Bearsden surprised me. She was really nice. She apologised for what she had said to Mary. It was all a mistake. Don't worry, we've sorted it out. Or at least, we will do.'

'What about Izzy? You said this was about Izzy,' said Belinda, thinking, she only cares about the racing. She's incredible. I would have thought that after what happened today, with the horse being killed, that she might feel differently.

'Izzy will be all right. We did talk about her and, well, Karen is cool about it,' said Jess, putting milk in a saucepan. 'Anybody want any hot chocolate?' They both shook their heads.

Cool about it? thought Belinda, not understanding. Did Jess mean that Karen did not mind that her husband's illegitimate child was living virtually next door? Had they discussed it – amicably, it seemed – and Karen was *cool* about it? She remembered Victor finding his daughter incomprehensible and thought, I feel the same about Jess.

Jess sat down with her cold steak on a plate, smeared it with a mixture of mustard and horseradish sauce and then sandwiched it between two slices of bread. She began to eat ravenously. 'Thanks, Tom,' she said, looking up. 'This is delicious. I can enjoy it now that I've got all that business off my mind.'

I don't know her, thought Tom, watching her concentrating on her food with an almost fierce hunger. Can she really brush things off like that? All that happened today? Dolly, and then all the rest? He knew there was no point in asking more questions tonight. He could sense that Jess had put up a shield of chirpiness to deflect probing or personal questions. He stood up. 'I'll be off, then,' he said wearily. 'I'll see you tomorrow.'

'Was Iz all right?' asked Jess looking up, her mouth full, and Tom felt glad that she had asked. It softened his feeling towards her.

'Yes. We saw a bit of her video and then she was happy to go to bed after a dose of *The Water Babies*.'

'Did she talk about today? About Dolly?'

'No,' said Tom. 'She never mentioned it and so I didn't either.'

'That's good,' said Jess, taking another mouthful. 'It can't have bothered her much then.'

Tom had put a hand on her shoulder as he left but he did not kiss her goodbye. He realised that he did not feel like it.

Now he drove out of the yard and turned into the lane, past the dairy farm where the black and white cows all stood in the yard. It would be a few weeks yet before they would be out on the new grass. On either side of the lane, the dark winter hedges were laced about with tiny furls of new leaves and the verges were showing the first tender, singing green of spring, clotted here and there with the pale yellow of primroses. Ewes and lambs dotted the fields, their fleeces very white against the new, surging green, enjoying the sun on their backs, the lambs leaping and skipping and racing about their mothers. It was the sort of morning that made your spirits rise, thought Tom, and it was grand to be going racing but the atmosphere in the Land Rover between him and Jess felt loaded with things unsaid.

He broke the silence as they turned onto the main road. 'Well, are you going to tell me what really happened last night?'

'Yeah,' said Jess quietly. 'I'm sorry, Tom. I could see you were annoyed with me, but I couldn't say anything with Mum there. I thought about it last night after I'd gone to bed, whether I should tell you the whole truth or not, and I came to the conclusion that you had to know. It's a really, really big thing, Tom, and it's like handing you a burden to carry and I didn't know whether it was fair, but Karen has made us an offer and I can't talk about it with you unless you know everything. OK?'

'OK,' said Tom, feeling his stomach tighten with anxiety. What the hell was coming now?

Belinda put the apple crumble on the table, happy that lunch was a success. Bursts of sunshine moved across the kitchen, making it look cheerful rather than shabby and the apple-green checked curtains blew bright and fresh in the breeze from the open window.

Izzy had picked flowers for the little pottery cream jug on the table – primroses and tiny violets and celandines from the edge of the wood behind the cottage, and although she was shy with Victor, Belinda was pleased to find that he was kind and natural with her. He didn't behave in that silly arch manner that some men adopted around small children. He made Izzy blush with pleasure when he remarked on her drawings on display round the room. Thereafter he ignored her, letting her eat her lunch in peace.

He enjoyed the roast chicken and bread sauce and crisp little roast potatoes which Belinda rather prided herself on and she remembered the pleasure of cooking for an appreciative man.

'Delicious,' he said, accepting a second helping of everything. 'I can see that you're a good cook.'

'You lazy, greedy lubber,' said Izzy suddenly and they both looked at her in surprise.

'Izzy!' said Belinda. 'That's rude!'

'No, it's not,' she protested. 'It's not rude, Granny. It's in *The Water Babies*. Tom read it to me last night.'

'Oh, Izzy,' said Belinda, laughing. 'But you mustn't *say* it to people. It's not polite. They might think you were being rude.' Izzy looked downcast but Victor laughed and said he didn't mind one bit and that she was probably quite right anyway.

When they had finished and cleared the table, Belinda made coffee while Izzy sat on the sitting-room floor with a pair of scissors and sticky tape, making a horse lorry out of an old shoebox. Victor turned over the pages of the Sunday newspaper and Belinda, glancing at him, knew exactly why she found him attractive. She looked at him as he sat there in his navy sweater and checked shirt and corduroy trousers, at his large, square brown hands holding the paper, at the bulk of his body and his long legs folded under her table, as comfortable and at home as if he had sat there all his life.

There was an easiness about him in any situation and this made him restful company. His actions were rather slow and deliberate as is often the case with big men. He took his time, never seemed to hurry, and there was something authoritative about him without any suggestion of being overbearing or controlling. She watched him as he browsed through the paper, his head tilted slightly back, the better

382

to see through the reading spectacles on the end of his nose, and with a serious expression on his face. His thick silver hair was too short to look untidy but rather as if he had carelessly run his fingers through it. He is a man who is comfortable in his own skin, she thought, and at that moment he looked up and caught her watching him. He smiled at her over his glasses and she put down the coffee pot and went to his side. Glancing through to the sitting room she saw that Izzy was absorbed in what she was doing and she kicked the door closed with her foot at the same time as she put her arms round the seated figure and dropped her chin onto Victor's head.

'What's all this?' he said and pulled her down to sit on his knee. Oh God, thought Belinda in a panic. I'm too heavy and too old for this, it's undignified and absurd, but for a moment it was wonderful to perch there with her arms round his neck and him holding her tightly. She forgot she was not young, and felt girlish and carefree. But it *was* absurd. Whatever would Izzy think if she came in? She quickly got off his knee and said, 'It's such a lovely after-noon, do you feel like coming for a walk along the ridge? We're so high up here that on a day like this, it feels like being on top of the world.'

'I'd like that very much,' he said, taking off his glasses and folding up the newspaper. 'Although there are other things I would rather do.' They smiled at one another in recognition and Belinda remembered how intoxicating it was to feel desired and desirable.

Tom pulled into a service station on the A303 towards

Taunton. He could not concentrate on his driving as Jess unfolded her incredible story. He listened gravely as she talked, not looking at her, gazing instead at his hands which rested on the steering wheel.

When she had finished, he shook his head and closed his eyes for a moment.

'I can hardly believe it,' he said. They sat in silence, Jess watching cars pulling in to the petrol pumps, full of families out for the day. Have I really told him? she thought. Is everything changed for ever? He was so still that she wanted to jump out and bang the door and walk away. Anything to break the tension. Eventually Tom looked over at her and reached across and took her hand. He held it in both of his.

'Oh, Jess,' he said sadly.

Jess sniffed and turned her head away. She did not want to look at him when she said, 'It's the second time in two days I've had to go through all of this. It takes a bit of getting used to when I haven't talked about it for six years or more.'

'I know. It must do.'

'So what do you think?' She turned back to study his face.

Tom half shrugged and shook his head. 'I don't know what to think, except that James Redpath was a bastard. You were eighteen, Jess. How old was he? Forty-five?'

'He didn't rape me, Tom. It was consensual – or whatever you call it. I didn't want to do it, but he didn't force me. I just gave way in the end because he was so persuasive. It was like drip, drip on a stone. He wore me down.'

'And you couldn't tell your mother?'

'She was mad about him! How could I? I felt so ashamed of what I'd done. You know, after Dad died, she had a tough time. It had been years and years since she'd felt anything for a man, and what did I go and do? Fuck it up for her. Literally!'

'Couldn't you have told Jo?'

'Tom! You know what Jo's like! We're not exactly close, and I couldn't trust her not to tell Mum. It would be typical of her. At school she was the goody two-shoes and I was the naughty little sister and she was always telling the head-mistress about me. Jo would have been the last person I would have told. After James was killed I didn't see that I had to tell anybody. It was nobody's business except Izzy's and mine and when the time was right, I knew that Iz would want to know, but until then, I wasn't telling anybody.'

'And now?'

'Karen's even more keen than I am to keep it quiet. You can see why. It must feel like sitting on a volcano, but she prefers it that way to coming clean with Johnnie. That's why she's offered us this farm.'

'I can't believe it,' said Tom again.

'I've got the stuff here,' said Jess, pulling her old denim bag from the floor and taking out the folder. She handed it to Tom who leafed through the sheets and looked at the photographs in silence, then gave them back to Jess.

'What do you think?' she asked.

'I don't know,' he said slowly. 'Yes, it looks fabulous. A dream come true in many ways, but I don't think it's for me. I don't want to build my life on an arrangement like that. You know I want to marry you, I still do, but I don't want all of this as well.' He indicated the folder. 'If we're going to be together I would rather start with everything in the clear. Not much to live on and even fewer prospects, but no skeletons in the cupboard.'

'Even if it means I have to tell Mum about James Redpath?'

'Yes.'

'But what about Izzy? How will Mum feel about Izzy when she knows the truth?'

'Do you really think it will make the slightest bit of difference to how much she loves Izzy? You underestimate your mother if you think that.'

'I hoped it wouldn't, but I didn't dare risk it, not on my own. You knowing too makes all the difference.'

'Oh, Jess.' Tom leaned across and put his arm round her and pulled her towards him. She hid her face against his fleece jacket. It smelled strongly and comfortingly of horses and sheep.

Belinda and Victor walked slowly along the lane, the trees thick and dark on one side and the fields sloping away into the vale on the other. Along the wood the ditch was full of dark water and smelled pungently of rot and bog. The spiky marsh grass was starting to shoot a vicious acid green from the brown clumps left from the winter and the mossy bank was green too, where tight coils of fresh new bracken were forcing their way through the broken branches and dead leaves. The primroses were a sight. Victor had never seen so many as starred the bank, pale and delicate amongst the bright gold cups and glossy leaves of the celandines, and the tiny, pale lemon trumpets of the slender wild daffodils.

On the other side, a wire fence ran along the ridge, tufted here and there by scraps of sheep wool caught on the barbs. The gate Belinda stopped to lean on was warm in the sun, the wood silver grey after years of wind and rain. She and Victor leaned side by side, taking in the view. The grass of the sloping field was still thin and sparse. It had not started to grow much yet, up here on the exposed side of the hill, and the sheep and lambs were gathered halfway down round the feeders where the shepherd left them hay and nuts.

The gate was sheltered from the keen wind by the wood at their backs and they could feel the warmth of the spring sun when it sprang from behind the racing clouds. In front of them, dark lines of shadow passed swiftly across the vale so that on one side, where the sun still shone, the trees and fields and hidden villages were bright with colour and, on the other, plunged into sombre shade.

A blackbird was singing quite close to them from the top of a tall pine. Belinda could see him there, bobbing about as the wind rocked the tree, and as she listened to his lovely music she became aware of all the other birds singing too, and realised that they were all at it, spilling their song up to the rolling, high wind which carried it even higher into the blue sky. Larks, too, she could hear them now, although she couldn't see them. She screwed her eyes into the white of the sun above, but the little birds were too far up, their throbbing notes, held trembling for minutes without a pause, cascading joyfully down to her.

Beneath the birdsong, closer to the earth and drifting up from the hills and fields, were the voices of the sheep and lambs, urgent, plaintive, keeping up the incessant dialogue of reassurance between mother and young.

Suddenly a pheasant burst out of the wood behind them, rocketing upwards and then gliding away on down-turned wings, followed by another and another. 'That's Snowy,' said Belinda. 'The naughty dog. They've stopped shooting but I'll still have to get him back.' She called and called and at last he appeared out of the wood, jaunty and pleased with himself, even when she scolded him and put him on his lead in disgrace.

'It's a lovely place, Dorset,' said Victor, still leaning on the gate. 'I've lived here all my life, you know. My father had the garage before me. His father was a wheelwright on the same premises. I went to school in Sherborne and did my apprenticeship in Yeovil. I went to Australia for a year as a young man and thought I might settle there but my mother sent me a telegram to come home when Dad had a heart attack.'

'Do you think you really might have stayed there if that hadn't happened?'

'I don't know. Probably not. I felt I needed to get away from what I'd known all my life as much as anything else. Sometimes a big, close family can seem a bit suffocating when you're young.'

Belinda was watching Izzy, wobbling along the lane on her bicycle. She had been so odd when Belinda had asked her if she wanted to ride Bonnet. She had said no so determinedly, and when Belinda said that the old pony really should have a little exercise, Izzy had looked close to tears.

Was it because of what she had seen yesterday? wondered Belinda. The lovely grey mare crashing to the ground with Jess? It seemed wisest not to ask, at least not in front of Victor, and so she'd taken the bicycle out of the shed and Izzy had been happy to ride that instead. In fact, she was peddling so furiously that she was about to disappear from view.

'Sorry, Victor,' she said, putting her hand on his arm, feeling she was cutting him short. 'This isn't a very peaceful walk with me bellowing every few minutes, but I must call Izzy. Izzy!' she shouted while Snowy pulled at the lead and whined. 'Izzy, don't go so fast! Izzy! Come back!'

'I've got something to ask you,' said Victor, turning to lean his back on the gate and to take her hand. He put it to his lips for a moment.

'What?' said Belinda, alarmed.

'You asked me yesterday about whether I had had many relationships since Sally died. Can I ask you the same question?'

'Yes,' said Belinda, 'and no, I haven't. A few flirtations, a few married men, the husbands of friends who, because I was on my own, thought I must be gagging for it – horrible expression – who I had to see off, and then one man who meant a great deal to me. I loved him, I suppose, or was infatuated, but he had to go abroad and then he got cold feet and broke it off. It was the best of times and the worst of times and it left me feeling I could never, ever, put myself through something like that again. He was killed – he was a soldier like my husband, David – and that was that. I couldn't go on resenting a dead man. But all this was years ago.'

Victor looked thoughtful and then leaned forward and kissed her forehead. 'I won't hurt you,' he said slowly. 'I promise.'

Cothelstone was a favourite course of Tom's. Not far from Taunton, set in a beautiful valley with hills rising steeply beyond, it had an old-fashioned, country fair atmosphere. Whole families were out for the day, to put a pound or two on the horses and have a bit of fun, and there was nothing smart or swanky about it, although the runners were as good as you would get anywhere in the south-west.

Ken had a good day. Carl had another winner for him in the men's open race and Jess was placed twice, a second in the ladies' race on Fenny Princess and a third in the restricted on a tricky old horse called Shivermytimbers, who jumped to the right and pulled hard. In due time his owner, a local vet, would be sent the thirty pound prize money and meanwhile he was as pleased as if he had won a classic.

'He's a dreadful old rogue,' he said. 'A real old sod. I only put him into training because it was that or the knacker's yard. You've done wonders, Ken, and as for how you rode him, Jess, well, I'm flabbergasted that you got him round, let alone won a place.'

Tom was especially pleased. He knew that Jess needed to get back on a horse and ride and she had shown that she could do that, and be as determined as ever. She looked tired though, he thought, with dark rings under her eyes and strain showing round her mouth. It was not surprising when he thought about what she had told him on the way. Now that he had had time to consider the astonishing truth, and he had walked to the far end of the course on his own to get away from everyone, he realised that he felt glad that Johnnie Bearsden was not Izzy's father. From his point of view it cleared the ground and he could see now what he wanted for the future. He was sure he was right about declining Karen's offer. In fact, he did not really even have to think about it again.

He also knew with certainty that he loved Jess and that he wanted to marry her and from what she had said in the Land Rover about the future, he felt he had reason to hope that she wanted it too. He was moved when he thought about her courage in facing all that had happened on her own. A different sort of girl would have wept and wailed, and seen herself as a victim of that bastard, Redpath, whereas Jess had taken responsibility for what she had done and tried to protect her mother.

Then there was Izzy. Now, knowing what he did, he hoped that if they married he could adopt her and she could one day be the older sister of the children he and Jess would have. He remembered Jess in hospital with Izzy and imagined what it would be like when the baby in her arms was his, and his heart felt full of love and tenderness.

He was glad he had turned down rides for today. He did not have the stomach for it and certainly not to ride against Jess and Fancy in the maiden race, the last race on the card. Earlier he had bumped into Pete Dawlish in the beer tent having a pint with Moira, who was not supposed to drink until the last race was over. It was one of the things that Ken was strict about.

He must have looked at her disapprovingly because she aimed a kick at his shin and said, 'What's the matter with you? I'm only having a half.'

'I don't care what you do,' he said coldly. 'It's not my business.'

Pete had obviously been drinking for some time. His speech was slightly slurred and his face red. He gripped Tom by the arm and drew him to one side to say confidentially, 'Do you want the ride? Do you want the fucking ride?'

'What do you mean?'

'What I said. I want someone else on board the mare. That girl of yours is no fucking good. How many falls has she had in a row, eh? And what's all this about Ken's owners not wanting her to ride their horses?' He looked at Moira for confirmation and she shrugged and pulled a face. Tom could have hit her. 'What about the horse Ken lost yesterday?' Pete went on. 'She brought that down and all, didn't she?'

'Don't be ridiculous! That horse had an old injury – a star fracture. Ken had it confirmed this morning from the kennelman at the hunt kennels who took the body. No way was that Jess's fault.'

'Then I'm asking Nick Martin,' said Pete. 'I'm getting Nick to take the ride.'

'That's your business,' said Tom and walked away.

Ken's horsebox was leaving the lorry park on its way home when the runners were declared for the last race. Tom jotted them down as their names came over the loudspeaker. Twelve horses. Quite a good field. He glanced at their form. 'Pulled up, sixth, fell,' he read. 'Pulled up, unseated rider, fourth; unseated rider; pulled up, third; ran out, third, pulled up.' The usual bunch of beginners. Amongst them Fancy did not look so bad with her 'fell, unseated rider'. What did the card say about her? 'Well bred. Uncertain start. May do better in time.'

He made his way to the lorry park where Ted Dawlish had unboxed Fancy early from his battered old trailer and had been walking her up and down for the last ten minutes, but she was sweating and nervous, dancing round on the end of the lead rope, spooking and half rearing. Tom could not see that she was any better behaved than the first time. In fact, she looked worse, if anything.

Pete was sitting in the cab of the truck talking on his mobile telephone and then Tom saw him get out and lumber off towards the bookies, so he helped with the mare himself, putting on the bridle and adjusting the orange rubber nose-band so that it held her mouth shut. She rolled her eyes at him, showing the whites and snaking her head. She's mad, he thought. She's got a screw loose. I wish it was me riding her and not Jess. For the second time, he felt real fear.

He kept away from the paddock and did not even watch as Jess was given a leg-up or wish her luck as she cantered sideways down to the start. She and Ted Dawlish had discussed tactics and agreed that this time she should get in front and try to stay there in the hope that the little mare would jump better if she was not fighting the bit but Tom did not want to watch any of it. Later, he saw old man

Dawlish walk along the line of bookies looking at the starting prices. Who is he putting his money on? he wondered. It won't be his own horse, that's for sure.

Tom wandered towards the bouncy castle and the candyfloss stall, where the shrieks of the excited children drowned out the commentary. He tried not to listen, chewing at the inside of his lip and tearing with nervous fingers at the edge of the racecard in his hand, but the penetrating voice carried across to him.

He was aware that the horses were under starter's orders and then that they were off. The children's merry-go-round started up near him and the hurdy-gurdy music blotted out the rest. Tom moved away. Minutes went past and then he heard the loudspeaker again and the words began to make a connection. 'Flying Fancy well in the lead,' said the urgent, West Country voice, 'setting a cracking pace for the rest of the field . . . Flying Fancy safely over the open ditch and coming round for the back straight . . . Flying Fancy jumps the plain fence ahead of Bow Tie. It's still Flying Fancy well in the lead as they come to the turn.' Tom stood still, staring at the trodden grass around his feet, the litter of betting slips, the discarded candyfloss sticks. She was going too fast. She would make a mistake. There would be another disaster. Five minutes or so and it would all be over, he told himself. Only five more minutes.

The commentary droned on and there seemed to be little change in the race although the favourite had come up to challenge the mare. 'It's Flying Fancy and Bow Tie, and there's not much between them.' Tom could not help it. He had to see. He started to jog through the crowds towards the track and then he heard, 'Flying Fancy made a bad mistake at that one, and it's Bow Tie now in the lead from River Craft and Bazooka . . .'

Tom began to run, dodging through the crowds who, not interested in the racing, were wandering towards the trade tents and the hot dog trailer. By the time he reached the rails there were two fences left to jump and it was Bow Tie still in the lead, but down the course he could see Jess and Fancy, still there behind the first three horses, could see the bright blue silk moving up fast on the inside. The little mare was streaking along and Jess was riding her as if her life depended on it, head down, arms and legs pumping and she was coming fast, catching the others. As they met the next fence she was only a length or two behind and she outjumped River Craft into third place and hit the ground galloping. There was still a lot to do to catch the leaders but Fancy stretched out and fairly flew towards the last fence and the finish, and she was there, right behind Bazooka at the last. He was tired and faltered, put in a short stride and only clambered over and she took off when he did, way out, and Tom shut his eyes knowing that she would never make it. She would hit the fence and come down. Tom had a vision of her catapulting through the air, but when he opened his eyes, she was flying, bold and fast, ears pricked, and Jess was crouching over her shoulder and the fence looked nothing to her. Nothing at all.

'And Flying Fancy recovered well from that earlier mistake and is now in second place. It's Bow Tie from Flying Fancy. Bow Tie from Flying Fancy at the finish . . .'

Tom started to shout, to run and shout as Fancy galloped

for the line. Ahead, Bow Tie thought he had it in the bag. His jockey did not look behind, was already raising his arm in victory when the roar of the crowd made him glance over his shoulder and he saw the hurtling chestnut horse and the bright blue silk streaking up behind. The next moment he had made it, he was safe over the finish, his tired horse stretching out his neck and blowing hard while Flying Fancy galloped past in second place.

Tom worked his way through the crowd and then ducked under the rails as the last runners straggled past. A loose horse galloped by, broken reins dangling, stirrups flying, and up in front he could see Jess pulling Fancy to a canter and then to a trot and flinging herself forward to grasp her round the neck. He saw old Ted Dawlish come hurrying, despite his skewed farmer's gait and his bowed legs, and clasp Jess's arm and pat his little mare and begin to lead her in towards the paddock and the winners' enclosure. There was no sign of Pete Dawlish. The course was emptying now the last race was over and well-wishers crowded round them. Ted Dawlish had been in point-to-pointing all his life and was well known in Devon. Someone offered him a price for the mare, but he shook his head. 'Don't be a daft bugger,' he said. 'This is a champion in the making, this is. I've waited all my life for a horse like this!'

When Tom caught up with them, they had reached the paddock and Jess had jumped down and they were unsaddling the mare, who was blowing but still full of running, although her neck and belly dripped with sweat. Her fine little head was up, her ears pricked and she stood quietly for once beside Bow Tie.

'Oh, Jess!' cried Tom. 'Well done! Well done! You rode a scorcher!'

She turned, her face scarlet with emotion and exertion. 'It was her. She was bloody wonderful! She did it all. I knew she could! I'm just so chuffed we did it . . .' She was gabbling with excitement.

Mrs Toynbee appeared in her usual shabby quilted jacket and tweed hat decorated with a pheasant feather.

'Well done, Jess. That was a wonderful race you rode. My word, this little horse has improved. I liked what I saw the other day when she was working alongside Cinders. I guessed she could do it. I've made a packet on you. Got you for a place at sixty to one!'

'You backed me?' asked Jess, astonished.

'I most certainly did. I wasn't the only one either.' Mrs Toynbee's eyes sparkled and she looked mischievously at Ted Dawlish. The old man's face was impassive but from the way he was rubbing the mare's ears, Tom could see how pleased he was.

'Well done, Mr Dawlish,' he said. 'I'd never have thought she could run a race like that.'

'You're a fool, then,' said the old man sourly. 'Get on with you, maid, and get weighed in.'

Jess laughed and pulled Tom away. 'Come with me,' she said and they walked together towards the tent where Jess had to present herself immediately after the race to be weighed in with her saddle, before she could officially take up the second place. She turned to him, her face bright with happiness.

'She was so great, Tom. The best I've ever ridden. She'll

win. I know she will. Next season she'll be unstoppable.'

'You rode her so well.'

'We just had one awful mistake. We took off miles out but she is scopey enough to recover.'

'Will you marry me?'

'What?' said Jess, turning to him and laughing. 'I thought for a minute you said will you marry me.'

'I did. Will you?'

'Tom! Don't be silly!'

'Why's it silly?'

'It just is.'

'Will you?'

They stopped and looked at one another. People were pushing past them, back to their cars, anxious to get into the queue to leave the race ground.

'Do you really mean it?'

'Of course I do! You know I've always wanted it.'

'OK. Yes. Yes, I will!' She bent down to put her saddle carefully on the ground at her feet and then reached to put her arms round Tom's neck. Her helmet got in the way when he tried to find her mouth. He could feel her hot face against his and smelled the scent of her skin. He held her so tight that she complained he was squeezing her to death and he felt so deliriously happy that he wanted to shout. The crowd divided round them as they kissed. A passing acquaintance made a loud, joking comment and soon people were laughing and calling, happy to see the pretty girl jockey in her bright blue silk and the tall, curly-haired young man lost in each other's arms.

'He's just asked me to marry him!' Jess broke off to inform anyone listening.

'Aaaah. What was the answer?' called a fat young woman, laughing, her hands on a double pushchair and with a labrador on a lead.

'Yes!' said Jess. 'I said yes!' and someone cheered and clapped and they kissed again.

'When? When shall we marry?' Tom asked later as they drove home in his Land Rover. It was a beautiful evening, still blustery and bright with late sun that glittered on the new green of the fields.

'Summer? I don't know. I don't care. Whenever. Soon, though.'

'Oh, Jess, I wouldn't have believed I could be this happy. Do you want a proper wedding? You know, with a big dress and bridesmaids and all that stuff?'

'God, no,' said Jess. 'Let's just slide off and do it. You and me and the vicar.'

'Suits me.' Tom felt light-headed, drunk almost. 'It's what I've wanted for so long,' he said.

'Me too,' said Jess. 'But you know, this other stuff, this James Redpath stuff, got in the way. It's such a relief now that I've told you, that it's in the open, and that you still want Izzy and me.'

'We'll be very poor. Do you mind? I've made a bit of money this year, from the horses I've sold, and the cattle. I'm quite optimistic that I can build on that, but your mother may think I'm not in a position to marry. My parents certainly will.'

'Tom! I don't care about them. You know I don't care about being hard up. I never have.'

'But we'll have to be a bit realistic, Jess. And there's Izzy. I want to support Izzy, too.'

'Don't worry. We'll manage. I know we will!'

'How are you going to tell your mother?'

'What about? Us getting married? I suppose we should do it together. We'll have to tell your parents at more or less the same time or there will be an international incident, won't there?'

'No, I mean about Izzy's father?'

Jess pulled a face. 'Can't it be done in one fell swoop?' she asked. 'Tell her both things at once?'

'Hardly. One is very, very private, Jess. I can't imagine how she'll react. Can you?'

'No. Not really. I dread it. I suppose I must do it, though. Get it over with. But I do think our other news will help. Hearing about us will cheer her up and make her think about the future and not the past.'

'When, though?'

'I'll have to choose my moment, won't I? Shit! The thought of being exported to Yorkshire seems almost a preferable option.'

'We couldn't do it, though, Jess. Could we? Be bought off by Karen Bearsden?'

'No, you're right. This is harder, but in the long run it's the right thing to do.'

'We'll have to tell Karen. I wonder what she'll do when she hears we don't want her offer.'

'I don't know. I don't think she'll tell Johnnie. She seemed adamant about that. I'll telephone her from work tomorrow. She won't be happy. She was banking on this arrangement.'

'Christ, Jess. "What a tangled web we weave when first we practise to deceive."'

'Yeah, well, that particular web is her own making. I've got enough problems of my own to worry about. As she pointed out, money is a facilitator, and she seems to have that in buckets. She'll have to facilitate herself out of trouble.'

They drove on in thoughtful silence and then Tom said, 'Did you know that Ted Dawlish made a packet on you this afternoon?'

'He did? The crafty old bugger! He never said anything to me.'

'He put a hundred on you.'

'Jesus!'

'Pete was spitting mad he hadn't backed you.'

'Good,' laughed Jess. 'Serves him sodding right. He'd done his best to get me jocked off. Nick Martin told me. Nick said he laughed in his face. He said that I was mad to sit on such a lunatic and that he wouldn't touch her with a bargepole.'

'What will they do with Fancy now? Are they going to run her again?'

'They won't if they've got any sense. She's made her debut. She needs to be turned away to grow up a bit.'

They lapsed into silence again. The cab was filled with flashing golden evening light as they passed between the trees that lined the road. Tom drove with one hand and found Jess's hand with the other. It felt warm and rough and dry in his, and he brought it to his lips and kissed it.

'I love you,' he said.

Jess nodded and smiled back but her thoughts were not of Tom or marriage. Instead she was thinking about her mother.

Chapter Sixteen

Looking back on it, Belinda should have known that there was something brewing. At the beginning of the following week, Jess was strangely solicitous and careful of her, cooking supper, cleaning the kitchen unasked, inquiring about her grandparents, even saying that when racing was over she and Tom and Izzy would drive to Suffolk to see them. She could see now that she was softening her up, preparing her for the bombshell she was about to drop.

At first Belinda had thought that Jess's mood was because of her success on Fancy. She could understand how much it meant to her to have turned round a difficult horse and shown that she was a jockey to be reckoned with.

Then on Wednesday night, after Izzy had gone to bed, Belinda came down from having a bath and found Jess helping herself to a measure of whisky from the bottle in the sitting room.

'What's that you're drinking, Jess?' she'd asked, unnecessarily. 'Whisky?'

Jess knocked it back in one go, grimaced, wiped her mouth and said, 'Sit down, Mum. I've got something to tell you.'

Belinda's heart sank. She did not know what was coming,

had absolutely no idea, but the look on Jess's face told her she wasn't going to like it.

'What?' she said in alarm. 'What is it?'

As Jess started to speak, Belinda sat, solemn-faced, working at the pile of her dressing gown with her fingers. She listened, saying nothing, hearing words which spun through her mind and seemed to make no connection anywhere. It couldn't be true, she told herself, this rewriting of history, this sudden altering of the landscape of their lives. It couldn't be true, and yet, as Jess talked, events from the past unravelled and took on a different shape, came together as a whole, made sense of so much that had been a mystery.

When she had finished, they sat in silence and looked at one another. Belinda's face was frozen, expressionless. She felt at a loss, utterly bewildered. Her heart was beating fast but giving her no clues as to how she should be feeling, how she should react. Numb, that was all she felt, as if she had been knocked down and winded.

'Mum?' said Jess, coming to sit beside her and taking her hand. 'Mum? Say something. Please.'

Belinda gave her head a little shake. 'I don't know what to say,' she said. Even her voice was flat and unemotional. Jess got up and poured another whisky and gave it to her, but she shook her head. She just wanted to sit there, on her own, devoid of feeling. What Jess had told her had thrown her life violently off balance. It was like being trapped in a car crash, the vehicle that was her life abruptly overturned, wheels helplessly spinning. Until the spinning stopped, she could not tell how she would feel or what she would do with the information she had just received.

Somehow or other she got to bed and found herself lying there, stiff and straight, still in her dressing gown. Slowly, as the night wore on, she was able to take small episodes of what Jess had said and turn them over in her mind. She began to see what Jess had had to bear for her sake, while all the time she had blamed and criticised her. She was able now to understand so many aspects of James's behaviour, but at the time she had been blinded by his glamour and how good he made her feel. Throughout that whole period she had been focused so much on herself, with all the introspection of being in love, that she had ignored what was happening to her own daughter.

If James was to be recast, then so was David, who had been a decent, honest and good man. How wrongly she had allowed her memories of him to be tarnished in retrospect by her foolish love for James. David had been a million times the better man and yet she had thought of him contemptuously because he was ordinary and had disappointed her own view of herself.

As the night wore on, Belinda wondered to whom she could turn for comfort. She wanted to confess her terrible shortcomings to someone who would understand. Dinka, of course, would listen, but she would be quick to say that there was no point in brooding on the past, or to blame James, and that none of this was her fault. What she needed was someone who would accept her guilt as real and justified, but who could offer her forgiveness and the hope of redemption.

As dawn broke, she got out of bed and went downstairs to make a cup of tea. She paused on the landing outside Izzy's door. She could hear her noisy, regular breathing and, pushing the door open, she went to stand by her bed. The little girl was curled on her side, her hair tousled on the pillow, her thumb nearly in her mouth. *The Water Babies* was open on the floor beside her bed. Belinda watched her for a few minutes, moved by her innocence and vulnerability, and her heart was burdened by love and sadness as if a stone had wedged in her chest.

As she waited for the kettle to boil, it suddenly came to her what she would do. She would go to her mother. It was her mother who would help her.

Karen Bearsden received Jess's telephone call and reacted with a calm dignity. She waited until Jess had finished speaking and said, 'Very well, Jess. I imagine that you and Tom have given this a lot of thought, and I have to respect your decision. I confess that I'm disappointed, and it will make things very awkward, but that's my problem.'

'Yes,' said Jess shortly.

'As for the future, I mean for Isobel and Mikey, I can't predict. We'll just have to cross that bridge when we come to it.'

'Yes.'

'So, good luck. I don't think there's anything else to say, and obviously if we need to be in touch, we will be.'

'Yes. Goodbye, Karen.'

'Goodbye, Jess.'

Jess and Tom argued mildly about when was the best time to tell their families that they were getting married.

'I want Izzy to know first,' said Jess, lying on Tom's sofa, with her head on his lap. 'That's only right, and then when she knows, we can tell our parents. Mum has just frozen over since I told her about James. She looks as if she's sleep-walking. I hope this will stop her thinking about the past all the time.'

'You can understand how she must feel,' said Tom. 'It must have been a hell of a shock.'

'She looked winded by it. You know, sort of gasping for breath and as white as a sheet. I don't think she slept at all that night. I heard her walking about. She went into work looking like a ghost and now she says she's taking a couple of days off to go and see Gran and Grandfather. I think she just needs to get away. Her boyfriend even offered to drive her but she wouldn't let him.'

'He's good news, isn't he? A bit of a surprise maybe?'

'Yeah. He seems nice. He's kind to her, anyway. It's all round the village now. Her romance. You can imagine how the old biddies will gossip.'

'Do you want an engagement ring?' asked Tom suddenly. 'Well, of course you do, but I mean, I ought to get that organised, I suppose. Aren't you meant to flash a diamond about when we break the news?'

'I don't care about a ring,' said Jess. 'It's a waste of money. Get me one from Woolworth's. A stonking great glass diamond. Will you come over to the yard and break the news with me? I'm longing to see Moira's face. She's leaving, you know. She's handed in her notice. She'll be gone by the end of the month. It's typical of her, isn't it, to jack it in halfway through the season and leave us short-staffed.'

'I'm not surprised,' said Tom. 'She's never been cut out for working in a racing yard. Where's she going?'

'I don't know and I don't care,' said Jess. 'There's something I haven't told you, Tom,' she said suddenly, sitting up and facing him, pushing her hair behind her ears. Her face looked hot and pink and she could not look him in the eye. 'I don't know how you'll take it. I'm not sure myself, even.'

'What, Jess? What?'

'Actually,' said Jess, 'I'm pregnant. I went to the doctor today. I'm two months up the spout, and I hasten to add that this is your baby, Tom. This one definitely is!'

Belinda asked for two days' holiday and although it was an inconvenient time there was something about her manner and her white, drawn face that suggested it would be unwise to refuse her request. She apologised to Jenny, explaining that it was a family crisis, and left the office in as best order as she could.

Telling Victor was a problem because she did not know how she could face him after what Jess had told her and she did not feel she knew him well enough to unburden herself to him. She didn't even feel like telling Dinka. There was a place inside her which felt too raw to expose to anyone. In the end she sent Victor an email saying that she was going to Suffolk for a few days. He emailed back to ask if she would like him to drive her there but she politely declined, saying that her parents were too elderly and eccentric to cope with strangers. 'I'll be back by the weekend,' she wrote, 'and perhaps I can see you then?'

She had underestimated him. That evening he telephoned and said, 'Look here, Belinda. One of the advantages of running my own business is that I can take time off when I want. I don't like to think of you driving all that way in that old car of yours. Why don't you let me take you? I'm not putting any pressure on you. I'll drop you off at your parents' and go and find somewhere to stay and come back and collect you when you want. I quite fancy a day or two away.'

Belinda closed her eyes. He was only being kind, but she felt suffocated by his attention.

'Please understand, Victor,' she said. 'I've been independent for years and am perfectly capable of driving to Suffolk. It's terribly kind of you but I will go on my own, if you don't mind.'

There was silence on the other end of the telephone. Oh, God, she thought. I've hurt his feelings now.

'Just as you like,' he said. 'I hope you didn't mind me suggesting . . . and if there's something wrong . . .'

'Please, Victor,' she pleaded. 'I'll telephone you when I get back.'

Izzy, too, begged to go with her and Belinda found it hard to say no.

'Sorry, darling. This time I must go on my own and, besides, you have to go to school. But I'll send them your love and tell them we will come and see them again in the holidays. I know, why don't you do Great-Gran one of your drawings? She'd like that.'

Izzy hung her head and looked miserable.

'Cheer up, Iz. I'll only be gone for two days and you will have Mummy here to look after you.'

'But I don't want to go riding,' whispered Izzy. 'I don't want to. Will you tell Mummy, Gran? Will you tell Mummy I don't have to?'

Belinda knelt down and gathered her into her arms. 'Of course you don't have to, Iz, not if you don't want to, but why? Don't you like riding Bonnet any more?'

Izzy shook her head.

'Why? You love Bonnet, don't you?'

Izzy nodded vigorously.

'What is it then, Iz? Tell Gran.'

'I don't want her to die,' she whispered, hanging her head.

Belinda held her close and lifted her chin so that she could look into her face. 'Of course she won't die, Izzy. Why do you think that? Because of Mummy's horse?'

Izzy nodded.

'But that poor horse had something wrong with its leg. Didn't Mummy tell you? It wasn't because she was riding it. There's nothing at all wrong with Bonnet. Just look how well she is. And greedy, and calling for her hay and her pony nuts and being naughty when you ride her. Bonnet is as fit as a flea!'

Izzy looked at her. Her blue eyes behind her spectacles were very large and luminous. She put her hand out to touch Belinda's face.

'Are you sure, Granny?' she said doubtfully.

'Of course I'm sure.' This is my fault, thought Belinda. If I hadn't insisted on going to London, Izzy would have been spared all this.

That evening, when Jess and Tom, both rather awkward, smiling and embarrassed, came to tell her that they were intending to get married and that Jess was expecting a baby, all thoughts of Izzy and Bonnet went straight out of her head.

She had to be pleased for them, of course she was, it would have been impossible not to be when she saw the sheer joy on Tom's bony, gaunt face as he held Jess's hand and fixed his gentle, loving eyes on her face. At the same time she hoped he knew what he was taking on, that Jess would always be stubborn and difficult, that he would forever be the one who had to compromise. But he must realise that. He could hardly have any illusions about her after all these years.

Jess surprised her. She looked happier than Belinda had ever remembered seeing her, and excited too, even about the baby. The studied lack of interest which had so distressed Belinda when she had been expecting Izzy was replaced by a new softness.

'Yes,' she admitted. 'I'm really happy. We'll be a family. It will be nice for Izzy, too, and Mum, in case you're wondering, Tom asked me to marry him before we knew I was pregnant.'

Belinda looked at her daughter sitting there at the kitchen table in her old work clothes. Tom was holding her hand, with its rough skin and dirt-rimmed fingernails, and her hair was pulled back in a careless knot. Her face glowed with happiness and Belinda thought, with a shock, that it was the first time she had ever seen her look content and at peace. Thinking this reminded her of the reason why this was so. This baby, although unplanned, would be loved and wanted by both its parents.

'When will you tell Izzy?' she asked. It would mean a new life for Izzy, with Tom as her adopted father – surely a good thing, because she loved him and he was so fond of her – and a half-sibling to look forward to. It would mean

Izzy growing up in a proper family as Belinda had always wanted, and yet she felt a lurching, downward drag of spirits at the thought.

'I wanted to tell her at once but I thought it was better to wait until you get back from Suffolk. You know, so you're around. She'll be so excited.'

I don't want to lose her, thought Belinda. I don't want her to go. She imagined Izzy's bedroom where she now lay sleeping, empty, stripped of her toys and books, and saw herself coming in from work to a silent and tidy house. How could she live without seeing that bright shining head bent over her drawing and her sweet face, like a little flower, looking up with a beaming smile to greet her? You can't take her from me, her heart screamed, and she felt shameful tears, brimming and hot. She got up to hide them and went to the sink to get a glass of water.

Would Izzy be all right with these two? she wondered, as the tap gushed and the glass overflowed. Would Jess really be a better mother when she had a baby to look after as well? What would life be like in Tom's dirty, cold farmhouse? How would they manage financially? Would Izzy be fed properly, sent to school in clean clothes, have her television viewing supervised? So many anxieties began to creep into Belinda's mind that she had a struggle to keep smiling and to turn back and take the glass of champagne which Tom handed to her.

'We're going on to tell my parents next,' he said, 'so we need a drink first!'

Yes, thought Belinda, they won't be very happy at the news. Once again Tom will have disappointed their expectations of him. Jess, unmarried mother, now pregnant again;

Jess, a stable girl with few social graces and no social standing, would not be their ideal daughter-in-law. She thought of Tom's mother with her stiff blonde hair and careful make-up, her pearls and frilled blouses and Christmas drinks parties with tiny, perfect canapés. No, Diana Hodges would not be pleased.

Telling the yard was another matter. Tom arrived at coffee time when everyone was in the kitchen and he had to pull Jess into the room to stop her hiding amongst the coats and boots in the scullery. Holding her hand, he made the announcement, while she blushed scarlet and then everyone clapped and there was kissing and laughter and Ken went and found a bottle of champagne won at the races and opened it there and then.

Jess was embarrassed and kept saying, 'But I'm sorry because I'm letting you down. The baby and everything. I'll go on riding, Ken, up until the end.'

'We'll see about that, my girl,' said Mary. 'Don't start thinking you're the only one who can sit on a horse!' and there was more laughter.

Moira sat looking sour and when she had drained her glass she went back out to the yard, muttering, 'Once a slapper, always a slapper!' Rhona followed her and what words were exchanged nobody knew, but Moira sulked the rest of the day and Rhona went into her caravan and banged the door.

Timidly, Jess went to look for her. She knocked and opened the door a crack. Rhona was sitting on the bunk with the big tabby cat on her knee.

413

'Can I come in a minute?' she said.

Rhona looked up. Behind her glasses her brown eyes looked unnaturally large and liquid.

'Yeah,' she said gruffly. 'What do you want?'

'I just wanted . . .' Jess floundered. She did not know how to say what she felt. She and Rhona had never talked like this. 'I just wanted to thank you, Rhona. You've always been fair to me. Well, more than that. You've always been a real friend and I don't know whether I've ever thanked you, or even if you know that I notice. Well, I do, and now that, you know, with Tom and everything, and the baby, well, I'm so happy and . . .'

'So now you feel sorry for me, do you?' snapped Rhona. 'Sorry for poor old Rhona?'

'No! Nothing like that!' Jess protested, stung. 'Oh, no, Rhona. Oh, shit.' She stood, blushing. 'Sorry, I'll go.'

'No, there's no need,' said Rhona in a different tone. 'Sorry I snapped. I'm turning into a bloody old bitch, aren't I? Thanks, Jess. I appreciate it. In the long run it's only the horses I care about and I've always seen that you care too. That's why I've always had time for you.'

'Oh, right, well, thanks,' said Jess, turning to go, still feeling rebuffed.

'And congratulations,' said Rhona, less gruffly. 'I don't want to be your bloody bridesmaid but I'd like to be that baby's godmother!'

'You would?' Jess beamed. 'That's a deal! Thanks, Rhona. Thanks for everything.'

Further south, in the kitchen of the small farmhouse in the

shadow of the open downs, the two Dawlish men were engaged in a fierce argument.

'We should run her Saturday week at Bratton Down,' said Pete. 'There's no rain forecast and she'll like the top of the ground. She should have one more run this season, and without the girl on board. Give the mare a chance to win, Dad!'

The old man poured himself another cup of tea from the brown pot which was always ready on the top of the stove. His wife cut a thick slice of sponge cake and pushed it across the table to him.

He took his time, stirring his tea, cutting his cake in four, wiping his mouth, stirring his tea again, before he said, 'The mare's done enough. We'll turn her away next week. Turn her on the hill. I'll not have her running again, not on the firm. I'll not have her buggered because you're too hasty. She needs time to mature, to let her bones harden. Another year and she'll be a different horse, her will, and that's the end to it.'

'Bloody hell, Dad,' complained Pete. 'She'd win next time out. Get a proper jock on her and she'd win!'

'The maid did well. You'll not get a better. Not many as wanted the ride, was there? But the mare'll not run again this year and that's that, my son,' and he put a piece of cake in his mouth and worked it about thoughtfully. 'Lovely bit of sponge, Mother,' he said and Nita, scuttling about between table and sink, gave a small nod of acknowledgement and pleasure.

Pete banged out of the back door and went across the yard, shoulders hunched. He'd had it with the old man. Had it up to here. There was no way he would get him to change his mind now. Maybe I'll go, thought Pete. Just bugger off and leave the old bastard and see how well he gets on without me. For all he knew the old man would live to ninety just to spite him and he'd never get the chance to take over and do things his way. They live too long, that's their trouble, he thought bitterly. These old bastards, they just go on and on. Nothing seems to knock them off their perches these days. They live too bloody long.

As Belinda turned into the no through lane and then into her parents' drive, the first thing she noticed was her father's car drawn up with a dented wing and a scrape all along the side. Goodness, she thought. How did that happen? She could guess. His driving had become more and more hair-raising lately and although she and her brothers had had a go at him about it, he insisted that he was still perfectly capable. He drove about slowly now, in the middle of the road, but still swearing under his breath and banging the wheel impatiently, as he had always done.

As she stood there, the front door opened and her mother came out on the step, holding on to the door jamb with one hand, leaning on her stick with the other. She was wearing an old blouse under a child's navy blue school sweatshirt and a shapeless skirt. Her stick legs were encased in navy tights and on her feet was a pair of rather dirty trainers. Her straight, silver hair was clipped back on one side with the usual childish plastic slide.

'Who is it?' she called loudly. 'I thought I heard a car!'
'It's me, Ma. Belinda.'

'Belinda! Whatever are you doing here? Has something happened?'

'No, nothing.' Belinda went forward quickly to hug her. As she put her arms round her, she felt even more frail and insubstantial than on her last visit. Her mother drew back to look at her again. The shrewd pale blue eyes were searching her face for clues.

'Well, what's all this about? A surprise visit?'

'I had two days' holiday,' lied Belinda, 'and I thought I'd just come and see you. I didn't let you know because I didn't want you to do anything. I've got food in the car.'

'Well, I don't know. What a surprise. Jim!' she shouted into the house. 'Jim! It's Belinda! Belinda's here!' There was no answer. Belinda heard the furious banging of the type-writer in the distance.

'The car?' she asked, making a face and indicating the damaged side.

'The post van,' said her mother. 'They met in the lane. Your father says it was the postman's fault but since he was stationary at the time I don't see how that could be possible.'

'Your fat-ball one?'

'Indeed. Your father was entirely in the wrong and I told him so. I won't have the postman get into trouble over it. I'm afraid that your father's eyesight isn't as good as it used to be. He won't accept it, of course, but I know he has trouble judging distances.'

'Mother!' said Belinda, horrified. 'Then he must stop driving. He really must.'

'Oh, there's no question of that. He has passed the vet, as he puts it, but young Dr Burns is bullied by him, I'm sure,

417

and he confessed to me that he had a good look at the letters on the board for the sight test and memorised the bottom line in advance. He was very pleased with himself.'

'Oh, God,' said Belinda despairingly. 'Does he have to kill someone, then, before he'll accept that he must stop?' She would have to speak to her brothers about it and see what they could do on a united front. She could not tackle this on her own. This breakdown of good sense was alarming and disturbing. It seemed no time ago that it was their father they relied on for good judgement.

Ernie, hearing voices and sensing a potential victim, trotted round the corner, ball in mouth, his stump of a tail wagging in greeting. Carefully he laid the ball at Belinda's feet, cocked his head and fixed it with a beady eye. 'Hello, Ernie,' said Belinda and obliged him by kicking the ball sharply across the gravel. In a flurry of flying stones, he shot after it, while her mother turned to lead the way inside. Belinda saw that on the back of her sweat-shirt was written, in large white letters, 'St Faith's Netball Team'.

Later, sitting in the kitchen with a mug of tea, Belinda wondered whether she was mistaken in thinking she could unburden herself to her mother. She always forgot how it was between them, how she felt instantly restrained in her company. Could the terrible truth ever be spoken here in this house where excesses of feeling had always been frowned upon, self-indulgence despised, where duty to others came before everything else and two lives had been lived selflessly to the end? Although in her father's case that no longer seemed to be true.

Would her mother, whose preoccupations in life had been her primary school, the Church and her various good works, ever understand what it had been like to be in love so passionately with James Redpath; that giddy, sick, intoxicated feeling? Probably not. But it must be spoken of, thought Belinda. I must find the words to tell her and then the great burden that she felt she carried would somehow be lifted from her shoulders.

'We should tell your father that you're here,' said her mother, reaching for the chipped brown teapot. 'It will be a lovely surprise for him. And take him a cup of tea. He'll enjoy these biscuits you've brought.'

'Just a minute, Ma. Could we just leave Dad, for a moment? There's something I need to tell you.' There, she had said it. Now she must go on.

Her mother looked at her across the table and cocked her head knowingly. 'I guessed there might be,' she said. 'I thought there must be a reason why you came.'

When she had finished talking, the tea in the pot had grown quite cold and her mother got up stiffly to refill the kettle. She had said nothing while Belinda spoke, her face becoming infinitely thoughtful as the story unwound. Now Belinda sat silently, feeling the same sense of emptiness as she had before, as if she was scraped clean of any emotion, and worn out by the telling.

Her mother moved between the stove and the table, one hand always seeking support, like a sailor on a leaning ship. Her eyes no longer looked sharp and bright. There seemed to be a cloudiness across the blue, a yellow in the whites, that lent them a faraway expression. It was as if they were focusing on something quite beyond the untidy kitchen or Belinda herself, sitting expectantly across the table.

'Did you want to tell me all this because you thought I would be your sternest judge?' she asked at last.

Belinda hesitated. 'I suppose so. A bit like making a confession must be for Catholics. I felt that you should know because in a way you are the last person I want to think badly of me. I've always wanted your good opinion, Ma. I knew you would be truthful and not necessarily kind, and perhaps be able to tell me what to do, although I realise there is nothing that can be put right. I feel so devastated, you see. I don't know how to go on from here. It seems to change everything I had taken for granted about the past.'

'I can see what a shock this must have been to you. I'm old enough not to be surprised much by anything, but I have to admit, this is an extraordinary story. And you blame yourself very much for what happened to Jess?'

'Yes, I do, Ma. Of course I do. If I hadn't been so blinded by this infatuation and so in love with myself, too, I would have seen it, wouldn't I? I would have realised the sort of man James was. I should have protected Jess. Instead, I spent the next six years blaming her.'

'Hmmm.' Her mother rubbed the rope-veined back of her right hand. 'Jess was eighteen. She was responsible for her own actions. She wasn't a child. He must have been a seductive man, this Redpath, and utterly unscrupulous, of course. You weren't alone in succumbing to his charms, were you?'

'That doesn't excuse me.'

'No, I'm not saying it does. It doesn't excuse any of you. Karen, you, Jess, each in your own way made mistakes.'

'So?'

'So what? Belinda, it is not for me to be your judge and jury. This thing happened, was highly regrettable, but it's now in the past. Jess is going to be married and have another baby, which should be a reason for rejoicing. Izzy will one day know who her father was and learn to be proud of the brave and distinguished soldier he evidently was, and she will also live in a proper family, which you've always wanted for her. It seems to me that things are very much better now than they were before.'

'And me?' said Belinda in a choked voice. 'They're not better for me, are they? Imagine how I feel. For the first and only time in my life I was wildly in love and I have held those weeks which we shared, James and me, as evidence that whatever else happened to me, or didn't, rather, I had had that amazing and wonderful experience. I know that later on it all fell flat, but that didn't matter, because in my heart I knew it wasn't a sustainable relationship. Now I find I've lost all that.'

'Everything has its price. To be properly grown up, one just has to accept that sometimes, and usually with hind-sight, the price can seem rather too high. I wonder, though, would you rather not have had any of that experience?'

Belinda thought. 'No,' she said sadly. 'I suppose not.'

'Self-knowledge, you see, is usually painfully acquired, but is very well worth it in the long term. It generally means one doesn't make the same mistakes again. I don't think you will. Now you must stop judging yourself so harshly. You've always done that, since you were a little girl, and it's time you grew out of it.'

Belinda looked at her mother in astonishment. This was not what she imagined at all. She had seen herself at the very heart of a tragic personal drama, and was anticipating a scene of tearful confession, and eventually, she hoped, forgiveness and absolution. It was what she needed and what she had come for. Instead she had been given a sort of bracing-up talking-to.

She sat at the kitchen table, wondering at her mother's response and feeling disappointed and let down. She had been right to suspect that she would not understand. Her mother had no idea of the pain and humiliation she suffered. It was quite outside her experience.

Then gradually she felt something moving and slipping in the wall of stony misery that had built inside her. The stout, pragmatic view expressed by her mother was so typical, if only she had thought about it, that she almost had to smile, and when she did, she felt much better, refreshed, as if she had been doused with cold water, which in a way she had.

'Thank you, Ma,' she said eventually. 'I knew I could rely on you to help me see things a bit differently. I was devastated when Jess first told me. It was hard to come to terms with. I suppose you're right and that there is a lot to look forward to and be positive about, and it *is* lovely for Izzy, although of course I shall worry dreadfully about her, and miss her, too. I've got to get used to the idea of being on my own for the first time.' Suddenly she thought of Victor.

There was no need to be on her own completely. Not if she didn't want to be.

'Good,' said her mother. 'I'm glad of that. But Belinda, I am interested in something you said. Have I been unkind in the past?'

Belinda paused. This was not what she wanted to get into. 'Well, chilly, perhaps. Unsympathetic at times. You were never a cosy sort of mother, were you? You must admit.'

'No. I realise that and it is a source of sadness to me. I hope that nevertheless you felt loved, because you all were. Deeply. But it was a gift I did not have, to be spontaneously warm and affectionate. I see you with your children and with Izzy and I envy you that. I simply never had it, that form of expression.'

Belinda got up and went to where her mother stood at the other side of the table and put her arms round her carefully. She felt her stiffen very slightly, as if the embrace was something to be warded off.

'You were a wonderful mother,' she said, gently. 'And still are.'

There, that was enough. They disengaged and stood looking at one another.

'I'll make the tea,' said Belinda to recover from the moment of awkward tenderness. 'And take Dad through a cup. It must be thirsty work, bashing that poor typewriter.'

'Oh, blow the tea,' said her mother unexpectedly. 'We'll go into the drawing room and get Jim to open a bottle. We both need a bit of a stiffener and I think he'll agree that we have something to celebrate.'

*

'So that was that,' Belinda reported to Dinka on the telephone. 'She's a woman after your own heart, my mother! Get up and get on with it, was what she told me effectively. Just as you would have done.'

'Too true,' said Dinka. 'I could have guessed you would want a good wallow in guilt. It *is* a tiresome trait of yours. Your mother is quite right. James Redpath was a bastard but if I went under every time I was kicked in the teeth by one of his ilk, I would have topped myself years ago.'

'Dinka, that's so unfair. About me wallowing in guilt, I mean.'

'Being almost entirely impervious to guilt myself, I detect it easily in others,' said Dinka, 'and if you're not careful, it becomes a bloody boring refrain – "Oh no, I couldn't do that, I'd feel so guilty" is often the excuse for doing nothing, and before too long it starts to sound like self-righteousness speaking. It's a modern form of self-flagellation and it's quite possible to become hooked on it.'

'Dinka! How can you be so horrible?'

'I'm not talking about you, sweetie. Just in general terms. I suppose I get a basinful of people hoping to make me feel guilty – you know, I'm single, childless, selfish, vain, indulgent, I have a hedonistic lifestyle, a young lover . . .'

All true, thought Belinda. She had thought it herself at times.

'Frankly, sod the lot of them. Self-righteous pricks. It's nobody's business but mine how I live my life and none of those things I'm accused of are illegal or harmful to anyone but me in the long run. I'm not a child abuser or a football hooligan or a crooked banker and I like to think that I make the world a marginally better place. At least, through the magazine, I try to promulgate good taste. No, there are far too many dodgy people out there peddling guilt for their own nefarious ends. Your mother was spot on.'

'But surely it's a good thing, too? Isn't it there to help us make the right decisions and show us when they are wrong?'

'Of course, but it can get out of hand,' said Dinka shortly. 'Now stop being bloody Sister Immaculata!'

'How is Javier?' asked Belinda, to change the subject. 'What does he think of the new you?'

'He's been bliss,' said Dinka. 'He missed me terribly in Barcelona and couldn't wait to get back. He said I looked amazing. So there. All worth it. Now I want to hear more about Jess and Tom. When will Jess move out of Rosebay Cottage?'

'They plan to marry as soon as the pointing season is over in June, after Umberley, the last meeting in Devon. Knowing Jess, she'll want to get married at the open ditch after the last race. She'll be six months pregnant by then, but they don't seem the slightest bit concerned about that, although thank goodness she isn't going to race again this season. Ken won't let her, for which I am eternally grateful to him. She's not going to move in with Tom until then. They're going to do a bit of work on his house. His land-lord has agreed to put in central heating and make it a bit more habitable. As it is at the moment I think she'd have the social services on to her if she took a baby to live there.'

'So,' said Dinka, with emphasis. 'At last. You'll be able to have a life of your own.'

'Yes,' said Belinda, in what she hoped sounded like a bright and cheery tone. 'Won't it be wonderful!'

Mikey Bearsden was glad when his mother told him that he and his family were going back to live in the United States. She had gone on and on about how she hoped he wasn't disappointed not to be living in the country and that although they would have to sell his pony, they would take the dogs with them. He didn't care, anyway. He didn't much like the dogs and although shooting was cool, it was always wet and cold and his father kept telling him what to do and the keeper was grumpy.

He didn't care that they were going to sell the house too. His mother said that it was going to cost too much to run. It wasn't feasible, she said. She wasn't made of money. They were going to buy a ranch in Virginia and he could go back to his old school which he much preferred to the prep school he had been sent to in England. He hated the food and he hated rugby and he hated the way his dad wanted him to be, like, English, when he thought that England sucked.

Really, none of them minded about going home, except Ludmylla. She was the only one who cried when his mom told her they were leaving. Not for long, though. 'You can go home for a holiday,' she told her, 'and I'll try and get a work permit for you to come out to the States. You and your daughter.' She'd cheered up then all right. None of them, not even his dad, minded. They'd all had enough of poxy old England.

Chapter Seventeen

When Izzy came out of school she was pleased to see Jess already waiting for her by the gate, dressed in her old work clothes, her long, thick hair in a ponytail. More often, Izzy had to hang around and wait for her mother to turn up and she was usually one of the last children to be collected.

'Hi, Izzbug,' Jess said, taking her school bag from her and giving her a hug. Izzy looked round hopefully. She wanted the other mothers and children to notice. She was proud of having a mother like Jess, who she thought was the prettiest by far, and she liked it that she came in her riding clothes and looked sporty and jaunty.

'Hello, Mummy,' she said. She sensed at once that Jess was in a good mood. She could tell from the way she said hello and her mouth dimpled into a smile and Izzy felt a surge of reciprocal happiness.

'I thought you and me might go somewhere together. Somewhere nice,' said Jess, catching Izzy's hand and swinging her arm back and forth as they walked to where the old car was parked. Izzy could see Snowy's alert, pointy black and white face looking out of the passenger window. His turned-over ears were cocked anxiously and then he seemed to smile when he saw them coming and started to

427

weave excitedly backwards and forwards before hopping onto the driver's seat and resting his paws on the steering wheel.

'Where? To see a horse?'

'No, nothing to do with horses, Iz. Just you and me. Wherever you want to go.'

'To see Ludmylla?' asked Izzy, remembering the biscuits.

'No. Ludmylla's gone home for a few weeks.'

'To her little girl?' asked Izzy, interested. 'The one like me?'

'That's right,' said Jess. 'She was very, very happy to be doing that. She hopes that she won't have to leave her again. She thinks that maybe they will both go and live in America. No, we'll go somewhere else. Somewhere you like. Where would you like to go?'

'Is Tom coming too?' asked Izzy, puzzled. The afternoon had a strange, unexpected shape to it. It was like going through a door, she thought, into a place you hadn't been before.

'Later, perhaps. Maybe we'll meet him later for a pizza. So have a good think.'

Izzy climbed into the back of the car and Snowy hopped over the front seats to greet her and Izzy kissed his head. She was afraid that she wouldn't be able to think of anywhere she wanted to go, apart from places like the South Pole, and that if she couldn't, her mother would change her mind and they would go straight home as usual and the special afternoon would disappear and be lost.

A sudden thought rescued her. 'The sea!' she cried, her face brightening. 'That's where I would like to go, Mummy.

Like Tom, the chimney sweep. Down the river, looking for the water babies.'

'OK!' said Jess, pleased by Izzy's excitement. 'If that's what you'd like, we'll go to the sea. Where? Which bit of the seaside would you like to go to?'

'Durdle Door!' shouted Izzy. 'Let's go to Durdle Door.'

As Jess started the engine, Izzy, sitting up straight in the back seat, thought of the high, ragged cliffs dropping down sheer into the grey sea, the black teeth of rocks circled with white foaming water and the great door itself, the soaring arch of rock through which the sea churned and rushed. It was a frightening, thrilling place and Izzy felt her breath blocked in her chest when she thought about it. The last time she had been there, last summer, she had been too timid to climb down the steep steps cut into the side of the cliff, but now she was older and bolder and she wanted her mother to see that she wasn't scared any more.

It took over an hour to get there, going cross-country south through the threadwork of lanes, high over Bulbarrow Hill, past the radio masts where patches of gorse darkened the blond, bleached winter grass, and the whole of the Blackmore Vale lay spread out below. Down the other side it was a different world of pastel cottages and sleepy villages and water meadows bounding the slow streams. Twice they got stuck behind tractors and had to follow several agonising miles at a snail's pace and Izzy felt the excitement might fizz out of her, like a gassy overflow from a shaken bottle. It seemed strange in the car, just her and her mother, going somewhere especially because she wanted to, and she sat, poised and important, in the back, holding on to Snowy's black ear which was like a triangle of thick, warm satin between her fingers.

Jess played a tape and sang along to it and did a funny noise in her throat for the bit of the tune which went 'cher-choo choo-choo', and which came round again and again, and dipped and rolled her shoulders to the beat. When she caught Izzy watching her in the driver's mirror, she laughed and trilled her fingers at her. They stopped to fill up with petrol before they left the busy coastal road and Jess bought some chocolate in the garage. Then they turned onto a winding lane, twisting through the pretty villages before racing out along the straighter road through the bare rolling hills where the ploughed fields were white with broken chalk.

At last Izzy saw the stand of tall pines which marked the caravan park where she remembered they would turn off. The site was empty and silent, the shop closed, the cafe boarded up, the rubbish bins stored upside down for the winter. The painting contractors, preparing for the spring, had finished work for the day and their white van passed them at the entrance. The men looked without curiosity at the car and its occupants. There were plenty of dog-walkers and hikers who used the cliff car park at this time of the year. One of the men wearing a baseball cap waved at Izzy through the back window.

The succession of speed bumps hardly slowed Jess down and the old car bucked and rattled and Izzy screamed with laughter as she bounced high on the back seat. Then between the vans she saw the start of the high grassy field and fell silent with apprehension.

Jess drew up as close to the edge as she could. From here

all that could be seen was the grass dipping and rolling gently away and then the steel-grey sea which filled the horizon. A white path wound down and disappeared from view as it followed the rolling slope towards where the cliff plunged suddenly away to the shingle beach far below.

'So,' she said, switching off the engine and turning to Izzy. 'Here we are. Shall we have some chocolate and then go down to the sea?'

'Yes, please!' shouted Izzy, pushing her face between the front seats, thoroughly excited now, her cheeks glazed pink and her eyes sparkling behind her glasses. 'Then we must go and look for the water babies! They live under the sea and Tom the chimney sweep found them there. He went to live with them.'

'You're very keen on these old water babies, aren't you, Izzy?' said Jess, unwrapping the chocolate and handing her a bit. Izzy nodded, cramming the chunk into her mouth. 'You know that I'm having a baby, don't you? Will you be pleased about that?

Izzy nodded again, suddenly thoughtful. She looked out across the sea. A large gull hung motionless in front of the car as if suspended on a string, and way out two little boats were moving slowly through the grey water.

'Careful, Izzy, the steps start here.' Jess held Izzy's hand as they reached the narrow wedges cut straight into the cliff face. Snowy hopped and bounded down the path like a rubber ball but Izzy held on tight, her face pale with fear, her woollen hat pulled low. Now she could see far down below to the shingled beach and hear the suck and hiss of the waves. Closer to the shore the sea was glass-green, frilled with white, and the wind, which was stronger here, pulled and tugged at the waves and sent the strong smell of ozone and seaweed up to where she hesitated on the path.

To the left of them the steps zig-zagged down to St Oswald's Bay and to the right dropped to Durdle Door. In front was a narrow bridge of sheer-sided cliff which, sticking straight out into the sea like an outflung arm, formed the apex of the great arch. Its grassy top was scored by rabbit tracks, and erosion had carved mysterious paths which meandered along the edge and then appeared to plunge over the dizzying drop to the sea below.

Izzy clung to Jess's hand. The treads of the steps were narrow and the drops were deep. Some she could only manage by scrabbling on her knees. She had never been brave enough to get this far before and she felt torn between terror and joy. The path wound on down and as it turned, first on one side and then the other, the cliff sheered away, and all the time the wind blew and the sea dragged and raked the beach with a roar and a sigh and the gulls hung above them, croaking and cawing.

'Don't look down,' said Jess. 'You're doing so well, Iz. Only look at your feet. It's not so far now.' And when Izzy was brave enough to lift her head, she could see the ledges of pebbles running along the beach, piled up with dark seaweed and littered with the rubbish brought in by the winter storms.

'Only a few more steps and then you can jump,' said Jess and the next moment they were down on the beach and Izzy's shoes were filled with shingle and Jess's boots were sinking. It was hard to walk and they staggered along hand in hand, laughing, and Izzy said, 'I was brave, wasn't I? I was really, really brave!' Now they could look up at the great rock arch, standing with its feet in the churning sea and its open doorway filled with sky and wheeling gulls.

Further down along the beach, they stopped when Izzy found a tiny yellow plastic flip-flop amongst the seaweed.

'Look,' she said, pulling it out. 'I think this must belong to a water baby, don't you?' and Jess, sitting on the pebbles with her arms round her knees, nodded.

'I think it does,' said Izzy dreamily. 'The water babies must be very near here.' She shaded her eyes and looked out to sea. Although it was a dull day, the horizon was a shining pearly grey, shot through with spokes of brilliant light. Slowly she began to slither and slide her way over the deep falling terraces of shingle towards the water.

Jess sat and watched her go. She was a small, stocky figure on the deserted beach in her blue school coat and knitted hat pulled low over her spectacles, tendrils of her tangerine hair whipping in the wind. Jess could see her lips moving and she realised that Izzy was talking to herself as she kicked her feet through the seams of washed-up pebbles, lost in some world of her own. She stopped and looked out to sea again, and then squatted down, her fat little knees round in her black tights, and raised a hand to shield her eyes from the light on the horizon. She's looking for the water babies, Jess thought, and her heart suddenly contracted with such an intense shock of love that tears started to her eyes.

Oh, Izzy! she thought tenderly. Funny little Iz. So much

had happened over the last few weeks that sometimes it had felt as though the fabric of their lives had been torn wide open and so much of the upheaval centred on the little girl. Jess's present happiness, her racing success, Tom, the baby, all the good things that had come out of the dreadful mess she had made of everything else were so consuming that she had hardly stopped to consider Izzy or how she felt. She was so uncomplaining, so stoical and accepting, that it was easy to forget how sensitive she was. Jess felt as if a dam had broken inside her and that her head was flooding with something hot and congesting, which pressed against the back of her eyes and throat, choking her. Anguished, she brushed tears hastily away with the back of her hand. The solitary little figure, squatting by the edge of the sighing sea, was so unbearably dear that the love she felt was like a great burden pressing down on her. She struggled to her feet, her hands on either side of her hot face. Gulping and wiping her eyes on the edge of her scarf, she went to join Izzy. She hunkered down and put her arms tight round her as if she was sheltering her from the sea wind and buried her hot face against Izzy's cold cheek.

'Izzy!' she blurted out, and Izzy turned, surprised, and put both hands in her mother's thick hair and filled her fists with the brown mass.

'Mummy, what's the matter? Are you crying?'

'Nothing. Nothing's the matter. I'm not crying. It's just the wind.' Jess sniffed loudly and wiped her nose again. 'Can you see the water babies, Iz? I thought maybe you could show them to me.'

Izzy looked serious. The cold air and her mother's warm face had misted her glasses. 'I'm not sure, Mummy. I thought maybe I could. Look. Right out there,' and she turned back and pointed. Jess looked but there was nothing except the choppy, glistening water and the white foam in the distance where the waves were breaking.

'Can you see anything, Mummy? Can you?'

'Maybe,' said Jess, screwing up her eyes. 'Maybe I can,' and she held Izzy so tightly that she lost her balance and they toppled, laughing, onto the wet pebbles of the shore.

When Belinda got back from work she was annoyed that Jess had Izzy out somewhere when, in her view, Izzy should have been bathed and ready for bed. I'm going to have to stop this, she thought. I can't go on pretending I can supervise Izzy's life. I have to get used to living without her. Nevertheless, as she lit the fire and started making some supper, she found herself glancing at the kitchen clock and a knot of tension formed in her stomach. Several times she leaned over the sink to open the kitchen curtains and peer out into the dark but there were no lights along the lane.

Where is she? she thought, exasperated, and visions of car accidents and twisted metal and flashing blue police lights filled her head. She tried Jess's mobile but it was switched off and it was after eight o'clock when she heard a car. She went to the table and sat down and began to go through a pile of bills. She did not want to reveal herself immediately because it would antagonise Jess, but later on she would tell her how Izzy must take a more important place in her life, especially when she was in danger of feeling crowded out by marriage and a new baby.

The kitchen door banged open and Snowy and Izzy burst in and both hurled themselves at Belinda in a joyful homecoming. Izzy's face was pink and there was something tomato coloured round her mouth. Her hands were very warm and sticky as she caught at her grandmother.

'Granny! Granny! We went to the sea! Mummy and me! I climbed down, Granny. Down the giant's steps to the beach at Durdle Door! I did, Granny!' She caught Belinda's face and drew it down between her hands so that she had her full attention. 'We had a lovely, lovely time, and then we bought a pizza and ate it at Tom's house and he showed me my room, Granny. My new bedroom! And we fed the lambs!'

Belinda hugged her back and swivelled her eyes to look for Jess. She was standing watching Izzy and the only thing that Belinda noticed was that her smile as she listened to her daughter transformed her face. She does love her, thought Belinda, and her anxiety and anger melted away and she stretched out a hand towards her. She felt Jess's dry, rough hand take hers and she pulled her gently to her and put her arm round her waist and hugged her tight and for a moment the three of them were held in an awkward triangular embrace. Then Jess said, 'Mum, what's all this about? I thought you'd give me a bollocking for having Iz out late.'

'I had to be glad that she'd been with Izzy,' Belinda told Victor as they sat over the remains of dinner two nights later. 'Even though she had her out disgracefully late and

I had to drag her out of bed for school the next day. It's been easy to overlook Izzy in all of this, what with the racing, and Jess getting engaged and finding she was pregnant, and me too, I've been terribly distracted. Izzy has been pushed to one side by both of us.'

Victor nodded. 'I realised that there was something the matter when you went off to Suffolk like that.'

'I'm sorry, Victor. I didn't want to hurt you, but I had to go alone.'

'I understand. I thought that maybe I was pushing my luck by suggesting I would take you, but it was because I was worried about you, that's all.'

'I know. But I was in a state of shock, I suppose, finding out about Izzy's father like that. I couldn't bear to be with you because I could hardly bear myself, if you know what I mean.'

'You can put all that behind you now,' he said, leaning back. The flickering candles cast his shadow huge on the wall behind him. 'Like your mother said. Close the chapter.' He leaned across the table and took her hand. Belinda smiled at him and filled his glass from the bottle of wine he had brought with him.

'I've got to drive,' he reminded her gently.

'Why? Why have you got to drive? There's nobody here but us. Izzy and Jess are staying over with Tom. Even Snowy has gone with them.'

Victor did not move. The significance of her remark did not escape him.

'Belinda,' he said softly. 'My little love.'

*

'You know Mummy is having a baby,' Izzy said to Belinda a few nights later when she was putting her to bed. 'You know that, don't you, Granny?'

'Yes, Izzy. This baby will be your brother or sister, so it's your baby as well.'

'You have to love babies, don't you?'

'People usually do, I think. I certainly did. I loved my babies very much and I loved you when you were a baby. At once. The minute you were born.'

'How much did you love me?' Izzy asked, always interested in quantities. 'To the end of the world? As much as that?'

Belinda nodded. 'Yes, easily as much as that. And I still do.'

Izzy reached under her bed for *The Water Babies* and turned the pages to find the place she wanted. '"From Peacepool to the Other-end-of-Nowhere!"' she recited in triumph.

'Yes,' said Belinda. 'From Peacepool to the Other-end-of-Nowhere.'

'Does Mummy want a baby more than anything else?'

'What do you think?'

Izzy didn't answer. She pushed the book into Belinda's hands.

'Read this,' she commanded. 'Please.'

Belinda read, '"And all her delight was, whenever she had a spare moment, to play with babies, in which she showed herself a woman of sense; for babies are the best company and the pleasantest playfellows in the world; at least, so all the wise people in the world think."'

'That's Mrs Doasyouwouldbedoneby,' Izzy informed her importantly. 'She's the one who loves babies.' She lay back on her pillow and turned slightly to look at the wall, twiddling a strand of hair round a finger. 'Do you think Mummy loves babies more than she loves girls?' she asked in a small, careless voice.

Belinda looked at her. 'No, I don't think so at all,' she said gently. 'I think she probably prefers girls, because they're more fun to be with than boring old babies who don't do much but eat or sleep. Your mummy has always liked doing things rather than just holding babies.'

Izzy turned her head to look at her grandmother thoughtfully. Then her face fell. 'But the book says—'

'Yes,' said Belinda, 'but look at the pictures. Tom was quite a big boy when he became a water baby. Look, quite as big as you. The book just calls them babies.'

'That's silly then,' said Izzy, sitting up again and turning the pages to study the colour plates. 'It's silly to call them babies when they're not. When they're as big as me. It's silly, isn't it, Granny?'

'Very silly.'

Belinda closed the book and held it for a moment on her lap. This was where it had all begun, she thought. This battered old book and a small boy's name in childish handwriting on the flyleaf. And now it was over. Gently, she put the book on the floor under Izzy's bed and bent to kiss her goodnight.

If you have enjoyed *Jumping to Conclusions*,
you may enjoy the following titles also available
from your bookshop or *direct from the publisher*.

FREE P&P AND UK DELIVERY
(Overseas and Ireland £3.50 per book)

Killing Helen	Sarah Challis	£7.99
Turning for Home	Sarah Challis	£7.99
Blackthorn Winter	Sarah Challis	£6.99
On Dancing Hill	Sarah Challis	£6.99
The Wedding Day	Catherine Alliott	£6.99
A Married Man	Catherine Alliott	£6.99
Rosie Meadows Regrets	Catherine Alliott	£6.99
Play It Again?	Julie Highmore	£6.99
Searching for Home	Mary Stanley	£7.99
Children of Eve	Deirdre Purcell	£6.99

TO ORDER SIMPLY CALL THIS NUMBER

01235 400 414

or visit our website: www.madaboutbooks.com

Prices and availability subject to change without notice.